How
in the
Wilderness

ALSO BY DIANA HARRIS

Johnny Jones: A Colonial Saga

Guardian of the Bridge (children's story)

Litterbugs (children's story)

The Kiwi Fact Book

Howling in the Wilderness

DIANA HARRIS

MARY EGAN PUBLISHING

MARY EGAN PUBLISHING

Published by Mary Egan Publishing
© Diana Harris 2023
The moral right of the author has been asserted

Designed and typeset by Anna Egan-Reid
Produced by Mary Egan Publishing
www.maryegan.co.nz

Printed in China

All rights reserved. Without limiting the rights under copyright above, no part of this publication may be reproduced, stored in or introduced into a retrieval system, or transmitted, in any form or by any means (electronic, mechanical, photocopying, recording or otherwise), without the prior written permission of both the copyright owner and the above publisher of this book.

ISBN 978-1-99-117981-4

Stay alert! Watch out for your great enemy, the Devil. He prowls around like a roaring lion, looking for someone to devour.

1 PETER, CHAPTER 5, VERSE 8

PART ONE
Bay of Islands, 1824

1

Henry Williams, missionary, faced Tohitapu, chief.

Tohitapu, clad in just a mat around his loins, crouched and swung his long spear so that the end, sharpened to inflict maximum damage, pointed directly at Henry.

Dear Lord, thought Henry, keep me calm in my hour of need.

His heart pounded and sweat congealed under his heavy clothes. But instead of retreating to the back door of his house, he moved towards the chief.

Tohitapu was shaking, presumably with rage.

'He aha te mate?' What is the matter? asked Henry.

Tohitapu thrust out his foot. Drops of bright red blood trickled from a long cut in the brown flesh.

'I hurt it,' he said in Māori. 'Jumping over your fence.'

Seeing the chief coming William Fairburn the carpenter had locked the gate and so the chief had sprung over the fence and scratched his leg. Whatever the original issue was that had made him so angry, Henry had no idea. Which was not unusual.

Tohitapu jabbed his spear in Henry's direction. He let fly a tirade in Māori.

Henry could not follow the rapid delivery. But he heard one word repeated – 'Utu.'

'No payment,' said Henry. 'Kāhore he utu.'

The chief ran towards the storehouse and grabbed a black iron pot – presumably this was to be the utu. He tried to spring back over the fence, but the heavy pot weighed him down.

He went to open the gate.

Henry leapt upon him and grabbed the pot from his hand. He stood against the gate so the chief could not escape.

'Someone take this!' he shouted.

Tohitapu thrust his face against Henry's, at the same time trying to snatch back the pot. The distinctive smell of shark oil was strong in his nostrils. The chief's face was covered in red ochre and close up, the whorls and lines of his moko made his face even more intimidating.

He whirled his greenstone club, the mere, over the missionary's head and made throat-cutting gestures.

Henry folded his arms across his chest, keeping his face impassive.

Like most Māori men, Tohitapu was tall and strongly built. He towered over the missionary's nuggety but much shorter frame like a massive tree of the forest, flourishing his spear and his mere.

Henry resisted the attempts of the chief to snatch the pot. Instead he tried to out-stare his opponent, repeating at intervals, 'Kāti, e mara – heoi anō.' Stop, sir – that is enough.

And from the window of their little house he saw the worried face of Marianne, gazing at the scene with horror.

This was the first time they'd been attacked. Of course they knew they were vulnerable: the hut, made of raupō stalks and a roof of raupō leaves, kept out the rain – most of the time – but it was no fortified castle.

The closest white people were across the bay, at Kororāreka. But they were unlikely to come to their aid — more likely to rejoice if those annoying missionaries were done away with.

There was a missionary enclave at Rangihoua, on the northern part of the Bay of Islands, and another at Kerikeri.

But no soldiers, no police — no protection at all. All that would have to come from Sydney, and the powers that be there would probably be no more enthusiastic about rescuing them than the escaped convicts and ship deserters at Kororāreka.

The Williams family had thrown themselves on the mercy of the Māori people at the Bay of Islands, who on the whole had shown them kindness and help, even if they were mystified at the reasons of this group of 'Pākehā' for coming to their country. All white people, in their experience, were only interested in taking their land and making it like Port Jackson, that is, Sydney — not in saving their souls.

But now Satan had shown his face in the form of Tohitapu, the chief who lived about two miles from their little settlement at Paihia, who was renowned for erupting into a fit of rage over the merest slight, and who according to reports from the other missionaries had already tasted the flesh of a white man.

Henry, ex-Royal Navy, knew danger. He'd served as a midshipman in the war against the French and been wounded, and in the war against America had participated in a hand-to-hand battle on board ship with prisoners who tried to take over.

But now it was different. Now he had a wife, Marianne, three children and a baby: he had no gun, and his only means of defending his family was to remain calm and refuse to be intimidated.

It was getting dark.

Fairburn came out of the house, walked up behind Tohitapu and snatched the pot.

Now the chief began to prepare for a fight. He pranced backwards and forwards, sideways, in front of the house, leaping in the air and stamping on the ground with measured steps. He whacked his sides with sharp slaps of his hands. His hair stood out in fiery curls, his eyes were wide and staring and his tongue protruded as far down as it would go, licking and curling in Henry's direction.

Now and again he stopped to crouch on the ground, beating his breast and panting loudly – not for lack of breath, but to increase his rage even further.

Then Fairburn returned and he, Henry and Tohitapu sat down to talk.

The chief said he wanted his utu and until he received it he would remain there – today, tomorrow and five days more. There would be a great fight. Tomorrow ten men – he held up his fingers – and ten more – more fingers – and ten more besides would come and set fire to Henry's house.

Henry went inside to reassure his family.

After he had finished evening prayers Tohitapu thrust his leg through the window, pointing to his foot and shouting that he wanted utu.

Henry moved towards the window. 'Me haere atu koe, e mara,' he said. 'You must go away now. Tomorrow you come back like a rangatira, a gentleman, and knock at our gate. Then I will say, "How do you do, Mr Tohitapu?" and you can come in and have breakfast with us.'

'No!' shouted the chief. His foot was so sore he could not walk. He would stay here for many more days and Henry's house would be burnt.

He became more and more enraged and threw off the mat he was wearing. Now he was stripped for battle.

Henry went outside.

It was dark apart from a lantern hanging at the corner of the house and in this half-light Tohitapu almost did seem like a devil: a huge man, running from one side of the yard to the other, leaping in the air with great agility and making terrifying faces.

His supporters called through the windows of the house to Marianne, marooned inside with her children: 'Oh Mother, tomorrow you will see a big fire in the house. Oh yes, the children all dead – all dead. Many, many men, plenty of muskets – a great fight!'

Then Tohitapu stood still. He began to intone a chant, very rapid and incomprehensible to Henry. The words were as staccato as gunshots.

'Auē!' Those standing by put their hands to their mouths and gazed from Tohitapu to Henry. 'Oh Karu-whā, he is karakia-ing you. Now you will surely die.'

The chief was a known tohunga or priest, renowned for his ability to curse someone to death.

But Henry stood still and faced the chief.

Tohitapu chanted. And Henry stood.

And he did not fall down dead as Tohitapu intended.

With two of the friendly chiefs he went into the cottage and closed the windows, comforting Marianne and telling her to go to bed. Fairburn remained in the house too, as did the chiefs, who wrapped their cloaks around themselves and settled down for the night.

First thing in the morning there was a row outside. Henry went to see.

Many people came pouring into the yard, Tohitapu amongst them, until they surrounded the cottage. Tohitapu grabbed a young goat, obviously intending to take it away, and Henry ran at him and pushed him out of the yard.

The chief sat outside the paling fence, surrounded by his followers.

Marianne boiled water over the fire and made a pot of tea to give to their supporters, and she also sent some out to Tohitapu, hoping this might appease him.

The chief drank the tea, but, then, followed by his tribesmen, forced his way back into the yard. Henry stood among them as they milled about, waving spears and mere. Some had muskets.

The noise as the Māori shouted and threatened seemed like thunder.

The sun rose higher and higher, blazing like fire upon their heads. And inside the cottage Marianne and the children roasted, the windows blocked by tattooed faces peering in.

But Tohitapu's rage was beginning to subside and by five o'clock the intruders seemed to be in a more peaceful mood. From outside Henry leaned into one of the windows and called to Marianne to pass out the children so they could get some fresh air. He had just set his daughter on the ground when there was a sound of banging. 'They're into the storehouse!' someone called.

He pushed Samuel and Marianne back headfirst back through the window and raced to the store.

The noise from their attackers became even louder.

Then he saw a man pointing a musket at the cottage, apparently intending to shoot his way in.

Five-year-old Teddy was still outside, surrounded by hostile Māori. Henry grabbed the terrified child and pushed him into the arms of one of the friendly chiefs, telling him to take the boy inside. He rushed to where the man with the gun stood and placed himself between him and the house.

He remained there, eyeballing the man, until he lowered his gun and walked away.

People were pushing on the hut, shaking it, and the walls, all that remained to protect his family, bent like reeds in the wind. But the house stood firm.

Finally the attackers dispersed and everything was quiet.

During this latest disturbance Tohitapu had not said a word. The friendly chiefs approached Henry in a group and indicated it would be a good idea to give him the iron pot that had caused all the trouble in the first place. He hadn't sided with the attacking Māori, but stood to one side, and the pot would be a reward for his support.

His pride assuaged, the chief took the pot and departed.

Finally Henry was able to enter the cottage and see to his family.

When he opened the bedroom door, his heart lurched. Marianne sat in the chair, nursing the baby. He could see from the way her head drooped that she was exhausted from worry and trying to keep the children calm. Teddy stood beside her looking solemn and frightened. And the two younger ones, thumbs in their mouths, eyes swimming with tears, clung to their mother's skirts.

Henry hugged each child in turn and then knelt and pulled Marianne to him. They remained, their arms round each other, for several minutes.

She raised her head and he stood back.

'Are you hurt?' she asked.

He shook his head. 'Praise the Lord,' he said. 'He was always with me.'

'I felt it!' said Marianne. 'You know I saw when you stood in the way of that man with the gun – I saw it! – and I was so afraid, but at the same time I experienced the most extreme sense of euphoria. It's hard to explain –'

'Sometimes one cannot put it into words.'

'And then it was back to reality, with the children crying and screaming. But they were very good. I could not have asked for more.'

'Poor Teddy was in the thick of things.' Henry gazed at his eldest son, the tears now dry on his round cheeks. 'You were very brave.'

'He was so worried for you. But I heard him tell little Marianne that a woman and four little children could do nothing, but we could pray to God and he would keep the people from hurting poor Papa.'

Henry nodded. 'And you must remember, Teddy, that many of these people do not wish to hurt us at all. In fact, they have protected us.'

Teddy said, 'I saw Aden snatch a gun away from one man.'

Aden was Marianne's best Māori servant-girl. She looked questioningly at Henry.

'You are quite right,' said Henry. 'I saw her too.'

'And Apo told us not to be frightened. She said she has been fighting for us,' piped up little Marianne.

'There you are,' said her mother. 'Even here in this wild place we have friends who will look after us.'

'But oh Mama,' said Teddy, 'what scary friends they are.'

2

While Marianne was calming the children and putting them to bed, Henry flung himself out of the hut and pushed open the gate.

Outside Māori people stood in groups, faces alight in excitement, arms waving, no doubt discussing the events that had just occurred. They could be sympathetic towards him or they could be plotting another attack.

He stepped onto the sand. Waves slapped the shore, withdrawing with the gurgle of a dying man. The islands out from the beach floated like upturned ships and clouds billowed like smoke over the oily sea.

His heart was pounding and his hands were shaking. He'd had a shock, even though he'd not let anyone see.

He began to walk along the beach. He had put his family in danger: the people who were most dependent upon him. Defenceless children, Marianne. Of course his wife knew their mission was dangerous yet she'd encouraged him to come to New Zealand. She was as convinced as he that this was the place where they must do the Lord's work. But the children — those with whom he was now blessed and those still to come — did he have the right to risk their lives too and subject them to such frightening scenes as those they had witnessed today?

But if he gave up now and returned home to where they would be safe and secure it meant the end of his vision. It was the reason he and Marianne had been brought together, each so suited to the task, and the reason they found themselves in this place.

He was near the end of the beach, where the sharp-pointed stick fence and thatch-roofed huts proclaimed the site of the pā. He would not go any further.

He turned and faced the inscrutable sea and the puffed-up clouds – a lone white man on the shore of a strange land. Dear Lord, he cried, thank you for being with me in my time of trouble. Thank you for softening the hearts of our attackers so they did not inflict the damage they surely could have. And, oh Lord, help me to know I am on the right path, and if I am, give me strength to continue and to let my family know you will protect them.

By the time he reached the cottage Teddy was ready to say his prayers:

'Gentle Jesus, meek and mild,

Look upon a little child ...'

Afterwards, instead of going back outside to see to the many matters that needed attention, he remained sitting on his eldest son's bed.

'When I was your age,' he began, 'my life was very different. My father owned a factory –'

'What's a factory, Papa?'

'It's a place with machines that make things in large numbers. In my father's factory they made stockings and he became successful and respected in the town of Nottingham. In fact, eventually he was made the sheriff.'

'Was he rich?'

'He was quite rich. Certainly as a family we did not want for money, nor did we have anything in particular to worry about. But then, when

I was twelve years old, my father died.'

'Why did he die?'

'He went to visit a friend who was dying of typhus, which is a very serious disease, and my father contracted it too.'

'Were you sad, Papa?'

'I was very sad. But my poor mother was even sadder, because she had eight children to support. She worked very hard to try to keep the factory going but in the end she had to sell it. And then she turned our house into a school for young women, to bring in some money to pay the bills. But she was always worried because she did not have enough money, and I wished and wished I could do something to help her.'

'But what could you do? You were only a boy.'

'Even little boys can do their bit to help, Teddy. Now, in those days Great Britain was fighting Napoleon. You've heard of Napoleon Bonaparte, haven't you?'

'I think he was a bad man.'

'He was a very bad man. In fact, everyone in Britain thought he was a monster. He wanted to invade our country.'

'Why did he want to do that?'

'Because he knew if he could conquer the British he would be able to take over all the lands and sea around us as well.'

'Were you frightened?'

'Not really, because I knew that Great Britain was very powerful, and we have the best navy in the world. And my grandfather and my uncles were all in the Royal Navy and they used to tell me stories about the adventures they had at sea, and it sounded very grand and exciting. I even made a little ship myself – I showed you the model I made, didn't I, of a man-o'-war? And so I thought I would join the Navy too so I could earn some money to send home to my mama.'

'And so you did!'

'As soon as I turned fourteen, that is indeed what I did.'

Teddy looked up, beaming. 'How brave you were, Papa.'

'I wasn't brave at all. In fact, sometimes I was very much afraid. But I knew I had to do my duty, and more than that I knew that the good Lord would always be with me.'

He reached out and touched his son's head, his fair, fine hair making him seem so fragile and other-worldly compared to the crowds that had surrounded and mocked them.

'And that is what I wanted to tell you, Teddy. You were very brave today and I am proud of you. But what I am most proud of is that you took care of your brother and sister and encouraged them to pray – because that is the most important thing you can do, and what you must continue to do whenever you are in need of help.'

He stood up from the bed and turned to go.

'Papa!'

'Yes?'

'Was it fun – the fighting?'

Henry looked at his son and shook his head.

It wasn't fun. It was horrible.

Oh yes, like any boy he'd wanted to serve his king and country, spurred on by the tales of his grandfather and his uncles of danger and adventure on the high seas, of wild storms lashing the decks and the daring of sailors as Great Britain fought her age-old enemy. The French had taken over England under William the Conqueror in 1066, and three hundred years later fought them in various conflicts for one hundred years. And now they'd rallied again, stirred up this time by the bogeyman Napoleon who'd risen to power on the back of the French Revolution and announced he wanted to annihilate England. Nelson had managed to stop them at Trafalgar in 1805 and they thought they'd seen the last of the French, but lo and behold they bounced back again. So then it was down to a battle between the two great nations of the world and this battle was fought at sea.

He joined the Navy in 1806. For his first engagement they'd put him on a ship as a midshipman, bound for Denmark. At Copenhagen he was told to go on land. As instructed he helped set up the cannons that surrounded the town and then the shelling started. He'd watched, astounded, as bombs and rockets tore into the lovely old city. Its ancient buildings caught fire or crumbled under the onslaught: the air was full of dust and flames and smoke, the pounding of the bombs and the screams of mortally wounded people.

'Why are we doing this?' he asked one of the older midshipmen.

'We wants their ships, son.'

'Haven't we plenty of our own?'

The old sailor looked at him sideways. 'You're in the Navy, now, lad. And y' doesn't ask questions. Y' just does.'

He later learnt that the British politicians, although they had no hard evidence, believed that Denmark, which had always claimed to be neutral, was about to let France use their navy. The shelling lasted four days, after which the Danes capitulated and surrendered their fleet to Britain. Most of the citizens of Copenhagen were evacuated before the battle, but even so as well as the militia, 195 civilians were killed and nearly 800 wounded, and a thousand buildings were destroyed.

Next he spent two years on one of the captured Danish ships, blockading the French coast. Word came that three French ships were stranded: the British attacked and killed the men in the open rowing boats sent out to defend them. Then they bombed the stranded ships.

After that he was assigned to intercept a French squadron sailing from Brest. In the melée his frigate took on water and all three of its masts, its bowsprit and its rigging were badly damaged. Forty six men, including Henry, were wounded and sixteen died. The British captured two of the French ships and they gave him a medal for his part in the battle.

Then the United States, who had been backed by France in its first War of Independence from Britain, again declared war. Now a lieutenant, Henry was transferred to the famous 'black frigate' – the *Endymion*. He was on board when in January 1815 it was off the coast from New York, helping to blockade an American squadron at anchor in the port. One of the American ships, the *President*, managed to escape through the blockade and the *Endymion* chased it. A battle ensued, ending when another British ship arrived as back-up, and the *President* surrendered.

The American ship was much larger than the *Endymion*, but she'd lost all her masts and there was six feet of water in her hold, caused by a hole made when scraping on a sandbank during the escape. Henry was one of those chosen to keep the *President* afloat and sail her to Bermuda, together with the American prisoners taken during the battle.

The crew rushed to remove the water that kept pouring into the ship. A roaring gale blew up and when the British called all hands on deck the Americans broke out of their quarters and tried to take back their ship. British and American sailors fought each other, man to man and hand to hand, while the ship rocked madly in the eye of the storm and the hold filled up with water once more.

They could have been wrecked and all perished, British and Americans alike. But Henry and his fellow sailors managed to overpower their prisoners and bring the ship safely to Bermuda. And then they had to sail the unseaworthy vessel back to Britain across the mountainous seas of the Atlantic.

Henry was shocked by the close encounter with the Americans. He'd seen the whites of their eyes and smelt their fear, not to mention his own. Yet were they not of British stock, like himself? – God-fearing men who spoke English and who simply wanted to run their colony the way they wished?

And yes, he had killed. Not just one man, but several. They came at him with all the vigour of men in their prime, fuelled by adrenalin and anger, and he had raised his gun – in self-defence, of course, but still he had done it – and he had fired that gun until they lay around him, limp corpses lacerated by wounds he himself had inflicted: young people who would never rise again.

To add to his disillusionment a peace treaty had been ratified by Britain a month before the battle, and by the United States a month after. It was the last engagement of the second War of Independence, and the *President* was returned to the Americans.

In 1815 Napoleon was finally conquered at Waterloo. The British had won the war against the French and were now the foremost power in the world. There was no longer the need to maintain a full-scale navy, and Henry was discharged on half pay.

So there he was back home in Nottingham: twenty three years old and what had he learnt?

Discipline, certainly.

But now he also knew the futility of war, its cruelty and chaos.

He thought of the man-o'-war that he'd fashioned from a picture in an encyclopedia. He still loved ships and hoped to sail in one again some day.

But he was no longer a man of war.

He wanted to be a man of peace.

3

What does a retired naval officer on half pay do for a living? Why – become an art teacher, of course!

After the war had finished England was full of returned soldiers and sailors roaming the countryside, hungry and desperate for work. Henry was fortunate in that the head of a girls' school in Cheltenham, impressed by his steady personality and pleasant manner, took him on as a drawing master. He was good at art and felt he had enough skills to impart his knowledge to others.

But there was a force that was drawing him in another direction altogether.

At the end of the eighteenth century there was a religious movement in Europe called The Great Awakening. In England this took the form of a group of clergy and lay people from the Anglican church banding together to form the Church Missionary Society. Its immediate aim was to stop the snatching of African people from their homes and taking them across the Atlantic to America where they were forced to work on huge plantations as slaves. Eventually the society was successful in achieving this, but it also had other aims: to improve the conditions at home and to spread the word to every corner of the world so that all people would love God and each other.

Edward Marsh, Anglican vicar of Aylesford, became an enthusiastic member of the CMS, as the Church Missionary Society was known. He was Henry's first cousin and also became his brother-in-law when he married his sister Lydia. After the passing of his own father, the person Henry looked up to the most was Edward.

During the war Henry's reading had been limited to the *Naval Chronicle*. But Edward persuaded him to broaden his horizon and take the *Missionary Register*, put out by the CMS. There Henry learned of the exciting progress that had been made in the southern seas of the Pacific Ocean, in particular Tahiti. In 1797 a group of missionaries had voyaged there and had at first endured great hardship and difficulties. But little by little they managed to win over the Tahitians from worshipping pagan gods who demanded human sacrifices. Instead the islanders were now well on the way to learning to love God and God's children, their fellow men.

The CMS also had missionaries in other parts of the world where the Gospel – the good news about Jesus Christ who died to save God's beloved children from going to hell – was, if not eagerly received, at least gradually being accepted.

But there was one place in the Pacific where the missionaries hesitated to go. The Māori in New Zealand were the fiercest people in the South Pacific, preoccupied with fighting each other or repelling any strangers who might land on their shores. In 1809 a British ship, the *Boyd*, anchored in a harbour in the far north of the country and almost all the seventy crew and passengers were killed and eaten. The reason eventually surfaced: a Māori man had been taken on board in Sydney and agreed to work his passage back. But he was taken ill and could not work, whereupon the captain of the ship had him tied to the gangway and flogged. Once in the midst of his own people the Māori took his revenge.

However, in 1814 the CMS sent three men – Messrs Kendall, King and Hall – to teach 'the arts of life' to the natives: boatbuilding, navigation and spinning flax to make rope. It appeared the Māori were already competent in these matters and to date no progress had been made in bringing them to Christ. Instead the lay missionaries' lives were constantly in danger: they were forever being robbed and attacked and threatened with death.

New Zealand, it appeared, was a no-go land.

And that was what made it so appealing to Henry. The more impossible the task, the more he liked the sound of it. The more difficult, the better!

New Zealand was where his future lay – but to that scheme there was a major impediment.

Her name was Marianne. Marianne Coldham, to be precise and she was a year younger than he. She lived in Nottingham, Henry's home town. Her father had arrived there to set up a business making hosiery or legwear, just like Henry's father, and like his father he had become an alderman and then a sheriff. And they had more in common than that: Marianne loved music, as did Henry. And she was a good artist. Furthermore, she had lost her mother at an early age and then, even more tragically, her father as well.

There were plenty of confidences to share when Henry began to travel regularly from Cheltenham to pay Miss Coldham a visit. Not that he expected the relationship to develop into anything more: they were simply two people who had already lost a great deal in their lives and gained comfort from the other's presence. Why else would a tall young woman, so beautiful and talented, condescend to entertain a shortish, bespectacled young man with no prospects?

Henry was content to sit and watch while Marianne played for him on the piano. With the eye of an artist he observed her clear skin and the graceful curve of her neck as she bent over the keyboard. As a man he saw her slender figure and shapely breasts, accentuated by her high-waisted muslin gown and puffed sleeves. As a musician he appreciated her skill upon the pianoforte. But when she finished a piece and turned towards him for his opinion, at the same time bringing to bear the gaze of her large blue eyes, he was so overcome he could barely speak a word.

Was there a hint of mischievousness in those big blue eyes? Was Miss Coldham well aware of the effect her presence had upon this battle-hardened officer and indeed gratified by it?

If amusement was something to go on he would accept that. And then he found that Miss Coldham was interested in the life of her admirer. She wanted to know what he'd done as a midshipman and then lieutenant in the Royal Navy: at first he was reluctant, not wanting to shock, but she insisted, and when he found her interest was genuine he came out with the story of his experiences that he'd never before shared with anyone.

He told her of his distress as a fourteen-year-old involved in the debacle of the battle of Copenhagen and in the subsequent campaigns the bloody slaughter he witnessed at close quarters, and at times had participated in himself. Finally he whispered that although he had participated in a conflict that was regarded as a triumph for the people of Great Britain, the main emotion that he felt was guilt.

They were sitting in the elegant drawing room at Marianne's house, each on separate chairs, a respectable distance apart. But when Henry finished speaking Marianne leant across the space that separated them and laid her hand upon his.

'Of course you thought you were doing the right thing, fighting to protect us from being invaded,' she said. 'But the Bible tells us, Thou shalt not kill.'

Henry was overwhelmed. This young woman went to the heart of the problem. She understood immediately his predicament; and she did not hesitate to utter sentiments that were at complete variance with the mood of their compatriots.

Was this what God intended? – by some miracle to choose for him as his wife a person of such empathy, ability and strength of character that she would make a perfect companion in the enterprise that he had so far barely articulated, even to himself?

He looked at Marianne, who by now had folded her hands demurely in her lap and was gazing at the floor. 'I wonder, Miss Coldham,' he said tentatively, 'if you have heard of the *Missionary Register*?'

'I'm sorry, Mr Williams, I don't believe I have.'

'It is the journal of the Church Missionary –'

Marianne became enlivened again. 'The Church Missionary Society! Ah yes indeed I have heard of that organisation. My father took a great interest in it and from him I learnt of the wonderful things they are accomplishing. Do you take their journal?'

Their conversation became very animated as Henry described to her the latest developments in the missionary field in the Pacific, and, finally, divulged his innermost ambition.

By the time the pair had finished they were talking as old friends. But this was not enough for Henry. From that time onward he determined to lay siege to the heart of Miss Marianne Coldham, and then, when he was sure of that, to ask for her hand in marriage.

'You wish to marry my granddaughter?' Mrs Temple gazed at Henry in surprise verging on horror.

Descended from Lady Godiva, the woman who in the eleventh

century was reputed to have ridden naked through the streets of Coventry in order to persuade her husband, the Earl of Mercia, to relieve his tenants of the high taxes he charged, Marianne's grandmother had a commanding personality.

Today they were sitting in the same stiff, high-backed chairs in the room where the relationship of Marianne and Henry first blossomed. But today the atmosphere was not humming with the joy and mystery of young love, but was icy with disapproval.

Henry was not to be intimidated. 'I know full well that Marianne is a very special person,' he said.

'Quite, Mr Williams. She has borne losses that no young woman should endure. First her mother dying in childbirth when Marianne was only sixteen and then supporting her father in his important work as sheriff. She has managed the entire household on her own – which is no easy task, I assure you – and as well as that she has had to bring up her three younger sisters. And then the death of her father two years ago, which made a double tragedy. I cannot conceive how she has coped.'

'But as you and I know, she has managed extremely well. In fact, I think it is this –'

'And then there is the matter of – I believe you have a tutoring position at Cheltenham. But how will this enable you to support her as she is used?'

Mrs Temple spread her hands outward to take in the beautifully furnished room in the comfortable, three-storeyed house that was Marianne's family home.

'I have my half pay from the Navy –'

'Half pay!'

'I admit that my circumstances do not permit me to live in luxury, which is, as you point out, the way of life to which Miss Coldham is accustomed. But we have discussed these matters and I believe she has accepted my proposal.'

'She has accepted already!' cried the grandmother.

'Shall we invite her in to hear what she has to say?'

'This is very irregular! How I wish Marianne's father were here, or my poor dear daughter, and then all would be conducted in the correct manner.'

'I realise this is an unusual situation, Mrs Temple,' said Henry. 'But Miss Coldham is an exceptional person and I think you can trust her judgement.'

'Her judgement! I don't know about that! Oh – very well.'

Mrs Temple rang a bell and a servant appeared. 'Ask Miss Marianne to step in,' she said.

And then she was there, poised in the doorway, her eyes bright with resolution and suppressed excitement.

'Please come and sit down,' said her grandmother.

Marianne perched on a chair that was shaped like a lozenge and demurely arranged the folds of her long dress.

'Mr Williams here has made an offer of marriage, of which I understand you are aware –'

'Indeed that is the case, Grandmama. He has done me a great honour and I would be very pleased to accept.'

'Marianne! You must remember you are a beautiful young woman and very accomplished. You need not take the first suitor that comes along. Obviously he is a brave soldier who has defended our great country. But as your grandmother I must be blunt. With the loss of your father, although for now he has made sure you are provided for, in the future you will face certain difficulties with regard to income. I think your parents would agree, if they were here, that the best course of action for you would be to accept a proposal from a gentleman of means and substance – someone who would best be able to support you. Whereas Mr Williams here —'

'Grandmama! I appreciate your concern — I really do — but I think you are well enough acquainted with me to know that I would never marry anyone for their money.'

'That's not quite what I —'

'I have absolute faith in the ability of Mr Williams to provide for me. He is a man of great integrity and I respect him enormously,' she said solemnly. Then her expression softened. 'And — and if I am honest I must say that I love him,' she said turning her head and smiling shyly at Henry '— and I dare to believe that he loves me.'

Henry gazed back at her and for a moment they were lost in the wonder of each other's presence.

'Love is all very well' said Mrs Temple. 'But —'

Marianne turned back to her grandmother. 'It is the most important thing. As you say, I have not led a sheltered life — in fact, at times it has been very demanding. But I feel that I have become a stronger person as a result and am well able to make a decision that will affect the rest of my life.'

'And your sisters? What will happen if you are not here to take care of them and help them find suitable husbands?'

'After we are married we will live at Cheltenham, which is not so far away. And when it is time for us to leave I will make sure arrangements are in place for their care. We have a large family and among them I'm sure there will be kindhearted people who have their best interests at heart.'

'As for that . . . But what did you say? Leave? Where would you be leaving for?'

Henry and Marianne looked at each other. Henry would have preferred to skirt the question at this delicate time, but Marianne was not so constrained.

'My husband-to-be,' she said, 'has a noble ambition.'

Mrs Temple relaxed slightly. 'He wishes to be an alderman, perhaps a sheriff, like his father?'

'He wishes to fulfil the calling of God. He is seriously considering offering his services to the Church Missionary Society.'

'A missionary society! Surely he would not take you to Africa!'

'Not to Africa, Grandmama. The place where he feels his skills are most needed is – New Zealand.'

'New Zealand? I do not know where that is.'

'It is at the farthest end of the earth.'

Mrs Temple was searching for her smelling salts. 'And how long, pray, would you be off on this adventure?' she said faintly.

'It is quite possible,' said Marianne, 'that we may never return.'

Her grandmother rose to her feet. 'Never return! What nonsense is this?'

Marianne also stood, and Henry followed her.

'It is not nonsense at all. We are merely doing our duty in taking the good news of forgiveness and redemption to people –'

'Who are no doubt perfectly happy as they are and have no need of your tender ministrations! Your duty is here, my girl, looking after your family and not leaving me to bear the burden.'

Mrs Temple made for the door. Then she turned. 'In my opinion you must not even consider marrying this man. Instead you should think of your poor orphaned sisters who depend upon you to see they marry well and have a secure future. You would be extremely selfish – not to mention foolish – to throw yourself away on a half-pay officer!'

4

The wedding did not take place in Nottingham, but at Nuneham Courtenay in Oxfordshire. Henry sketched the house from where they were married: its three storeys, with tiny attic windows in the slate roof, where the servants dwelt, a curving path leading to the front door, prettily festooned with creeping plants and the whole neatly fenced from the road.

He knew they would probably never again have the luxury of staying in such a place.

They had chosen Nuneham because it was where Edward Marsh, whose parish it now was, could officiate. The day was dark, grey, cold, the winter-bare branches beseeching the clouds with frail hands.

Marianne wore a simple white muslin gown with puffed sleeves and a ribbon tied high beneath her breasts; there were beads and flowers in her hair. She looked like a nymph, a goddess, thought Henry, in spite of knowing such a pagan symbol was not entirely appropriate. Afterwards she put on a long pelisse over her dress to keep her warm, but as they strolled back from the church together, followed by the wedding guests, the hand she slipped into Henry's was icy.

'You're frozen,' he said. 'We must hurry indoors.'

She flashed a smile at him, her eyes sparkling. 'Just imagine,' she said, 'in New Zealand at this very moment it is full summer. The sun is at its height and the skies are blue. I can feel its warmth already.'

Their first baby, whom they named Edward Marsh, was born in November. Then, with Marianne enthusiastically supporting him, in 1819 Henry offered his services to the CMS.

He had read in the *Missionary Register* that the Society was thinking of buying a ship to transport missionaries and supplies to their small settlement in New Zealand. What an ideal opportunity that would be: with his experience in the Navy he could command the ship. And they would not need to pay him, for he and Marianne thought they could manage on the half pay he was still receiving.

Thank you, but no said the CMS: the idea of sending a ship had been abandoned. But as Henry was so interested in New Zealand, would he consider going there as a lay missionary?

Henry and Marianne conferred and made up their minds. Henry threw himself into learning the skills the CMS thought he would need: he went to Oxford to study medicine and to London to study surgery. He also learnt the practical arts of boatbuilding: he might not sail a ship to New Zealand, but once he was there he would need to build a boat in order to travel around. As far as he knew there were no roads and the only way to reach the local villages was by sea.

He wrote to tell Edward Marsh of his progress. His cousin must have been having his doubts, or maybe he just wanted to sound a warning.

He had heard, Edward said, from the Reverend Josiah Pratt, the secretary of the CMS, and it appeared all was going well. He liked the sound of the pursuits in which Henry was engaged, although he thought that in boatbuilding the Māori might know more than he. But he warned Henry to count the cost of the project on which he and his wife were embarking. Once in New Zealand he needed to be prepared for all situations and hazards and he would be cut off from direct communication with the people most familiar to him. 'Your companions will be ignorant, may be perverse, or may even misinterpret or reject what you design for their good. Even those who ought to co-operate with you may often disappoint you. And when this happens you will have no retreat, few persons to consult and no other avenues to take your mind off your problems.

'But if you can contemplate this and yet still want to persevere, if knowing that you must not look back and will still put your hand to the plough, then I have nothing more to do than wish you good success in the name of the Lord.'

In fact, they were again prevented. This time the Society said there'd been trouble among the lay settlers themselves who were already installed in New Zealand. And the Māori people had become more hostile and were attacking them. The settlers' recall was imminent.

Henry wrote to Edward Marsh advising him of the delay. 'Whilst I bow in submission to his will, I rejoice that the Lord has called me out of darkness into his marvellous light, and from the pursuit of war to an earnest desire to lend my feeble efforts to convey the gospel of peace to a far-distant nation.'

'Why is there so much trouble among the settlers?' asked Marianne.

'I suppose it all began with the Reverend Samuel Marsden.'

'The gentleman who set up the mission?'

'He was, and still is as far as I know, a chaplain to the New South Wales convict settlement. He struck up a friendship with a Māori chief, Ruatara, whom he met on board a ship travelling from London to Sydney. The chief was in a pitiable state, having wished to visit England and see the king and instead had been treated most grievously by the sailors. Samuel Marsden saw that he was well looked after while on board until he recovered, and when he arrived in Sydney he took the chief into his home for several months.'

'But how did that lead to the mission?'

'Evidently the Lord was preparing the way. Ruatara was extremely grateful for the kindness shown to him. He returned to New Zealand, where the Reverend Marsden had always had hopes of eventually taking the Word of God. And in 1814, having established there were enough people among the Māori who were well disposed towards himself and a mission settlement, Marsden took the three settlers of whom we have been speaking, and their families, to a place called the Bay of Islands, in the northern part of the North Island of New Zealand.'

'Are they of the Evangelical persuasion?'

'Mr Kendall is – he was born again of the Spirit while in London, and is very fervent. In fact, this may have exacerbated the problems between them as the other two are more practical men. Mr Hall was a carpenter and Mr King a ropemaker. Kendall was a schoolteacher and regarded himself as the leader of the mission. The Reverend Marsden's idea was that these men and their families would act as forerunners –'

'Like St John the Baptist before the coming of Jesus Christ?'

'"The voice in the wilderness." Yes, that is an interesting comparison.' Henry gazed fondly at his wife. She was so clever, so good at putting things in a way that made them clearer.

Then he collected himself. 'But these gentlemen fell far short of the standard set by St John. The idea of the Reverend Marsden was that they would teach the civilised arts to the Māori people, such as growing crops, trading and European manners in general. This, I believe, is what Ruatara, the chief he befriended, hoped for also. Then, having discovered what knowledge and benefits we have to offer, Mr Marsden expected the Māori would be more receptive to the Christian faith.'

'But that has not eventuated?'

'Unfortunately not. A major problem, as I understand from the CMS people here, is the calibre of the lay settlers. One or two of them are not of strong enough character to withstand the temptations and difficulties of living in such an isolated place, far from their own race. They have sold muskets to the native people and some have resorted to drunkenness. The worst of it, in my opinion, is that they have not been able to work together.'

'And thus show the virtue of the Christian religion — that we are all the children of God and should love each other as brothers and sisters?'

Henry nodded. 'So now the CMS has decided to proceed in a different direction; they have engaged an ordained man, the Reverend John Gare Butler, to proceed to the Bay of Islands. And with his presence they hope the mission will proceed on a surer footing and that once more the light of Christ will shine brightly in that dark place.'

'I do hope so.' Marianne had been listening intently. Then it struck her. 'So — what does that mean for us?'

'This is what I was leading up to.' Henry put his arm around his wife, now pregnant with their second child. 'I have had a communication from Josiah Pratt and he asks if, in line with the new direction the mission is taking, I would consider becoming ordained.'

'Ordained! You would become a minister in the Anglican church!'

'Is that so ridiculous? I admit I'm not academically inclined — I may have to learn Latin and Greek —'

'You know I have absolute faith in you. It's just such a surprise —'

'It would mean a lot of study and then I would have to do my apprenticeship — serve in a parish.'

'How long would it take?'

'Two years.'

'So long!' Marianne put her head in her hands.

Henry gazed at her anxiously. 'It is disappointing, I know. But Mr Pratt says otherwise they will not let us go.'

'I feel that we are urgently required in New Zealand – that we are being drawn there.'

'And one day we will be there. But this way I will learn a great deal and be a much more effective servant of God.'

Marianne pressed her palms together and looked up. 'Yes of course, you are right. You must do it.'

'I knew you would understand.'

'Oh, I do, I do! And in the meantime I can learn more about nursing and teaching and –'

'You can contribute so much. If you are not happy I will not go. For you are my right hand, my rock and my angel. If you are with me, I can do anything.'

He knelt before her and held her hand.

'Oh Henry,' said Marianne, 'we are truly blessed.'

Edward Marsh was appointed his counsellor and tutor, so they moved to Balden, where he was now the vicar. Then, when he moved to Hampstead in London they followed him again; here Henry was able to help his cousin in the parish and gain some practical experience. He also immersed himself in study: he was spared the Latin and Greek, seeing it was unlikely he would need those languages in New Zealand, but he learnt in depth the principles of Christianity and the theology behind them, in order to give the spiritual leadership that was required.

Marianne too decided she needed more practical skills. She learned to cook, which was something so far she had left to servants. And because there would be no doctors or nurses or hospitals in the faraway world to which they were going, she learnt nursing and midwifery.

She put her newfound skills to the test when she produced her second child, a daughter this time, whom they named Marianne.

And because she would need to educate their children, and also, she hoped the children of the Māori people, she learnt to be a teacher.

Josiah Pratt asked Henry to step in and see him.

The secretary of the CMS, normally a cultured and serious man, was red with rage. 'I have just received a letter from the Reverend Samuel Marsden,' he said, 'and I regret to say it is the bearer of terrible news. The situation in New Zealand, as regards the lay settlers, has become even more difficult, if that is possible.'

'Please enlighten me,' said Henry.

'Thomas Kendall has refused to accept the leadership of the Reverend Butler and nor will he take instructions from the Reverend Marsden. Instead he and most of the other settlers as well have been trading muskets and powder with the Māori chiefs.'

'Lining their pockets by selling arms! That is despicable.'

'Quite. But worse is to come. We have now heard that Mr Kendall has arrived in England –'

'In England! What – he is in London?'

'Completely against our orders and without our permission. And he has brought with him two chiefs, Hongi Hika and Waikato.'

'Indeed? Perhaps I should meet them. It might be advantageous –'

'Perhaps not, Mr Williams,' said Pratt hurriedly. 'While in Sydney, on his way to England, Mr Kendall bought muskets in Sydney and sent them back to the Bay of Islands. We fear – we fear very much – that the aim of these two chiefs is to obtain more arms while in England.'

'But how could they achieve that? Do they have money?'

'Not at present. But the chiefs have caused a great deal of interest and they are being showered with gifts. And they are to be presented to the king, who will no doubt also be very generous.'

'You think they would sell the gifts?'

Pratt nodded. 'With the help, I suspect, of Mr Kendall. And then they will buy the muskets.'

'But whom would they attack?'

'Their fellow countrymen. In New Zealand, and, in fact, throughout the Pacific, there is a strong ethos of revenge. There are scores to settle...'

Henry gazed at Josiah Pratt.

'And these other people – do any of them have guns?'

'As far as I know, they do not. They have spears and suchlike.'

'As a former military man I can tell you – soldiers with spears, no matter how skilled they are, have no chance at all against men with guns.'

The two men's eyes met.

'Precisely, Mr Williams,' said Josiah Pratt. 'There would be a bloodbath.'

5

Their second son, and third child, was born in January 1822. They called him Samuel, which was prophetic: the little boy became very ill and was expected to die. Henry and Marianne dedicated the baby to the Lord, just as the Samuel in the Bible had been, promising he would be brought up to carry out the Lord's wishes. In time, Samuel Williams recovered.

As well as studying for his ordination, Henry set to finding out more about the Māori people amongst whom he would be working.

He bought the two-volume *Nicholas's New Zealand*, an account by John Nicholas who went with Samuel Marsden on the *Active* in 1814 when he took the lay settlers and the chiefs to New Zealand.

The chiefs had been staying with Samuel Marsden on his farm, in order that they might learn something of the new way of life that was being offered to them. Nicholas first met them here.

One was Ruatara, whom Marsden had befriended and on whose account the mission in New Zealand had been established. Nicholas described Ruatara as 'a man in the full bloom of youth, of tall and commanding stature, great muscular strength, and a marked expression of countenance'; dignified and noble, 'while the fire and animation of his eye might betray, even to the ordinary beholder, the elevated rank he held among his countrymen'.

The other was Hongi Hika. He was not as muscular, said Nicholas, but was a chief of superior rank to Ruatara. Although he was reputed to be one of the greatest warriors in his country, his natural disposition seemed to be mild and inoffensive. He appeared to be much more inclined to peaceful habits than to strife.

Henry looked up from his reading. Peaceful habits? This was not borne out by what he'd heard from Josiah Pratt. Perhaps this Hongi Hika was a dissembler, able to project himself as well-intentioned. Or perhaps something had happened to change his disposition?

He went back to his reading.

Everyone was loaded onto the *Active*: Hongi Hika, Ruatara and Korokoro and their relations; Marsden and Nicholas; and the missionaries Kendall, Hall and King and their wives and families.

But then it was discovered that the chiefs, who previously had been cheerful and duly impressed by the workings of civilised life, were gloomy, sullen and reserved.

Marsden asked what was the matter.

'We fear that if your people come to our country we will lose our independence, our mana, our freedom and maybe even our lives,' they said.

'Why do you think that?' asked Marsden.

'A white man told us. He said, "Look at the way your people have treated the Aborigines. They have been dispersed and killed and chased out of their own lands. Soon they will disappear altogether." And the same will happen to us.'

There was dismay in the ship. The whole expedition was based on the expectation that Ruatara and the other chiefs would protect and support the missionaries. If the chiefs were not happy with their presence in the country, it would be dangerous to proceed any further.

Marsden spoke to Ruatara. He told the chief if he preferred, the ship would turn around then and there and return to Sydney. The missionaries and their families would disembark and there would be no further attempt to send anyone to New Zealand.

The chiefs discussed the matter amongst themselves and with Marsden. They told him also that while in Sydney they'd heard rumours there were plans to create large settlements in their country where many white men would come to live. They feared the Māori people would be overrun.

In spite of their misgivings the chiefs decided they wanted the *Active* to continue on to New Zealand.

On 22 December 1814 the ship anchored in the Bay of Islands, just off Rangihoua, the village of which Ruatara was chief. On the following Sunday, which was Christmas Day, Samuel Marsden gave the first sermon to be preached in New Zealand. The text he used for his teaching was the tenth verse of the second chapter of St Luke's Gospel: 'Behold, I bring you good tidings of great joy.'

Ruatara translated Marsden's words. The chiefs affirmed their support and the people seemed to want to follow their chiefs.

But then Ruatara became ill with a severe cold. Marsden tried to help, but only a few people and the tohunga, or priest, were allowed near him, and then it was time for Marsden to depart.

Four days after Marsden left the Bay of Islands, Ruatara died. This was a disaster of the highest magnitude, and not just for the tribe of Ruatara. It meant the little missionary settlement was now entirely dependent upon the goodwill of that other chief – Hongi Hika.

In June 1822 Henry was ordained a priest of the Anglican Church.

At last they could make definite preparations for their voyage. In the house they rented Marianne had been busy putting aside items they absolutely needed for the voyage, plus things it would be nice to take if there was room. She went about with a smile on her face and the children, catching her mood, were excited too.

Then Henry received a message from Josiah Pratt: would Henry be good enough to call in and see him?

When he entered the secretary leapt from behind his desk and came to shake Henry's hand, holding it in both of his. 'The Reverend Henry Williams!' he exclaimed. 'It has a fine ring, does it not?'

He retreated back behind his desk and gestured to the chair for Henry to sit.

Then he wiped his forehead and sighed. 'If only matters in New Zealand had progressed as smoothly as your ordination.'

Henry waited.

Pratt picked out a letter from the papers scattered on his desk and passed it across to Henry. 'Would you care to read this, sir. I have just received it from the Reverend Marsden.'

Marsden's letter ran: 'Very unpleasant news from New Zealand. The visit of the chiefs to England has been productive of great evil. All the presents Hongi received were changed in New South Wales for muskets. He is supposed to have a thousand stand of arms. Mr Kendall is implicated. The natives despise those missionaries who obey the instructions of the Society and refuse to sell muskets.'

Pratt watched as Henry read the letter. 'What we feared is now coming to pass.'

'A thousand stand of arms!' he said. 'How could he have amassed so many?'

'While he was here in England,' said Pratt, 'He, along with Mr Kendall, met a Frenchman who offered to buy land and paid him in muskets.'

'How much land?'

Pratt sifted through papers on his desk. Then he looked up. 'It says here that Charles Philippe Hippolyte de Thierry bought thirty thousand acres in the Hokianga district of New Zealand.'

'That's a huge amount — a whole county, in fact — obtained by a Frenchman! Who is he?'

'He is a baron, or some such — one of those emigrés who scuttled over to England during the Revolution. But we cannot concern ourselves with what the French are doing. The main fact is de Thierry promised Hongi Hika five hundred muskets, gunpowder, ball, swords and daggers.'

'And he received them?'

'He uplifted the cache once he got to Sydney.'

'And Mr Kendall is implicated?'

'I regret to say he is. In fact, he bought the land on de Thierry's behalf. And now he has been using his friendship with Hongi Hika to claim his position as head of the mission. Naturally this upsets the other missionaries, who have already been disturbed by his behaviour. Kendall has also been instrumental in persuading them there is nothing wrong in selling arms. He even wrote a letter to the CMS, which he got the other men to sign, insisting they had to trade in guns in order to remain on side with the Māori. Here —' Pratt rifled among the papers on his desk. 'Ah yes.' He read out, 'The Māori dictate to us! It is evident that ambition and self-interest are amongst the principal causes of our security amongst them.'

'And this was written by Mr Kendall? He is clearly a bad influence on the lay settlers.'

'But that's not all our Mr Kendall has done. He has been very interested in learning the Māori language, which is what we hoped. But in learning about Māori culture he has become rather too involved.' Pratt leant forward and hissed: 'The Reverend Marsden informs me that

Mr Kendall has been guilty of the basest behaviour.'

Henry stared at him.

'Adultery, Mr Williams – adultery! One of the Ten Commandments that we take most seriously – of course we take them all seriously, but –'

'With whom? Surely not the other settlers' wives?'

Pratt shook his head. 'With a young Māori woman who was a pupil at his school. She was also a servant in his house. Marsden tells me Kendall has left his wife and is living with the woman.' Pratt ran his fingers through his hair. 'He said he needed a close relationship in order to learn more about the culture of the Māori.'

'Hmmm!'

'And now he even claims he has found the beliefs of the Māori so compelling he is quite turned from being a Christian to a heathen!'

Henry stared at him. 'Your news is indeed extraordinary.'

Pratt sat back. 'Of course one has to accept that the pressures these people have been under are immense – greater, I may say, than we anticipated. But also it appears they were not of the calibre that was required to withstand the forces and temptations encountered in a non-Christian society.'

'They need strong leadership. The sooner we depart the better.'

'That is what I wanted to discuss with you. I – we, that is, the Church Missionary Society, now feel that New Zealand is not the place to which we wish to send our people. The soil is not yet ready to receive the seed of the Gospel.'

Henry opened his mouth to speak.

Pratt held up his hand. 'Pray allow me to continue, Mr Williams. We are well aware of, and very grateful for, the time and effort you have put into preparing for mission. We feel in yourself we have an excellent candidate. But with the lack of success of our mission in New Zealand – not one soul has been brought to God in the eight years they have been there – and the disarray they are in …' Pratt distractedly ran a hand over the top of his head. 'But apart from that, it must be remembered that New Zealand is a wild and dangerous place. And with Hongi Hika now so heavily armed, it has become even more dangerous. You and your family could find yourselves in a very serious situation.'

'We have always been aware of that, Mr Pratt. But we have the best and greatest protector – the good Lord himself.'

'Oh, I quite agree, Mr Williams. But even so, there are many other fields of endeavour – places where people are crying out for the Gospel to be brought to them – Africa, for example. It is a good deal closer to home and would mean Mrs Williams is not so far –'

Marianne. What would she think?

He knew, straightaway.

He leapt to his feet and advanced towards the desk where Josiah Pratt was frowning, gazing down at his desk with his chin resting on his clasped hands.

'Mr Pratt, I fully appreciate your concern for my wife and myself. Your solicitude for our safety and well-being is much appreciated. But from what you have just told me it seems more evident than ever before where we are needed.'

Pratt raised his head.

'Our minds are quite made up. All our planning – all our efforts – have been focused on this one place. We are sure in our hearts that New Zealand is where the Lord intends us to carry out our endeavours. Furthermore, I think I can speak for my wife when I say the difficulties that have manifested themselves in the mission do not deter us. We merely see them as a challenge that we are all too ready to accept. And so, Mr Pratt –'

Henry stood up and thumped on the table, making Josiah jump.

'New Zealand is the place where we will go.'

The CMS called a special meeting to farewell them.

Henry walked into a room where a semicircle of earnest men in sober suits were seated on hard-backed chairs. Edward Marsh was also present.

He was invited to be seated. Then Josiah Pratt, as secretary, rose and walked to the centre of the room to address them.

'Gentlemen,' he said, 'I need not remind you of the importance of this meeting. It is an occasion both serious and joyful. Serious, because of the high calling of the expedition on which Mr and Mrs Williams are about to embark; and joyful, because in sending a missionary of his calibre to New Zealand the Society is furthering the agenda it set out so long ago. We admire enormously his persistence in acquiring the best qualifications possible for the work that lies ahead: also his determination to set sail for New Zealand in spite of the undoubted hurdles and the quite possible danger that he and his wife and children will encounter.

'I now have a few words to address to Mr Williams.' He turned and faced Henry. 'I must warn you, sir, not to fall into the trap which has unfortunately ensnared the earlier lay settlers – of paying too much attention to worldly matters and not spending enough time on religious instruction. This has led them to be tempted to provide for themselves and their families in a way that might lead them astray. However,' said Pratt, 'with regard to this, provided that all the time and labour of yourself and your family are devoted to promoting the aim of the mission, the Committee does not wish to interfere with any property that a missionary might acquire through his private means.'

There was silence as they waited for Henry to reply.

He looked around at the men who had been his supporters for so long and who were sending him out to act on their behalf.

'I am well aware of your great anxiety with regard to this mission,' he said. 'I feel anxiety myself. My main aim will be to repair the breaches that have occurred in the mission community. I will achieve this by promoting unity and Christian affection for one another.

'I believe also that you are concerned at how much it will cost to run the enterprise. To this end Mrs Williams and I feel that we are well able to live on the money I receive from the Navy, and we hope this will relieve the burden upon you.

'As for myself, I have long been aware of the state of the people among whom I hope to live and die. It is my desire, even to the end of my days, to spend the rest of my life in the service of my God in bringing them to the knowledge of his ways.'

He told the Society they need not fear the lawlessness and disobedience that had previously been shown. 'I will observe the orders you may send to me from time to time just as rigidly as I ever did those of my senior officer while I was in His Majesty's service. However, I am aware I have many faults, and I hope that when my conduct does not meet with your approval you will tell me with all possible plainness.

'With regard to Mrs Williams, I wish to say that she does not accompany me merely as my wife, but as a fellow-helper in the work of the mission. Although for some time she will be occupied with the care of our children, these too have been dedicated to the Lord and we hope you will consider them as part of your missionary household.'

Edward Marsh then gave a long exhortation on the conduct of a missionary. He praised Henry for his devotion to the cause and his enthusiastic study of medicine and surgery, and the crafts that would teach the natives how to improve their condition and take their minds off the pursuit of war. And he reminded him that he was entering the territory of a powerful people against whom it would be useless to try protecting oneself by force: 'As your object is peaceful, so should your hand be unarmed.'

At the end of the meeting all stood. Henry moved round the circle, shaking hands. Each man murmured words of support and good wishes.

Then he went to leave the room, but Edward Marsh followed. Henry turned and Edward held out his arms, gripping him on both shoulders.

Henry gazed into the eyes of the man who had been his friend, mentor, advisor and father figure and whom he may now – probably would – never see again.

'Edward ...' he began, and then emotion overcame him. The cousins embraced and Henry left with tears pricking his eyes.

The vessel Henry and Marianne embarked on for the first leg of their voyage to New Zealand was not one in which most people would have considered travelling. The *Lord Sidmouth* was a convict ship, carrying ninety seven women convicts plus nineteen free women and their children going out to join their convict husbands in Sydney. But it was the earliest passage they could take, and after waiting so long to carry out the mission to which they had dedicated themselves they did not want to lose a day more.

Before he left Henry spent precious time with his God. He asked him to watch over his mother, and also over the family of Marianne. He asked for his special protection as they made their way across the seas to the other side of the world and he asked his blessing on the enterprise. And, most particularly, he asked the good Lord to take care of his family – Marianne, Teddy, little Marianne and Samuel – as they sailed into the unknown.

6

The Marsh family gathered to see them off.

'It looks very old,' said Lydia, gazing doubtfully at the *Lord Sidmouth* – named, probably in jest, after a former prime minister. 'Do you think it's safe?'

Henry surveyed the vessel to which he was entrusting the lives of those who were dearest to him in the world.

'It is old,' he said, 'but it will serve the purpose. And we have the greatest of all protectors to see that we reach our journey's end in safety.'

'We will be thinking of you all the time. You will write, won't you?'

'I shall write – Marianne will write, I assure you,' said Henry.

'Teddy will see that you do,' said Lydia, putting her arm around her nephew.

'Yes I will, I will, Aunt Marsh!' the little boy assured her.

A bell rang.

The ship's main complement of ninety seven convict women and their twenty two children, plus nineteen free women and their children – all forty four of them – had already been stowed in the hold.

Now it was time for the Williams family to make their final farewells and to stand for the last time on the soil of Old England.

In the Channel the sea was so rough and the ship so poorly balanced that everyone – that is, the prisoners, the free women, Marianne and the children were sick – even Henry.

He would have said – if he was capable between bouts of retching, vomiting and generally feeling extremely miserable – that he was not insensible to the absurdity of the situation.

In spite of her own misery, Marianne teased him. 'Is this a British sailor I see before me?' she said. 'Perchance not the kind that sails upon the ocean!'

'It's seven years since I was on a ship,' he retorted between spasms. 'But that seems to have been forgotten by my brain.'

In spite of his wretchedness, at the end of the first week of the voyage Henry resolved to take a service on Sunday evening. He had given sermons before, when he was assistant to his cousin at his parish in Hampstead. But this would be the first time he had preached to the unconverted.

The service was to have been held on deck, which suited Henry as he had no desire at all to clamber down into the dark hold where the women and their children had been vomiting for the past week.

One by one the crew and the free women and their children began to appear through the hatchway. Henry's heart lifted. They wore clean clothes, hats and shoes and there were smiles on their faces. But then a squall swept across the deck and the captain ordered that the service be moved below decks. It would first be held in the prison.

Resigned, Henry climbed down the ladder as the ship lurched and rolled. It was like descending into a dungeon – which of course it was. At first he could see nothing, and then by the light of the one lantern swinging violently back and forth he made out low wooden beams above his head and, skittering across the floor under his feet, slimy brown cockroaches. He crunched some under his boot.

The stench of urine, faeces and rotten vomit hit his nostrils. From the darkness came the sound of children crying; some women were wailing too, while others were shrieking abuse and oaths at each other.

His legs were unsteady and he felt queasy and nauseous, but he kept his face composed.

'Good evening, everybody,' he bellowed. 'I have come to take a service!'

There was a sudden quiet.

The capricious light of the lantern as it swung picked up the faces of the convict women who moved towards him – their faces pinched by illness and lack of food, hardened by misery and despair. Children, still grizzling, clutched their mothers' skirts, eyes large with malnutrition. They would already have spent weeks or even months in prison in London, or on one of the hulks that lay at sea, abandoned ships now used for a prison.

Henry asked for God's blessing: 'In the name of the Father, the Son and the Holy Ghost.'

'Blimey! ... He's seen a ghost already!' came out of the darkness.

There was a burst of cynical laughter.

Henry held up his Bible. 'I'm not sure how familiar you are with the Holy Book –'

'Only when we 'as to swear on it in court,' called the same voice. 'An' look where it got us!'

Another titter from the women.

The ship gave a mighty shudder and everyone collapsed upon each other.

Henry waited until they had righted themselves.

'I thought I would begin,' he said, 'by reading you some verses that mean a great deal to me. They are from the Book of Ezekiel, which is found in the Old Testament. They are, in fact, instructions from God to Ezekiel, but I regard them as my commission, that is, my instructions from God to do the work on which I am now engaged.'

Another lurch and more shrieks and curses from the women.

He stood astride to steady himself and opened his Bible at the place he had marked.

'This reading,' he began, 'is taken from Ezekiel, chapter three, verses seventeen to nineteen: "Mortal man, he said, I am making you a watchman for the nation of Israel. You will pass on to them the warnings I give you. If I announce that an evil man is going to die but you do not warn him to change his ways so that he can save his life, he will die, still a sinner, and I will hold you responsible for his death. If you do warn an evil man and he does not stop sinning, he will die, still a sinner, but your life will be spared."'

'So what does that mean, Mister?' asked a woman close to him.

'It means,' said Henry, 'turning to her, pleased he seemed to have a receptive listener, 'that I must warn you to repent of your sins.'

'What sins?' she asked.

'For that you must ask your own conscience. But first and foremost I would say it is the sin or sins you have committed that have led you to being incarcerated in this ship.' The woman's face convulsed. 'Was it a sin I committed, to take food so my poor starving children had something to eat? Where is the sin in that, you tell me!'

There were murmurings from the women around him. They began to close in on him.

'Yes, Mister Bible-man,' cried another. 'Who are the sinners – the women who had to steal to keep their families alive – or those that had food in plenty but did not share it with them, and instead sent us off in this damned old hulk?'

'Yes, tell us that, mister!' The women crowded closer, grimacing, snarling.

'No one forced you to steal,' said Henry.

There was a growl from the women. They thrust their faces into his. 'No one forced us! What do you know, you –'

A face appeared at the hatch. 'Shut y'r faces, you whores!' he roared. 'Or I'll get the doctor on t' ya!'

The threat of the doctor's attentions seemed to strike fear into their hearts and the women backed away.

To calm them Henry read the psalm for the day, which was particularly appropriate for those facing difficulties. 'And so,' he finished, 'although it may appear that we are in trouble, we know that if we call upon the Lord he will have mercy upon us.'

He prayed aloud for God to keep them safe on the voyage. And then, with the creaking of the ship's timbers and the groaning of her straining sheets overhead as his accompaniment, he sang the Evening Hymn.

Some of the women joined him:

Now, now that the sun hath veil'd his light
And bid the world goodnight;
To the soft bed my body I dispose,
But where shall my soul repose?
Dear, dear God, even in thy arms …

No one had a soft bed on which to 'dispose their bodies', least of all the poor creatures surrounding him. And yet, that evening, it almost seemed that something divine occurred.

When he finished some of the women came forward to grasp his hand and thank him.

Finally he was able to climb up the steps and out of the hold, gulping in mouthfuls of pure air.

Then he paused.

From below a sound floated up.

Of their own accord, the convict women were singing another hymn.

When they struck out into the Atlantic, the sea became even rougher. The ship reared up, climbing to the top of a wave and then crashing down the other side, its bow buried in the water. The sea was hammering them like a blacksmith on his anvil.

Within all was chaos. To keep plates on the table in the family's cabin two strips of rolled up cloth, called puddings, were strapped crosswise and lengthwise. The table was also crisscrossed with string to hold the glasses in place: even so, they had to down the glasses' content in one gulp and hold their soup plates in their hands.

Like everyone else poor Teddy was dreadfully sick and lay on the couch without moving.

Marianne tried to soothe him by applying a cold compress to his forehead.

He began to stir.

'Can I sit up?'

'Not just now, Teddy. The ship is still rocking.'

'I was thinking,' he said. 'Could we go by coach to New Zealand? It would be so much easier.'

'I'm afraid that's not possible, Teddy. Didn't I show you a globe and you saw the great seas that we must cross?'

'I think so, Mama, but I didn't know there was so much water in the sea. How many more days will it be before we arrive?'

Marianne shook her head. 'Many, many more days. But it will not always be as rough as this and I'm sure that soon you'll be feeling better.'

'Will I see my dear little cousins again? I miss them so.'

Marianne stroked his head. 'Let's write them a letter and tell them all about our adventures. I'm sure they will be terribly interested.'

They had been on board for ten days and to get to Sydney it would take, the captain said, about five months.

As they moved south, heading across the Atlantic to South America, the weather grew warmer. The ship became hot as an oven and the cockroaches began to multiply.

Whenever he entered their cabin in the evening the first thing Henry did was to lay about him with the heel of his shoe, squashing as many as he could. Eventually they disappeared.

But for those in the hold there was no escape. The infestation was worst among the free women, some of whom became ill and were too weak to move and brush away the creatures that crawled all over them.

Sometimes there was what the sailors called a 'wedding': thousands of cockroaches swarmed from every part of the ship like locusts, eating everything they could find – food, books, clothes, boots and paper parcels.

And then on 15 October the ship was becalmed.

Marianne became ill, with a very high fever and severe headache.

The doctor and the captain did all they could for her, and with the help of Kitty, one of the convict women, Henry took over the care of the children. The baby Samuel was weaned.

The captain only just tolerated the children; and when he was suffering an attack of gout not at all, so everything had to be done to stop them crying.

Teddy was forever asking his father to write letters – to his grandmother, his cousins, or whoever else he could think of in England. Little Marianne wanted him to write to 'Uncle Marsh'. But unless they met a ship going the opposite way to England, there was no means of sending a letter back.

Henry also continued to read the Bible and pray with the convict women. But in the intense heat and the lack of sanitation the conditions in which they were gaoled became worse and the women even more defiant. When he spoke they crowded up close beside him, coughing and laughing and killing cockroaches. And if they sang a hymn at all it was with vulgar words to the tune.

For two weeks the ship was becalmed – 'in irons', as the sailors called it, after the iron shackles that prevented convicts from running away.

Then at last the wind began to blow and the boat to move. They passed close to the Grand Canary and Cape Verde Islands. And then the cool trade wind picked them up and blew them straight to the coast of Brazil.

By now Marianne had recovered and resumed her duties with the women. But she was dismayed by their behaviour. 'I do believe,' she said to Henry, 'that most of them are dissolute and careless – in fact, downright bad. I hope you haven't been wasting your time, putting all this effort into preaching to them.'

'Not at all,' he replied. 'For one thing, there are some among them who are quiet and listen carefully to what I have to say. And for the rest – at least I have taught them something of the way to salvation. The rest is up to God.'

When they finally reached Rio de Janeiro they were invited by an English family to stay in their house on the shore of the harbour.

Marianne was in heaven and so were the children. They delighted in the big rooms, the green trees, being able to walk on the beach, play in the garden and sit at a proper table. How precious these things were, that formerly they had taken for granted!

But while wandering around the market they were brought back to earth.

'Come and look,' said Henry. He beckoned to Marianne.

Displayed on a stall, much like a row of oranges or apples, were the preserved heads of people. Their eyes were wide open and their mouths drawn back in what seemed like a sneer, or more likely was an expression of terror. Their faces were adorned with strange markings – spirals and wavy lines – and they were cut off at the neck.

She recoiled. 'Are they real?'

'Only too real. They are regarded as curiosities, because of the way the faces are decorated.'

'People buy them for ornaments?'

'So I have heard. I believe they fetch high prices in England.'

'How absolutely appalling! But whose? – why? Where have they come from?'

'That's what is so worrying. I've been told they're from New Zealand. These are Māori people, killed and sold to traders visiting the country. Possibly the heads have been decorated after death. And I think that what we are witnessing here are the fruits of the evil that was done when muskets were given to Hongi Hika.'

And then they were back on the ship.

After a break away, conditions on the *Lord Sidmouth* seemed even worse than when they had endured them for months on end. But at least now they were, not exactly on the homeward stretch, but nearing the end of their journey.

Marianne found it hardest to bear, because she was pregnant again and ill to boot.

They skirted the coast of Brazil and rounded Cape Horn. Then they were in the Pacific: 'Our Pacific Ocean,' said Marianne. 'I feel as if I'm home already.'

And then they were passing New Zealand, which lay to the south.

'Why are we going past?' asked Teddy. 'Why not stop there?'

'First we have to call upon the Reverend Marsden,' Marianne told him. 'It is he who has invited us here so we must call in to pay our respects. And besides, he has people waiting in New South Wales so they can come with us – help build a house and so on.'

'Aren't there any houses in New Zealand?' asked little Marianne. 'What do people live in?'

'I'm sure they have their own houses,' said Henry. 'But we'll need an extra big one, won't we? Especially now that Mama is expecting a new baby.'

'A new baby! Will it be a girl this time? I would so like a sister.'

'We will just have to wait and see. But whichever it is we will love them very much.'

Henry had been conscientious about holding a service every Sunday (numbers increased markedly when there was a storm and dropped off in fine weather), had taken Bible classes and assembled as many as wanted every evening for prayers. The captain assured him that thanks to his efforts the behaviour on board was far better than usual. Even so, Henry had to admit the seed of the Word of God appeared to have fallen on stony ground.

After passing New Zealand they dropped down into the Tasman Sea, bound for Hobart.

And then, finally, they were there.

Everyone crowded on deck, including the women. The free women were excited, waiting to be reunited at last with their husbands, but the convict women were terrified. In spite of having endured for months what must have seemed like eternal torment, they now had to face their sentences: fifty nine of them had been sentenced to seven years, eighteen to fourteen years, and twenty to life – in a place that was known as the hellhole beyond the seas.

The Reverend Samuel Marsden was a man in a hurry.

The ship had barely docked before he was up the ladder and striding across the deck: a portly gentleman with a large, pudding-shaped face from which glittered sharp dark eyes.

'My dear Mr Marsden,' Henry cried, suddenly emotional. 'I cannot believe it is you I am seeing after this long, long voyage. We had no idea –'

'That I would be in Hobart? Pure coincidence, my dear fellow. I am here on a matter of public duty.'

'I must find Marianne. She will be overjoyed to meet you. There is so much to –'

'I regret, Mr Williams, I have only a few minutes, then I must be off. I just wanted to greet you. Also to inform you that I shan't be at my estate at Parramatta when you arrive, but here is a letter to my agent.' He handed Henry an envelope. 'In it I tell him to make available any money you may require both here in Hobart and in Parramatta, and that I expect you to be accommodated in my own house.'

'I very much appreciate your thoughtfulness, Mr Marsden, but I hope we will not presume upon your hospitality for very long.'

'Once I return we will have plenty of time to discuss future plans.'

The Yorkshireman, as from his accent he appeared to be, turned to go.

'There is some urgency, sir,' said Henry. 'My wife is with child –'

Marsden turned back. 'You are welcome to remain with me for as long as you wish.'

'We are both impatient to reach the end of our journey.'

Marsden faced him. 'The truth is that problems have arisen in New Zealand.'

'We were expecting challenges. I'm sure we can take those in our stride.'

'The problems lie with the missionaries themselves.'

'Mr Pratt did mention something of the sort.'

'The situation has become worse. I have had to suspend Kendall – the man is refusing to admit the error of his ways and is still living with the Māori woman in question. And then there is Butler –'

'The superintendent of the mission? Surely he –'

'He has forced me to lose confidence. I shall go into more detail later.'

'And the other missionaries?'

'Mr and Mrs Clarke are still in New South Wales and have not yet been able to leave. Unfortunately, Mrs Clarke has been experiencing problems with her health. But none of these problems are insurmountable – I regard them as merely hurdles put in our way by the Arch-enemy of Our Lord and I do not intend to allow him to scupper this mighty enterprise. In fact, I had decided that if for some reason the CMS chose not to pursue the mission in New Zealand I would go there myself.'

'I should hope that now we are here there would be no more talk of ending the mission.'

'Quite!' Marsden clapped him on the shoulder. 'And when I see with my own eyes the calibre of the person they have sent me in the form of your good self, I have no fear on that point. But in the meantime, Mr Williams, until certain matters are resolved I must ask you to be patient. You will need to remain in New South Wales for several months to come.'

7

How tantalising! Now they must wait some more, tiptoed on the edge of reaching the place that had occupied their thoughts and endeavours for so long.

They were not put up in Marsden's house but in a cottage on a steep bank on the opposite side of the river, where the whole family was squashed into one and a half rooms. It was a long way from the place for which Henry yearned, with a 'nook' where he could retire and write letters, or just simply think, or pray, on his own, in peace.

He occupied himself by beginning to learn the Māori language with the two servants now living in their house; and visiting the establishment where George Clarke was ministering to the needs of the Aboriginal people. Marianne, meantime, was busy supporting Mrs Clarke, who in addition to problems connected with her pregnancy, was suffering fainting fits.

Finally Marsden returned to Parramatta. A few days later he appeared at the door of their cottage and Henry invited him in. The two men sat in the living area, with Edward and little Marianne playing in a corner.

In the tiny house Marsden's presence seemed to be magnified. Henry had heard he'd begun life as assistant to a blacksmith: certainly he had the bulk for such work. There was a certain aura about him – of energy, determination and sheer force, that dominated the room.

The Yorkshireman began by heaving a sigh that seemed to be of annoyance. 'I regret I have not called upon you sooner. I am a very busy man.'

'I can see that, sir.'

'My parish is enormous and my duties are many.' He leaned back in his chair and spread his arms out on the table. 'Tell me, from where do you hail, Mr Williams?'

'Nottingham.'

'Well, let me tell you that Nottinghamshire could fit several times into the district of New South Wales.'

Yorkshire too? thought Henry. But now was not the time to compare counties.

'As well as my duty as senior chaplain of this vast area,' continued Marsden, 'I am also a magistrate. That is not perhaps a position I would have chosen myself, but I was invited to accept and I did so. It is another way where I can render service to God, by seeing justice is done – not always easy in this benighted country. There is criticism, of which I am well aware.'

Henry gave a faint nod. He'd read negative reports in the newspaper and heard references to 'the flogging parson'.

'It seems very unfair –'

Marsden thumped his ample thigh. 'Lies and slander, Mr Williams!' he shouted. 'Lies and slander!'

The children stopped playing and turned to stare.

Marsden lowered his voice. 'And you know from whence that emanates? The Devil! You know as well as I do, Mr Williams, the more successful a man is in spreading the word of the Lord, the more Satan is determined to destroy him.' He began to shout again. His face, normally a ruddy colour, grew even redder and his double chin wobbled. 'And I will not allow men of a base nature to destroy me. I will maintain the highest of standards! Do you know, Mr Williams, that some of the magistrates with whom I must share the bench are of the same ilk as those upon whom they sit in judgement? Men who have been convicted of crimes! Of course I must stand up for what is right. My duty demands it.'

He leaned forward, speaking in confidential tones. 'I tell you, Mr Williams, even the governors of New South Wales are not immune to the general corruption. I have had occasion to speak strongly with one or two and I assure you it does not go down well.'

'I can see you are in a difficult position.'

'But I do not allow this to stand in the way of administering punishment. If a crime calls for a hundred lashes I will not flinch to order the same. Justice must be done! And for that I am the victim of lies and slander, which are the currency of this colony. I urge you to be aware of these things, Mr Williams, and to take them into account.'

'I assure you, Mr Marsden, I do not pay heed to idle talk.'

'I am also a man of pity. I feel for the women and children, who are innocent victims. In fact, I have done much for them – set up orphan schools for both boys and girls, and the Female Factory to house convict women, most of whom, I regret to say, are of loose morals.'

'And the natives of this land?'

'I have tried, Mr Williams. I have done my best, as have others. I brought an Aboriginal child into my family, took him straight from his mother's breast and treated him as one of my own. But he was never sensible of the opportunity this gave him, never responded to the affection that was lavished upon him and indeed he could not give up his native ways. It would appear that the Aboriginals of Australia do not want or are unable to absorb the basics of our civilisation.'

'Whereas in New Zealand –'

'Now there we are speaking of a different matter entirely. The

Māori are a noble race, vastly superior to anything you can imagine in a savage nation. I have spent much time among them, both in their country and here, where I have brought some individuals to my home and taught them the civilising arts such as reading and writing. They have responded well to my teaching; in fact, they are eager to learn all they can and that is why I am anxious for you to carry on the good work that I have begun.'

'Now that you mention it, both Marianne and I feel we must not lose any more time. We would like to proceed to New Zealand as soon as possible.'

'I understand that, Mr Williams. I must say you are by far the best informed of all that I have employed on the mission, and I am delighted to have you on board.'

'In that case, let us depart without delay.'

'Of course, as you would expect I should go with you when you first arrive in New Zealand, but I am not yet free to travel. And then there is the matter of the Clarkes: Mr Clarke is still engaged with the mission for the Aborigines, while Mrs Clarke, whose confinement is imminent, is still very much in need of the help provided by your inestimable wife.'

'Fortunately at present my wife enjoys good health, but this will not be the case as she draws nearer to her time. I will tell you plain, Mr Marsden. We urgently need to be on our way so I can get on with building a house where she can give birth in comfort and have a suitable place in which to attend to the baby.'

Marsden rose.

'I appreciate Mrs Williams' predicament, but I am anxious that your arrival in New Zealand is prepared in the best way possible. I can only advise you to trust the Lord will make sure that all will take place at the optimum time. And now, Mr Williams, I must bid you adieu.'

The door closed and Henry sighed. The trouble with Marsden, he thought, was that, an independent man himself, he had absolutely no conception of the vulnerability of women and children and of the extreme necessity to find a settled place for his family.

Marianne was always so positive, so ready to give of herself, as she was now with Mrs Clarke. But she was also fragile – a special, precious person with whose care he had been entrusted and who right now needed to be established in her own home.

Fortunately, Mrs Clarke was delivered of a healthy child, so that Marianne's help was no longer needed. Marsden decided the Williams family could now go to New Zealand, but the Clarkes would remain behind – and so would he, as he was still occupied by matters in New South Wales. They would not sail in the *Active*, the ship he owned, which was in service elsewhere. He told them to embark on the *Brampton* on the nineteenth of July and they would sail on the Sunday. Henry expressed his concern: departing on the Lord's Day, when all work should cease and all thoughts turn to God, seemed an inauspicious beginning for a Christian endeavour. But Marsden assured him this was the general day of sailing in these parts.

Farewells were said and the luggage and furniture they had brought with them half way round the world were loaded onto the ship, which was moored at Mr Marsden's own wharf on the Parramatta.

Accompanying them were Mr and Mrs William Fairburn and their two children. The Fairburns had already been in New Zealand: Mr Fairburn was a carpenter who would be of great use to Henry, Marsden told him, and he also had a tolerable grasp of the Māori language. They seemed a pleasant, quiet couple. There were also three Wesleyan missionaries, whose religious movement sprang from the Methodist church, and the two chiefs who had been at Parramatta.

The ship was about to cast off when who should appear but Mr Marsden himself, puffing up the gangplank and lugging a small travelling trunk. 'Something has come up,' he announced, 'and I shall be sailing with you. I will explain at a later opportunity.'

And then once again they threw themselves upon the deep and the mercy of the Lord.

A massive gale blew up and drove them across the Tasman Sea, buffeting the ship and causing the waves to rise up and carry them forward, as if they could not wait to ferry them as fast as possible to their final destination.

One evening Marsden called Henry into his cabin. He waved him to a seat at his table.

Henry faced him. Marsden's face was set and his large eyes gleamed in the light thrown by the ship's lantern in the dark, wood-panelled room.

'I shall now lay before you the difficult circumstances you are about to face.'

'We expect challenges. The native people –'

'With regard to the missionaries.'

'Mr Kendall?'

'It is true that he presents a problem, and I intend to deal with that. But there is also Mr Butler. I fear he is not made of stern enough mettle to carry out the task I set him.'

'May I ask how you have come to this conclusion?'

'His character is not suitable. He is a nervous, excitable man, unable to exercise authority. As you have heard, he has no control over the behaviour of Mr Kendall. But he has also not been able to work with the missionaries at Rangihoua, either. Even his relations with Hongi Hika, who is the protective chief of his own mission, have deteriorated.'

'So what is your intention?'

'I have just received authority from the CMS, in the form of a letter.

I now intend to dismiss both Mr Butler and Mr Kendall from the mission at the Bay of Islands.'

For a minute Henry stared at him open-mouthed. 'Without a superintendent, how can the mission function effectively?'

Marsden leant forward, emphasising each point with a blow of his index finger on the table. 'I am depending upon you, Mr Williams, to correct the many evils that have caused this most important mission to falter. I believe you and your family will prove to be a great blessing to the Society, and you will be an example to the others as to what they as missionaries should do.'

The same blustery westerly wind that had whisked them across the Tasman Sea was still blowing when they arrived: it was August 1823 and here they were, finally, in New Zealand. They stood off the entrance to the Bay of Islands, waiting for the wind to die down.

Henry and Marsden had studied a map of the country they were about to enter. The Bay, named by Cook because of its many islands, rocks and islets, lay on the northeast coast of the North Island. As the place of his first mission, Marsden had chosen Rangihoua, just inside the entrance to the bay, because that was where Ruatara lived and he knew they would have his protection. Even though that chief had now died the mission was still on good relations with the local people. At Kerikeri the mission had the support of Hongi Hika, who had sold them the land there. But Henry and Marianne were to be stationed further north, at Whangaroa Harbour where, as far as he was aware, no chief as yet had offered protection.

Then they entered a wide bay. In the distance low hills and valleys, everywhere smoothed in green, enclosed the sea like a rumpled blanket. The islands they passed bore a cape of tangled trees and creepers, verdant and luxurious, that sprawled down to rocks and little bays of golden sand, against which crashed the still-furious waves. Dark clouds hovered and the wind howled about them. Was it a welcome – or a warning?

The captain pointed out Rangihoua on their starboard side, but they continued on, the sea being too rough to allow them to anchor. Henry and Marianne stood with their children on the slippery deck, looking out at the land that had called them from so far away.

Marianne gripped the rail and turned to Henry. 'We are here! We are truly here at last! Oh my dearest love, can you quite believe it?'

Henry put his arm around his wife and hugged her as closely as her swollen body and bulky clothes would allow him. 'You've done so well. I was afraid this final journey would be too much for you.'

'I knew our dear Lord would take care of us,' she said. 'But the baby is beginning to kick. I feel my time is approaching.'

'I know,' he said. 'It is uppermost in my mind.'

'How quickly, do you think –?'

'I will make a house for us as soon as possible. You can be sure of that.'

But there were many things of which he was not sure.

They waited until the afternoon, when the wind had abated and the ship could hove to, to celebrate their arrival in New Zealand. They would also give thanks to God by taking communion, re-enacting the Last Supper when Jesus Christ broke bread and took wine with his disciples before he was led out to be tried and broken on the cross.

In his cabin Marsden placed on the table a bottle of wine and a loaf of bread. He broke the bread into several pieces, which he laid out on a plate, and poured the wine into a cup.

The ship rocked to the tune played by the wind and waves. Around them ropes wheezed and strained and the ship's timbers groaned.

Henry, Marianne, the Fairburns and the Wesleyan missionaries sat around the table, just as Jesus and the disciples would have done on that holy evening. Everyone was solemn; everyone was aware that this was a momentous occasion.

Marsden raised the prayer book: 'Almighty God, unto whom all hearts be open, all desires known, and from whom no secrets are hidden –'

From outside came a sound. It sounded like a shout.

Marsden hesitated.

Again it came, louder, and repeated. 'Nau mai!'

'It is the people,' he said. 'They have come to welcome me.'

He laid down the prayer book and all took turns to peer through the porthole. Below the ship, rocking in the waves, was a long, narrow canoe made of carved wood with a tall, curving prow. It was manned by men waving their paddles in the air and shouting, 'Mātenga! Mātenga!'

'Is it you they are calling, Mr Marsden?' asked Marianne.

Marsden nodded. 'It is encouraging, is it not, Mrs Williams, to know that our hosts are glad to see us?'

Marianne clasped her hands. 'It warms my heart to hear this joyous sound. The Lord has sent us a wonderful sign.'

Marsden went out and stood at the rail, waving back. 'It's too rough for now,' he shouted against the wind. 'Āpōpō! Come to the ship tomorrow!'

'Hei āpōpō!' they replied. 'Nau mai, e kara! Nau mai ki Ipipiri!'

In the morning they looked out to find the ship surrounded by several graceful canoes. Marsden leaned out over the gunwale and waved and immediately came the response: a shout of joy. The occupants of the canoes clambered on board, greeting Samuel Marsden with exclamations of delight, throwing themselves back, then leaning forward to press their nose to his, making a humming sound as they did so.

Soon the deck and the main cabin were full of men, women and children. There was a strong odour accompanying them – shark oil, Henry was told. In spite of the smell and the strangeness of the new arrivals, his own children moved happily among them, offering raisins all round, and the people reached out and touched and stroked them. He saw some of the chiefs bending down and touching noses with Teddy.

These were tall, well-built people, obviously strong, fit and confident. Their faces were marked with patterns that swirled across their cheekbones and round their eyes – just like the tattooed heads he had seen in Rio de Janeiro, went the unwelcome thought through his mind, except these designs were more intricate. They strode across the deck with dignity and grace, their fringed cloaks swinging as they walked.

There was a great deal of noise – laughter and chattering. Marsden seemed well able to communicate with his friends, with the help of gesticulations. Henry watched his mentor. He had already been impressed by Marsden's ardour for the cause of bringing Christianity to the Māori people, but now here was the proof that even if his message had not yet been accepted, the man himself was welcome, even apparently loved, by the people here.

How could it be that a man so revered, as he obviously was by these fierce chiefs, so dedicated to the cause of saving their souls, should be denigrated by his own people?

Marsden beckoned him over to introduce him to the chiefs. Most of the others, including Hongi Hika, were away fighting. No doubt decimating yet more of their kin with the guns Kendall had obtained, thought Henry: a problem that needed to be sorted out forthwith.

Each chief bent down to press his nose to his. Henry was enveloped by the fishy, oily odour, and he saw at close quarters the smooth brownness of their skin and the tattoos that adorned it. One chief stood out from the others because he was covered from head to foot in a red preparation: his name was Tohitapu and he was stamping his feet and shouting at Marsden.

'What's the problem?' Henry asked when Tohitapu disappeared over the side of the ship and Marsden was able to move away.

'He tells me the Wesleyans have set up a settlement at Whangaroa and he is angry because his missionary has gone with them.'

'He thinks the missionary belongs to him?'

'The chiefs regard the missionaries as their own. They are the source of all the things they want. And they in turn need the chiefs to protect them.'

'Is God not enough?'

Marsden shook his fat cheeks and waggled his forefinger at Henry.

'You will learn, Mr Williams. You will learn.'

Everyone wanted missionaries. Henry and Marianne found themselves ensconced in the main cabin with three chiefs from the Firth of Thames, begging them to come to their area.

'They are so eager to have us. Perhaps we should go with them,' said Marianne, looking at Henry.

'The Firth of Thames is a long way from here. And as you have pointed out we are running out of time to find you a place for your confinement. I think we should be guided by Mr Marsden.'

They were interrupted by a wailing sound. Māori women, tears flowing down their faces, were peering through the window of the cabin.

Marsden went outside, then returned. 'They are relations of the three men here,' he said. 'The women were taken prisoner by Hongi Hika and brought here as slaves, and now they have seen their chiefs, they are overcome. They are also remembering the fate of another major chief, who was killed by Hongi.'

It was decided they should visit Rangihoua, which was just inside the heads, on the northern side of the bay.

Henry, along with Marsden, Fairburn and two of the Wesleyans, stepped into the boat and was rowed into a small bay dominated on the left by a steep hill on which perched a fortified settlement, or pā. It was ringed with ditches and ridges on which were placed rows of sharp wooden sticks to act as palisades. Within these could be seen the tops of thatched huts, while seeming to hang down the sides of the hill were neat cultivations, also fenced. This was the pā of Rangihoua, where Ruatara had reigned as chief.

On the right lay another hill, not as steep, but covered in ferns and trees. Between these two hills, almost at sea level, on the banks of a stream that ran through the valley lay the settlement of the missionaries. This seemed to consist mainly of a long, low building made of reeds and without any windows.

On the pebbled beach they were met by two missionaries, John King and William Hall. They greeted Samuel Marsden first and then turned to Henry.

King grasped his hand with both of his. 'My dear Mr Williams, I am delighted to see you. In fact, I might almost say I feel like a survivor who has landed on a desert island and now finds himself rescued.'

'Your presence is much needed,' said John Hall, offering his hand. 'You have no idea the ordeals we have been through.' He turned to King. 'Though no doubt he'll find out quick enough.'

They took him to the house in which they and their families lived communally, a situation Marsden believed was important for the mission.

However, it appeared the missionaries themselves were not happy with this arrangement, as there were tensions between the families. Further, Hall pointed out that the stream flooded when there was heavy rain and in winter the house was permanently damp.

Marsden looked around. 'Where's Kendall?'

The two men looked at each other. 'There have been difficulties, as we've already informed you,' said King.

Marsden nodded.

'Thinks he's cleverer than we are,' put in Hall. 'Just 'cos he was a schoolmaster. Throws his weight around, tries to give us orders. And when you think what he's –'

'I am well aware of Mr Kendall's shortcomings,' said Marsden. 'But where is he now?'

'At Matauwhi, on the other side of the Bay. Gone back to his wife and children.'

'Praise the Lord,' said Marsden 'Not that it makes any difference.'

'He says he wants to live at Kerikeri.'

'Kerikeri! Over my dead body! The man is a disgrace to the mission, to himself and to the Lord.'

There was silence. Marsden stood there, his arms folded.

Then he said, 'Now, is it correct the Wesleyans have set up in Whangaroa?'

'They've beaten us to it.'

'We must not begrudge them, Mr Hall.' He jerked his head in the direction of the Wesleyan missionaries who were standing a little way off. 'There is plenty of room for missionary endeavour in New Zealand.' He turned to Henry. 'We shall have to find you somewhere else.'

'Begging your pardon, sir,' put in King, 'but I reckon Paihia's the place. More shelter and no problem with flooding. There's space to grow crops, too.'

'Much better than here,' said Hall. 'I was half a mind to move there myself, but they wouldn't let me.'

'Who wouldn't let you?' asked Henry.

'Why, the people, of course. Said they'd tie me hand and foot and bring me back. So 'ere we stay in this miserable valley and –'

Marsden broke in. 'I promised the chief there, Te Koki, that I'd send him a missionary after his son died when he was living with me at Parramatta.' He turned to Henry. 'It appears Paihia might be the solution. What do you say, Mr Williams?'

'Of course I know nothing of this place,' said Henry. 'Is it far from here?'

'Not ten miles south,' said King. 'It faces northeast across to Kororāreka where there's a Māori settlement and also where the whalers come and go. And it's near the mouth of the Waitangi and Kawakawa Rivers, which are entry points to the inland settlements. Altogether, I'd say an excellent position for a mission station.'

They returned to the ship and found that John Butler had arrived. He was a solidly built man, full of good cheer and apparently entirely ignorant of the fate that was about to befall him.

'Well, well, Mr Williams,' he said, slapping Henry on the back, 'what d' you say to our little paradise? Is it not the best place in the world?'

'From what I've seen it offers many possibilities.'

'One day New Zealand will be an agricultural centre, mark my words. And I'll be remembered with gratitude by every person coming after me, because I was the first person to set up a plough and turn the first sod. And – not to take anything from your good self, sir – I am the first ordained clergyman to live in this heathen land.' He turned to Marsden and banged him on the back too. 'Isn't that right, eh, eh?'

'I agree you've made your mark,' said Marsden. 'But as you are well aware there have been major difficulties.'

Butler began to shout. 'Water under the bridge! I wrote you a letter putting all that right.'

Marsden was silent.

Butler turned to Henry. 'Forgiveness, that's what it's all about, eh Mr Williams?'

'Once a man's reputation has been sullied,' said Marsden, 'no amount of forgiveness will put it right.'

8

And now it was evening. All about the ship were the sounds of chatter and bustle as people packed their belongings into their trunks and prepared for going ashore the next day.

Henry found Marianne in their cabin. She wasn't busying herself with packing; she was reclining on the bed, pen and paper in hand.

He sat down beside her. 'It has been a wearying day,' he said. 'I hope it wasn't too much for you.'

She gave him one of her brilliant smiles. 'Oh, absolutely not! I kept saying to Mr Marsden, "If only our dear friends in England could see us now!" I will put our things together ready for tomorrow, but right now I want to describe the wonderful scenes we witnessed while they're fresh in my mind.' She shook her head. 'I would like to tell them about every look – every conversation – but I know I must be careful with how much paper I use, otherwise we will have scarcely been here any time at all and I will have used up all our paper. But see how thrifty I'm being.'

She showed him the paper she was writing on, with both front and back covered so that there was a cross-hatched effect. 'I hope they'll be able to read it. Is it clear enough, do you think?'

'Of course,' he said, 'and I know they'll be fascinated to read your accounts of our experiences. They would be astonished to see you mingling with our chiefly friends.'

'But they were magnificent, those Māori chiefs, don't you think? – so tall and handsome, striding about the ship in their feathered cloaks. As I was watching them I had a picture in my mind's eye of how our British ancestors must have appeared to the Romans when they invaded Britain. I can just see Caractacus among these people, dressed in his animal furs.'

'What an imagination you have!' said Henry, laughing.

'However, the people here are caught in the chains of Satan. I have just been describing their plight; but as I have said to our friends, What could be a nobler ambition than to rescue them from their evil foe?'

'And with the strength of Almighty God behind us, we will.'

'We will, Henry, won't we?' Marianne clasped both his hands in his, her blue eyes shining. 'And now that I've met them and seen what fine people they are, so worthy of being saved, I feel surer of that than ever before.'

'It will take time – we must be patient.'

'We must be very patient! But I firmly believe our Lord will teach us how to work with them, and in his own good time he will cause the seed to spring up and they will be free.'

Henry felt as if his heart would melt as he smiled at his beloved Marianne, so enthusiastic and optimistic. If anything, she was stronger than he and the best helpmeet he could possibly have in this venture. 'You see things so clearly, and you are so brave,' he said. He took her hand and stroked it. 'Now, for tomorrow – William Fairburn says he and I could row over to this place called Pie-here, and as I'm keen to see it as soon as possible I thought I'd ask for the use of one of the ship's boats. But that would mean you and the children going on your own with Mr Butler to Kerikeri. Would you mind?'

'Oh, you must go! I am just as keen as you to know if we have a place where we can begin our labours. And never fear for me – I am in good hands.'

Henry left her to her writing and headed for the cabin of Samuel Marsden. But when he reached the door, he stopped. From behind it came a sound, not of merriment and relief, but of raised voices. And then there was sobbing – hysterical, broken-hearted. It did not sound like Marsden; it must, he presumed, be John Butler.

In the morning it was a case of marshalling the troops. Butler offered to transport the missionaries in his boat back to Rangihoua and then he would return to the ship to take Marianne and the children to his house at Kerikeri, where he said he could accommodate them all. He seemed confident and eager to help, showing no sign of the broken man of the night before.

There was a commotion. The chief covered in red paint, by name Tohitapu, had arrived and was stamping round the boat, shouting out in Māori. Samuel Marsden had a word with him and the chief disappeared over the side.

'What's the problem?' Henry asked.

'He wanted you to live at his place,' said Marsden. 'He's very angry you're going to Paihia. But I pacified him by saying I'll send Mr Shepherd instead, so he's left to collect some raupō to build him a house.'

After breakfast, a boat was brought round for Henry and Fairburn. They climbed down the rope ladder and settled themselves into the boat, waving up to the people watching from on board. 'You don't waste any time!' someone called.

He wasn't there to waste time. This place – William Fairburn had told him it was Paihia, not Pie-here – sounded promising, but he would only believe it when he saw it with his own eyes. And if it wasn't suitable they would immediately have to start searching elsewhere.

Fairburn began rowing, heading in a southerly direction. The storm had died down and the waves transformed to a gentle swell. Everything was in sharp focus, delineated by the bright morning sun. The oars splashed into a sea of clear blue-green that sparkled in the sunlight and the clouds following above were extra white, as if freshly washed by the passing storm. Above them seagulls wheeled and called.

As the boat moved along the land opened itself up. On their starboard side was a series of low hills; on their port, in the distance, what appeared to be a large island, but which Fairburn said was a peninsula.

Fairburn continued to row until he began to slow. Then Henry took over.

They continued heading south. 'Are we still on track?' Henry asked, laying down his oars and turning to look behind him. A large, flat piece of land projecting out into the sea looked inviting. He indicated with his oar. 'What do you think?'

'Maybe. But it's not Paihia.'

'How much further?'

'Not far at all. See – over there, past those islands.'

Fairburn pointed.

Between the islands had appeared a beach – in fact, Henry could see two beaches of golden sand, on which lay canoes with their curving prows. Between the beaches was a small, rocky headland topped with a village sporting spiky palisades and thatched roofs in the manner of Rangihoua. Behind the beaches a series of hills covered in ferns and small trees rose in layers of chartreuse and olive, up to a sky of cerulean blue. Henry's painterly eye registered the scene, even as his practical side reasserted itself.

'Which is Paihia?'

'It's on the left.'

'Let's go!'

His oars dug into the translucent sea, the ripples seeming to run with the boat, hurrying them towards the beach. Through the clear water he saw the sand below, scattered with shells and stones. Then the boat hit the land.

Henry took off his shoes and rolled up his trousers. He climbed out and grabbed the painter, pulling the boat further in.

'What's the tide variation here?'

'About six to ten feet,' Fairburn told him, 'and I'd say it's half way in now.'

'Better take her up a bit, then.'

They each took a side of the boat and carried it up the beach, their feet digging into the sun-warmed sand.

Henry stood on the beach and surveyed his surroundings, hands on hips. Maybe, in this very spot might be the place where he could make his home.

Between the beach and the hills was an area covered in sparse vegetation. He narrowed his eyes and then began striding across it towards the sheltering hills, counting his steps. He returned to Fairburn. 'There's a good hundred yards of flat land here.' He turned round and searched for the sun in its unfamiliar place in the north. The site faced towards it.

He looked out to sea. Before him were the three little islands they had passed on their way in, tufted with grasses and trees. If it were not for those islands the beach would be directly exposed to the waves rolling in from the entrance to the whole bay. As well as providing protection, with their pleasing outlines the islands added to the vista.

Further out, to the northeast, along the south side of the peninsula they had seen on their way in, were the spiky masts of a few ships and what appeared to be huts along the foreshore.

'And over there?' he asked, pointing.

'Kororāreka,' said Fairburn. 'That's where the whalers stop after they've been on long voyages. They call it rest and relaxation – you and I would call it sin and shame.'

'I'm an old sailor,' said Henry. 'I can imagine. Drinking and carousing.'

'And the rest.'

'Prostitution? Not the Māori girls?'

'Aye, sir.'

Henry sighed. How sad that the first-comers of the great British Empire should be the least impressive members of that society. Furthermore, the whalers had chosen exactly the spot where he intended to carry out his work. But that was fine by him: the Devil might send a warning shot across his bow, but with the Lord's help he would give him a strong riposte.

'At least I shall have them in my sights,' he said. 'And it would be useful to see any ships that are coming and going. Now, let's do some reconnaissance.'

They walked along the beach to the village on the headland, which seemed to be deserted, apart from the canoes drawn up on the beach beside it. They skirted the headland and crossed to the next beach, equally golden and inviting, but lacking the same amount of flat land. Then they came to a river.

'This is the Waitangi,' said Fairburn. '– means sounding water, or even crying water.'

'Why would they call it that?'

'There'll be a story behind it – that's how they remember things that have happened in the past.'

Talking of crying . . . thought Henry. Aloud he said, 'Mr Butler seems a good fellow. It was kind of him to take Marianne and the children and to offer to put us up.'

'Yes, we're all here to help each other.'

'But I understand there's a problem. Mr Marsden and he –'

Fairburn gave him a sideways glance. 'I don't rightly know what's happening in that regard, not having been here myself recently.'

'You didn't have trouble with him?'

'Not usually. He is a good man, is Mr Butler, and there's no doubting his faith. But he used to lose his temper a fair bit, over things that didn't seem important.'

'What, with the other missionaries?'

'He reckoned they were shirking.'

'It is true, isn't it, that they have not brought one soul to Christ in the nine years they've been here?'

'Not for want of trying! It's a hard life, Mr Williams, as no doubt you'll discover, and we have to work together. If we can't get on we're no better than those we've come to save.'

'Quite! In any case, I'm sure Mr Marsden will sort it out.'

'I'm sure he will, sir. But I'd be obliged if you didn't pass on to anyone the things I just said.'

'Of course I won't,' said Henry. 'Now, what about the land over there?' He pointed to the other side of the river.

'There is a large, flat area up higher, certainly,' said Fairburn, 'but it doesn't have easy access to the sea like Paihia.'

Henry shook his head: 'Let's go back.'

When they turned round they found a group of Māori people were walking towards them.

'They'll be from the village we passed,' said Fairburn.

'The owners of the land?'

'It could well be the chieftainess, Hamu, who is the wife of Te Koki.'

'Can you talk to her?'

'I'll do my best. Now, sir,' said Fairburn hurriedly, 'they may want to greet us the way you saw them do it yesterday – by pressing their nose to ours. It's something to do with exchanging breath.'

Exchanging breath, so two people became one. He could understand that.

84

'And also,' said Fairburn, 'could you not stare into their eyes as you do it.'

'Why not?'

'It's the custom, sir. Just look down.'

The group consisted of about ten people, women and old men, dressed in cloaks and with feathers in their hair. Playing round them were naked children who stared at their visitors with wondering eyes. For a minute the people stood in stately silence and appraised the white strangers who had appeared uninvited on their shores. For their part the two men regarded them cautiously.

Then, as Fairburn had predicted, they stepped forward to exchange greetings.

Henry gestured for Fairburn to speak. It appeared that Hamu, the owner of the land on which they were proposing to settle, was indeed among them. Fairburn addressed himself to her, using the words 'Mātenga' and 'Paihia' and she smiled and nodded. He spoke some more to Hamu and then called Henry over.

'Ko Mr Williams tēnei,' he told them with a wave of his hand.

Henry bowed.

To his surprise they began laughing and pointing.

He looked questioningly at Fairburn.

'I think it's your glasses, sir. They've never seen such a thing.'

Henry whipped off his round, steel-rimmed spectacles.

At this there was even more hilarity. 'Ko tā tātou ingoa kārangaranga mōna ko Te Karu-whā!'

'I think they've decided to call you Karu-whā.'

'What does that mean?'

'Four Eyes.'

'Oh!' Henry replaced his glasses. 'Yes, very appropriate.' To the Māori he probably did appear a comical figure, with his receding hairline surmounted by a halo of curly hair – and the spectacles. He bowed again, this time in an exaggerated manner, and then there was laughter from everyone, Māori and white man alike.

The interview, for that was how it seemed, was now over and the people moved away.

The two men continued walking back towards the boat. 'Hamu told me her husband, Te Koki, is away fighting, as are most of the chiefs,' said Fairburn.

'Whereabouts?'

'I believe quite a way south.'

'Is Hamu happy for us to settle here?'

'I think so. As soon as I mentioned Mr Marsden's name all was well.'

They returned to the beach where they had landed, and then continued on to the south end and up a headland. They climbed to the top, pushing through trees and undergrowth along the cliff. Finally they reached a point where they could see along the coast to the south and east.

Here the sea formed an inlet, snaking between the mainland and another, smaller peninsula. There appeared to be no flat land.

'Doesn't look very promising,' said Henry. They beat their way back until again they were looking down over the beach.

'Do you know what Paihia means?' he asked.

'I'm not sure, but "pai" means good, so maybe it means "Good has been done here," or maybe "Doing good".'

'That seems auspicious, don't you think?' said Henry.

'And here's another thing, sir,' said Fairburn. 'You've got the Waikare Inlet and the Kawakawa River to the south, as well as the Waitangi to the north. For the Māori, those are their roads. In peacetime they come down them for fishing, and when they're fighting that's how they get their war canoes to the sea.'

'Mr King mentioned that.' Henry shaded his eyes, taking in the scene anew. 'So it's at the crossroads, so to speak – perfect for making contact with the tribes living inland. But of course we wouldn't just sit here. We ourselves could reach the people inland, by the very same means.'

'Indeed we could, sir. If you're sure this is the right place?'

Again Henry looked down at the bay. More Māori had joined the group they'd first met and they were inspecting the boat in which he and Fairburn had arrived. These were the people he would minister to; these were the people he would save.

There was a tide of excitement rising within him. From a practical point of view the gentleness of the land, the hills behind for shelter and the trees for wood, and the easy access to the sea made it an ideal spot. But there was something more. He felt he could love this place and it would be his home.

'You know, Brother Fairburn – I believe it is. The Lord has truly blessed us.'

He put his hand on the younger man's shoulder and began to chant the One Hundredth Psalm, and Fairburn joined him:

'Make a joyful noise unto the Lord, all ye lands.

Serve the Lord with gladness; come before his presence with a song.

Know ye that the Lord he is God: it is he that hath made us, and not we ourselves: we are his people, and the sheep of his pasture.

Enter into his gates with thanksgiving, and into his courts with praise: be thankful unto him, and bless his name.'

Down on the beach the people must have heard them, for they looked up at the two men standing on the headland, chanting their unknown song.

'I think, sir, we should be heading back to Kerikeri,' said Fairburn. 'It's a long row.'

Together they lugged the boat down to the water and Henry pushed off before climbing in. For the first few miles Fairburn rowed and then

Henry took over. Soon he could feel the muscles in his arms beginning to rebel.

'I'm not used to this! How long since you've been in a boat?'

'Not recently – but I've got strong arms. As you will too after you've been here for a while.'

'I can see a lot of rowing would be required.'

'It's our main form of transport.'

Henry looked at his companion thoughtfully. William Fairburn was a stocky, well-built young man with a jaw that spoke of determination and character, yet he also had a kind face. Today he'd shown himself to be pleasant company and the source of good advice.

'Tell me, Brother Fairburn,' he said, 'would you help me build a house at Paihia?'

Fairburn grunted as he heaved on the oars and sent the boat whistling through the water. 'I'm a carpenter, Mr Williams – that's what I do.'

'We would have to share accommodation, to begin with, at least – your wife and my wife, your children and our children, all under the same roof. It could be difficult . . .'

'We're not here to take the easy path, are we? We're here to do the Lord's work. So I'll not complain and I know my dear wife won't either.'

They rowed for hours. Henry's arms and wrists were aching continuously, but he was eager to arrive at Kerikeri before it was dark. Also, he was anxious about Marianne in her condition having to settle the children on her own in yet another strange place. The land they were passing was devoid of any habitation – just the burgeoning ferns and dense forest, tumbling down to the water's edge. The mission station would likely be quite primitive, he thought, and it would be interesting to see what kind of building the missionaries there had come up with.

Eventually they reached a channel between the mainland and an island Fairburn said was Motuora. They turned to port and began to follow an inlet that had opened up. It wound past pretty bays and land covered in the tree-ferns and the myriad kinds of strange plants that seemed to be a feature of the landscape everywhere.

The river twisted and wound between the forested banks. Then it made a sudden and complete turn. On their left, sprawling over a ridge, was a large native settlement. 'Kororipo Pā,' said Fairburn, pointing. 'Though we call it "Hongi's Palace", because that's where he lives.'

The inlet became narrower. They turned round a sharp headland.

'And there's the mission station! What do you think?'

Henry, who was rowing, laid down his oars and turned around.

The light was beginning to fade, but even so the sight before him was breathtaking. They were in a round basin of water into the right of which poured a waterfall, the frothing water glistening in the evening light. The hills behind rose in ridges to form an amphitheatre round this placid pool and on the lowest slopes, facing them were English-looking buildings. The main one, directly in front of them, was quite a large edifice, double-storeyed, with two chimneys and a verandah.

It was so unexpected to come upon such a scene when the only buildings he had seen so far were the flimsy, if picturesque, huts of the Māori, or the reed hut at Rangihoua.

'I'm very impressed,' said Henry. He pointed to the larger house, noting it was in the Georgian style so fashionable at home, with three symmetrical, rectangular windows along the front of the upper storey. The walls were white. 'What is it made of? – it looks like stucco.'

'Just painted planks, sir. We sawed them here in a pit from trees felled in the bush. That's how we get all our timber.'

'Did you build it?'

'I did, alongside William Bean, who's now left the country, and William Puckey.'

'It's a credit to you and everyone involved,' said Henry. 'Although of course we must not forget the foresight of Mr Marsden in choosing this site in the first place.'

'He was lucky to get Hongi Hika to agree – forty eight axes he paid him.'

Henry wondered what would have to be paid for the land at Paihia: 'Were the axes just for this valley?'

'Oh no! Thirteen thousand acres is what Mr Marsden's bought. Though I'm not sure what Hongi would do if he tried to take possession.'

Marianne must have been watching out, for she came running down to the beach to welcome them.

'You've been such a long time! I was beginning to worry.' She hugged him, then pointed up the hill. 'Is it not the prettiest scene?'

'When we rounded the bend I could scarcely believe my eyes.'

She grabbed his arm and they began walking up a path to the house. 'Did you find Pie-here? What's it like?'

'Just a minute! I'm sorry it took so long. It was a long row. But yes, we did find Paihia, as it's called. And yes, it is very suitable. In fact, I could say I am delighted.'

'Did you meet any people? Were they happy for us to settle there?'

'I think that has already been sorted out by Mr Marsden and there is no problem in that regard. Certainly they were very friendly and I pressed my nose to those of several.'

'The people here are very helpful and friendly too. Mr and Mrs Butler have been extremely kind and welcoming. And Mr and Mrs Kemp – they live in that house there.' She pointed at the smaller house near the water. 'Mr Kemp is a blacksmith but he's also a missionary. They keep everything neat as wax, and Mrs Kemp – I felt I loved her on first sight.'

'Where are we staying?'

'Up here, with the Butlers.'

She led him to a gate in a fence of high planks that surrounded the house. When she opened it they were in a small courtyard.

'See – that room on the left. We even have a fireplace all to ourselves. I sleep on a sofa and the children on the floor, on bedding and mattresses brought from the ship.'

'Is that all right?' he said suddenly. 'Are you all right?'

'I am perfectly comfortable. In fact, I have never felt better in all my life. And now, to know that you have found us a home . . .'

'There's a bit of work to do on that front before we could call it a home. But it is looking very promising.'

'Oh Henry!' Marianne turned to him with shining eyes. 'Aren't you so happy? It's much better than we expected.'

'There's only one thing that concerns me.'

'Which is?'

'Everything seems too easy.'

Marianne laughed. 'No need to worry about that! I'm sure there are plenty of surprises to come.'

9

The next morning Henry awoke to find himself in a small room with Marianne reposing on a sofa and the children, as he was too, on mattresses on the floor, and all of them still asleep.

She was lying on her back with her belly, now full with child, forming a graceful curve. How uncomfortable she must be! And yet, even after bearing three children and the fourth soon to eventuate, she was still the vivacious young woman with whom he had fallen in love. With his eyes he caressed her fine features – the turned-up nose and the strong chin. Well, she was determined all right! Sometimes he still looked at her with wonder, thinking how impossible it had seemed that she would consider him as a suitor. But she had not only accepted him, she had embraced his cause. And now here she was, with him in New Zealand.

Marianne gave a sigh, or was it a groan, and shifted her body to ease the weight. It was unlike her to sleep longer than he, but he could see the dark lines that pooled under her eyes; in spite of the excitement of their arrival and her delight in the unexpectedly pleasant and civilised surroundings at Kerikeri, she was exhausted.

He needed to find a settled place for her and their family where they could regain their strength and then embark on the venture for which they had come. He'd already made a significant step along the way in deciding upon Paihia; but he also needed to find out more about the mission operation itself and why up till now it had not been successful.

While everyone was still asleep he would do a little exploring: suss out the lay of the land.

He had slept in his shirt and trousers. Over his shirt he pulled on a waistcoat, with both hands smoothed back his curly hair and moved silently to the door. He stepped onto the verandah of the Butlers' house.

A circular garden plot lay before him, its array of English country flowers seeming as incongruous here as would an embroidered sampler in the mess of a man-o'-war. And yet Henry was drawn to them: in the drawing classes he gave to the young ladies the subject was often garden flowers and he recognised marigolds flaunting their brassy yellows and oranges; columbines in shades of smoky pink, cream and mauve; and the cheerful blue of cornflowers. Here, in this place, the garden was an act of optimism.

The paling fence shut out the surrounding land and Henry opened the sturdy gate, made from planks like the fence. He stepped out. From here the ground sloped down to the beach and the placid 'lake' before it that was really the sea, backed by the high ridge on which were scattered the tufted huts of the Māori inhabitants. What struck him was the brightness of the light: he had noticed it before, at Paihia. In contrast to the industrial midlands where factories enveloped all with their smoky waste, here everything in this brand new world stood out with crystal clarity. The air was completely still and the only sounds were the rushing of the waterfall to his left, the cries of seabirds whirling high in the air above him and from the trees that surrounded the clearing the gurgles and clear, bell-like chimes of the native birds.

There was a bench outside, handily positioned for anyone to rest awhile and take stock of their surroundings, and Henry accepted the invitation. As he gazed around, for a minute he had a sensation of utter and all-encompassing peace. 'The peace that passeth all understanding': was this the Lord's way of offering him a glimpse of the richness of life that lay in store for those who gave themselves completely to him?

There was the sound of shoes crunching on the shell path.

The gate opened and in its space stood John Butler.

'Good morning, Mr Williams. I do hope your first night in this fair land was a peaceful one?'

Henry stood up. 'It was indeed, thanks to your kind hospitality. I must say I'm most impressed with the way you have set up the mission. The house is considerably more solid than I expected, and your garden is delightful. The whole settlement is a credit to you.'

Butler ducked his head and grimaced in the manner of a man unused to receiving compliments. He moved forward, settled on the seat next to Henry and folded his arms.

'I'm glad you noticed the flower garden, Mr Williams. One could be forgiven for such a frivolous thing when we are embarked on a glorious but challenging enterprise, but when it comes to one's wife these matters assume an importance out of all proportion.'

'When it comes to our wives, Mr Butler, I think anything we can do to make their lives happier is extremely important.'

'Ah! I do believe we are in agreement on this matter. If only Mr Marsden could see it in the same light.'

'He doesn't approve?'

'Let's just say I think he felt our home should have been a little more spartan. At any rate he did not see the need to contribute to the cost of building the store down there.' He gestured to a modest building on their right. 'But that's another story I shall not weary you with, at least –'

He paused and looked sideways at Henry, as if hoping he would ask further questions.

Instead Henry gestured behind him. 'Mr Fairburn tells me he and two others were responsible for this house.'

'I oversaw its building, and they were aided by the local Māori men.'

'They are competent?'

'With supervision. Although they're apt to down tools —'

From the smaller house below on the left another man had appeared and was walking up the hill towards them.

'Good morning, Brother Kemp!' called Butler. 'Do come and join us.'

Ah, this must be the blacksmith. He certainly looked the part — strong and solid with a kindly face.

He shook hands solemnly with Henry and then they were three on the bench. What a crew! — Butler, originally an office clerk in London, Kemp the blacksmith from Norfolk and himself the pensioned-off sailor from the East Midlands, all brought together to tell the people of this strange land how much God loved them.

Kemp took out a pipe.

'Mr Williams was asking after the capability of Māori men.'

'In what respect?'

'In the matter of carpentering. I was about to say they will down tools on account of any distraction.'

'Well they're off on a big distraction now.' Kemp pointed with his pipe to the village on the hills surrounding the lake. 'Not a single man of fighting age left.'

'I thought it seemed very quiet,' said Henry. 'In fact, I've not seen many young men, either at Rangihoua, or at Paihia.'

'Only women and old men left. Hongi Hika's rounded 'em up and taken them off to do battle — if you can call it that, with all the guns on one side only.'

'What kind of guns?'

Butler stared at him. 'Why, the kind that kills people — does it matter?' Then his face cleared. 'Ah, of course, you being a military man, Mr Williams — you would be interested in such things.'

'Mostly flintlock muskets,' said Kemp. 'Cheap and nasty, but they're light and easy to use. And, believe it or not, the warriors like them because they're shiny – good for brandishing about and striking fear in the enemy's heart.'

Warfare was ever thus – the art of one-upmanship. And the flintlock, known in the trade as the 'sham damn iron', was cheap and nasty, as Kemp said, but none the less lethal. British manufacturers produced them by the ton especially for places like Africa and the Pacific, where indigenous peoples were bent on fighting each other, quite possibly to extinction. But what cared the arms dealers?

'There are people in our own land,' said Henry, 'who are profiting from a vile trade. They have much to answer for. As you rightly say, Mr Butler, I was a sailor in the Royal Navy and as such I bore arms, which I deeply regret. But I can assure you that now I am vehemently opposed to the bearing of arms, by anyone.'

'If you'd seen what happened when Hongi Hika came back from his wars down south, you would feel even more strongly.'

'Can you tell me,' said Henry.

'Horrific,' said Butler, shaking his head. 'Mr Kemp here was a first-hand witness.'

Henry looked at the blacksmith.

''Tis true, I saw it all and how I wish I had not.' Kemp leant forward and buried his face in his hands. Then he sat up again, aware that the other two men were waiting.

He took a breath. 'With Brother Hall,' he said, 'I went down to the beach to see the canoes come in –'

'They had been where?'

'In the Hauraki Gulf, to Tāmaki, and then on to Te Tōtara pā, in the Firth of Thames,' said Kemp. 'I wanted to witness the ceremony when they brought in the bodies of the two chiefs Tete and Apu.'

'Tete was the husband of Hongi's eldest daughter,' put in Butler, 'and as such was an important personage. In fact I would say of all the chiefs he was the most pleasant and civilised that I have known, so it was indeed a great loss to the tribe. Apu, his brother, was also a very fine young man. But I interrupt. Pray continue, Brother Kemp.'

'And so the waka came, and they kept on coming until they'd filled up the lagoon here. I'd say there would have been about forty boats.'

'It must have been an impressive sight.'

'It was, it was! The noise was what you noticed above all. The warriors in the canoes were doing the haka, as they call their war dance – chanting real loud in unison and waving their guns in triumph – and those on shore were answering with another haka, and the women were doing their wailing like they always do when someone returns. But you also had the prisoners, and they were screaming equally loudly and crying too, poor miserable wretches.'

'They knew what was coming,' said Butler.

'As I was watching, suddenly there was silence. Not a peep from any of 'em – it was eerie. Then one of the canoes came forward and touched land, quite a small one but it was heaped up with dead bodies. Then a group of warriors in another canoe also moved forward and the noise began again. They jumped into the first canoe and trampled on the bodies, chanting all the while. They cut off the heads and threw them about as if they were balls, to play with. Then the daughter of Hongi and some other women from the pā ran up and began smashing the prows of the canoes –'

'Why they would do that?'

'I do not know, sir. I suppose it was their way of grieving. But then they got in a terrible frenzy. They dragged the live prisoners screaming and struggling out of the canoes and clubbed them to death right there and then. Just down here,' Kemp said, pointing to the beach where the gentle sea now lapped, 'until the water turned red.'

'The women killed them?'

'Oh yes, Mr Williams,' said Butler. 'One of the women was Jane – we call her Jane, but of course she has a Māori name – whom we employ in our house as a servant. She is not a bad girl, and in fact is generally as pleasant and helpful as one could wish. But she was one of the first to go down and slaughter a prisoner with her bare hands.' He turned to Kemp. 'Did she not?'

Kemp jerked his head in agreement.

Henry turned to Butler. 'Why, when they had won the battle, would they treat their prisoners so brutally?'

'I think it's all about utu – revenge. They know of no other way. But also they have a saying that war engenders a madness that takes over their souls, and this is what Mr Kemp witnessed.'

Yes, Henry knew that madness. He knew it all too well.

'If you don't mind, Mr Williams,' said Kemp, 'now that I've begun I would like to continue.'

There was more?

'The noise rings in my ears still when I think upon this scene: the prisoners screaming with terror, the shouts of the blood-hungry warriors. And then, when they brought the canoe containing the bodies of Tete and Apu, the howling and wailing, and all of it –' he waved his arm – 'echoing round this little valley here.'

'How many prisoners did they bring back?'

'I'd say there were about two thousand.'

'Two thousand! All men?'

Kemp shook his head. 'Some men, but mostly it was women and children.'

Henry gave a deep sigh. 'Did you not remonstrate with the people – try to calm them and make them understand the evil of what they were doing?'

Kemp nodded. 'Oh yes, we tried, but they were rabid with the spoils of war.'

Then, hardly daring to ask: 'What happened to the rest of the prisoners, do you know? – the ones that weren't . . .'

'Many were distributed around the tribes in the Bay of Islands. But that very night several were killed and eaten.'

'And where was Hongi Hika in all this?'

'Ah, Hongi Hika – our patron and guardian! Since we were unable to restrain the people, and the sights we had witnessed being so distressing, we withdrew. But it appears that Hongi personally slaughtered five of the prisoners by his own hand. And the next day . . .'

'Ah,' said Butler, 'the next day . . .'

'I came out of my house,' said Kemp, 'and found Hongi making a structure with pieces of a canoe, which he told me was to contain the bodies of Tete and Apu. Nearby there was a fire where dead bodies were being cooked, and beside that were baskets containing pieces that had already been cut up. The stench!' Kemp pressed his hands to his nose, as if trying to rid himself of the smell. 'Can you imagine what it is like, sir – human flesh cooking?'

Henry shook his head. 'Did you speak to the man?'

'To Hongi?' Kemp shrugged. 'I made it clear to him that such a sight filled me with horror and disgust. But he laughed and said I should try some. He said it was better than pork.'

'He had no respect for you?'

'He despised me.'

'And then you saw, just over there –' Butler indicated the side of the hill at the back of Kemp's house.

'I saw they were cooking one of the poor women who had been killed the previous day. Before they put her in the fire they cut off her head and rolled it down the hill.' He pointed. 'And then they took turns to throw stones at the head until they'd smashed it to pieces.'

For a minute the three men were silent.

Finally Kemp turned and looked Henry in the eye. 'So now you have it, Mr Williams, and it is not a pretty tale.'

'Since then, have there been any more battles?'

'Not two months after, off they went again, this time to attack the Waikato tribes, who live south of Tāmaki, because they had been allies of Ngāti Whātua, the people they'd just conquered.'

'Any pretext will do,' said Butler. 'In fact, I believe Hongi wants to decimate all other tribes while he still has the greater number of guns.'

'That is his aim, you think?'

'It has always been his aim. Ever since he saw the success of Te Morenga.'

'Te Morenga?'

'He was a chief of great mana living in these parts who obtained some muskets by bartering with the ships that visited the Bay of Islands. Through firearms he saw the means of getting revenge on a chief who had killed and eaten his niece some sixteen years before. And so with his tribe away he went, down the east coast – about three hundred miles, I might say, to Tauranga, where they attacked the tribe who had no defence against their guns, slaughtering and eating many people. Then they returned here with their prisoners.'

'And Hongi saw –'

'Hongi saw what had happened and the prisoners they brought back – as well as their canoes.'

'He wanted to be more powerful than Te Morenga –'

'And he realised that guns were the answer,' finished Henry. 'Do you think he went to England with the express desire of obtaining them?'

'I think he did,' said Butler, 'and our so-called Brother Kendall aided and abetted him, whether knowingly or not I wouldn't like to say.'

So that trip to England had led directly to the present situation, just as Josiah Pratt had feared. And now, yet again, even as they spoke there would be more killings, more people decimated. 'Was there any particular reason for this latest sortie?' he asked.

'They are going to Rotorua to avenge the death of a young Ngā Puhi chief, Te Pae-o-Te-Rangi. And he was killed because of the death of a chief at Ngā Puhi hands in the battle of Te Tōtara, even though Te Pae-o-Te-Rangi had not been present. The trouble is, they go to war and though they might have the upper hand, they will always lose some people.'

'And if a chief is killed his death must be avenged. There it is again – utu.'

'Please explain,' said Henry.

'I think it goes a long way back,' said Butler, 'to a custom that is common throughout Polynesia. If a wrong is done the balance must be restored, preferably, but not necessarily, with the death of the original perpetrator. But now, with guns being brought into the situation, the results are far more disastrous.'

'And the more they kill,' said Kemp, 'the more they come under the power of Satan.'

'Here we have the real enemy.'

Henry stood up. 'It seems clear to me, gentlemen, where our duty lies. We must break the cycle of utu, for in doing that we will break Satan's power over them. And the only way we can do that is by teaching them the gospel of the Lord Jesus Christ and the need for forgiveness, not revenge.'

Butler too stood up, arms raised and hands clenched. 'Easier said than done, Mr Williams! Do you not think we have been striving to this end for the last several years? And in fact we have made great progress. But while they have the thirst for blood –'

Kemp too stood. 'On this matter I am with Mr Butler. At present there is little we can do. We can only wait until the love of God makes itself known.'

'But –' said Henry.

'And now, if you will excuse me, sir,' said Kemp, 'I must be off.

Mr Marsden has called a meeting this morning.' He opened the gate in the fence.

Butler followed him, suddenly agitated. 'Mr Kemp, Mr Kemp! I must talk to you!'

The two men disappeared.

Henry remained standing and looked again down at the water, and over to the village astride the ridge of hills. Maybe it was his imagination, but the sparkling scene before him seemed darker. It was as if a shadow had passed over the little valley – the shadow of a menacing presence that was more real than many liked to admit.

It had become all too evident why the Lord had called him to this place. He was about to be locked in a hand-to-hand battle with the Devil.

10

Revelation, chapter 12, verses 7–12

Then war broke out in heaven. Michael and his angels fought against the dragon, who fought back with his angels; but the dragon was defeated, and he and his angels were not allowed to stay in heaven any longer. The huge dragon was thrown out – that ancient serpent, called the Devil, or Satan, that deceived the whole world. He was thrown down to earth, and all his angels with him.

Then I heard a loud voice in heaven saying, 'Now God's salvation has come! Now God has shown his power as King! Now his Messiah has shown his authority! For the one who stood before our God and accused our brothers day and night has been thrown out of heaven. Our brothers won the victory over him by the blood of the Lamb and by the truth which they proclaimed; and they were willing to give up their lives and die. And so be glad, you heavens, and all you that live there! But how terrible for the earth and the sea! For the Devil has come down to you, and he is filled with rage, because he knows that he has only a little time left.'

'Brother Williams,' said John Butler, 'I have received a letter.'

'Yes,' said Henry.

The two of them were at Paihia, preparing to carry a large plank of timber up from the beach; materials from the ship anchored out in the bay had been ferried to shore and now, finally, work had begun on building the quarters to which he could move his family.

'It is from Mr Marsden – I presume you are aware of its content?'

Henry gave the faintest jerk of his head, heaving up his end of the timber and settling it on his shoulder. He knew very well the content of Marsden's letter, but right now he was anxious to get on with the task to which Marianne and he had dedicated their lives.

'Mr Marsden has dismissed me.'

'I'm sorry –'

'In fact, you and all those I have regarded as my brothers-in-arms have dismissed me, on the basis of an entirely false accusation.'

'Now that's not fair, Mr Butler. I –'

'You were at the committee meeting and you agreed with him.'

Henry gave an exasperated sigh and let fall his end of the plank. 'Mr Marsden has made some very serious allegations. If they were not true why didn't you defend yourself?'

The two men faced each other, there on the golden sand where the sea rose and fell, unhurried, behind them.

Forced to look at Butler, Henry saw he had tears in his eyes.

'I knew it was a waste of time!' he shouted. 'Marsden wanted to get rid of me by whatever pretext he could rustle up!'

'I'm sure you are mistaken. The Reverend Marsden has given his all to set up the mission at great sacrifice to himself. In fact, I have so much regard for him that I am considering naming this new settlement in his honour.'

'You may name this place what you wish, Mr Williams. But I must inform you that in New South Wales Samuel Marsden is renowned for being a greedy, grasping man who uses his position to further his own interests.'

'Our brother in Christ has already apprised me of the lies and calumnies he has had to endure. But you must not take seriously the tittle-tattle of a convict settlement.'

He bent down to lift up the plank.

'It's true, Mr Williams, it's all too true!' screeched Butler. 'And the reason he is getting rid of me now is because I dared to challenge him on that very point.'

Reluctantly, Henry stood up again. He was not impressed by Butler, whom he regarded as boisterous and overbearing, and too unguarded in his way of speaking to be an effective member of the team. He wasn't surprised that he'd annoyed Marsden. But even so, as a Christian brother he had a right to be heard.

'Very well, Mr Butler, you'd better give me your side of the story.'

Butler sighed, and then began: 'I have come to know the Reverend Samuel Marsden very well. In fact, the two of us made a long journey together to the south of here and were the first white men to follow the portage route north from the Waitematā and see the great harbour of Kaipara on the west side of the island. I too, like you, believed Samuel Marsden to be a good man. But then there were disagreements. I began to have my doubts after two occasions, the first being at Parramatta. I was there when I heard him tell John Lee, who was as great a sot as ever lived, that if he remained in New South Wales he would be in prison again for drunkenness ere another month, and therefore he would take him to New Zealand. I thought that wonderful.'

'Wonderful?'

'I am being sarcastic. I'd have thought it was obvious that we need people of the highest calibre to carry on our great and blessed work. In spite of my objections Lee was brought here, where he duly got drunk and beat the sawyers. I sent him back to New South Wales but Marsden remonstrated with me, saying we cannot introduce civilisation without also bringing in the evils of civilised life, and he put Lee on a ship back here. But eventually he was forced to take the man back after he was found in bed with the carpenter's servant girl.'

Henry folded his arms. 'And the other occasion?'

'Marsden gave a Māori a bayonet, presumably in payment for something or other.'

'A bayonet! But that is —'

'Forbidden by the Society? Oh, when it comes to making money out of weapons of war, our saintly Mr Marsden has no scruples at all, I can assure you. And in this case there was a quarrel and that same bayonet was attached to the end of a spear and used to pierce Taiwhanga, my foreman. I am very fond of Taiwhanga, who is a great worker and picks things up very quickly, and I was extremely upset to see him so wounded.'

Henry stared at Butler.

'After that I heard that on his return to New South Wales Marsden had begun to speak ill of myself and my family, which as you can imagine hurt me deeply because there was no just cause. But the final straw was when he refused to reimburse me for timber —'

'Ah — now here is a situation where misunderstandings can easily arise, particularly when it is a matter of dealings in two different countries.'

'But surely you would expect dealings between Christians to be irreproachable no matter where they take place, particularly when it is between members of our small and faithful community?'

Touché! 'Pray continue, Mr Butler.'

'It was to do with the store for the mission station at Kerikeri. Mr King paid the Māori for the timber to build the store and then came to me for recompense, with which I acquiesced — Marsden had already told me he would pay any bills I incurred in order to carry on the Society's work. But when I forwarded him the bill he refused to pay it, thus making me look extremely mean.'

'On what grounds would he not pay?'

'He gave no reason.'

A thought struck Henry: 'How did Mr King pay the Māori?'

'With gunpowder and half a musket.'

'In that case surely Mr Marsden was within his rights to refuse to pay for items so gained.'

'But he recompensed Mr Hall for his timber purchased in the same way! And he himself gave a large teakettle filled with gunpowder to Hongi, and half a gallon to Rewa for land.'

'A teakettle full of gunpowder! That is preposterous!'

'This is New Zealand, Mr Williams, where the preposterous is always possible.'

'Did you take up the matter with Mr Marsden?'

'I did, but got nowhere. So then I wrote him a letter setting out my concerns, charging him with buying potatoes and flax with a musket, with buying cargo for the *Active* with muskets and bayonets, with procuring a native head —'

Into Henry's mind came the sight he had witnessed in Rio de Janeiro, of tattooed human heads, their lips drawn back in a ghastly smile, lined up for sale on a table like so many pumpkins. What sort of a person, he had wondered, could engage in such a trade?

'With selling the supplies intended by the CMS to clothe the Māori people, with —'

He put his fingertips to his head. 'Enough, Mr Butler, enough! You must not make these claims without proof.'

'Oh I have proof, sadly. As I wrote to Marsden, my very heart ached while I put those important questions. However, after receiving an unsatisfactory reply from him I felt I must apprise the Society of the unjust dealings of one in whom they had absolute faith.'

'You wrote to the Society?'

'You may say I was stepping beyond the bounds of my responsibilities, but I felt strongly it was my duty. And as a consequence of that, Mr Marsden has laid a plan to be rid of me and, as extra revenge, is sending me off in disgrace.'

Butler worked hard, there was no denying it. He and Fairburn sorted out the timber they needed, dug sawpits down on the beach and set to sawing the planks into the right lengths. Then they brought them over to the spot Henry had marked out. A storehouse was an extremely important building in an outpost like this: it was for keeping safe supplies such as grain and materials; it needed to be solid and strong to withstand the elements – and also, as Butler had warned him, raids by the local people.

Henry continued to take the boat, now rowed by a team of young Māori men, to and fro from the *Brampton*, bringing to shore the goods that would be kept in the storehouse once it was finished and carrying them up to the site.

Their activities were closely watched by the local people, members of the tribe of Te Koki. They leant on their spears or squatted on the ground, wrapped in their cloaks of flax, dogskin or feathers and looking for all the world like a flock of rather large birds. When they weren't chatting non-stop sometimes they sang.

There was a shout of laughter. Henry had tethered a goat given to him by Mrs Butler to a wooden, two-wheeled cart, which he filled with some of the lighter stores and now with a bit of coaxing the goat towed the cart up from the beach to the building site. The Māori ran down and followed the goat up the beach with whoops of delight, fascinated by this new method of haulage.

All the omens looked good for the relationship between the

missionaries and the people of Paihia. Te Koki was still away fighting – 'at the fight' as his people put it, but apparently he had previously expressed a desire to have a missionary settle on his land and as a powerful chief he would be able to protect them. And his wife, Hamu, who was also of high rank, had promised to look after their property, as far as she was able.

A black cloud that Henry had his eye on lived up to its appearance and emptied its contents on the bay. The three men ran to shelter under the old sail that covered the precious items brought from the ship. He found himself huddling with Butler in a hole formed by two piles of timber.

The rain pelted so hard on the sail it sounded like the rattle of gunfire.

'Tell me,' Henry shouted over the din, 'you say you are being sent off in disgrace, but surely that is your own doing.'

'The charge of drunkenness? Pure trumpery!'

'But the captains?'

'They are indebted to Marsden. Their witness was utterly false.'

'What – you say you weren't drunk?'

'All I had while I was on board their ship was a little gin in water that the captain begged me to take. And if that would make a man drunk then I'm a Dutchman.'

The rain was drowning his words. 'A Dutchman! What did you say?' shouted Henry.

Butler reached out and grabbed him by the shoulder. 'Look – I'm not a drunkard. Everyone knows that. And on this occasion my wife was with me, and my son, and they stated I was not drunk. And if they should be considered partial to my cause, there was the sailor James Spencer, who came to give evidence and was told by your man there was nothing else to add, that the meeting was over.'

Butler's grip on his shoulder tightened. Henry shifted uneasily. 'I didn't see it as necessary.'

'Not necessary! Not necessary to do all that you can to ensure an innocent man is not wrongly convicted!'

'I saw it as a disagreement between yourself and Mr Marsden that could only be cleared up with your departure.'

'Taking the easy way out!'

The downpour had ceased and the two stepped outside.

Henry faced John Butler. 'I still don't understand why you didn't speak in your own defence. It seemed as if you were tacitly admitting your guilt.'

Butler clenched his fists. 'I'll tell you why. I have laboured more than any other missionary for the good of New Zealand. My wife and I came here four years ago and since then we have worked so hard – in fact, I can safely say we have slaved – to set up this mission so it has reached the state you see today – a base all ready for you to step into. And having done our utmost in the service of the Lord, in working with people that we trusted, in facing grave danger alongside them every day, to be turned upon by those very people who sent me here, charged with a crime I did not commit . . . Can you imagine the shock and the hurt, Mr Williams, that I felt in that situation?'

Henry shook his head.

'So I said nothing. I was silenced by the enormity of it all. And that is why, now, I accept that the only thing left for me is to leave this place.'

After one week the storehouse was finished, minus its roof, and Henry was able to stow away most of the goods, not covered, but safely walled in.

Meanwhile the Māori people had been coming and going from the bush that carpeted the hills behind, bringing the materials they needed to build his house. With sticks Henry had marked out the site – next to the storehouse, forty feet long by eighteen feet wide, divided into four 'apartments'. Then it was his turn to be fascinated. He stood and watched as, all the while chatting together, with the occasional burst of laughter and sometimes snatches of song – quickly and dexterously they stuck the branches they had cut down into the ground to form the walls, and tied them together with vines that they plaited to make a strong framework. Then more poles made of branches were tied to the top of the walls to form a roof.

The walls were filled in with the upright stalks of a kind of bulrush they called 'raupō', and the leaves of this raupō were used to thatch the roof. Then more branch-poles were laid over the whole, to make a chequered pattern, and tied down. The whole house was completed in a day.

In shape it was an upturned boat, and a fragile-looking one at that, but as Henry surveyed it with a critical eye he decided that, barring an extreme event like a violent storm, it ought to be strong enough. He thought of the children's favourite story, the tale of the three little pigs, one of whom built his house of straw, one of sticks and one of bricks. His house stood on sand and was made of rushes, but it was built on the rock of his faith in the Lord and because of that it would stand.

The storehouse also received its thatched roof and then he, Butler and Fairburn set to building a fence around the whole complex.

When he arrived back at Kerikeri, in spite of being exhausted, like the other two men, by the hard physical work and nights of sleeping on the ground without even a blanket, Henry was in good spirits. The work had gone well, thanks in great part to the labour put in by Butler and Fairburn, and they now had a reasonably secure and comfortable shelter for the family – although the spaces where the windows were to go eventually were boarded over, and the floors were made of earth, packed down hard. He wasn't sure what Marianne would make of it.

She was delighted to see him, concerned to find him so tired.

'It's nothing,' he told her. 'I'm just pleased we've managed to complete this dwelling – more or less. What about you? Are you ready to move to Paihia?'

'Henry, do you doubt me? I can't wait to see it and in the meantime I've learned so much from Mrs Butler – how to manage goats, how to pay our servant girls – she gives them a hoe or an axe every three months, as do the other missionaries, and that seems to work very well.'

'Do you think you'll be able to manage with a Māori girl for a servant?'

'I think they will do a good job, under supervision, and Mrs Butler has been very helpful in giving me advice. The only thing that worries me –' She hesitated, looking Henry in the eye.

He gazed back at her steadily, waiting. Marianne did not usually admit to any doubts.

'While you were away there was a problem with one of the chiefs. He was demanding that Mr Kemp mend his gun –'

'It is a scourge we can only deal with by firmly refusing such requests. Mending a gun is the same as giving them one.'

'I know. And Mr Kemp was very patient, just politely refusing and explaining why. But then the chief became angry and accused the missionaries of trying to spread ourselves around and take over the land so that one day New Zealand will become like Sydney. He said we had no right to be going to Paihia.'

Henry folded his arms and looked at the ground. 'He was annoyed because we refuse to give him guns. But to look at it in a wider sense, we must expect opposition – this is Satan speaking and he's furious because he's being challenged in a place where up until the coming of the missionaries he has held total sway. It is a mighty battle in which we are engaged, and for the sake of the people we have come to save we must stand firm.'

'In a way could you say it's a sign we're on the right path, because we are encountering opposition?'

'Exactly that.'

Samuel Marsden was about to leave the mission. He would sail on the *Brampton*, departing on Sunday.

Marianne quoted the Fourth Commandment to the captain: 'Remember the Sabbath day, to keep it holy.' Why was he departing on the day the Lord had declared was holy and on which no one should work?

'The fairer the day the fairer the sail,' replied the captain, apparently not in the least bothered about profaning the Sabbath Day.

'Really,' said Marianne to Henry, 'I fear our own kind are just as much in need as the Māori people of the call to salvation.'

Marsden departed and the wind got up, blowing in strong gusts. Then it poured with rain and the Kerikeri River rose until they feared it would burst its banks and destroy the fences and paddocks of the Butlers' farm.

On Tuesday evening in the Butlers' sitting room all were on their knees, deep in celebrating the service of Evensong. There was a banging on the back window.

They turned round and saw Māori people making urgent faces, pointing to Mrs Butler. She went to them and made signs to be silent, that they were in the midst of prayers.

They forced open the window and spoke to her even more strongly. She ran out of the room and everyone else stood up, looking at each other, wondering what was going on.

The banging became louder and now one of the young men who rowed Henry's boat pushed forward, raising his arms and shouting at him. Still they did not understand. Then one of the Māori servants in the room cried out, 'He aituā nui!'

'He aituā? A disaster?' said John Butler.

'Āe!' said the servant. 'The ship is broke to pieces.'

'What ship?'

'The ship of Mātenga!'

'The *Brampton*?'

'Āe, koia nā!'

Butler turned to explain but there was no need. Everyone had their hands to their mouths.

The *Brampton* was wrecked.

11

Samuel Marsden was ensconced in a chair in the Kemps' house, availing himself of the scones being pressed upon him by Mrs Kemp. His chubby cheeks were perhaps less fulsome, and there were hollows under his large dark eyes to prove he had been through a most harrowing experience. However, when the missionaries burst in he seemed not to have lost his spirit.

He waved a scone in their direction. 'We meet again, dear friends, rather sooner than expected.'

'Brother Marsden!' said Henry, 'we've just heard –'

The chaplain grasped the scone with both hands and bit into it. 'I've had nothing to eat but a few potatoes for the last two days,' he said, his mouth full.

Henry knelt beside him.

'You've been through a great ordeal, sir.'

'Sometimes, Mr Williams, one needs to be reminded that when it comes to the sea and the weather we are but minnows.'

'So what happened?'

'The captain departed on Sunday, as you know, but the wind was against us –' Marsden stopped, breathing heavily '– and it was strong, blowing hard all evening.'

'So you continued to beat against the wind,' said Henry.

'Of course the captain tried to work out but it was to no avail. The gale began to push us back –' he paused again to puff – 'and suddenly there was a loud crash – in fact there were three shocks, and then we were on it.'

'On what?'

'A reef just off Waitangi.'

'As far back as that! Why didn't the crew drop anchor before they hit?'

'I believe they did, but it was too late. All was in turmoil, confusion reigned – and then we saw waves breaking on the rocky shoal and the anchor cable broke. I remained calm and encouraged the others to do so –'

'Did everyone get off?' asked Butler. 'And where have you been sheltering once you reached the shore?'

Mrs Kemp brought a mug of tea, which Marsden swallowed noisily while at the same time demolishing the last of the scones.

Finally he wiped his face with the napkin provided, and looked around at the people crowded into the Kemps' house. 'You have no idea, my friends,' he said, 'how gladdened I am to see you, even though our plans have been thwarted. Yes, somehow we managed to get everyone into the ship's boats and struggle to shore against alarmingly large waves. As some of you may know, there is a hut – a very simple one and not at all comfortable – on the island of Moturoa, and that is where we have been for the last two nights, waiting for the storm to abate. And now finally we have been able to reach you.' He turned to John Butler. 'However, until we can persuade another ship to come from Sydney and take us back, I fear we shall have to avail ourselves of your excellent hospitality.'

Their eyes met. Butler gave a smile that was more of a grimace.

'Which, of course, may take some time,' Marsden added.

There was silence.

'Is the ship salvageable?' asked Henry.

Marsden shook his head. 'She's in a very bad way. And as a shipwreck the Māori will claim her.'

'Why?'

'They regard any ship that founders on their land, which I suppose the rocks are, as their property. And what could we do to stop them? After the disaster, the vessel, our property on board, and indeed our own persons on the island, were completely in their power. They could have taken our lives at any moment.'

'But they didn't.'

'We were saved by a most fortuitous intervention. Captain Moore told me that when he was down below in the hold, trying to sort out the most important items to save, he heard a commotion and came up on deck. There he found the ship surrounded by some five or six hundred men on boats who were making a loud and threatening noise. But one of the head chiefs leapt on board and after motioning the captain to keep quiet and not interfere, he stood on the deck and harangued those men for an hour – told them they must not plunder it nor attack anyone on it.'

'And they obeyed?'

'Indeed they did! And then, for good measure the chief turned, took Moore's sword from him and held it aloft, saying he would cut down the first man who came on board.'

'Did anyone try?'

'They quietened at once and the captain and crew were able to remove everything they wished, without molestation. Now, this would not have happened in the past.'

'Would it not? So why –'

'I believe the only reason we are alive today is because our little missionary band has come among the Māori people and gained their confidence and goodwill.'

'Already your efforts are bearing fruit,' said Marianne, beaming at the Kemps and the Butlers.

'A large part of my energy and resources have been devoted to this project,' said Marsden, 'and I am of course gratified to see such an outcome.' He turned to Henry and Marianne. 'I now count upon you, Mr and Mrs Williams, to continue my sterling work and build a true Kingdom of God right here in New Zealand.'

The storm continued to batter the Bay of Islands with wind and rain, but finally, eight days after the *Brampton* had perished, the morning of 15 September dawned clear and calm. All was ready for the voyage to Paihia. The boat that was to ferry Marianne to her new home was drawn up on the beach and everything they would need in the way of bedding, clothes and food had been carefully stowed and lashed with ropes.

Accompanied by Marsden, John and Hannah Butler, and James Kemp, they made the procession down to the shore, Marianne walking slowly for she was now seven months pregnant. The children had been left in the care of Charlotte Kemp.

The little band stood together in a circle on the sand as Marsden prayed for the success of the mission of Henry and Marianne and their family and asked the Lord to keep them safe. Henry looked up at the Butlers' house, so attractive with its neat windows and verandah, and so solid: the place to which he was taking his wife was by no means in the same league. He hoped she would not be too disappointed.

Their crew of young Māori men were standing on the sand, waiting – in the same place, it flashed into Henry's mind, where Kemp had told him the prisoners brought by Hongi Hika were killed. Was the thought a shot across the bows from his enemy the Devil? It might be! But it was also a reminder of the task on which they were all engaged – to remove the evil that contaminated this beautiful land.

Marsden raised his hand. 'In the name of the Father, the Son and the Holy Spirit.'

'Amen!' responded the missionaries, loudly and in unison.

They dropped back as Marianne hitched up her skirts and climbed over the side of the canoe. With her sitting in it, the men dragged the boat down into the sea. Then Henry hopped in, positioning himself beside Marianne. The crew dug their paddles into the limpid water and round the hill they went, following the bends and twists of the Kerikeri Inlet. On the forest-covered banks fluttered birds of all kinds, singing like the choir of a cathedral, urging them on.

Then they were out of the inlet and passing through the narrow passage that separated the island of Moturoa from the mainland. Henry spotted the hut amongst trees on the side of a hill where Marsden had sheltered, and down on the shore the tent the captain had erected to protect the stores.

Then they were out in the broad sweep of the bay, heading towards the land to the south. And in the distance was the melancholy sight of the *Brampton*. She was sitting bolt upright in the middle of the water, stuck fast on the reef; her masts had gone and there was the sound of banging.

They drew closer. Now they could see men clambering all over the hull, yanking out planks and nails, dismembering the carcase. The figurehead stared out mournfully.

Marianne grasped his arm. 'I can't believe it,' she said, '– to see her like this. She brought us here without mishap and I had complete faith in her. But now . . .'

He squeezed her to him. 'I know – I'm sorry.'

'Only a few weeks ago we were hove to in that dreadful storm, not far from here – how close to danger we were.'

'We are always close to danger,' Henry said. 'But we must remember we are in the care of our Great Protector.'

'Look!' she cried, pointing. 'I can see the windows of our cabin!' The portholes hung low over the water, almost within reach of the breaking waves. 'Oh, the poor ship!'

'There is nothing sadder than a shipwreck. Especially when the disaster could easily have been avoided.'

'One good thing – I suppose now it marks the reef,' she said. 'Other ships will know not to go near.'

The wreck of the *Brampton* was more than just a marker on a rock – it was a warning to the captains who insisted on sailing on the day of sacred rest so they were paid more for extra working days.

'It's also a beacon to stupidity and greed,' he said.

Now they were truly on their way, across the sea of the Bay of Islands. The waves danced and sparkled in the sunlight and the dark heads around them moved forwards and backwards, paddling Marianne towards her new home.

They skirted the three small islands and then the handiwork of Henry and his helpers – Butler, Fairburn and the Māori people – was clearly visible, there on the beach.

Marianne gazed at the bay, fringed by pohutukawa trees, with the pā at one end and the rickety hut and its storehouse at the other, and, suddenly anxious, Henry watched her face.

She turned to him, her smile brilliant.

'It's so exciting – our very own home, at last!'

'It's not what you might have expected when you married me – not like, for example, a house in Nottingham.'

Her smile disappeared and she nodded gravely. 'No it is not – not at all.' She rested her chin in her hands.' I'll tell you what it's like – it's a beehive!'

Henry looked again at the their new house and, as she said, it looked just like one of those oval, upside-down pudding bowl-shaped shelters they used back home for bees to make their honey.

'It's just temporary – as soon as I am able I will build you a proper –'

She flung her arm around him and kissed him on the cheek. 'It's our very own beehive where we'll all work hard like busy bees and I love it – of course I love it!'

They were almost at the shore, where hundreds of people had gathered. Henry and the crew jumped into the water and the men began to drag the boat onto the land, with Marianne still sitting regally inside.

There was a roar as the people converged on the boat, shouting, and an overpowering smell of fish oil.

Henry was walking alongside. 'Why are they here?' she called to him.

'It's the tribe of Te Koki – Te Uri Ongaonga – come to welcome you!'

The crowd pressed around them. 'E te wahine! Hōmai te ringaringa!' they cried, stretching out their arms.

Marianne leaned out and touched as many as possible of the brown hands that reached towards her. Then she put her face in her hands and her whole body shook.

'What is it, my darling?' called Henry. 'Are you all right?'

She lifted her head but there were tears pouring down her cheeks.

'I'm so happy, really I am. It's just that I'm not used to such a fanfare.'

'They want to carry you in.'

'Like this?' She looked down at her belly, curving out in front of her. 'Oh – I don't really . . .'

'Would you mind? I'm sure they will be careful.'

'Very well, if you think it's all right.'

With Henry supporting her, Marianne stood up uncertainly. The boat lurched and the men steadied it. They reached up their arms and took her weight, some carrying her from behind under the armpits, others bearing her bulky body and legs, still demurely covered in her long skirts, and in a not exactly dignified and yet almost stately manner she was borne by the tribe up the beach and set in front of her new home.

There it was, surrounded by a paling fence. Henry opened the gate and ushered her in, with the people crowding round and watching from behind.

He opened the door with a flourish.

'It's very dark,' she said, peering in.

'The apertures where the windows are to go have been boarded up until the glass is ready,' said Henry.

'And there is no floor!'

'But there soon will be!' came a voice from the darkness. William Fairburn emerged. 'Good afternoon, Mrs Williams and welcome to your – or may I say our – new home.'

'Thank you,' said Marianne. 'I know we'll be sharing with you and your family, and I'm very much looking forward to having the company of Mrs Fairburn.'

'As for the floor,' said Fairburn, 'Mr Williams and I have that matter well in hand. In fact, I can assure you that by nightfall you will have the best floor in the whole of Paihia.'

Henry showed her round their house. It would be divided into two main areas, one for each family, each with a sitting room and a bedroom. The kitchen, as he had already warned her, would be a little lean-to outside the main hut because their 'rush palace' was far too flammable to risk setting up an open fire inside.

He produced for her one of the chairs they'd brought all the way from England and then, with Marianne recovering in the sitting room, he and Fairburn set to, sawing up the planks to make a floor for her bedroom.

By the evening they had finished. Henry insisted on cooking the meal himself and then he brought in the bedding. Proudly he set it out on the newly laid floor and Marianne slept, she said in the most comfortable bed on which she had ever reposed.

If Paihia was to be a mission it must also have a place of worship. Henry persuaded the Uri Ongaonga to build not only a house for the Williams and Fairburn families, but also a smaller hut to serve as a chapel.

On Sunday he erected a pole to which he attached a Union Jack. The red, white and blue flag made a bright spot on the beach and was intended, he told Marianne, to signify to the Uri Ongaonga that it was a sacred day. 'From now on,' he told her, 'we will do this every Sunday, when we hold a service for ourselves and the people to attend.'

'Do you think they will come?' she asked.

'Wait and see,' said Henry.

He fetched a hand bell, which he began to ring. For the next quarter of an hour, Henry, Marianne and William Fairburn stood outside their newly built chapel and waited.

And the people came. They carried with them chairs and planks, as Henry had explained they would need these for sitting on, rather than on the ground as was their custom. They walked along the sand in the sunshine, laughing and chattering among themselves, while the bell sounded sweetly and the flag fluttered in the breeze.

Marianne touched Henry's hand. 'What a delightful scene,' she murmured. 'I feel the Lord is with us, rejoicing to see his people come to him.'

They all squeezed into the raupō hut. Henry was not yet accomplished enough with the Māori language to be able to address his congregation, so he read from the Bible and asked God to bless all those who had gathered for the service: also to guide the missionaries as they brought the good news of God's love for all his children on earth, to the people of Paihia.

The two men continued to lay the floors of the hut and position the windows, so that suddenly sunlight streamed in. Marianne, eager to make their two rooms seem more like a home, unpacked their belongings and placed books on the shelves that William Fairburn had made. Then she set to work in the 'kitchen', producing bread made by kneading flour and water into a dough and baking it in a heavy black iron pot suspended over an open fire.

Little Marianne, Teddy and Samuel arrived, brought by boat from Kerikeri, as did Mrs Fairburn and her children, and then — this was the final touch — there was the sound of excited children running through the house.

But a week after their arrival, Marianne was exhausted from all the activity. In the evening after she'd finished ironing their clothes Henry helped her bath the children, but she said her back was sore and she needed to lie down.

He went outside to find people gathered on the beach in the evening sun, pointing out to sea. The silhouette of a canoe was approaching.

Along with the people he waited on the shore. The waka drew closer and he could see that apart from the crew those it was carrying were both British and Māori. Ah yes — now it was clear: one was Samuel Marsden and the other was James Kemp. But who was the Māori man with the black and white feathers in his hair?

Amidst the animated conversations that suddenly arose around him he was joined by William Fairburn.

'I see we're being paid a visit by our brother missionaries,' said Henry. 'But who is the chief?'

They went forward as the occupants clambered out of the waka.

Fairburn drew in a deep breath and whistled.

'The chief, sir, is none other than Hongi Hika!'

12

Henry rushed back to the hut.

'Marianne!' he called. 'Marianne!'

Teddy was sitting in the doorway. 'Mummy's inside,' he said, 'and she's crying.'

'What! Have you upset her?'

The boy shook his head. 'She's just crying like she always does.'

From within came the sounds of desperate sobbing: muffled howling, as though someone was emptying out the very depths of their soul.

Henry entered the door of the room. On her side on the mattress lay Marianne, the long skirts of her dress twisted round her voluminous belly. She was face down in the pillow.

He knelt beside her.

'Oh my love, my love!'

She turned and looked up and he saw that her eyes were blood-red and tears were coursing down her cheeks. 'Henry! I thought you were —'

'What is it? What's happened?'

Awkwardly she pushed herself up to a sitting position, wiping her eyes and nose with a handkerchief.

'It's nothing. Truly.' She gave a massive sniff. 'I get like this sometimes and it's best to let it all out. I feel so much better afterwards.'

He lowered himself down to the mattress and sat beside her, rubbing her back.

'But why?'

She shrugged. 'I don't know.'

'There must be a reason.'

'Maybe sometimes it all seems too much.'

And now he was about to burden her even further.

His head sank onto his knees.

'What is it, Henry?'

He raised his head.

'I'm so sorry – but we have visitors.'

She looked at him questioningly.

'Mr Marsden. Mr Kemp.'

'Oh!'

'And . . . Hongi Hika.'

Now Marianne's eyes were really wide.

'They'll be expecting something to eat,' Henry rushed on, 'and, and – presumably to stay and I don't know where –'

There was silence, then Marianne blew her nose again and smiled at him – her dazzling smile.

'We'll manage, don't worry.' She stood up awkwardly and patted down her skirts. 'And one thing's for certain – I can't keep lying here like a lazy whale!'

Henry and William Fairburn stood by the gate of their surrounding palisade, waiting.

The three men advanced up the beach: Samuel Marsden and James Kemp on either side of Hongi Hika, with the crew following behind. Marsden's figure could only be described as short and rotund; Kemp was of average height and solidly built, as befits a blacksmith, but the tall, wiry figure of Hongi, even though stooped now, towered over them both, his sharp eyes steadily fixed on Henry. The man certainly had presence, even if that was sinister.

Te Koki appeared, the news having already been relayed to him, and Hamu beside him made the karanga, that haunting call of welcome in which, as Henry understood it, she made mention of the people who had gone before, the dead of Hongi and of their own families, and asked for a blessing on the house that Hongi was about to enter.

The people of Paihia were in an uneasy partnership with Hongi's tribe, Ngā Puhi. These last were originally from a place in the inner stretches of the country called Kaikohe, but through intermarriage and fighting, at which they were particularly proficient, they had enlarged their territory to a kainga or village at Waimate, also inland, and from there had spread north to Kerikeri. The Ngā Puhi chief of Kerikeri was actually Rewa, Hongi's cousin, but Hongi liked to treat it as his own, and it was he who'd become the protector of the missionaries after Ruatara died, and had sold the land at Kerikeri to Samuel Marsden.

Now, because of his fighting prowess Hongi was the dominant chief in the whole area and tribes like the Uri Ongaonga had become subservient to him, and for fear of being annihilated themselves they joined him in his war initiatives. Te Koki therefore needed to appear welcoming, but Henry sensed there was an undercurrent of resentment.

The people of Te Uri Ongaonga had gathered round to exchange the hongi, or pressing of noses.

When it was Henry's turn, he could feel the power as Hongi bent to greet him and share his breath: the perfectly executed, symmetrical markings that completely covered his face at close quarters were even more distinctive, as well was also the earthy, oily smell of his body and his luxuriant hair, curling to his shoulders.

Marianne appeared at the door, making an urgent face. 'I'm not ready yet,' she whispered. 'Perhaps you could show them round?'

He began by taking them down to where he'd sown long rows of seed, occupying an area stretching in neat squares almost down to the beach. Already little shoots of green were showing through the fertile earth.

'And these are?' said Marsden.

'Oats and barley.'

'Barley! Don't tell me you are about to make beer!'

'Not at present, Mr Marsden. For now we are engaged only in producing the basic necessities, in this case to make flour.'

Marsden turned to Hongi. 'And from flour they will make bread.'

'He ōti, hei mahi pāreti,' said Hongi.

Henry looked questioningly at Marsden.

Kemp explained. '"And the oats are to make porridge." Hongi quite often breakfasts with us at Kerikeri.'

'Āe, he parakuihi! He tino reka tēnā kai ki ahau.'

Henry was somewhat taken aback at the familiarity of the chief with British customs. But of course, he was not speaking to an unschooled native. This was a man who'd been to England and met with King George, no less! – an honour unlikely to be conferred upon the majority of Henry's own countrymen.

He brought the men back within the palisade fence and showed them the carpenter's bench where Fairburn worked, and the fowl house. Everywhere chickens were pecking the earth, tethered goats were bleating and pairs of ducks were waddling about clacking to each other.

'I know it looks very random and ramshackle,' he said, 'but in fact everything has a purpose.'

'Survival,' said Marsden. 'I would expect nothing less of our missionaries. It is important to bring the Word of God to a place but one must also make sure one has the necessities to live and not be a burden on the CMS.' His gaze fell on a pile of boards and shingles.

'Those, sir, are for our next house,' said Henry.

'You have another building project?'

'That's for the future. Our Beehive, as we call it –' he gestured to the raupō hut '– will do us very well for now, but in the future we'll need something more substantial.'

He took them behind the hut to another palisaded area: the vegetable garden, where beans and peas were already growing vigorously, entwining themselves round the mānuka branches he'd placed in the earth to make a climbing frame. He had also planted seeds of cucumber and melon, as well as potatoes.

The three men stood there, looking round.

'I'm particularly proud of my gardening efforts,' he said. 'I've never done it before and it seems to me like a miracle – the way you can sow seeds in the ground and they grow up and provide you with food.'

'The seed sown in fertile ground . . .' said Kemp.

Hongi gestured to the forest clothing the hillside behind. 'Anei te kai o te ngahere.'

'The food of the forest! You are right to remind us of that, Mr Hongi,' said Marsden. 'But I think the way we grow food is more convenient.'

There was a laugh from the other Englishmen. Hongi swung round and walked off. Kemp followed him and Henry dropped back with Marsden.

'Soon we will have all the vegetables we need,' he said, 'but meat is a problem. We've been subsisting on salt beef for the last three weeks. The people catch wild pigs but they refuse to give us any unless we give them guns, no doubt on the orders of –' He jerked his head in the direction of Hongi. 'And that we will never do.'

Marsden was silent.

'Do you not agree with our stance on firearms, sir?'

Marsden started. 'Oh absolutely, yes! Inadmissible!'

'However, I have an idea on how to resolve that problem,' said Henry. He heard Marianne calling. 'But for now I believe Mrs Williams is ready for us.'

She greeted them at the door of the hut. 'Please do come in. I'm just baking a batch of fresh bread,' she said brightly. There was no sign of the distraught woman of only half an hour ago. Yet Henry knew that while he showed his visitors around there'd been frenzied activity behind the scenes as she bundled up the mattress, swept papers and books off the table in their little 'sitting room', whipped away all other furniture to goodness knows where and laid places at the table.

Te Koki set a chair at one end of the table and invited Hongi to sit, placing himself on the ground beside the great chief. Marsden, Fairburn and Kemp also sat on chairs, while the boat crew found space on the floor.

Henry asked Samuel Marsden to say grace, which he did so at length and in English, thanking God for having brought them all there together, for the house that would from now on shelter the Williamses and the Fairburns, and asking the Lord to aid them in the great project on which they were engaged.

Then Marianne brought out the bread she had baked, now sliced into pieces. She hesitated. Who would take precedence – Marsden or Hongi Hika?

Te Koki noted her hesitation. 'Ka nui ngā kai mā te rangatira,' he said, gesturing to Hongi. 'You must give him lots to eat.' He turned to the others. 'The Pākehā, he not eat much but the tangata Māori – he eat a great deal!'

There was a shout of laughter from the Māori with many vehement nods of the head, joined in by the Europeans when they understood the gist of his little joke.

Quickly, beginning with Hongi so he could take as many slices as he wished, and then passing the tray around, Marianne shared out the precious loaf.

From outside the evening sun crept in and illuminated the faces of those seated round the table. Henry looked from one of his extraordinary guests to the other: there was Samuel Marsden, the man who single-handedly had set up the mission in New Zealand in spite of the most compelling of obstacles, doing most of the talking, the jowls of his round face wobbling and his protuberant eyes gleaming.

And then there was Hongi Hika, whose teeth were now biting into a piece of bread but which could equally tear into a man's haunch with the same gusto. People had told Henry it was hard to believe that a man of such peaceful demeanour was capable of the deeds accredited to him. But now Hongi had joined in the conversation and taken offence, probably with something Kemp had said because the blacksmith was inclined to be tactless. The chief's whole expression changed: narrow eyes flashing, the lips drawn back and the mouth twisted. You would think he was inhabited by another creature, wild and ferocious – which of course he was. The mild exterior that Hongi exhibited was simply that of a man who believed he was in complete control of those around him.

Marianne again brought out another loaf and, as before, Hongi was given first choice.

Once they had finished it was a matter of organising the sleeping arrangements.

Marianne gave orders with the aplomb of a sergeant-major. She asked the crew to lift the table outside so the sitting room was free to become a bedroom for Marsden, Kemp and Hongi Hika. She directed the boat crew to the Fairburns' sitting room, while the five Māori girls who were acting as servants could sleep in the little hallway of the hut.

As for the Williams and Fairburn families, who numbered ten amongst them including the children, they would just have to find a space where they could.

In the midst of the chaos Marianne met Henry's eye and grinned triumphantly. 'I told you it would be all right,' she whispered. 'Even though I wasn't expecting our little house to become a hotel quite so soon!'

It transpired that Marsden and Kemp had come to stay for a week, which, with the cramped sleeping arrangements and the difficulties for Marianne of cooking outside on an open fire, sometimes in the rain, was a challenge to say the least.

Henry tried to help her as much as he could, and watched her carefully. But Marianne was as cheerful as ever, giving no sign at all of the turmoil he had witnessed just a few days ago.

When it was time for them to leave Marsden asked him to accompany him to Kerikeri for a meeting. Henry agreed, although he was reluctant to leave Marianne now that he knew she was in a fragile state.

'Do not worry, my darling,' she said.

'But . . .'

She put her arm around him. 'Honestly, I will be perfectly all right. I have Mrs Fairburn to attend to me, should the little one arrive before its time.'

'I'm worried – will it be "all too much" again without me here to help you?'

'I know, and so do you, that the Lord is always with me and from him will come strength.'

As it turned out Henry was not away long, and when again he clambered out of the boat on the beach at Paihia he was met by a smiling Marianne.

She held out her hands and he grasped them with both his. For a minute they stood there, gazing at each other. 'Are you all right?' he asked.

'I've been writing to your mother,' she replied, 'telling her about arriving here and the new house you've built for me and all the people we had to put up already.'

'She'll be horrified.'

'I think she will be glad to know that we now have our own place and all is well. In fact, I said to her I wished she could look in upon us, that we have never been more happy and comfortable since we were married. And it's true!' She pointed at the hut. 'Look at our own dear little rush cottage, so neat with its thatched roof, and our lovely vegetable garden at the back, full of good things to sustain us.'

Edward and Marianne were running down the beach to greet him. 'And the children! I hardly see them, they are having such fun paddling in the water and playing in the trees on the hill. And I set Tom, one of your boat crew, to scrubbing floors. Aden helped me show him what to do and we had such a time together. Everyone was laughing fit to burst, myself included.'

'Did he do a good job?'

'Yes, he managed very well.'

Edward and Marianne were upon him, clutching at his legs, insisting he come right this instant to come and see a hut they'd built in the forest.

Marianne put her arm through his as they walked up the beach together.

'Do you know,' she said, 'I've never been as happy as I am now. We're in a little romantic paradise in a barbarous land, and here I feel as safe and peaceful as can be. This is our home and I cannot give thanks enough to our gracious Lord, that he has brought us to a place where we can be truly useful.'

While in Kerikeri Henry had left a message for Captain Moore, whose ship was visiting the Bay of Islands, to call upon him.

Obtaining meat had become more and more difficult: on one occasion the local people brought down the river thirty pigs they'd caught inland, intending to exchange them for muskets with the captain of a ship that had put into the bay. The captain was uninterested in buying, having already more than enough pork on board, and when the missionaries refused to give them guns the people took the pigs back.

Now Moore had arrived and that evening Henry took the captain into their sitting room-cum-bedroom.

'Thank you for visiting me so promptly,' he said. He brought out a scroll of paper on which he'd drawn sketches. 'I believe you are a master of shipbuilding.'

Moore took out his pipe. 'I wouldn't say I'm an expert, but I have practical knowledge.'

'So I hear. As do I, a little – in fact I attended a boatbuilding course before I left England. But I would appreciate you running your eye over my proposed plans.'

Moore leant forward. 'A schooner!' He gave Henry a sharp look. 'You're an ambitious man, Mr Williams. Why such a large ship?'

'She needs to be big enough to get to Sydney, so we can replenish our supplies – meat, for example.'

'Sydney!' Moore leant forward with renewed interest. 'In that case . . .'

Finally Moore left. Immediately the outer door was shut Marianne rushed into the room, clutching towels, a pillow and a bowl.

'I thought he would never leave!'

'What's the matter?'

'The baby!'

'It's coming? Now? Are you sure?'

She turned to face him. 'Henry Williams! I do believe after giving birth three times already I ought to know when another is on its way. Now, please could you bring in the mattress so I have somewhere to lie down. Hurry!'

Obediently he brought in their mattress and helped Marianne to lower herself down on to it. He covered her with blankets but she threw them off.

'I've heated up water on the fire, so could you put some in another bowl and bring it in. Oh, oh!' She put her hand to her belly. 'The contractions have been going for some time.'

'You should have told me,' said Henry. 'I —'

'And scissors. I've cleaned them in the fire and left them beside it. And string!'

Scissors and string? Henry's heart was beating fast. This was the first time Marianne had given birth away from home, where she was attended by his mother or a midwife.

He brought them to her. Marianne was moving restlessly and grimacing. Then she began to vomit.

He gave her the bowl.

She cried out and Henry knelt beside her.

'It's coming! I'm pushing! Have a look to see!'

Henry rushed round to see a little dark head appearing. He grabbed the baby as it slithered out and held it up. 'It's a boy!'

'Quickly, turn him upside down!'

The baby duly obliged with a lusty wail and hastily Henry set him to rights again.

Marianne sat up. 'Wrap him in a towel and pass him to me.'

He gave her the baby. She hugged it to her breast, then its little head nuzzled into her and she pressed a nipple into its mouth. The baby began to suck and Marianne looked up at Henry.

'He's beautiful! Don't you think?'

He looked at the two of them, Marianne with her hair spreading down round her shoulders, her face flushed with the effort of bringing a whole new person into the world: and his perfect son, earnestly sucking on his mother's breast.

'You're both beautiful,' he said.

'You'll have to cut the umbilical cord.'

Henry looked at the bloody lifeline that attached the baby to its mother.

'With the scissors!'

She showed him. 'Look, right down here near my tummy button.'

Just then the door opened and Sarah Fairburn appeared.

'I thought I heard something! You should have called me! Is the baby –?' She stopped and looked down at Marianne cradling her precious little bundle. 'Now I see,' she said. 'He has arrived.'

'Could I ask you to deal with these?' said Henry, handing her the scissors.

Sarah took the scissors, carefully cut through the fleshy tube and tied it with string. In the bowl she caught the placenta, which had just appeared and with the other towels she set to wiping up the blood and faeces that had accompanied his son's birth.

Human beings had a very messy start in life, not to mention giving their mothers excruciating pain, Henry reflected.

Sarah gathered up the bowl and the towels and departed.

Then Marianne sank back against the pillows, looking up at him. He sat beside her, gazing anew at his son. Even after four births he was still taken aback by the wonder of it all – the sudden appearance of a human being in miniature.

'The Lord has given us another boy to aid us in our grand enterprise.'

Henry stroked her hair. 'He will be a member of the team.'

'For his name – I have been thinking about that, you know.'

'I know!'

'And I have decided – if it's all right with you – I would like to call him Henry, after the best papa in the world.'

He took a lantern and went outside to heat up some gruel. Fortunately the fire was still burning, probably stoked by Marianne. Even in the midst of her ordeal she thought of everything. Then he woke up the children to tell them they had a new baby brother.

They filed in, half asleep, and gazed open-mouthed at their mother, lying dishevelled on the mattress with the baby beside her.

Then they went back to bed and Marianne slept. Henry wrapped his boat cloak around him and watched, and prayed.

'Oh heavenly Father,' he said, 'I thank thee with all my heart that this birth has had such a happy outcome, and that my beloved wife is well.'

That was always the worry – would she survive the ordeal? After all, even women back home surrounded by people with the latest medical knowledge sometimes died in childbirth.

'I thank you for the miracle of the birth of this little one, whom Marianne wishes to name after me. And I ask that you bless this new little Henry and encourage him to be another messenger of the salvation you have offered to the world through your son Jesus Christ.'

There was a knock at the outer door.

'And now please pour out your blessings upon Marianne, and upon all our little family, when we are so far from home, family and friends. I ask this in the name of Jesus Christ our Lord. Amen.'

He went to the door and opened it, to find Te Koki standing there, majestic in his feather cloak.

'Kia ora e te hoa,' he said.

He'd seen their lamp shining and come to see if everything was all right.

Henry spoke softly so as not to wake Marianne: 'Our baby has just been born.'

'He tamaiti hou!' He looked at Henry questioningly. 'He tama, he kōtiro rānei?'

'He tama.'

'He rongo tino pai!' A smile spread over the chief's face. It appeared that a boy was extra good news. Te Koki held out his hand and Henry clasped it.

He turned to go. 'E pai ana ngā mea katoa?'

'Āe, e pai ana,' said Henry.

All was well, and all was very well.

He stood for a minute at the door of the hut as Te Koki vanished into the darkness. Then he looked up at the deep velvet sky of the Southern Hemisphere, sprinkled with myriads of diamonds glittering above him. To Henry's heightened awareness the stars seemed to be particularly bright tonight, winking and shining and sharing his joy.

And maybe it was because of the excitement of the birth, but he was also buoyed by the visit of Te Koki. He had just prayed for his family because they were far from those they loved, but now they had friends here, such as Te Koki, and he'd felt the warmth of the chief's concern and seen the kindness in his eyes. They were part of a new family now, right here in Paihia.

Marianne was right. They'd been wonderfully helped in being led to this place where they had every prospect of usefulness. Now they must help these noble people throw off the shackles of the Evil One.

He raised his arms to the firmament, a puny man in a vast universe, and his heart swelled with gratitude, love and determination.

13

And then had come the attack by Tohitapu.

The family held up well, but the attack came as a shock and a warning they could never take their safety for granted. Not that they did – they were always cautious, but they had hoped they would be safe under the protection of Te Koki.

After finishing his walk along the beach Henry turned his back on the sea and headed for the cottage. The Fairburns had now moved out, which gave them a great deal more room, and the carpenter had built a house made of wood a little further along the beach. Henry hoped to do the same for Marianne, when he had a chance, for it pained him to see her still standing outside, sometimes in the rain, cooking their meals.

She'd been so very patient, his darling wife, with hardly a word of complaint. However, she did remark to him recently how Samuel Marsden, when they were in Parramatta, had assured them they would want for nothing: house, ship, furniture, shoes, even – all would be made for them in New Zealand because there was a carpenter, a blacksmith and a shoemaker at the mission.

Henry replied, 'I do remember. I suppose they've come as missionaries and don't want to carry on their old trade.'

'But it does seem strange that in Mr King we have a shoemaker right here in the Bay of Islands, yet when my old ones are completely worn out I must send to England for a pair of shoes and wait several months for them to arrive.'

He understood. Shoes were important and without them life was difficult: but how he wished the lack of footwear was the only matter to distress them.

They were not making progress.

Once back in the cottage Henry sat down at the table in the sitting room; after finding one of the precious pieces of paper they were saving he began pouring out his heart to his cousin.

'Dear Edward,' he said, 'we work so hard, and yet we don't seem to have had any impact on the people in terms of bringing them the Good News. It is true that every day we say a prayer in the native language and sing a hymn, and some of the local people join in. But when we question them afterwards, via William Fairburn who has a good grasp of Māori, we find they have no sense of their fellow men being the children of God, and therefore to be loved and cherished. As one chief has told us, all they are interested in is eating and fighting, and attacking other tribes so they can bring back more slaves.

'We are continually being disappointed. Even Aden, Marianne's servant for whom we had high hopes and who was the only one she could permit to care for little Henry, we have had to dismiss because of her behaviour. She killed a slave woman who was married to one of her close relations, and now she has taken off to the ships. The women's parents and relations encourage them to work as prostitutes because the crews of the ships pay them with the things they want most in the world – muskets and gunpowder. The conduct of our countrymen in this respect is shocking: they are the destroyers of this people, in both soul and body.

'The desire for firearms gives rise to another problem. We refuse to give the people guns so they deny us food and we must rely on salt pork, which is not easy to stomach, particularly day after day. It is eleven months since a supply ship came from Sydney, and we have almost nothing left of flour, sugar, soap, wheat and peas, etc. Fortunately, the Wesleyans at Whangaroa gave us two casks of flour, but we have already finished the first.'

Henry put down his pen and put his head in his hands. Even writing was becoming an effort. He ate less than his share in order to give Marianne and the children more, and these days he was continually empty and tired. Soon they would be at crisis point. In fact, Marianne, while eyeing the bracken fern that flourished around them, had suggested she try cooking fern root to take the place of potatoes. 'You pound it to make it more tender and then you steam it,' she said.

'And lose our teeth because it's so hard,' he had retorted. 'Then we truly would starve.'

He should not have been so harsh. She was merely being practical and resourceful, and that was what was needed right now.

He took up his pen again.

But there was a knocking at the gate. Marianne was occupied with the baby so Henry went to open it and found four chiefs waiting.

One was Tohitapu.

Eyes narrowed, he surveyed the men. Dressed in their cloaks slung over one shoulder, their ever-present mere swinging at their side, it was difficult to tell if they had come as friend or foe.

But their tattooed faces were smiling and each, including Tohitapu, held out a hand, which Henry shook.

'Kia ora, Karu-whā,' one said. 'He parakuihi tāu?'

'You've come for breakfast? Well, my friends, if you would only sell us food for something other than muskets . . .'

He opened the door to the cottage and told them to sit at the table.

Then he went to find Marianne.

'My dear, four chiefs have honoured us with their presence.'

Marianne stood up from kneeling down to the baby. Hearing the tension in his voice she looked at him questioningly.

'Tohitapu . . .'

'Tohi is here! What does he —?'

'He appears to be friendly. But they say they want parakuihi.'

She gave a sigh. 'If only they would —'

'I told them so, but sometimes they have trouble understanding.'

She put her hands on her hips. 'I will make some stirabout.'

'Which is?'

'A mixture of flour, sugar and water.'

'Can we manage that?'

'I think so — just, thanks to our kind friends the Wesleyans.'

The chiefs installed themselves around the table and Marianne brought them the stirabout in a large bowl. Then she and Henry stood back.

The chiefs enthusiastically gulped down the concoction — apart from Te Koki, who sipped his with a teaspoon so as not to make a mess of his beard.

'They're very jolly,' murmured Marianne. 'Look at Tohi.'

Henry gazed at the chief, who grinned back and raised his spoon to say thank you.

'Maybe we are now friends.'

'Or we are simply the suppliers of a sweet treat.'

Marianne took Henry's arm and led him outside, leaving the chiefs to chatter and laugh.

'My darling,' she said, 'I think you could be more positive.'

'I am always positive,' he said. 'What do you mean?'

'About Tohi. He's undergone a transformation. You can see that — not long ago he was our deadly enemy, capering and strutting round here, bent on destroying us. And now he's sitting in the hut eating stirabout! I can hardly believe it's the same man.'

'Is that progress, do you think? He's still a million miles from accepting the Lord as his king. Like all the rest of them.'

'I think we must be patient. I realised this after Aden . . . when Aden left and I felt so cruelly let down because I had such high hopes of her. But then I decided to make this my lesson – not to rely on my own efforts but to leave it to the Holy Spirit to make its presence felt in its own way and its own good time. And I feel that these moments when we see a change, a shift, however small, in the right direction, is a sign the Spirit is working.'

Henry returned to his letter and read what he'd written to Edward Marsh. Yes, it was negative – Marianne was right. But was he not telling the truth, describing what their life here was like and how little hope there seemed to be? Also, right now his stomach gnawed within him like a ravening wolf. When he watched the chiefs eating the stirabout he had to restrain himself from snatching it from them and guzzling it down himself. And, for the first time he was so tired that doing anything at all seemed impossible.

From whence had come this blackness in his heart?

Immediately he knew the answer: the Great Enemy of Souls was goading him on all sides.

Henry sat up straight and clutched his tousled hair with both hands. That was it! He could not allow himself to become downhearted.

As Marianne had reminded him he should not be presumptuous and rely on his own efforts but allow the Holy Spirit of God to work through him. Maybe that was his trouble – he was too full of pride, too eager to show that he alone could turn around a whole people from being followers of Satan.

What was it she said to him recently? 'I think we are like the soldiers in the battle of Waterloo, taking hit after hit, casualty after casualty, but all the while standing their ground until finally they tasted victory.'

Well, he knew all about fighting – had renounced it for good and all. But now he was involved in another kind of battle, more insidious than the firing of guns, blood-and-guts sort of conflict, but a fight none the less. The Evil One had him in his sights and was determined to prevent him from achieving his goal.

From now on he would fight back with all his might. He would be stronger than ever before, because he knew he was aided by the Holy Spirit and right was on his side; and he would go on fighting until with God's help he had wrested the Māori people from evil and taught them to live in peace with each other.

Now he must report to the Church Missionary Society.

When he raised his pen a picture came into his mind: the day he opened the door to find Jacky Watu, a chief who lived nearby, standing there with Teddy in his arms, dripping with water. He explained he'd seen their son playing on the bank of the creek nearby when suddenly he disappeared. Watu had run over, reached into the water and pulled out the frightened little boy.

Henry began to write: 'When I consider the people of this land, their dignified appearance, their pertinent questions and remarks, their obliging disposition, with the high sense of honour which they possess, I cannot but view them as a most interesting people . . .'

Next it was time to put his ideas into action.

The first thing to do was to build the ship he had been planning for so long. Only when they had a vessel large enough to travel round New Zealand, and to cross the Tasman Sea, would they have the means to spread the Gospel to other parts of the land and also bring supplies and food from Sydney.

Using the plans he'd already drawn up he instructed the carpenters to pit-saw the timber for the keel. Once the correct lengths were ready they laid them out on the beach, erected a fence around the site so nothing could be pilfered, and set to work, hammering in the nails and gradually joining up each section until the curving, oblong shape of the keel began to rear up on the sand.

Watching with great interest every day were Te Koki and his son, Rangituke. The latter had recently returned from Sydney and announced he was a great admirer of European ways and wanted to possess and do everything like them. This had mostly consisted of turning up twice a day for meals, which put a great strain on their stretched resources; and asking for a great deal of things for his wife and child.

Occasionally Te Koki attended the daily services that Henry and Marianne had commenced. One day he joined in and it was very affecting to hear the voice of the chief joining in and harmonising with the young people. Seizing the opportunity, Marianne explained to him about their beliefs on life after death.

'Anyone could go to heaven,' she said, 'as long as they accept the Word of God.'

'Anyone?' cried the chief. 'Children?'

Marianne nodded.

'Taurekareka?'

'Yes, slaves too.'

'He aha?' Te Koki threw back his head, horrified. 'Taukuri e!'

However, he understood the concept of the payment Christ had made for the sins of the world in sacrificing himself on the Cross. To Te Koki this was utu. But he said Christianity was not for him: 'It is good for the children to understand these things,' he said, 'but I am too old.'

And then 'utu' took another form.

Te Koki entered the enclosure around the shipyard, and went to sit on the chest of tools belonging to the carpenter, as was his wont. But the chest was not set level on the ground and when Te Koki sat on one side there was a crash as it overturned, spilling out the tools inside.

At the noise one of the carpenters, who was a sullen, bad-tempered man, looked up from his work to see what had happened. When he saw his tools scattered on the ground and realised whose fault it was, he swore loudly at Te Koki. From the expression on his face Henry could see the old chief was angry – he wasn't sure if it was because he'd been made to feel embarrassed or because he had been sworn at: probably the latter because Māori took swearing very seriously.

Henry called out to Te Koki and asked him to come into the house and talk over the matter, but he refused.

The next day, as usual, the chief and his son came to watch the building of the ship and all seemed well. It was beautiful weather and Henry was supervising the men working on the vessel. He gained enormous pleasure to see the craft taking shape, even if progress was much slower than he'd hoped. Marianne was busy inside the cottage, the children were playing on the beach and the Māori girls were engaged in hanging out the washing, laughing and singing together.

Then they gave a scream: 'Kua tae mai he taua!'

He taua? A war party?

The Māori lads began shouting. The girls climbed onto the roof of the cottage and called to Marianne, 'Te Matua, kia tere – close your door!'

The cottage was surrounded by a group of naked warriors. They were armed with muskets, axes and mere, pouring into the house and laying their hands on anything they could find. The washing the girls had just hung out was pulled off the line; even the pot in which peas were being cooked was snatched off the fire.

Inside the cottage the lads fought back. Jacky Watu grabbed the pot of boiling water from one of the assailants and threw it over him, burning himself in doing so. Then he stood at the window of the bedroom, where some were trying to clamber in, and shoved his spear in their faces. From the intruders the girls grabbed back what they could, flinging saucepans, clothes and bed linen into the sitting room.

Outside, Henry with Fairburn and the other men stood in front of the cottage, trying to protect it. They were wrestling with the mob when someone knocked him over. He wiped the sweat from his forehead, struggled to his feet and went back to the fight, trying to push the intruders away. Then William Fairburn was flattened.

An Englishman who was living further along the beach appeared and ran to help Fairburn, but one of the attackers came up from behind and chopped at his heel with an axe.

William Puckey, the carpenter who'd been working on the ship, grabbed the man and helped him, hobbling painfully, into the cottage.

Meanwhile William Fairburn was back on his feet, laying about him with all his strength.

Henry recognised Moka and Hepatahi, two chiefs who seemed to be leading the attack. He went to speak to them. Moka saw him staring at him and raised his mere. Then he thought better of it and dropped his weapon, but ran at Henry and gave him a shove.

On the ground again. Henry sat up.

'Moka! Hepatahi!' he shouted. 'Haere mai ki kōnei!'

The two chiefs hesitated. They looked at each other, released the men in their holds and came over.

Henry sprang to his feet and faced them, panting with exertion – and rage.

'Why are you doing this taua? Why have you attacked us?'

The chiefs stood staring at him.

Eventually Hepatahi replied. 'Your carpenter swore at Te Koki.'

'But what has that to do with me? I have not sworn at anybody!'

This time it was the turn of Moka. 'The carpenter has nothing for us to take – but you have plenty.'

The other warriors stopped fighting and gathered round.

Fairburn translated as Henry shouted, 'You came at us with great violence! You attacked our house and you took our belongings!' He eyeballed the two chiefs. 'The carpenter was wrong to swear at Te Koki and I am as angry with him as you are. If you had come here in peace I would have made him apologise and pay utu. But instead you came here in a cowardly manner, without giving us any warning. My heart is very sad that you have treated us in such a way.'

'The fight is over,' said one, 'and now we will make peace.'

'There will be no peace,' said Henry, 'until you have returned all the property you've stolen and paid us utu for that and the injuries you have inflicted.'

The Englishman's wound was more critical than Henry had realised: he was on the verge of fainting and copious amounts of blood were pouring from his foot. However, quite by chance two doctors who were visiting the Bay arrived on the scene and quickly dressed the gash and made the man comfortable.

In all the years since the mission had been established in New Zealand, this was the first time that blood had been spilt. Henry resolved it would be the last.

He gave orders that no further work was to be done on the ship and his men began dismantling the fence to the dockyard. This obviously rattled Te Koki and Rangituke, who came to see him on the beach, begging that the vessel not be destroyed. These two had not participated in the fight, but afterwards they had sat down with the offending chiefs and did not try to remonstrate with them. He shook his head at them without speaking.

On Monday morning, early, he left for Kerikeri to inform the other missionaries. Samuel Marsden had now departed to Sydney, taking John Butler and his family with him; but William Hall, Richard Davis, James Shepherd and George Clarke listened with grim attention while he described the attack on his settlement. Then they accompanied him back to Paihia.

When Henry stepped out of the boat he was met by Marianne, who told him their servants were terrified they would depart. 'The girls have been crying all day and the boys keep saying, "Please don't go, Mother — wait and see!" And do you know, shortly after you left for Kerikeri, Tohi appeared.'

'What! That rascal! You should not have —'

Marianne put her arm round his waist as they walked back to the cottage. 'He told me he'd been sent by Te Koki to look after the white people. He said Te Koki had given him instructions that even if I scolded him he must not mind; if we turned him out of the yard, if we beat him or swore at him, still he must not mind; but he must stay and take care of us.'

'Well!' said Henry. 'I suppose that's an improvement.'

'And then it appeared he had a problem.'

'Ah!'

'His son was burnt, presumably by the pot of boiling water.'

'And he wanted you to heal him.'

She nodded. 'And Rangituke said his female slave was burnt also. So they brought them in and it was terrible to see — the woman's skin was so badly damaged that it fell from her in shreds and she could not walk — she had to crawl into the cottage. It chilled our blood just to look at her. And do you know —'

He shook his head.

'Rangituke laughed at her. And when we took those two out to the back of the house to dress their terrible wounds, our girls would not help the woman because she was a slave.'

Henry sighed. 'We have a long way to go.'

That evening the committee of missionaries sat around the table in the cottage, surrounded by the Māori staff who crowded into the room, anxiously trying to follow the conversation.

They began with a prayer, asking the Lord to look upon them with mercy and guide them to make the right decision.

Once again Henry outlined the situation.

'It's a problem we all face,' said one. 'We are open to attack whenever the people have the inclination, or if we have unwittingly transgressed one of their customs.'

'Here we are particularly vulnerable,' said Henry, 'living as we do in a house made of highly combustible materials. If the men and I had not been here when the attack occurred I dread to think what might have happened. I need to know my family is safe, particularly once my ship is built and I will be away for some time.

'Somehow we have to teach them their behaviour is unacceptable.'

George Clarke indicated the people surrounding them, listening intently. 'Your friends here are obviously very concerned that you might leave.'

'And that is your strength, is it not?' said Richard Davis. 'It does appear the most effective course of action is to close down the settlement and move elsewhere. This will establish a precedent and be a protection, we hope, not just for yourselves, but for the mission as a whole. What is your opinion, Mr Williams?'

'I entirely agree,' said Henry. 'We must stand firm and demand reparation; otherwise, sadly, we will have to go elsewhere. I shall speak to them in the morning.'

The next day he looked out to see several of the chiefs standing about, waiting to hear what decision had been reached.

He and the missionaries went out to face them. Marianne remained in the background, watching from the gate.

'Are you not ashamed,' he began, 'to come against me with weapons of war when you knew I had nothing in my hands – not even a stick? I do not allow the men working for me to carry any weapons in case one day they lose their temper and use them – because I hate violence. Whereas you allowed one of your slaves to nearly chop a man's leg right off!'

There were murmurings among the chiefs. 'It's true, what you say, Karu-whā,' said one. 'We are bad people.'

'I was a soldier once,' said Henry, 'and I know how to fight.'

They nodded. Yes, they believed him.

'But I have not come to your land to fight, and neither will I fight. I just want to stay here and give you my message – or else I will go away to another place.'

At this there was an outcry. 'Do not go, Karu-whā!' they cried. 'Stay here, Te Matua!' they called to Marianne. 'Do not leave us!'

At this the staff, who were crowded behind Marianne, began crying and sobbing. 'Oh do not go, Te Matua, your heart will be sad to depart from us.'

It was decided to set up a formal meeting between the committee and the chiefs. The table and chairs were taken outside the fence and paper, pens and ink were brought also and arranged on the table.

Henry looked around. 'Where are Moka and Hepetahi? They were the worst offenders and we cannot make peace if they are not here.'

'The sea was too rough for them to come,' said one of the chiefs.

'Let us have the boat and we will go and fetch them,' said the Māori crew.

This was agreed and in the afternoon, Moka and Hepetahi came up the beach.

As Henry waited for them to join the meeting, he reflected that it made quite a scene: the chiefs, colourful in their russet and gold cloaks, dignified as ever, holding their spears upright beside them and solemnly waiting to hear what he had to say.

For them, too, it was a moment of great significance.

'Very well,' said Henry. 'To make it clear we begin by asking, What was the cause of the attack?'

'The carpenter swore at Te Koki,' said Moka.

'And for that utu was required,' said Hepetahi. 'It is our custom.'

Henry looked at James Shepherd, who began writing and the chiefs watched as his pen scratched marks on the white paper.

'As a result you attacked us with great violence and blood was shed. For that we too need utu. We have therefore decided that you must make us a payment – in this case two pigs, five mats and five large baskets of potatoes – and you must also return all the property that was stolen. If that is not done within three days, we will leave.'

All the chiefs were nodding, except the two renegades, who stood apart, their faces sullen and looking down their noses in haughty disdain.

Now Tohitapu leapt up, flourishing his spear in front of the two, running up and down and haranguing them about how they must support the white people.

The missionaries looked at each other. 'I think we should depart,' said Clarke, 'to make it clear that negotiations are now over and it's up to them to decide if they want us to stay.'

The missionaries walked to the boat and Henry and Marianne followed them, waving as the boat lurched into the choppy water.

William Puckey remained. They were having dinner inside the cottage when Marianne spied Moka and Hepetahi sitting outside.

'Maybe they've come to talk sense,' said Henry. With Puckey beside him and Marianne watching from the door of the cottage, he walked towards the chiefs.

They stood up and came towards the two white men. Moka held out his hand and Henry grasped it, put his left hand on the chief's shoulder and pressed his nose to his. Then it was the turn of Hepetahi.

'Ai!' There was a great shout of joy from the Māori people gathered outside the cottage.

It was echoed by those inside. 'Haramai te pai!' they cried. 'Karuwhā has made peace and our white people will stay with us!'

The pork, potatoes and mats were brought out. Henry eyed them, his mouth already watering. Food at last! The Lord had truly helped them.

He went towards Marianne, who put her arms around him. 'So we are staying,' she said.

Henry looked into her eyes. 'Are you happy with that?'

'I am so, so happy, and relieved – for you, for us, for myself. I don't think I could face starting all over again.'

14

Henry and Marianne were in their little sitting room, pouring over the precious letters that arrived in a cask and were opened with such care – thin, almost transparent pages neatly folded and etched on each side by rows and rows of handwriting, full of news of home. It was hard to know where to begin but when Henry saw his brother William's familiar hand, he reached for the letter immediately.

'Oh!' he read the lines again, and then re-read them. 'Oh!'

Marianne looked up from the letter into which she had dived and rushed to his side. 'What is it? Has someone died?' Immediately she began to consider who it might be. 'Not your dear mother!'

'Your mind is running away with you. No one has died. Look!' He passed her William's letter and sat back.

She began to read: 'You may remember a young lady who has been assisting our mother as a teacher at her school by the name of Jane Nelson. To me it seemed she would make a delightful companion and helpmeet on my journey through life, and accordingly I proposed a closer relationship. But to my great distress she turned me down! It transpired she had no objection to my poor self, in fact quite the contrary, but her mother, who had heard of my plans to follow the missionary path, was very loathe to allow her daughter to marry someone who might venture from these shores. However, knowing that our Lord is always with me and will help to further my goals, providing they are in line with his intentions, I asked Miss Nelson if I could speak to her mother. And then, somehow I managed to persuade this good lady that I would take the greatest care of her precious daughter.'

Marianne put down the letter. 'So he talked her mother into it! Well, that is wonderful news. Do you know Jane?'

'Only slightly. From what I remember she is a very intelligent person, full of life and energy and a devout Christian.'

'Just right for William.'

There was a pause. 'You haven't finished reading.'

She glanced down and gave a start. 'There was talk of him going to India –'

'Which is where the CMS wanted to send him.'

'But he was determined to join us.' She put her hand to her mouth. 'No! They're coming here!'

She put down the letter and they hugged each other.

Then Henry held her away from him and grasped both her hands in his. 'You know, my dear,' he said in a voice that, for him, was unusually emotional, 'my brother's presence here, in this place, will be the greatest boon that could possibly occur.' It was as if, now he knew that he was to be relieved, he was suddenly aware of the huge burden under which he had been struggling. 'The Lord knew we needed help and he has sent it.'

'You've done so well –'

'We have both done well. But now I shall have William's support and he will have mine. Each will bear up the other and together we'll make much better progress with the work we have come here to do. For you, too – I know you have put in such an effort to make this place a home, but there is so much more –'

'I want to help the Māori women. Their circumstances are so distressing.'

'Now Jane will be here to assist you.'

Once more Marianne took up the letter and re-read it. 'Goodness me! William was told his ship would be sailing on the twelfth of August so they had to marry in a hurry – on the eleventh of July. I wonder what Jane's family thought of that!'

Henry shrugged. 'Not much, probably. But it's typical of William – once he's made a decision he likes to get on with it.'

She turned to him. 'So they are already on the high seas, sails unfurled, hastening towards us?'

Henry nodded, a broad smile on his face.

'How long will they take?'

'Four months, maybe. They could be in New South Wales by December.'

'And here by . . .'

Marianne gazed around her. Henry had finally finished building their new house, made of 'wattle and daub', that is to say thin branches placed closely together and covered with layers of plaster, and topped with a roof of wooden shingles. It was more substantial than the Beehive, and what's more it housed an indoor kitchen and chimney; but it was small, not to mention cold – in bad weather wind and rain filtered through the shingles.

'I know what you're thinking,' he said. 'There isn't a great deal of space, but we'll manage somehow. And when I get a chance I'll clear out the Beehive to give them more room.'

His brother William, younger than he by eight years, was the ideal person to aid them in their venture. For a start, he was a qualified doctor and surgeon and thus had skills that were desperately needed in their isolated situation. Also, he too had been ordained and so was eminently suitable to bring the Good News to the people of New Zealand and officiate at services; and he was an accomplished linguist. At Oxford University he'd gained a BA in Latin and Ancient Greek, required to fully understand the Bible, which was originally translated from Hebrew into those languages.

Henry was aware that in order to make progress in teaching the Gospel to the Māori people it was necessary to learn their language properly – not just the 'missionary Māori' with which he got by – and thanks to his training William was perfectly suited to tackle this task.

He'd always hoped his brother would join them: they'd talked of this even before he and Marianne had departed for New Zealand. However, once they knew just how far the journey was and how full of peril, not to mention the testing times that awaited them here, it seemed too much to expect his brother to make the sacrifice when a distinguished career awaited him in any field he chose. Not to mention his very new wife, who was forsaking home and family for an entirely unknown land.

The main project at present was the completion of his ship so he could go to Sydney to meet them. Also, he needed to obtain food and supplies to provide for not only the missionaries who would soon include William and Jane among them, but also for the children they wanted to attract to their school. For if they could not feed and clothe their young ones the Māori people would not allow them to come.

But right now there was another, even more pressing, matter. His mother would be losing another son to the Antipodes. She'd always understood and supported Henry's calling, but even so, to say goodbye to William and Jane, knowing that, like Henry and Marianne she would never see them again, might break her heart. He went into the bedroom, closed the door against the tumult of his children and the chatter and laughter of the Māori servants, and took up his pen.

It was difficult to know what to say. To describe the situation for what it was might be too much; it was best to emphasise the big picture: 'We feel the trial you will be called upon to endure in the separation from these, your youngest children,' he wrote, 'but trust your views extend far beyond this present vale of tears to that glorious period when we may all assemble around our Father's throne.' He put down his pen and gazed out at the beach, where the sun highlighted a turquoise sea. 'This vale of tears'? In fact at this moment, because of the relief of William's news, he felt optimistic, even cheerful, and at home in the beautiful vale in which it had pleased his Lord to place him.

But he could not admit to Mother that he was actually quite happy where he was. And she needed to know that William was making the right decision. 'It is meet they should be about their Father's business,' he added. 'The work is great and the day is far spent.'

Finally it was time. For several days beforehand crowds of people from the interior of the island had begun gathering on the beach, come to witness the 'tōanga waka' – the launching of the largest vessel ever to have been built in the Bay of Islands.

They were woken early in the morning by the sound of many voices. Marianne looked out the window and exclaimed, 'Look at all the canoes!'

Henry strode out the front door and gazed seawards. In the foreground the solid figure of his ship sat upright on her dogshores, or wedges, waiting expectantly.

And off the beach the sea bristled with waka taua. He counted forty, and more were rounding the point all the time. Sleek and graceful, the vessels bobbed upon the gentle waves that broke upon the beach and he could see the topknots and waving spears of their excited occupants. Some were swimming ashore to join those who thronged the beach.

As he stood at his gate some of the warriors came up to him. 'Our waka are this big,' they said, holding their hands shoulder width, 'engari tou waka, ka tino nui' – then spreading their arms wide to indicate the relative size of his ship. 'Nō reira, ka nui te utu, nē?'

They were pointing out that his 'waka' was a monster compared to their narrow craft, fashioned as they were from the trunk of one tōtara tree; and they expected the payment for towing it into the water to be equally large.

However, he maintained a quiet smile, and said nothing.

Others approached: 'Te utu – mo he waka tino nui, ka nui ngā rīwai – ngā pēkē e tekau, nē?'

'No!' said others, shaking their heads. 'Not ten bags of potatoes – twenty!'

Still Henry was silent. He walked up to his ship and circled her, scanning the vessel out of habit to check for imperfections. There she was, all sixty feet of her – just the hull, for the masts would be added later. It had been one and a half years since he first laid down the keel and he'd persevered in spite of the lack of facilities and construction difficulties, plus the complications of working with people of another culture – conditions that would have seemed challenging if not impossible to any dockyard manager in London or Scotland. In spite of that he'd completed the task and in his opinion she was as good as any ship built back home.

But the real test was yet to come: was his precious vessel seaworthy? Well, soon he would find out.

After breakfast the Williams and Fairburn families issued forth, joined by other missionaries who'd arrived for the occasion. Henry had erected a small platform on which the women could stand to watch the launch. It made quite a picture, with the missionary wives, pretty in their full skirts and bonnets, making a tiny splash of pastel colour among the thousands of Māori spectators in their mats and blankets milling around on the sand.

He beckoned to William Fairburn and together the two men stood side by side at the prow of the ship. Henry had a bottle of wine in his hand which he'd been hoarding for this purpose.

He smashed the bottle against the hull of the ship. 'I name you *Herald* – the herald of redeeming grace!'

Then it was Fairburn's turn. 'May God bless all who sail in her!' he shouted.

The people surrounded the ship, jostling to be the first to help pull her down to the sea.

Henry motioned to Fairburn and the two men began removing the dogshores that held her in place. The people pushed closer.

Quickly Henry lifted the last wedge and stood up. There was a hesitant creaking sound, and then, slowly but steadily, the ship budged.

The crowd stepped back, startled. Then with one thunderous voice they roared, 'Anā nā, anā naaa!'

As stately as her name, the *Herald* moved majestically down the slipway and with a splash entered the water.

The young men followed after, waving their spears in excitement at seeing such a huge waka move down the beach by itself. They rushed into the waves with her, flinging their spears against the hull of the ship. Henry watched anxiously as the men clambered up her sides and stomped a haka on her deck. The *Herald* was quite high in the water, for she had no ballast and could still at this delicate stage keel over.

But the ship remained upright. The older men on shore crouched on their knees at the water's edge, arms raised in excitement. They thrust out their tongues and rolled their eyes. Then they jumped to their feet and gave an answering haka to those on the ship. The whole beach resounded with their shouts.

The missionaries gave three cheers. Then they gathered round, shaking hands and congratulating Henry. Various warriors also came up to 'hariru' his hand. All were smiling and there were no more requests for payment – they'd had their reward in witnessing such an impressive event.

But it was not finished. The *Herald* was stuck on a sandbank.

Quickly some of the young Māori men swam out and grabbed the ropes trailing from the ship, dragging her over the bank and out to deeper water.

And there she lay, his now named and blessed craft, ready for whatever awaited.

It was time to go.

On the morning of 16 February Henry woke to the howl of a gale and saw sheets of rain driving across the bay. He was exhausted: he'd had very little sleep for the last week, busy preparing for the trip to Sydney and making sure everything necessary for the journey was on board and neatly stowed. But every time he saw more goods appear and directed them to the place he'd provided for them, he felt a warm glow of pride.

Food to sustain them on the voyage was important and Te Koki had been generous, bringing pork and potatoes. Since the launching there'd been a feeling of success, of brothers working together and achieving something extraordinary – a 'we're in this together' sort of comradeship that was deeply encouraging.

He too had a newfound respect for the people who had helped him build the ship, an initiative that was new to them and at which, with direction from him, they had excelled.

Marianne came to him as he stood at the door of the cottage, surveying the storm. 'It's terrible out there,' she said. 'Don't you think you should delay?'

'I be not made of salt nor sugar,' said Henry, adopting a broad Nottingham accent, and affecting an exaggerated swagger, 'and a bit o' weather don't keep me off my job.'

'Wouldn't it be wonderful if you were able to bring William and Jane back with you.'

'Ooh er, that be bluidy marvellous!'

'Henry! Seriously! Do you think that's possible?'

'It's entirely possible. But it depends what speed we make on crossing the Tasman Sea, and whether they have already arrived in Sydney and are even now on their way here.'

The *Herald* was on the move. 'Weigh anchor and men to the masts!' shouted the captain. The crew pulled on the ropes to turn the capstan and bring the anchor up the last few fathoms; others loosened the sheets so sails the colour of clotted cream billowed out above their heads.

Then down came the rain – and the wind. The sails flapped and the men rushed to trim them. Then the ship heeled over. They could not see ahead for the shroud of rain. Mountains of sea reared above them, one driving in after the other.

Henry was not the captain. To this position he'd appointed Gilbert Mair, a young Scotsman who'd helped with the building of the ship and had impressed him with his ability.

He clawed his way to the wheelhouse and stood beside Mair. 'Doing all right?' he shouted.

'Not showing any vices so far. She's a fine little vessel, sir – does you proud.'

Henry checked the compass. 'Heading north: rocks at the entrance!'

Mair nodded and grinned at Henry. 'Wouldn't want to run aground on our first trip!'

Once they were out of the bay they set sail along the north-eastern coast of the North Island until they were round North Cape and out in the open sea.

The winds became light and Henry took the opportunity to write to

Edward Marsh. 'I have already mentioned my intention to visit Sydney and am now on my way. This is the first time I have been separated from my family and I feel it very acutely. We have had frequent calms and are now making little or no advance. I fear William and Jane may have sailed from Sydney before we arrive . . .'

But finally they reached Sydney, where on enquiry he found his brother had not yet sailed, but was booked to leave on the *Sir George Osborne* that evening. Immediately Henry called on the captain of this ship and asked if he could wait a few days longer, when he would have transacted his business in the town and could join them. The *Herald* was to remain in Sydney until she was filled with goods, then Gilbert Mair would take her back to Paihia.

So strange to see his brother in these surroundings: the brilliant light of Australia and the crowded shanties of The Rocks. The brothers embraced and then stood back to have a better look at each other. They were not an alike pair, in build anyway: in spite of all his exertions, Henry could only be called short and stout. William was tall and thin.

'I cannot tell you –' Henry began.

'No need. After so long . . .'

A woman joined them: she had bright eyes and a sweet expression and it was evident her body was a great deal thicker than normal.

'My dear wife Jane,' said William.

Henry looked from one to the other, and they nodded.

'She is eight months with child.'

Again Henry embraced his brother. 'Wonderful news! – wonderful!'

'She found the voyage rather trying, but in spite of that she managed to keep up her spirits,' said William, beaming at her proudly.

Henry turned to her. 'I trust you had a good physician?'

Jane smiled. 'The best possible!'

There was the sound of hoofs clattering on paving stones and a carriage drew up beside them.

'We've found some reasonable accommodation and hope you will join us,' said William. As they drove through Sydney Henry looked around him at the merchants' houses lining the main street, the workshops and the market.

'It's strange to be back in civilisation again – if you can call it that,' he said, noting the many grog shops. 'In Paihia it's very simple – just our little house and the Māori people for neighbours. You do realise that where you're going there are no carriages, no roads and even –'

'You can't put us off now, Brother,' said William, thumping him on the back. 'It's much too late for that!'

Back across the Tasman, this time with his brother and sister-in-law. He had scarcely thought it possible but now it was real. The wind lifted up the sails and the ship sprang forward. 'This is the first westerly wind we've had for months,' he remarked to William. 'You are indeed being hurried home.'

As they rounded the heads on 26 March 1826, the friendly wind died down, as if it felt it had done its work and now could rest. The *Sir George Osborne* moved slowly into the Bay of Islands and a full moon began to rise, illuminating with its other-worldly light the swells of the darkening sea.

It was the evening of Easter Saturday. On board, since it was Good Friday they had prayed together and read from the Bible the account of Jesus' trial at the hands of Pontius Pilate: at the behest of the mob the Son of God, who had come to earth to bring the Gospel of Love to all people, was forced to walk the streets of Jerusalem, carrying his cross. And then the Roman soldiers nailed him to that cross, where he was left to die in agony.

'Lower the anchors!' came the call, and the men rushed to unwind the capstan.

Henry instructed one of the crew to run up a flag which he had agreed would be the signal to those on shore that he had arrived. However, now with the light gone, he doubted anyone would see.

However, someone must have been keeping a lookout because about fifteen minutes later he heard the sound of oars and Richard Davis appeared out of the darkness.

With both of them supporting Jane, awkward in her pregnancy, and with someone on deck holding a lantern to light their way, they climbed down a rope ladder and into the rocking boat.

The oars made a splash in the inky sea — it might have looked black but it was so much cleaner than that in Sydney Harbour, thought Henry, which was contaminated with the detritus of shipping. He hoped William would appreciate the beauty and unspoilt nature of his new home.

And then they were near to shore. Jane gathered up her skirts and prepared to step into the water, with Henry and William steadying her by holding her elbows. Bodes well for the future, Henry thought, watching as she waded without complaint through the waves to the land.

The lights were on in the house but still no one was aware of their arrival. Ah — yes they were! The Māori girls had spotted them and were even now shouting the good news to Marianne.

Henry rushed forward through the gate to the front door, which at the same time he reached it was flung open.

'Henry!'

Marianne fell into his arms. 'It was you! Mr Davis said you had come — I doubted it but he insisted it was your signal — and now it is indeed you!'

Henry waved to the others, calling them on.

And then there really was a commotion.

'My first priority,' said William, 'is to learn the language.'

'I was hoping you would say that,' said Henry. 'We have made some progress – we've been meeting weekly with Brother Shepherd to consolidate what we have learnt and of course we learn much from our daily discourse with the people.'

'It needs to be set out in a scholarly order – ascertaining the rules by which the language is governed and listing the vocabulary. We must also compile a dictionary.'

Henry sat back. William's presence was such a relief. Even now he could scarcely believe his good fortune to have his brother alongside him. Together they would make strides not only in the language, but in so many other areas as well. And it was a huge boost for Marianne to have the company of Jane, with whom she'd immediately fashioned a bond.

The final touches to the wattle and daub cottage had been made in time for their arrival, and now here they all were, sitting round the table in their new sitting room, hearing firsthand the news of home.

Tomorrow would be Easter Sunday, when they would remember the day that Jesus Christ rose from the dead and proved he was indeed the Son of God. And now William and Jane would be here to celebrate with them.

His heart was fair bursting with gratitude.

He stood up. 'As you know, William, I am not one to waste words. And until now I have really not expressed how delighted Marianne and I are that you and Jane have crossed the world in order to join us in our endeavours. To have you here, with us in person and not just via a letter, is the greatest blessing that could possibly be showered on our heads. In fact, I can truly say . . .' Suddenly he was aware that tears were welling up in his eyes. Marianne came to stand beside him, holding his hand. 'I can truly say' – and now the tears were flowing copiously and his voice broke – 'that this is one of the happiest days of my life!'

15

'It really is a miracle,' said William, as he came in to join Henry, 'that Jane and I have been enabled to join you here.'

Henry, in the midst of sending his usual report to the Church Missionary Society, swung round in his chair. 'Although I think that was always your intention?'

'To come to New Zealand, yes; but we would happily have accepted a posting to a place that wasn't already developed. Here we're profiting from all the work put in by you and Marianne, and we're very grateful to you, Brother.' He put his hand on Henry's shoulder.

Henry motioned with his pen for William to sit in the only other chair. 'And we to you! I can't tell you how much your company means to us – you know that.'

William sat down and stretched out his long legs. 'It's the company that makes the difference, isn't it? To be with like-minded people who know the joy of walking with the Lord and doing his will. Otherwise I can see how hard it would be to work alone in this waste howling wilderness.'

Henry turned to gaze at his brother. 'Waste howling . . .?!'

William quoted from the Bible. '"He found him in a desert land, and in the waste howling wilderness.'"

Henry finished the verse. '"He led him about, he instructed him, he kept him as the apple of his eye."'

'Deuteronomy, chapter thirty two, verse ten!' they chorused.

'But surely,' said Henry, 'you don't see our surroundings as a wasteland?'

'All I've seen so far are hills covered with bracken fern and scrubby trees.'

'When you begin to explore further afield you will be astounded by magnificent forests with trees stretching more than fifty yards into the sky. And beyond them mountains topped with the purest of white snow. Then there are clear-running rivers and –'

William held up both his hands. 'Enough, dear brother – you've proved your point! Of course you're looking with the eye of an artist, and no doubt in time I too will come to appreciate the finer points of my new home. But in speaking of wilderness I didn't just mean the vegetation. The Māori people appear to be presided over by the powers of darkness.'

'That is for us to combat. However, when you get to know them, as of course you will, you'll find they are a very impressive race of people. Marianne and I now have many close friends among those who were initially opposed to us. And even their customs, once you understand their point of view, are entirely logical. It's just they are founded on a different set of beliefs from our own.'

'You're not going down the path of Mr Kendall?'

'Ah, Mr Kendall!'

'What happened to him, by the way?'

'He has now left the country. In fact, in spite of the warnings he didn't cause me any trouble. For a while we had a problem in that he thought he should move into Mr Butler's house after that gentleman departed, but the missionaries and I spoke firmly to him and he understood our position. After that he returned to his wife and children and for the rest of his time here remained at Matauwhi, across the Bay.'

'And his ideas on Māori traditional beliefs?'

'At one point he may have lost his belief in the salvation of his soul. Unlike Thomas Kendall, I would never do that! But I do believe we should tolerate most Māori customs, apart from the bloodthirsty ones. What I want to do is show the people a better way of living – in peace rather than war.'

'So what are you going to do about the main instigator of war in these parts?'

'Hongi Hika?'

William nodded.

Henry laid down the pen. 'The first thing to do, in his instance, and in all things to do with this wilderness, as you call it, is to understand. To that end I've had discussions with the chiefs here, who have explained to me the reasons behind the warlike behaviour of Hongi. I could share this with you, if you wish.'

William leaned back and put his hands behind his head. 'I'm listening.'

'It goes back to the beginning of this century, to the battles between Ngā Puhi, the tribe of Hongi, and the tribe of Ngāti Whātua.'

'Where were they?'

'Ngāti Whātua controlled the land from the Tāmaki isthmus right up the west coast to north of the Kaipara Harbour.'

'So it was a battle between the east coast and the west coast?'

'In a way, although in places the lands of Ngāti Whātua stretched right across to the east, and Ngā Puhi had the centre north. It's a complicated story, but from what I understand – and I may not have it entirely correct – the bad blood between them began with a case of unrequited love.'

'Something from which Mr William Shakespeare could have made a good play?'

'Quite possibly! So . . . a chief named Pōkaia, a Ngā Puhi chief and cousin of Hongi, fell in love with the latter's half sister, who did not return his tender feelings and rejected him. This slight, so the story goes, in the eyes of Pōkaia required revenge, or utu, but he could hardly attack Hongi and instead he joined with the tribe of Te Roroa, with whom he was friendly, to fight Ngāti Whātua.'

'Why were these two tribes fighting?'

'A Ngāti Whātua chief had seduced the wife of Pīnaki, whose father was a Te Rōroa chief called Te Toko.'

'Again, the culprit is love.'

'The Māori have a saying, "He wahine, he whenua, ka ngaro te tangata": For women, for land, men die.'

'Common causes of war! Our own enemy, Napoleon, for example . . .'

'Napoleon!'

'I don't know about love, but he certainly wanted land –'

'More and more of it, although I think he was merely opportunistic when he took over nearly the whole of Europe. But, as you say, perhaps there are parallels. Hongi is a great leader of men, as was Napoleon, able to inspire them and rally them to his cause. Both are, or were in the case of Napoleon, very astute in battle, and Hongi too when he leads a successful conquest finds his prestige enhanced in the eyes of his people. But Hongi does not appear to want to take the land of those he conquers.'

'Just as well! Otherwise he might take over the whole of the North Island.'

There was a pause.

'Sorry – I was digressing. Do continue.'

'Accordingly there was a battle, and I don't know the outcome, but during the skirmish the son of Pōkaia was killed by a sub-tribe fighting on the side of Ngāti Whātua. Pōkaia then expected Te Rōroa to join him in avenging the death of his son, but they refused.'

'Because?'

'They were related to that particular sub-tribe.'

'So Pōkaia now had a quarrel against not only Ngāti Whātua but also Te Rōroa?'

'Correct! The situation was aggravated when a Ngā Puhi woman was killed by someone from Te Rōroa and during that skirmish Ngā Puhi were defeated. There were several battles between the two tribes –'

'Was Hongi involved in all this?'

'I think he was present at some, although not all, of the battles. But the one that affected him the most was that of Moremonui.'

'Which is where?'

'I am not sure precisely, but it is on the sea and north of the Kaipara Harbour. Probably within the land that Ngāti Whātua considered their own.'

'What were Ngā Puhi doing there?'

'They'd decided to mobilise for a massive battle against Te Rōroa, so with five hundred men they began to move from the north down the west coast. But by now Te Rōroa and Ngāti Whātua had joined forces against their common enemy, and when they heard from their spies that Ngā Puhi were on the move, heading for Moremonui, they decided to ambush them. They arrived there the day before and during the night hid among the flax bushes that lined the stream flowing onto the beach.'

'I see!'

'When Ngā Puhi arrived they were hungry, so they took off their fighting gear and began to prepare a meal.

'Which left them defenceless!'

'The other tribes attacked and Ngā Puhi went to grab their weapons, but it was too late. There ensued what must have been a truly frightful scene: the stream is apparently surrounded by high cliffs so escape would have been difficult and the Ngā Puhi men were slaughtered. Among those killed were Pōkaia –'

'Poetic justice, perhaps?'

'But also the brother of Hongi, and his half-brother. And – this is what affected Hongi the most – his sister. It seems that when she saw the two other men in the family fall, she told Hongi to flee, saying that she would distract the enemy. Hongi escaped to the top of a cliff, from where he had to watch as his sister was killed. But not only that: he saw them cut out her uterus, leaving a bleeding hole, which they filled with sand.'

William buried his head in his hands. 'Oh, that is horrific! Why would they do such a thing?'

'It might have been symbolic, as these matters often are: in this case, to show there would be no more issue. But that action was the reason Hongi was eager to obtain firearms during his voyage to England – he wanted utu.'

'But you say the battle of which you speak took place in eighteen hundred and seven – and now it's eighteen twenty five. That battle at Moremonui happened eighteen years ago!'

'Hongi, so I am told, has been biding his time. His other battles were practice runs, to see how well his tribe managed the firearms. There were also other matters to settle with the tribes he decimated. But now, he is preparing for an all-out war with Ngāti Whātua, in which he will finally redress the balance.'

William let out a sigh. 'More bloodshed. Then his enemies will reply with more violence, and so on and so on.'

'That is why, I now believe, the Lord has brought us here – to break the cycle.'

'And to do that –'

'We must persevere with teaching the Gospel of Love.'

'But this battle may be imminent!'

'That's why I have resolved to take the only course open to us.'

'Which is?'

'We are preparing to talk to Hongi and his other chiefs.'

'What would you say?'

'We will try to dissuade them from war. Hongi is an intelligent man and the original protector of our mission, along with Ruatara. I think he might listen – although of course whether or not he pays any heed to our advice is another matter altogether.'

William departed and Henry again took up his pen.

But it remained poised in the air as he stared unseeing out the window. Calling a meeting with the chiefs was a long shot, certainly as far as Hongi Hika was concerned, and probably with the others as well. The problem was, the missionaries had not made much progress in raising themselves in the people's estimation. He began to write: 'As far as the Māori people are concerned, they generally think we come here on account of the goodness of their land, and to purchase their pigs and potatoes. In all our efforts to civilise them, they do not see that we have any aims other than to benefit ourselves.'

He paused again. On the other hand, thanks to William, who had been appointed the leading translator of the Scriptures, the missionaries were making good progress with the Māori language. They met from nine till twelve each morning, generally translating one chapter of the Bible and revising it the next; which in turn meant they were better able to communicate with the people around them.

The children's school too was flourishing, thanks to the *Herald* – and whenever Henry saw the ship he'd built appear over the horizon his heart gave a burst of pride – bringing supplies from Sydney. Apart from fulfilling their own needs, it meant they could provide food for those who came, and now the people saw that their children were being fed and housed they were happy to send them.

However, as Hongi pointed out, school seemed to be a burden for

Māori children, who did not like staying still and needed, as the chief said, 'to move around a lot'.

All the same, he had much to be thankful for. William and Jane's daughter was born in April, a healthy child they named Mary after Henry and William's mother. The child was thriving – although not to the same extent as Henry's own children, who William said were the largest he'd ever seen. Their brood numbered five, with Thomas Coldham having been born in July. However, now the older children were growing up, as Marianne reminded him they needed to be thinking about their education: maybe they should send them for further education to Sydney? But to have them travel so far away, and to such a lawless place, might only invite disaster.

He sighed and turned once more to writing to the CMS: 'The people seem to be obsessed with making war, which occupies all their thoughts and activities. They are therefore not at all receptive to the commandment "Thou shall not kill" and even less to the notion of forgiveness. They are now mobilising, yet again, for war, and we have decided to mount a deputation to try to dissuade them. However, I am not hopeful about the outcome as they cling to their customs with more tenacity than a conservative Englishman.

'We ask that you pray for us.'

16

They met at Kerikeri, in the Mission House where Henry and Marianne had sheltered two years ago. All the missionaries except John King were there: James Shepherd, who had a good command of the Māori language, was to be the translator and Richard Davis would record what was said.

Hongi Hika arrived. He was accompanied by the chiefs Rewa, Tītore, Hihi, Ururoa, Pākira and Te Nānā.

Hongi would now be in his early fifties and you could see the ravages war had wrought on his body – he was quite stooped and leaned heavily to one side. Surely that must have been a warning to him that it was time to stop fighting. Even so, his presence dominated the room and his sharp black eyes flickered from one to the other of the faces of the missionaries.

'I suppose you have come to try to stop us going to fight,' he said.

Trust him to take the initiative! But Henry was not going to be ambushed and he took a different line.

'Once we were as you are, dressed as you are, living in houses similar to yours, but now, you see that we possess all things –'

Hongi pointed to a chief wearing a dogskin cloak, 'Yes! Their ancestors clothed themselves with dogskins the same as you wear now.'

'We missionaries came amongst you so that you could learn to farm and instead of being poor and having nothing to eat except fern root – and sometimes even very little of that – you may have farms and houses, clothes, cows and horses just as the English have in Sydney and Europe. We came at the hazard of our lives –'

'What!' said Rewa.

'We knew the whole of the crew of the *Boyd* had been murdered by the people of Whangaroa, which caused great alarm in our country, and were it not for the presence of us missionaries here for the last ten years, the ships would not have come here again.'

'E tikana tērā! That's true!' said the chiefs.

'And now we have been with you for ten years – sufficiently long for many of you to learn skills such as carpentering, blacksmithing, reading and writing. But you have not!'

'The children are best to learn these things,' came the answer.

Kemp, plain-speaking as usual, stepped in. 'From us you have received many tools. But where are they? You've had vast quantities of potatoes. But where are they? You've had many pigs, and where are they? Well, I will tell you. Your potatoes and pigs have all been sold to the shipping to buy muskets and powder. The powder is gone to smoke and your muskets are continually breaking, and the reason you have not learnt the useful arts of life from us is because every season you have all gone south to make war.

'Now we hear that you're preparing another expedition and we're afraid that many of you will be killed. The field of battle is the field of death, and if you go to kill the enemy you know they will try to kill you. Had you remained at home the last time as we wished you to do, your friends who were killed would have been with you now. If you continue on your current path, you may fight your enemies and they you, until there are hardly any of you left.'

Hihi stamped his foot. 'Your words press ours down! You do not give us time to speak for ourselves.'

Henry tried a change of tack: 'Are you sure none of you here present will be killed if you go to fight?'

'Can you tell which of us will be killed?' asked Hongi.

Cunning fellow, thought Henry. Trying to put me in a position where I could easily be proved wrong. 'No, we cannot,' he replied. 'But in going to war, do you not rush as it were in the arms of death – like jumping from a high cliff?'

'A man who has a large and loving heart for his dead friends,' said Hongi, 'will bid the world farewell and jump from that cliff.'

'Where is the satisfaction to you in thus going to fight when you know some of you will be killed?'

'When we fight there are but few of us killed and many of our enemies, and that is a satisfaction. And when we have killed our enemies we will be at rest.'

'If three of you, here present, should be killed in the fight, what will the others do?'

'Why, go and fight again,' replied Hongi, 'and if they should be killed also they will rejoice to go into the other world to be with their departed friends, and those who are left alive must make peace.'

'Those of you who are killed will go to the place of fire and be slaves to the Devil. This we know to be true, as it is written in the book of God. That is why we are here today, to turn you away from evil things: is it not from love – from aroha – that we are speaking to you in this way?'

The chiefs looked at each other and then back at Henry. 'Yes, it is indeed aroha.'

At this several missionaries chimed in: 'We pray for you every day that God may bless you with new hearts and give you grace to leave off fighting.'

Titore was not to be swayed. 'The person who was killed in the last fight was a great man, so our present preparations for battle cannot be delayed or stopped.'

Hongi agreed. 'My heart is as hard as a piece of wood. I cannot stop, I must go. I must kill that one man, Toko, the principal chief of Kaipara. However –' his expression softened slightly as he looked at the downcast faces of the missionaries '– I do believe you have spoken to us out of aroha.'

'In addition to our love for you,' said Henry, 'we know that if we did not point out the danger you run by going to war, and the terrible sin you commit against God by doing so, he would punish us for neglecting our duty. Therefore we would have to bear, in part, the burden of your wrongdoing.'

After their meeting with the chiefs, whom they hosted to a meal before they departed to their respective dwellings, the missionaries gathered round.

'Well, gentlemen?'

George Clarke was the first to speak. 'Obviously we have not succeeded in achieving our objective, which does not surprise me.'

'They were, however, receptive to what we had to say,' said Henry.

'I agree,' said another. 'Up till now they have been suspicious that we are pretending to care about them when all we want is something for ourselves. But now it does seem they appreciate what we're trying to do.'

'But they still intend to carry on fighting and kill as many as possible,' said Clarke. 'And they will keep on doing so. To put it bluntly, for one thing, attacking other tribes and taking their food means they don't need to do their own planting or hunt wild pigs. For another, they get a new influx of slaves. Generally these poor things do not bear children and so the supply needs to be replenished.'

There was silence. Henry looked around at the little group. He saw depression, even despair in their eyes – these people who had given up all creature comforts, sacrificed themselves and their families and in some cases suffered, in order to bring the Good News to New Zealand.

Then he thought of his own family – and Marianne – and inspiration filled his heart. What would his wife have said? Would she accept they were wasting their time?

He prayed silently: 'Oh Lord, I know you are here and that you want us to continue with this work on your behalf. May your Holy Spirit come into my mind and guide me with the words with which to inspire my brethren.'

He stood up and cleared his throat. 'You paint a bleak picture, Mr Clarke,' he said. 'But you know – we all know – that no challenge is so great the love of God cannot overcome it. And there are glimmers of hope. Firstly, as you say the chiefs do appear to appreciate what we are doing and accept we are acting out of love for them. Even Hongi himself has said as much. Secondly, they are by no means united when it comes to war and several have told me they don't want to go on any more of Hongi's expeditions.'

'They say they have no choice. But is that really true?'

'If that is what they say we should believe them. And in the meantime we must pray to the Lord for guidance and strength, and carry out his work even more diligently than before. The one thing we must not do is retreat and leave the field open for the Prince of Darkness to reclaim his evil kingdom.'

There was another possible ray of sunshine. Because of Hongi's depredations in Tāmaki, Thames and Rotorua, the people as far south as Bream Bay, who were allied to the Bay of Islands tribes, found themselves in a no-man's land where they became a target for those from the south seeking vengeance. They had therefore moved north and settled not far from the mission at Paihia.

Henry spent much time visiting this community of refugees, whose numbers had doubled since his arrival at Paihia. He had not had much response to his teaching, and in fact most were indifferent to the message he brought. But among them was an old chief, Rangi, whose heart, it appeared, had been touched by the Holy Spirit.

Rangi listened with great attentiveness to Henry's teaching about a God who loved him and wanted him to turn from sin and love all people, even his enemies. Every Sunday he hoisted a piece of red cloth on a pole to remind his fellows that it was God's sacred day.

Eventually the chief contracted a cough that he was unable to shake off, and after some months of suffering and loss of weight it became apparent he was fading.

Henry went to visit the old man. He knelt down beside him as he lay on his sick bed: 'You are not well, my friend.'

'I am dying, Karu-whā – I know that.'

'Do you have any thoughts about death?'

'My thoughts,' replied the chief, 'are always in heaven, in the morning, at midday and at night.'

'That is very good, for there is no pain in heaven, neither for the mind or the body; no fear of the enemy coming to kill you, but a quiet and happy rest for ever.'

Rangi nodded.

But Henry wanted to examine him further, to see if he really believed in the Christian God. 'Do you sometimes think that our God is not your God, and that you will not go to heaven?'

'That is what I sometimes think when I am alone. I think I shall go to heaven, and then I think perhaps I will not go there, and possibly this God of the white people may not be my God. And then my heart is cast down.'

'And then?'

'I feel more cheerful and the thought that I shall go to heaven remains last.'

'Ah! I am pleased to hear that. And you know, those bad thoughts are put in your heart by Satan. You must ask God to give you his Holy Spirit to enlighten your heart – and, you can be sure he will do this, for he gives his Spirit to all who ask for it.'

On returning to the mission, Henry found Marianne and William waiting for him.

'How is Rangi?' asked Marianne.

'He is not well – at least in his body. However, his mind is in heaven, he says, and he finds comfort in that thought. He says he prays several times a day and he will ask God to give him his Spirit, that he may dwell in his heart. And having heard him say that, it struck me that we may at last have a candidate for baptism.'

'Praise the Lord!' cried Marianne. 'I always knew that God had a plan for our work here, and now we are seeing the beginning of its fruition.'

'But can you be sure Rangi is sincere?' asked William. 'Might it not be that he is ill and is clutching at any straw that can help him believe he will suffer no more?'

'I will visit him again tomorrow,' replied Henry.

The next day Rangi seemed cheerful. He assured Henry, 'Even though my flesh is falling off my bones and I shall soon die, my heart is full of light and peace.'

'And why is that?'

'I think I will go to heaven because I have believed everything you have told me about God and his son Jesus Christ.'

'Have you made any payment for the bad things you have done?'

'I have nothing to give him – only I believe he is the true God, and I believe in Jesus Christ.'

'Do you know who was the payment for our sins?'

The old man shook his head. 'I do not understand.'

'Do you remember I told you that the Son of God came into this world and gave his life for us? It was he who paid for our sins, and because of that we can look forward to eternal life.'

'I remember!'

'And do you wish to be a Christian – a follower of Jesus Christ, like us?'

'Āe, koia nā! – yes!'

Everyone in the mission walked along Paihia beach to the settlement where Rangi lived. He was now too weak to walk, but his people brought him out of his whare and laid him on a mat on the sand. They gathered round, observing as Henry blessed the bowl of water he had brought. He called on God to sanctify the water within it for the washing away of sin and asked that the person who was to be baptised might receive the fullness of his grace.

Then he cried out with a loud voice, 'Rangi! I baptise thee in the name of the Father, and of the Son, and of the Holy Spirit.'

'Amen! – so be it!' chorused the people of the mission.

Henry knelt down and with the water made the sign of the cross on Rangi's forehead. 'We receive this man into the congregation of Christ's flock, and sign him with the sign of the Cross, in token that hereafter he shall not be ashamed to confess the faith of Christ crucified, and manfully to fight under his banner, against sin, the world and the Devil; and to continue as Christ's faithful soldier and servant unto his life's end.'

Rangi's people backed away as the missionaries and their families knelt upon the ground and together recited the Lord's Prayer, the one that, eighteen hundred years before, Jesus had taught his disciples to pray:

> Our Father, which art in heaven,
> Hallowed be thy name.
> Thy kingdom come.
> Thy will be done on earth, as it is in heaven.
> Give us this day our daily bread.
> And forgive us our trespasses, as we forgive those who trespass
>   against us.
> And lead us not into temptation;
> But deliver us from evil:
> For thine is the kingdom,
> The power and the glory,
> For ever and ever.
> Amen

Henry and Marianne walked back along the beach with William and Jane.

'It was amazing to see Rangi witnessing so bravely in front of his people,' said Marianne.

'Do you think there are others that will follow?' asked Jane.

'I think it will take time,' said Henry, 'but who is to know whom the Lord will touch next?'

'I must say I have noticed,' said William, 'that as I go about my work as a doctor, tending to people, they are asking me more about spiritual things.'

'All the missionaries are finding we're being treated with greater respect,' said Marianne, 'and now wherever we go we are received with much kindness.'

'All things for which to thank our dear Lord,' said Henry.

They stopped walking and held hands in a circle, there on the beach.

'Especially today we thank him for the miracle he has wrought,' said William.

'Amen to that!' said Marianne, as she stepped back from the circle and spread out her arms wide. Henry gazed at her with love and pride: she was his figurehead, the one who led him on through rough waters and storms even when he wondered if there was any point in continuing.

'One soul has been saved,' she cried, 'and in heaven the angels are rejoicing!'

PART TWO
Sydney, 1839

17

Captain William Hobson leaned intently on the gunwale of the ship. There before him reared the North and South Heads of Sydney Harbour, the gateway to what he hoped was a bright future and recognition at last of his abilities. But then he frowned and rubbed his eyes: the blazing December sun of Australia was giving him a headache.

His wife Eliza joined him and the tension in his body receded a little.

'We are here?'

He nodded. They were passing between the heads now and enclosed in the harbour of Port Jackson.

'Finally!' she said. 'I thought the journey would never end.'

He gave her a tight smile, although his eyes were still anxious. 'We still have a way to go, my dear. This is not the end of our journey – or at least mine, for the time being.'

'Oh, I know – there is still New Zealand. However, I shall be glad to relax in some comfort. I presume the governor will put us up in his house? And I can remain while you continue on? How long do you think you will be away?'

'So many questions!' He put his arm round her and drew her close to him, taking comfort in the swelling of her breasts against his body and the fullness of the silk skirts of her dress. He adored this young woman whom he'd married twelve years ago when she was only sixteen and he thirty four, and had taken her away from her home in the West Indies, where she lived the undemanding life of the daughter of a merchant. Since then life had been a challenge, for almost immediately he'd lost the command of his ship and therefore his wages and had been forced to rely on the hospitality of family and friends. Then, thanks to the beneficence of the First Lord of the Admiralty, Lord Auckland, he'd been offered the command of the *Rattlesnake*, which brought him to Australia three years ago; and from where he visited New Zealand on a reconnaissance expedition. Now he was repeating the journey, but this time his family was with him and so much more was at stake.

Eliza lay her head on his shoulder and he inclined his head to hers. For a moment they remained thus as the ship bore them onwards. He drew his strength from her and her resilience never failed to surprise him: she'd given birth only eleven days before, to another daughter to add to their two daughters and one son, but already, in spite of the difficulties of caring for a new baby on board a ship, she was up and about and trying to organise their future.

'What about the children? Can they remain with us? Now that we have four we really need a house of our own.'

'Do not be anxious about such things, my dearest. I am sure Sir George is in a position to offer us comfortable accommodation.'

'Because he's the governor of Australia?'

'Of New South Wales, in fact, which is a part of Australia. It is a very large country.'

'Well, he should treat us with respect. After all, you are the governor of New Zealand.'

'Oh Liz, Liz!' He wailed in mock despair. 'You must not say such things. If all goes according to plan I shall be the lieutenant-governor, but at present my title is consul.'

'Do I have a title too? Perhaps I will be the consulesse!' She looked up at him with laughter in her lively eyes. 'Oh William, I do think this will be loads of fun!'

Major Sir George Gipps received Captain William Hobson RN in what passed for grandeur in the colonies, in Government House.

The governor was a tall and imposing man who used his height to emphasise his superiority over Hobson, who felt his slight figure, emaciated from the illness he'd picked up in the West Indies, wilt under the hawk-eyed gaze of a battle-hardened bureaucrat.

Gipps shook his hand without smiling. 'Captain Hobson,' he said, 'I am delighted to see you here in Sydney.' He indicated a table on which a chart was spread out. 'If you wouldn't mind I feel our time is short and we should waste no time in devoting ourselves to the matter in hand.'

'There is a time constraint?'

'We are at present awaiting a ship to ferry you to New Zealand, and I understand there may be a slight delay. However, we cannot presume that this will be the case and therefore I feel we should consider your assignment an urgent matter.'

'Because of the situation?'

Gipps inclined his head and with a wave of the arm indicated they should sit at the table.

'We have here,' said Gipps, 'a copy of the chart by Captain James Cook. I presume it is familiar to you?'

'It is indeed,' said Hobson, gazing at the map of New Zealand, which was drawn on sepia-coloured paper with jagged lines round the outside of the land to mark Cook's explorations in 1769 and 1770. The northern island he had named 'Eahei No Mauwe' and the southern, 'T'avai Poenammoo'.

'Now tell me,' said Gipps, leaning back and folding his arms, 'what precisely is your knowledge of this part of the world?'

'I arrived here in eighteen thirty six, began Hobson, 'on the frigate HMS *Rattlesnake* –'

'By here you mean Sydney?'

'Yes, I –'

'You had discussions with my predecessor, Sir Richard Bourke?'

'I did, early in eighteen thirty seven. And he informed me there was a problem in New Zealand. The British Resident, Mr James Busby, who had been sent there by the Colonial Office, was requesting help.'

'Oh, Busby!' Gipps sniffed dismissively.

'He was concerned about the fighting between the tribes.'

'So he said. But then he tells us he's solved the problem by setting up a sort of parliament of natives. Called it the Confederation of United Tribes of New Zealand – even gave them a flag.'

'That was two years previously, was it not?'

'And said from now on they would run the country by themselves. What poppycock! Everyone knows the Māoris are a warlike people and before long of course they were again at each other's throats.'

'I believe not many of them signed his confederation, and those mostly were from the Bay of Islands, just here.' Hobson leaned over and put his finger on the spot in the north-east of the North Island, where it hollowed into a bay scattered with little dots.

'Anyway, Bourke sent you over.'

'He asked me to reconnoitre the situation and make recommendations.'

Gipps surveyed Hobson from under his very thick and bushy brows. 'At this point, Captain Hobson, would you care to outline for me your previous experience before you were offered the command of the *Rattlesnake*?'

'Well, I was in the Royal Navy, fighting the French –'

'As were we all!' exclaimed Gipps, his black eyes showing animation for the first time. 'I was in the Peninsular War, and what a show that was

– drove the French back over the Pyrenees and that was the beginning of Boney's downfall. Missed Waterloo, unfortunately – preparing fortifications in Belgium. And you, sir?'

'I saw action against the enemy in eighteen hundred and nine, when I was on blockade and convoy duty.'

'I see!'

Hobson leaned forward. 'I was in the squadron that escorted Napoleon Bonaparte to his final prison.'

'You took him to St Helena?'

Hobson nodded.

'Jumped up little toad. And now he's gone and good riddance! But he certainly kept us occupied – and gave us all gainful employment, it must be said.' Gipps cleared his throat. 'In respect of which, pray continue.'

'After a break of eighteen months I was finally given my own command, chasing pirates from the West Indies. I succeeded in capturing thirteen pirate vessels.'

Gipps slowly expelled the breath from his nose. 'Catching pirates is all very well, but in my opinion it hardly constitutes training as a diplomat. And then?'

'There was a period of ... inactivity,' said Hobson, 'after which I was appointed commander of the *Rattlesnake*.'

'For how long were you ... inactive?'

'About six years.'

The brows of Gipps drew together like dark clouds in a thunderstorm as he gazed down at Hobson. 'Six years! Well, well. And now you are a consul, with no diplomatic experience whatsoever.'

'As the commander of a vessel –'

'The men on board a ship are disciplined, on the whole, to obey orders and accept without question the command of the master. But on land I can assure you it is a different kettle of fish altogether.'

There was silence, and Gipps' demeanour became even frostier. He gave an exaggerated sigh: 'Now, sir, pray recount your experiences in New Zealand.'

'I arrived in the Bay of Islands in May eighteen thirty seven, and spoke to the chiefs Pōmare II and Tītore, about whom Mr Busby had voiced his concerns, and tried to reconcile them. However, that battle ended with the death of Tītore.'

'A storm in a teacup! I knew Busby was exaggerating.'

'I also spoke with the missionaries and some of the settlers.'

'Who are another part of the problem.'

'The missionaries?'

'No doubt they are capable of causing us difficulties. But I meant the 'settlers': they are the very scum of the earth, are they not?'

'It would be fair to say,' said Hobson, 'they are not the fine and upstanding examples one would wish to represent our fair nation.'

'Convicts, escaped from Sydney!' shouted Gipps . 'Others that should have been incarcerated, layabouts, sailors who've jumped ship. And all two thousand of 'em carousing and causing mayhem because they think they're beyond the arm of British law. Well, they've another think coming, do they not, Captain Hobson?'

'If I have anything to do with it, I believe they will.'

Gipps stood up and patted him on the shoulder. 'You and I will see to that. But for now I think we have discussed the matter sufficiently. This is the first day of your arrival in Sydney and I'm sure you would like to make sure your family are well settled.' He rang a bell and a servant appeared. 'Kindly show Captain Hobson to his quarters.'

Hobson stood and they shook hands.

'I look forward to a further discussion tomorrow.'

'Shall we return to your little trip to New Zealand,' said Gipps. 'Whom else did you contact?'

'As I have already apprised you, I met with the missionaries, among them the Reverend Samuel Marsden –'

'The Flogging Parson!'

Hobson stared at him, bemused.

'The good reverend is also a magistrate, known chiefly in these parts for his love of handing down sentences for flogging far in excess of the standard punishment. He has also managed to amass a large amount of land. However, I believe in New Zealand he has quite a saintly reputation.'

'He was very helpful to me,' said Hobson, 'with regard to meeting the chiefs.'

'Whose disagreement you were, in fact, unable to resolve.'

'I also of course discussed the situation with Mr Busby, who was still very enthusiastic to promote his Confederation. I then sailed around the North Island, returned to the Bay of Islands and set sail on the fourth of July, bringing the Reverend Marsden back with me to Sydney.'

'So you were there for about six weeks. Was that long enough, do you think, to make a fair assessment?'

'I believe it was. For example, I could see that with the enmity between the tribes being so intense, there was no possibility of them acting together to run the country, which is what Mr Busby envisaged.'

Gipps emitted an assenting grunt.

'In fact,' Hobson lent forward, 'what is more likely is that at the rate they are fighting, eventually they will decimate each other, and there will be no natives left at all.'

'I think that is highly likely, Captain Hobson.'

'In my opinion,' said Hobson, 'the day is not far distant when New Zealand will be wholly occupied by white people.'

The two men's eyes met and Gipps nodded his head slowly. 'There I am in total agreement.'

'I therefore proposed in my report,' said Hobson, 'that Great Britain should assume the sovereignty of the whole country.'

'Ah – the sovereignty!'

'You think I am too ambitious?'

'Not at all. But in my opinion we already have sovereignty.'

'In what respect, Your Excellency?'

'New Zealand was discovered by Captain James Cook in seventeen sixty nine and –'

'But –'

Gipps stood up and began to pace around. 'Oh, I know the Dutchman Abel Tasman was there in sixteen forty two – but he did not set foot. He was attacked by the natives and ran away. Whereas our great explorer Cook circumnavigated both islands and landed at several places. And since then people from our country, both from here and from Britain, have visited and carried on trade.'

'You think we have a strong case? The French, too . . .'

'There you have put your finger on the matter, Captain Hobson. Yes, the Napoleonic Wars may be over and Britain has well and truly put the damned French to rout, but we are by no means rid of them. Already they are in Tahiti, New Caledonia and the New Hebrides.'

'Their explorers were in New Zealand last century.'

'Oh yes, they've been sniffing about. But that was after Cook.'

'Baron de Thierry?'

'Another storm in a teacup. The good baron did not materialise. However, we have a much more immediate threat.'

'The French have plans for settlement?'

'There have been rumours. In fact, according to my sources they are more than rumours.'

The governor rang for tea and when it came the two men sipped in silence.

This time Hobson initiated the conversation.

'So it is a matter of urgency?'

'Urgency! But try telling that to the Colonial Office. With all respect to our masters in London – not that I think of them as my masters but that is their belief – instead of assisting and supporting their representatives overseas they seem determined to make matters as difficult as possible.'

'They have no idea of the problems you face.'

'None whatsoever! That office is populated by ditherers and bunglers. The politicians have one opinion, the bureaucrats another. Some of them don't want to take on another place to run – too expensive, they say, and we shouldn't be moving into someone else's country. The Protection of Aborigines Society insists on putting in their oar, worried about the natives. But when in New Zealand we have the French poised to take it over, plus the riffraff of Sydney using it as a carousing place and who eventually will cause problems with the natives, who are themselves at loggerheads . . .'

'The word anarchy comes to mind.'

'On the other hand I do see the point of view of the Protection of Aborigines people. Are you familiar with the attitude of the settlers here to the Aborigines of Australia?'

Hobson shook his head.

'They say the only good Abo is a dead one! They will kill them, shoot them, poison them – all to get them off the land – their own land – so the Whites can take it over. There was a very sad case last year – two massacres – and I use the word advisedly, when hundreds of Aborigines were killed. I was so incensed I dealt with the perpetrators in the most effective manner available.'

'By?'

'I had them all hanged.'

Hanged! Hobson put down his cup. The room was stuffy in the heat of a Sydney summer and his old headache had returned. 'What did the settlers say to that!'

'Hanging is not uncommon here – it is, after all, a prison settlement.

But yes, there was an outcry. They hate me, you know.' Gipps put his hand to his brow and suddenly Hobson was aware his superior looked old and tired. 'The role of governor is not easy, if you want to carry it out responsibly. My health has suffered.'

'I am sorry to hear it, Your Excellency.'

'New South Wales is a hotbed of haters and stirrers. The "free" settlers – those who've come here of their own accord – hate the convicts and their descendants and that sentiment is returned. But the overriding urge on both sides is to acquire land, because that gives them a livelihood and social status, the last probably being more important than the first. Hence the fate of the original occupiers.'

'At least in New Zealand I will not have the convict problem.'

'Maybe not. But I think nonetheless you are about to face a challenge. Up till now the Colonial Office has been in two minds about settlement, as I have said. But their attitude has hardened and they are all for taking over, because of the New Zealand Company.'

'Set up by a certain Mr Wakefield.'

'Edward Gibbon Wakefield,' said Gipps with emphasis. 'An adventurer and a confidence trickster. He has spent time in prison, you know – a matter of abducting an heiress.'

'I believe he has quite a reputation.'

'And now he's come up with a plan for an organised settlement in New Zealand – without the blessing and in spite of the refusal of the British Government. The cheek of the man knows no bounds!'

Once more Gipps returned to the chart and jabbed the south end of the North Island with his index finger. 'His settlers arrived here in August and they're calling it Port Nicholson. Did you know about this?'

'The Colonial Office has forewarned me.'

'Another reason for a speedy resolution. Now, back to your report. As I have said, I believe we already have the right to claim sovereignty over the country, but the native inhabitants are entirely unaware of this, naturally, and they are a very fierce and warlike people. How will you deal with that?'

Hobson did his best to ignore his giddy head, but his voice, when he spoke sounded even to himself as weak and not particularly impressive.

'I have instructions along these lines from Lord Normanby.'

'I too have received a copy, but these same instructions seem to me to have been hastily put together. I don't think too much attention has been devoted to the detail. Would you not agree?'

When he received the instructions Hobson had been surprised to see they looked very much like the recommendations he himself made to the Colonial Secretary in 1837, albeit hastily rehashed. 'I think . . . possibly, that may be the case.'

'You are of course wary of criticising our masters, and quite rightly so. I too tend to treat them with caution. However, in my experience the main thing they are concerned about is the financial side, and that is what you must remember if you become lieutenant-governor. You may criticise them as much as you like, but woe betide you if your colony gets into debt.

'But back to Normanby's instructions. The main thrust, from what I see, is that he wishes you to draw up a treaty, which you must get the chiefs to sign.'

'That is what I intend to do.'

'Normanby says you can only claim sovereignty over the lands belonging to the chiefs who put their names on that treaty.'

'True – although I do not believe they can write. It will be a matter of me appending their names and then they will put a cross.'

'Very well. But how will you induce the chiefs to put a cross next to their names by which they sign away their territory? And if you cannot, it appears to me that if you do not have jurisdiction over any land you cannot be Lieutenant-Governor of New Zealand.'

Hobson stared at the governor. 'I hadn't . . . I don't . . .' He had an urgent need to lie down.

'I see you are a little overcome by our climate, Captain Hobson, and I think it is time to call a halt to our conversation. But I'm sure you will agree you have a difficult task ahead. I suggest you return tomorrow so we can chart a path by which you may achieve success in your mission.'

'The problem as I see it,' said Gipps, 'is this. On the one hand you have the do-gooders in the Colonial Office concerned about us appropriating someone else's land. The missionaries are all for the British Government taking over, but they don't want large-scale settlement – which of course there will be. To add to the complications, from the legal point of view we have, thanks to Busby's Declaration, already accepted the natives have sovereignty over their own country, so the Colonial Office wishes you to persuade them to relinquish it, without appearing to trample on their rights.'

Hobson passed his hand over his forehead. 'That appears to be a good description.'

'Now with Wakefield's New Zealand Company we already have settlers arriving in the Cook Strait area. If we don't do anything the trickle of new settlers will become a torrent and once the floodgates are opened the British Government will lose control of the situation.

'Then there is the very real possibility the French might try to beat us to it, so you will need to act speedily. I suggest to obtain the consent of the chiefs you make signing this treaty attractive to them, and by that there needs to be a carrot. In this case I think you should offer them British citizenship.'

'I wonder if they would understand the significance.'

'The rights and privileges of British citizens: to be treated as equals with our people. I think they would comprehend that. Also, it would appease the missionaries, whose help we need to persuade the chiefs to sign.

'Secondly, we must control the land sharks. Some Sydney businessmen are inducing the Māori chiefs to part with large areas of land. There is a forthcoming auction to be held in Sydney and I will immediately put a stop to that. Then the day after you depart I shall issue a proclamation to the effect that all sales of land in New Zealand are to be declared null and void and will only be valid if they are derived from or confirmed by the Crown.'

'What about the purchasers of land who are already there?'

'I will give you a copy of the proclamation and I suggest you present it as soon as you arrive in the Bay of Islands; that should resolve the situation there.' Gipps gave a wry smile. 'Although you may not be received with open arms.'

'The white settlers?' Hobson shifted uneasily. 'Surely in order to enforce these measures I will require back-up — financial and military. I shall need to appoint officers, and magistrates as well.'

'You may recommend to me such persons you think fit to be appointed, Captain Hobson,' said Gipps smoothly. 'I will provide you with a few police and some JPs, and on the financial side I could spare you a small amount from the exchequer. But there will be no troops.'

'No troops! But wasn't that the problem Mr Busby had, with no one to support him?'

'I will also provide you with a group of officials who can advise you.'

'I shall need good people with experience —'

'Having bureaucrats on whom one can rely is crucial to a successful ministry. I myself have spent many years gathering together a very able coterie of men who are loyal to me and me alone. It is up to you to train your advisors to the same standard.'

'But —'

'When or if the treaty is signed and you become lieutenant-governor, the colony of New Zealand will be a dependency of New South Wales and I shall be the governor in chief. We will enact the laws and control the finances, while you set up your own administration.'

At this Hobson stood up abruptly. 'Thank you for your assistance, Your Excellency. No doubt you have done everything in your power to support me.'

He turned to leave the room.

'Oh, and one last thing,' said Gipps. 'When you present the treaty to the chiefs, I suggest you wear your best uniform and make sure the other officials do the same. Lots of flags and bunting – put on a good show. It's the sort of thing that appeals to the natives.'

Finally, after three weeks, the ship to bear him to New Zealand was ready. It was captained by Joseph Nias, who immediately made it clear who was in charge. Of course, as a Royal Navy man Hobson knew that the captain of a ship always has sole command of the vessel, but he was not prepared for the unpleasantness and total lack of respect the man showed him. It appeared Nias's ill humour was due to the fact that his ship had been diverted from its journey to China, where a war was raging, and Nias had therefore lost the opportunity for promotion.

The officials Gipps selected proved to be entirely unsuited. None of them had any experience in public business and there was not one 'advisor' in whom Hobson could place any confidence at all.

When the ship reached the Bay of Islands he requested Nias to fire a fifteen-gun salute, to alert the Resident James Busby that he had arrived. But Nias insisted on limiting the number of salutes to eleven, pointing out that a fifteen-gun volley was only appropriate for a lieutenant-governor, whereas Hobson was still just a consul.

And when they finally hove to in the little cove of Kororāreka, there, fluttering onshore was a flag with three vertical bands of blue, white and red – the flag of the Republic of France.

18

Ratatat!

In the distance, someone was hammering – building something, maybe.

Ratata*tat*!

Deep in sleep, Henry shifted in his bed and with an effort opened his eyes. It was dark – too dark for someone to be working.

There was the sound of footsteps, hurrying, and the mutter of hushed voices.

Where was he? Ah yes, he was at the Te Waimate mission station, about fifteen miles inland from Paihia. Marianne was lying beside him; he'd only just arrived that evening and fell into slumber as soon as he joined her because he was extremely tired.

Then someone was knocking on the door of their bedroom.

'Father! Father!'

He grabbed a lantern, went to the door and opened it, brain befuzzled, standing there in his nightshirt.

Before him was his son Edward. 'So sorry to awaken you. But someone has come from the Bay –'

'At this hour! What time is it?'

'I think it's about eleven o'clock. The messenger says Captain William Hobson arrived today on a man-o'-war.'

'Captain . . . Where?'

'At Kororāreka. And he's sent you a summons –'

Henry rubbed his eyes. 'Has he now!'

'He wants you to return as soon as possible.'

In the morning it was raining, but by lunchtime it had cleared and horses for himself, Marianne and some of the family were brought out and saddled up. Off he went, back on the track to Paihia that he'd only just traversed three days before. They were passing countryside that he knew so well and was his home; what would happen to it now that the British had arrived to take it over, if that was their aim? There'd been no intimation they were contemplating any move towards New Zealand: so what was Hobson expecting of him?

What's more he'd had no word from the CMS on what position to take, and yet they must have known about Hobson's voyage. He suspected they were at sixes and sevens on whether New Zealand becoming part of the British Empire was a good thing for the mission or not: but on an important matter like this he needed guidance.

His horse stumbled on a root and he loosened the reins and allowed the animal to find its own footing. Then he gathered them up again. At least it was fresh – not like himself. It seemed for the last four months he'd been continually striving: in October he left on a journey around the North Island, sailing first down to Port Nicholson and then up to Waikanae in order to accompany Octavius Hadfield to Te Rauparaha, the major chief of the area, who had requested a missionary. At his stronghold on the island of Kapiti he met the old chief, who assured him he would lay aside his evil ways and turn to the Bible.

From there he'd gone on foot across the heart of the North Island, stumbling through dense bush and massive forests: crawling under fallen branches or feeling his way along decaying trunks lying on the ground and smothered in creepers, wading through swamps and crossing turbulent rivers. By the time he arrived at Tauranga his shoes, clothes and hat were torn to pieces.

Along the way he saw the volcanoes of Tongariro and Ruapehu, their mighty summits covered in snow even in summer; the massive stretch of water of Lake Taupō and the boiling fountains of Rotorua. He stopped at settlements where mostly the Māori people were delighted to see him and although he was very tired after the day's journey he took services and talked to them about the Gospel of Jesus Christ, sometimes far into the night.

He'd arrived back in Paihia on 18 January 1840, heartily relieved to be home and find his family well after his absence of thirteen weeks. By now he'd managed to build a house that accommodated them in comfort; it was large, with four bedrooms and, to Henry's delight, at last a study to which he could retreat. There was also a verandah where Marianne and he could sit and gaze at the Bay of Islands spread out before them. Well, that was the idea, although so far they'd never managed to reach this peaceful stage.

Since his return home they were inundated with callers, both European and successive parties of Māori, who had urgent matters they needed to discuss. These last included Patuone and his wife, eager to be baptised. This was of course a wonderful step forward for which he gave thanks to God, for Patuone was one of the older chiefs, very influential, and with his leadership many others would surely follow. But he could have done with a little peace and quiet in which to gather his thoughts.

Even without visitors their house at Paihia was chaotic, the main reason being, he had to admit, they had so many children – now numbering eleven. They ranged in age from Teddy, known as Edward since he turned twenty one, to Joseph aged three. Where did they come from? Well, he knew the answer to that, he thought ruefully: he and Marianne still took such pleasure in each other and he had to admit it was a way of forgetting, for a moment, problems that sometimes seemed too much to bear.

Their huge brood needed to be housed and fed. Education was a problem and the best solution they had settled on was for Henry, with the help of Richard Davis, to teach the boys and Marianne and Jane to take the girls. They'd sent Edward to England to study medicine and learn there was more to the world than just New Zealand; but after four years he returned home, ill and unable to cope with the severity of the English climate.

To add to the numbers in the house, on 1 January William and Jane had left for the East Coast to set up their own mission station there, leaving four of their children with Henry and Marianne. So with all the children, plus the Māori servants and hangers-on, plus a constant stream of visitors, the place was like an ant-heap.

So on Friday he'd sent Marianne and the children off to Pakaraka, six miles to the south of Waimate, where he'd bought land six years ago, and where Edward and his brother Samuel were managing the farm. Patuone and his wife arrived at Paihia that evening, and the next day, Saturday, was spent engaging with the local Māori and trying to write letters in time to catch a vessel that was about to leave for England. On Sunday, at a service attended by many Māori people, he baptised Patuone and his wife; it was an emotional occasion, with much singing and rejoicing that the dear Lord had made this conversion possible. Henry was particularly moved because, at his suggestion, Patuone had taken on the names of his cousin, Edward Marsh, which translated into Māori was Eruera Maihi, and his wife became Lydia, or Riria.

Later that day he went over to Kororāreka to hold services in the church there. He returned late in the evening to an empty house. Which was worse, he mused – a house full to bursting or one that was silent and lonely?

On Monday, in spite of the stifling heat of summer, he rode to Pakaraka to be with his family. On Tuesday some of them went over to Waimate, where yesterday, 29 January, Henry joined them – only to get the order from Hobson the same day.

Marianne's voice startled him: 'Henry!'

'Oh!' He was drooping over the saddle and beginning to slip sideways. With a start he righted himself: he was exhausted, no doubt about that. As the outcome of all this he fervently hoped that under an effective consul or governor or whatever nomenclature Hobson held, he would sort out the problems at Kororāreka, where the behaviour of seamen using it as a port for 'recreation' had become intolerable. There was also the matter of land sales: William reckoned there was more land being sold than actually existed in New Zealand. Then there were the day-to-day problems Henry had to deal with as head of the mission and general problem-solver for the local population, both Māori and European, because everyone had lost faith in Busby.

Finally they reached the mouth of the Waitangi River. As the little cavalcade trotted along the golden sands of Waitangi Beach they were met by the dark-clad figure of William Colenso. This young man had arrived in Paihia six years ago to set up the printing press that was so badly needed by the mission. He set to work with great energy and determination and so far had printed the New Testament of the Bible, which Henry's brother William had painstakingly translated into Māori, and also the Book of Common Prayer.

Colenso was an intelligent man who rapidly grasped the Māori language, and his work had given an enormous boost to the mission; but his was an abrasive personality – seemingly almost obsessive – and he'd managed to upset most people, including the Māori themselves. In a place like this you needed to at least try to get along with others, although as Henry himself knew that wasn't always easy. But Colenso had been heard to criticise Marianne as a 'highly imperious woman'; and then had made a proposal of marriage to one of their daughters who hardly knew him. Henry did not consider the printer at all suitable and had promptly vetoed the match, and Colenso, being a man to hold a grudge, had never forgiven him.

Jesus said one should love one's neighbour as oneself; but sometimes in this wilderness of souls it was hard to love one's fellow men.

Colenso was standing on the sand, arms akimbo. 'Mr Williams! I've been waiting for you!'

Henry brought his horse to a halt and indicated for the family to continue. He dismounted and walked his horse alongside.

'How goes it?'

'You were so keen to go off and see all that land you've bought, you've missed out on the action.'

Henry decided to ignore the reference to his property. 'Just tell me what's been happening.'

'Yesterday,' said Colenso, 'I was invited on board Hobson's ship, along with Busby and Baker.'

'Mr Baker!'

'Hobson requested the presence of a missionary, and you were unavailable.'

'And ?'

'He wants to set up a meeting with the chiefs, and he asked Baker – well he asked Baker but in fact Busby did it – to write a letter to be sent to the chiefs inviting them to come to Busby's house on the fifth of February.'

'Why Mr Busby's?'

Colenso shrugged. 'I suppose he has a good large space in front of his house and it makes it look more official if it takes place on the resident's property. And then, what do you know but Hobson wanted another circular letter sent out, this time to invite all the Europeans in Kororāreka to attend the church there, to hear his proclamation. So I had to print that out as well, and what a chore that was.'

'Isn't that your job?'

'But it's in English!'

'So?'

'As you know full well my type cases are designed for Māori and there are English consonants they don't use – 'l', 's' 'v' and so on. I don't have room in my case for them. So I've had to –'

Henry wasn't of a mind to sympathise with the printer's problems. 'I'm sure you'll sort something out, Mr Colenso. But when is it to be read?'

'The proclamation? Today.'

'It seems very rushed.'

'Does it not! I tell you I was up all night in my office printing it out – and the invitations to the chiefs, of which I did one hundred. I might say along the way I improved Busby's Māori –'

'You have a copy of the chiefs' invitation?'

Colenso pulled a piece of paper from his pocket and Henry perused it as they walked over the headland and into Paihia.

Then he read it out, translating as he went: '. . . a ship of war has arrived with a Chief on board, who is from the Queen of England, to be a Governor for us. Now, he desires that there should be assembled together all the Chiefs of the Confederation of New Zealand on Wednesday of next holy week –'

He turned to Colenso. 'You say Mr Busby wrote it?'

Colenso pointed. 'See – he's put his name to it – not Hobson's.'

'I suppose Captain Hobson thinks – or maybe Mr Busby thought – it's better the invitation comes from someone already known to the Māori people. But in this letter Busby is still talking about his Confederation. Does he really think it has any chance now?'

'That's always been his vision – surely you're aware of that, Brother Williams!'

'I am, but in my opinion he must now relinquish it. We are about to enter an entirely new phase and everything has changed.'

'In any case perhaps you should not refer to 'Captain Hobson' any more. In his proclamation to the settlers he signs himself "Lieutenant-Governor".'

'How can he be? Britain has no jurisdiction here, no authority at all until the chiefs have agreed!'

Colenso glanced at him sideways. 'A minor detail when a nobody wishes to be a Somebody.'

By the time Henry had commandeered a crew to take him across to Kororāreka it was late afternoon. The gentle waves giggled and slapped against the boat as it cut through the water; the cloud and rain of the morning had retreated and the sun sparkled on an azure sea. The low, emerald-forested hills and islands of the Bay lay stretched out, basking in the warmth of summer. From a distance even the shacks of the settlement ahead of him looked picturesque. In spite of a concern at the back of his mind that this business might not turn out well, Henry's heart leapt: he was part of a momentous occasion when the lawless outpost in which he'd been living for the last seventeen years was being brought into the fold of the mighty British Empire.

He climbed the rope ladder let down by the man-o'-war and there to meet him on deck was Hobson. He'd last seen the captain when the *Rattlesnake* arrived in the Bay three years ago, ostensibly to quell the conflict between the rival chiefs Pōmare II and Tītore, who were fighting over the boundary set between them in Kororāreka. Henry was the one doing all the work, racing to and fro between the rivals in an effort to persuade them to stop fighting.

Hobson came towards him to shake hands. 'Mr Williams! We meet again, but in happier circumstances.'

'I regret I was fully occupied at your last visit. Welcome back to the Bay, sir.' Or should he have said 'Your Excellency'? He would wait and see on that one.

Nias, the captain of the ship, also came forward to shake his hand. Hurriedly Hobson ushered him away into his cabin and as Henry followed he noted that the governor-general-to-be, whom he had before noted as a slender, but pleasant young man, had deteriorated since his last visit. His head was inclined to one side and he appeared to have difficulty standing straight. He lacked the authority you would expect in a senior representative of the British Crown.

However, he was smiling warmly. 'I am delighted you could make the effort to come. I believe you have made quite a journey?'

'In the light of some of the journeys I have made around this country, it is as nothing. But allow me to say I in my turn am very relieved to see you in these waters. There has been a great deal of excitement here lately over the purchase of lands and it is time to put it at an end.'

Hobson indicated an armchair and Henry noticed his hand was trembling slightly.

The two men sat facing one another.

'The New Zealand Company . . .' said Hobson.

'I have recently been in Port Nicholson and I was very concerned at what I saw of the Company's activities. The tribes there, and elsewhere, are too inclined to sell their land for the sake of a little present gain. And if some protection is not given them by the British Government the whole country will be bought up and the Māori people will pass into a kind of slavery, or be completely destroyed.'

'Other parties have their eye on the place. I must say I was rather taken aback to see the French flag flying when I arrived, although I am told it is only a Roman Catholic bishop who has a small presence here.'

'Jean Baptiste François Pompallier is still a Frenchman,' said Henry, 'and as such should be regarded with caution.'

'A spy, you think – a forerunner to an attempted takeover by France?'

'Probably more likely a takeover by the Church of Rome. You are a member of the Church of England, sir ?'

'Most definitely.'

'May I remind you that our forefathers fought valiantly – were persecuted and in some cases burnt alive at the stake – to rid our nation of the yoke of the Pope in Rome. And now Pompallier wishes to impose it upon the Māori people.'

Hobson gave a little cough. 'He seems a decent enough fellow.'

'You have already met?'

'He came on board at midday.'

Henry stared, astounded.

Hurriedly Hobson changed the conversation. 'Returning to your concerns about the wholesale purchases of land – early this afternoon I have been on shore to Carry . . . Corry . . .'

'Kororāreka.'

'– and in the church there I read to the assembled Europeans firstly Her Majesty's commission appointing me lieutenant-governor over such part of the colony as may be acquired in sovereignty in New Zealand. I also read two proclamations, the one announcing that the queen's authority has been asserted over British subjects in New Zealand; and the other in which the settlers are informed Her Majesty does not deem it expedient to acknowledge as valid any titles which are not derived from or confirmed by a grant for the Crown.'

'And the reaction?'

'It would be fair to say my proclamations were not well received.'

'I am not surprised. The majority of Europeans in Kororāreka are rogues and vagabonds who are only out to feather their own nests. What's more, they've done everything they can to corrupt the local people and drag them down to their level of depravity.'

Hobson leant forward, his hands clasped. 'In spite of that I believe you have made a huge impact in terms of disseminating upright Christian values. How many souls would you say you have brought within the fold?'

Henry folded his arms.

'Every Sunday around the country we have at least thirty five to forty thousand Māori people assembling to worship. This figure includes about three thousand in the Bay of Islands.'

'As many as that! And who are the missionaries living here?'

'In terms of CMS missionaries, at Paihia as well as ourselves we have the Reverend Charles Baker, whom you have already met, and his wife Hannah, Mr Samuel Ford the surgeon and Martha, and Mr William Colenso, the printer for the mission. At Kerikeri, Mr James and Mrs Charlotte Kemp are in charge of in the Mission House, and Mr John and Mrs Hannah King are stationed at Te Puna, near Rangihoua. At Te Waimate, where a farm was begun with the encouragement of the Reverend Samuel Marsden –'

'Who, I believe, is now deceased.'

'He died two years ago, in May eighteen thirty eight.'

'A sad loss.'

'He was the father of our mission and there will never be another like him. However, I'm sure he would be pleased, in fact he knew, that Te Waimate is succeeding as he intended – it educates the Māori people in farming techniques and provides food for the mission stations. Three houses have now been built there, at present occupied by the Reverends Richard and Mary Davis, George and Martha Clarke, and Richard and Caroline Taylor. And on a wider scale, my brother William has just this very month departed for the East Coast –'

'Which is where?'

'By "the East Coast" I mean the East Cape down to Hawke's Bay, over four hundred miles south from here.'

'The perseverance and determination of yourself and the other missionaries, Mr Williams, is to be much admired. You must be delighted with your achievements.'

'It's not my doing, Captain Hobson – I am simply carrying out the wishes of our dear Lord, who wishes all his children to love each other and to live in peace. That is the main reason I came here – to turn the Māori people from Satan, who delights in fighting and violence, and to encourage them to make peace with one another. However, I must admit I have far to go in that respect.'

'Nonetheless, I believe they hold you in high regard, Mr Williams. And that is another reason I have requested your presence so precipitately. In order to instigate the law and order that you and I so ardently desire to see established among the European settlers in this place, I need to have the agreement of the Māori chiefs to allow Her Majesty to wield her authority here. Therefore I have requested Mr Colenso to print a circular letter inviting them to meet at Mr Busby's property next Thursday the fifth of February.'

'I have already heard as much from Mr Colenso himself.'

'Capital! So you are already up to date with the situation. The thing is –' and here Hobson leaned forward and locked eyes with Henry '– Mr Busby has already agreed to lend his support to any proposal I might put before them on that day, which is only right and proper for the departing resident to do. He is simply doing his duty for our great queen. But I understand that you, with all the influence that you wield with the chiefs, could also have a beneficial effect on the outcome.'

'You wish me to speak to the chiefs?'

'Not now, necessarily. But on the day, perhaps you could say a few words – encourage them to take the right path.'

Hobson was regarding him with an intent, almost pleading expression and Henry folded his arms and stared at the floor.

Eventually he said: 'I would like to point out, sir, firstly that your arrival has come as a surprise. We received no intimation that the government was contemplating such a move. Secondly, I have had no guidance from my superiors, the Church Missionary Society, on the subject. But perhaps you are bearing a letter from them for me?'

Hobson turned back to his desk and leafed through the mail lying there. 'I regret to say that I do not. However . . .' Hobson turned back and held out a letter. '. . . I do have a communication for you from the Bishop of Australia, the Right Reverend Broughton.'

Henry had already met the bishop when he visited the Bay at the end of 1838 and he had preached at his church at Paihia on Christmas Day; after that Broughton had sent a report to the CMS, praising the work of the missionaries.

He opened the letter while Hobson watched.

'You will without doubt have heard of the arrival of Captain Hobson, and of his destination for New Zealand where he is to exercise, it is supposed, more ample powers than were conferred on the British Resident . . . Among his first duties will be that of endeavouring to obtain from the chiefs a voluntary recognition of Her Majesty's sovereignty over the territory; as so far as that endeavour shall prove successful, the clergy of the United Church of England and Ireland who may be resident within the limits of that territory will belong to the diocese of Australia, and be subject to the jurisdiction of the bishop.'

In other words, the bishop was telling him he was, or soon would be, under his orders, as would all the missionaries of the Church of England in New Zealand.

He read on: 'Upon the fullest consideration, my judgement inclines me very strongly to recommend to you, and through you to all the other members of the mission, that your influence should be exercised among the chiefs attached to you to induce them to make the desired surrender of sovereignty to Her Majesty.'

He looked up. 'The bishop is giving a very strong direction.'

Hobson nodded, not showing surprise, and the thought went through Henry's mind that perhaps it was he who had instigated the letter and was already familiar with the contents.

The bishop continued: 'I am led to suppose that the immediate consequence of establishing the British dominion will be the settlement of titles to land according to the principles of law and equity.' Then he warned Henry there would be a 'judicial investigation' into the land bought by the missionaries.

He would think about that later. But for now, he needed to give Hobson an answer.

He folded the letter carefully.

'This is an occasion of the greatest importance and what you are proposing will have a very great effect not only on the white settlers in this country, but also on the Māori people, whose land it is. I would therefore like a little time to consider my role in the matter.'

On the trip back to Paihia Henry was in a more reflective mood. This was not what he had envisaged. He wanted the British Government to take charge of the country and appoint a governor, so that the lawless element could be controlled – yes, that was true. But he had not expected them to require the chiefs to relinquish their sovereignty. What he'd suggested was the formation of a general assembly of chiefs, along the lines of what Busby was proposing, with the back-up of a military force to enforce any laws that were made, and maintain order and peace.

Marianne must have seen him coming from afar, for she was waiting on the beach.

He described to her briefly his meeting with Hobson, and then, hand in hand, they walked to the chapel he had built next door. It was no longer the little building made of rushes he'd erected the year they arrived: the church of St Paul's, which he named after the apostle who spread Christ's gospel to the world, was a small, square building with a portico at the front and latticed windows. The interior was plain, if not spartan, with no decorations of any kind that might distract people from the reason they were there: the worship of Almighty God.

Both of them walked down the aisle and knelt before the altar. Henry bowed his head and clasped his hands together, and for a moment remained silent. Then out loud he prayed:

'Dear Lord and Father, you have brought Marianne and myself from far away to minister to the people here; I ask your forgiveness if our efforts have often seemed puny and inadequate to the task you have set before us. But we thank you that even in our darkest hours you have supported and encouraged us with your loving kindness, and that we have brought the mission to a point where many people listen to your Word and praise your Name.

'Now I have a major decision to make: should I support Captain Hobson and help persuade the chiefs of this land to allow their country to become part of the British Empire? It is a path that will have major consequences for those I am here to serve and I need your guidance, not only to make the right decision, but also, if you see fit, to accomplish my task in the best manner possible.

'I ask this through your Son, Jesus Christ our Lord.'

Here Marianne joined him: 'Amen,' they said together. 'So be it.'

They returned to the house and Henry made straight for his study, where he sat at the desk on which he kept his precious Bible – the Word of God. He opened it in front of him and began to leaf through the pages. Then one verse stood out.

That Sunday, 2 February, the bell was rung for the morning service. The chapel filled up with Māori people, all of whom Henry knew and most of whom he believed sincerely desired to learn about the true God and the path he wished them to follow. The majority wore European dress and they filed in quietly, participating in the service, reading from their service sheets, written in their language, and singing hymns. In the Māori fashion they sang as one, the sound so pleasing to his musical ear. Their voices rang out over the little settlement of Paihia and Henry's heart swelled with love for these, his people.

Then he stood before them to preach the sermon, the text for which he took from the book of John, chapter one, verse five:

'And the light shineth in darkness; and the darkness comprehended it not.'

19

On Monday 3 February the tall figure of James Busby appeared at his door. Henry was somewhat surprised to see the British Resident: he'd had hardly any contact during these last few months — Busby was yet another of his fellow countrymen with whom he found it difficult to maintain good relations.

'Mr Williams.'

'Mr Busby! Please come in.' Henry showed him into his study.

There Busby remained standing, gesticulating with a sheaf of papers. 'I ha' an important matter to discuss.' As always when under stress his Scottish accent became even more pronounced. 'This trrrreaty —'

'Mr Hobson has drawn up one already?'

'That is the crux of the matter. Captain Hobson has not drawn up a treaty — instead he has requested that I write it for him.'

Henry stared at Busby.

'You look at me askance, Mr Williams, but I assure you that is the case. Yesterday I was visited by two officials who informed me he was indisposed —'

'Indisposed?'

'Poorly.'

'He seemed in good spirits when I saw him on Thursday.'

'Be that as it may, he is now not up to the task. The officials brought notes that he had jotted down, and said Hobson would appreciate my advice. I assumed that what he meant was, Would this be a suitable proposition to which the chiefs would agree? I replied that these notes – which presumably he formed from previous treaties used elsewhere in the British Empire – would not be sufficient to achieve his aim and I offered to prepare a draft for his consideration. My offer was accepted and this is the result of my efforts – rather hurriedly executed last night.'

'Why the rush? If Captain Hobson is not fit enough, surely he should wait until he is in a better state.'

'My reply to that would be, firstly that I suspect – and here I may be doing him an injustice – this sudden indisposition is his means of employing me to do his work for him. After all, he has only just arrived in New Zealand and knows almost nothing of the situation, nor what would be acceptable to the chiefs. And secondly, he is in haste because until a formal agreement is signed he has no authority here to do anything, and – last but not least – he has called a meeting on the matter in two days' time.'

Busby handed Henry the sheets of paper. 'To that end, Mr Williams, would you be good enough to cast your eye over my rough draft.'

Henry sat down in his office chair and indicated to Busby to sit in the other. It was indeed a rough outline, with crossings out and new words added to the handwritten text. Busby's blue eyes, always intense, bored into him as he read out loud: 'First Article. The Chiefs of the Confederation of the United Tribes of New Zealand and the separate and independent chiefs who have not become members of the Confederation cede to Her Majesty the Queen of England absolutely and without reservation all the rights and powers of Sovereignty which the said Confederation or individual chiefs respectively exercise . . .'

He looked up. 'I see you are still talking about your Confederation.'

'It is not just *my* Confederation, Mr Williams. And I do not know why there has been such a commotion over a document I initiated for a very good reason. As you are well aware, it was in response to the plans of a certain Baron de Thierry to form a settlement on the Hokianga Harbour. You yourself witnessed it and –'

'Yes, yes, Mr Busby. I understand. And I see now this treaty also includes the independent chiefs. Does that mean those not from just here in the Bay?'

'It means all chiefs, everywhere in New Zealand.'

'Why is that?'

'Otherwise there could be pockets of tribes who fall prey to the wiles of foreign powers, such as France, and the country would be fragmented.'

Henry raised his head in understanding. Then he read on: 'Second Article. Her Majesty the Queen of England confirms and guarantees to the Chiefs and Tribes of New Zealand, and to the respective families and individuals thereof, the full, exclusive and undisturbed possession of their Lands and Estates, forests, fisheries and other properties, which they may collectively or severally possess so long as it is their wish and desire to retain the same in their possession.'

'I have heard talk of "waste land" being available for sale,' said Busby, 'meaning lands that are not inhabited or cultivated by Māori – but in fact every acre is accounted for.'

'Besides which,' said Henry, 'they would not agree to give the queen the sovereignty if they did not have control over their tribal lands.'

'Exactly.'

He continued to read: '. . . but the Chiefs of the United Tribes and the individual Chiefs yield to Her Majesty the exclusive right of Pre-emption over such lands as the proprietors may be disposed to alienate . . .'

'By 'pre-emption' do you mean the Crown has the first offer? But if the agents of the Crown don't want to accept the terms on which the land is offered, the Māori owners can sell it elsewhere?'

'Only the agents of the queen may buy it.'

'Does that not mean that if the Crown has no competitors, it can buy land on its own terms whenever it pleases? — say, a farthing an acre?'

'The chiefs are accustomed to receive a certain rate, and they would expect the same from the government. If they are not satisfied they have the right to refuse to sell.'

'Third Article,' read Henry. 'In consequence thereof Her Majesty the Queen of England extends to the Natives of New Zealand Her royal protection and imparts to them all the Rights and Privileges of British subjects.'

He nodded slowly. 'Yes — that is excellent. They may not appreciate immediately the importance of this last article, but I think in the future it will stand them in good stead. However . . .' He laid the papers in his lap. 'Realistically speaking, what do you think the chances are of them accepting this document?'

Busby shrugged. 'Some might. I am not sure. No doubt you have heard the saying "Ngā Puhi kōwhao rau" — the many holes of Ngā Puhi.'

'Meaning they have so many chiefs considering themselves equal to all the others, they cannot agree on anything?'

Busby inclined his head in agreement.

'Now, back to the treaty,' said Henry, 'to which Captain Hobson apparently expects us to lend our weight. Are you prepared to do this?'

'As soon as he arrived,' said Busby, 'I went on board to greet him and the first thing he did was hand me a letter from Sir George Gipps, announcing my dismissal.'

'How extraordinary! I'm very sorry —'

'I don't deny it was a shock to be stood down in this manner, but I had already had intimations of what was to come. However, I am aware of my duty and I therefore offered to continue to aid him with my experience and influence – as no doubt you will do likewise.'

'I have decided to give my support – yes.'

'Was that ever in doubt?'

'I've had no word from my superiors on the matter.'

'That has not prevented you from acting on your own behalf before, or so you have assured me.'

Henry gave Busby a long look. He knew to what he was referring: Busby had accused him, and the Church Missionary Society in London, of agitating for his removal and Henry had assured him that he had nothing to do with it; that he and the missionaries in the Bay of Islands were independent of the head society.

'Now, Mr Williams,' said Busby suddenly, 'there is something I should say to you. I was offered a place in the new administration but I have refused. Once this business of the treaty is over, my wife and I will be departing – we are bound for Sydney.' He cleared his throat. 'That being the case, there is a matter I would like to resolve.'

Henry sat up straighter.

'Your excellent and talented wife, Mrs Williams, saved our precious first bairn when he was born three weeks early. And then when our house at Waitangi was attacked not thirty six hours after the birth, you yourself rushed immediately to our aid. Shots were fired, one almost killing me, and it was a perilous situation.'

Henry nodded. It was indeed perilous. Busby was in a very isolated position on the Waitangi headland and he had no one to protect him.

'And then afterwards you returned to stand guard over our house. I seem to remember your only weapon was a garden rake.'

'I was relying on the element of surprise.'

'I believe you once routed some troublemakers with your umbrella – and very effective it was, too.'

'Just shows,' said Henry, 'you don't need a gun.'

Although it had occurred about six years ago he remembered the incident at Waitangi very well – the instigator of the attack on Busby's house was Rete, one of several owners who still had a claim on the land when Busby bought it from the missionary William Hall in 1833. Rete was banished, but later Henry and Busby met with the Māori owners of the land and Busby repurchased it from them.

'Both Agnes and I are extremely grateful to you for your support over the years,' said Busby, 'and I'm sorry I allowed the anxiety over the precariousness of my position to overshadow what should have been a warm friendship. Please accept my apologies – and my heartfelt gratitude.'

'I know it has been difficult for you, and perhaps I should have been more helpful.' The British Resident had been in an impossible situation from the start: underfunded by the Governor of New South Wales to the point where he could not afford new clothes – even in the midst of summer he wore a greatcoat to hide the hole torn in his only pair of trousers by one of his cattle; derided by the Bay of Islands Māori as a 'man-o'-war without guns' because he had no military back-up; and mocked by the Europeans, he had tried in spite of daunting obstacles to carry out his duty.

There was silence. 'So what now?' said Henry.

'If you approve of what I've written –'

'It's not at all the manner in which I would have thought such an important matter would be expedited. But from what you say it seems the best we can do in the circumstances.'

'In that case I will make a fair copy of the draft and return it to Captain Hobson today for his opinion.'

'Assuming he is in a fit state to read it.'

Busby raised his eyebrows and shrugged. He stood up, as did Henry, and the two men shook hands.

'May the Lord be with you and bless you,' said Henry.

'Amen to that!'

Henry followed him to the front door. As he stepped out Busby turned to him.

'By the way, sir, you will be pleased to know we have just received a shipment of clothes, sent by my brother Alexander from Sydney. So I shall have a decent pair of trousers to wear for the gathering on Wednesday.' His usually solemn face crinkled into the dazzling smile that one saw all too seldom. 'Agnes is overjoyed: she now has a selection of morning dresses and mob caps from which to choose for the big occasion!'

He was ready for a walk along the beach.

By the time Henry stepped out of his house Busby had already vanished over the headland, bound no doubt for his house at Waitangi where he would write out once more the treaty he had drawn up and take it back to Hobson. Busy man; busy times.

He needed to think. He began to pace along the beach, his shoes making indentations in the dry sand that would just as quickly disappear. At present in the Bay all seemed settled, under control, but he knew that, like the sand on the seashore things could shift and change in an instant.

What if the people refused to accept this treaty? What if the gathering at Waitangi degenerated into an argument among the chiefs and war broke out on the scale of the last battle between Pōmare and Tītore? Or, they could decide to turn on the Europeans.

At least Hongi Hika was no longer there. That chief would probably have regarded with scepticism any proposal by white people to diminish his authority and mana, and would have commanded his fellow chiefs to refuse likewise their co-operation.

And yet, of course, at the beginning it had been Hongi who'd sold the land at Kerikeri to Samuel Marsden and offered the missionaries his protection. And they had benefited from that, during his lifetime. Certainly when they received the news of his death the missionaries at Kerikeri were concerned that without the shelter the great chief provided they would be attacked, but this had not eventuated. In fact, for such a warlike and feared man, his passing had been surprisingly peaceful.

Patuone brought the news. In the Bay they knew Hongi was unwell. In late 1826 he had travelled with his fleet of waka to the harbour of Whangaroa, in order, it was believed, to seek utu for wrongs perpetrated against his mother's family, and in particular for the desecration of her father's bones. He had even announced that in order to do this he would turn against the people of Ngā Puhi, and been warned by a fellow chief: 'You are urinating on your own house. You will not survive!'

While Hongi was attacking the tribe of Ngāti Pou he was shot: a musket ball entered just below his right breast and came out near his backbone, leaving him severely wounded. The enemy closed in, thinking they could finish him off, but Hongi summoned up his strength and shouted as if to two hundred warriors. When twelve chiefs jumped out of the rushes where they had been hiding, the Ngāti Pou men panicked and ran.

It turned out that at the time Hongi was not wearing the chainmail coat given him by King George, which had been stolen by a slave although later returned. The attack left him with a hole through which his breath could be heard wheezing and he'd lost the use of his right arm. He must have been in great pain, but he carried on for another year. The last time Henry saw him was when he appeared at Paihia seeking medical attention from William. His brother had done what he could for the chief, but said he did not think he had long to go.

However, there were still rumours of battles that Hongi was planning: Te Koki at Paihia was terrified he would be attacked because he'd boasted of cutting off the heads of his rival Tohitapu, and Hongi's cousin Tāreha, and sticking them up on posts. Then there was the tribe of Kaitangata who were destroyed by Hongi's party because, weary of war, they had refused to join in the battle against Ngāti Pou. George Clarke said that fighting had become so habitual to Hongi that 'he will never cease until the cold hand of death arrest him.'

And so, eventually, it did, in March 1828. Patuone reported that he'd gone up to Pupuke, on the Whangaroa Harbour, to find Hongi had deteriorated and was very emaciated. Terrifying though he was in the eyes of many people, the chief nonetheless was very affectionate towards his children and now he saw their fear at his leaving them. 'Ka ora koutou! Ka ora koutou!' he assured them: You will be all right! You will live! He gave his sons his treasured possessions: his mere, his muskets and gunpowder, and — most precious of all — the coat of chainmail presented to him by the King of England.

Then, Patuone said, Hongi turned to the others in his party. Seeing the anxiety on their faces he rallied them in a half-humorous, half-serious manner: 'Ko wai mā te hiakai kia koutou? Kāhore!' — Who will want to eat you? No one!

He urged his followers to be brave and to repel anyone who might try to attack them; but he did not request that any slaves be sacrificed for his death, nor anyone else to be attacked, which up until then would have been the custom. He told his children and relations to be kind and look after the missionaries, because they had treated him with love; but he also warned them to hold onto their independence and their land, and not allow themselves to be diminished by other Europeans yet to arrive.

Hongi's last words to his family were: 'Kia toa! Kia toa!' — Be courageous!

In spite of his reassurances, when their great chief finally gave up his last breath and the Hokianga chiefs came to pay their respects, Hongi's people trembled 'like leaves in the wind', said Patuone; they were afraid of what the Hokianga Māori would do to them. The chiefs reassured them and they turned to expressing their grief in the traditional way of the tangi: orating, crying, cutting their skin with shells so the blood ran down: dancing and firing their muskets. On the day he died, however, no guns were discharged because it was a Sunday.

So ended the life of Hongi Hika.

None of the missionaries attended his funeral; but those at Kerikeri were sent a message assuring them they could remain where they were without being molested. Their reactions to news of the passing of Hongi were mixed: Richard Davis said he esteemed Hongi as the greatest man that ever lived on these islands. George Clarke, sceptical as ever, remarked that the Ngā Puhi chief had often heard of the Gospel of Peace, but it always interfered with his plans.

Henry, for his part, was relieved that Hongi had not died on the battlefield: his people would have felt obliged to exact massive revenge, and with utu and counter-utu being exacted the repercussions would have continued in battles for years.

Te Koki died a year after Hongi, but he was preceded by his son Rangituke, who was killed during the fighting at Tāmaki. After the death of Te Koki, Hamu came to live with the missionaries at Paihia and in 1834 was baptised by Henry.

Tohitapu, also, was no more. He too had killed many of his own race, but his powers as a tohunga held less sway after Henry vanquished him in the battle over the iron pot. Since then he'd been, on the whole, a staunch friend to the mission, although whenever Henry tried to speak to him of the love of his Redeemer, he went to sleep.

In death, as in life, the vociferous chief knew no peace: when he became ill he was neglected by his friends and whānau, and was brought to Paihia for the missionaries to care for him. When he died his body was taken up the river, but two other chiefs came firing their muskets and carried him back to Waitangi. Then, a week later, he was stolen again by Te Rōroa tribe, of whom he was a chief, and buried at Whangae.

Alas, poor Tohitapu!

At four o'clock in the afternoon of Tuesday 4 February Henry was in his vegetable garden. Later on he liked to remember that moment: his contentment at the sight of runner beans with scarlet flowers curling up the mānuka poles he had tied in a tent-like structure for them to climb, their slender stalks heavy with the long green beans he was in the process of picking for the evening meal. It was calm and warm here behind the house, with the ferny hill rising above him; and the bees humming happily among the flowers he had planted to attract them so they would fertilise the tomatoes, cucumbers and marrows. At the back of the garden bourgeoned fruit trees dripping with apples, pears and plums. Just for an instant, he had the sense that all was well.

Then he heard Marianne calling. He snipped off the last bean, placed it carefully in the bowl he carried and turned to go. But his wife had already come rushing out the back door of the house and behind her followed Captain William Hobson.

'Henry! We have a visitor.'

Henry put down his bowl and he and Hobson shook hands. Was it appropriate to ask after the Captain's well-being? Probably not – and anyway he seemed perfectly fine.

'I regret to come upon you so suddenly, Mr Williams,' he said. 'But I'm sure you are aware that now we are about to finalise proceedings, time is of the essence.'

Then Henry saw that he held in his hand a sheaf of papers.

'I have here the document in question. This treaty is in English, but we must make sure the chiefs understand what it is they are signing.'

'Of course.'

'It will need to be translated into Māori.'

Henry nodded.

'And I have been led to believe that the person best equipped to do this is your good self.'

There was silence.

Marianne stood looking from one man to the other.

'You are a fluent speaker of Māori, are you not, sir?'

'I am reasonably competent, but not at the level of translating an official document. My brother William is a scholar in the language and far better qualified.'

'But did you not say he is not in the vicinity – that he resides many miles from here?'

'That is true.'

'Mr Williams, I have been assured you are more than equal to the task and I'm sure you will accomplish it with aplomb.'

Gingerly Henry accepted the papers from Hobson.

The captain turned to go, then he wheeled around.

'The chiefs will assemble tomorrow in front of Mr Busby's house, where the treaty will be read to them in Māori. I would therefore be grateful if you could meet me at the house before ten o'clock tomorrow morning – with the translation.'

20

As soon as he'd gone Marianne turned to Henry, hands on hips.

'Before ten in the morning! Does he think you have nothing else to do?'

Henry shrugged and began to leaf through the pages densely filled with handwriting. 'I'll just have to work through it till I finish.'

'And that could be midnight! You need someone to help.'

'William would be the one, but he isn't here.'

'Who else? Mr Colenso, perhaps – he's very fluent.'

Henry shook his head. 'Too inflexible – he'd argue over every word. It will have to be Teddy.'

At five in the afternoon, after Henry had waited for his eldest son to return from fishing, Marianne brought them tea and they entered his study.

He faced his son, sturdy and bronzed from working on the farm at Pakaraka. 'Thank you for coming, Edward – I must say I'm very relieved to have your assistance. Now what we have here,' he said, turning to the paper on his desk, 'is the treaty Captain Hobson will present to the tribes tomorrow morning. It is an official document and as such needs to be carefully translated.'

'You know I'm not really up to this sort of thing, Father. Of course I can speak Māori but I don't write it.'

'Sometimes, Son, we are presented with a task that seems too much for us to handle. It's the Lord's way of giving us a challenge, and in these cases we can only call upon him to aid us.'

In his little room the two of them found space to kneel.

'O God our heavenly Father,' said Henry, 'we know that you are with us wherever we are, especially in a time of need. We therefore beg you to have mercy on us and give us the guidance we need for the important task ahead. We ask this in the name of Jesus Christ our Lord.'

'Amen,' said Edward.

They sat at his desk. Henry placed a sheet of paper in front of him and took up Hobson's papers.

'What we have here is a prologue, presumably written by Captain Hobson, followed by the three articles that were drafted by Mr Busby, and which I've already seen. We'll begin with the prologue, which I'll read out and you can be thinking about how it should be translated.'

He took a deep breath: 'Her Majesty Victoria Queen of the United Kingdom of Great Britain and Ireland regarding with Her Royal Favour the Native Chiefs and Tribes of New Zealand and anxious to protect their just Rights and Property and to secure to them the enjoyment of Peace and Good Order has deemed it necessary in consequence of the great number of Her Majesty's Subjects who have already settled in New Zealand and the rapid extension of Emigration both from Europe and Australia which is still in progress to constitute and appoint a functionary properly authorized to treat with the Aborigines of New Zealand for the recognition of Her Majesty's sovereign authority over the whole or any part of those islands – Her Majesty therefore being desirous to establish a settled form of Civil Government with a view to avert the evil consequences which must result from the absence of the necessary Laws and Institutions alike to the native population and to Her subjects has been graciously pleased to empower and to authorize me William Hobson a Captain in Her Majesty's Royal Navy Consul and Lieutenant-Governor of such parts of New Zealand as may be or hereafter shall be ceded to Her Majesty to invite the confederated and independent chiefs of New Zealand to concur in the following Articles and Conditions.'

Edward was gazing at him, aghast. 'Do we really have to translate all that? And there are things I don't understand – for example, how does Hobson know the wishes of Queen Victoria?'

Henry had dipped his quill in the pot of ink that stood on his desk and now he held it mid-air, considering. 'I suppose it's a convention. As you say, Captain Hobson has probably never met the queen and nor have I for that matter – in fact, she ascended the throne after we departed from England's shores. But nevertheless although she is young, from what we hear she is already a great queen who cares about her people. And she's anxious that those in the British Empire, or those who are about to become a part of it, should be protected.

'In any case, the sooner we begin the sooner we'll finish.' He put his pen to the paper. 'Now then: "Her Majesty Queen Victoria Queen of the United Kingdom of Great Britain and Ireland . . ." Shall we say "Ko Wikitoria te Kuini o Ingarani?"'

'What about the United Kingdom of Great Britain and Ireland?'

'Let's not make it too complicated. We've only got till tomorrow morning.'

'Very well, Father.' Edward was scanning the page. 'Now: ". . . regarding with Her Royal Favour . . ."?'

Henry sighed. 'I think we have to avoid all expressions in English for which there are no terms in Māori.'

'So we miss that out?'

'We do. Let's just say she is concerned to protect the chiefs and tribes of New Zealand – "i tana mahara atawai ki ngā Rangatira me ngā Hapū o Nū Tīrani."'

He began writing it down.

'"Hapū" means subtribe. Shouldn't we say "iwi"?'

'I think by saying hapū we make sure we include everybody.'

'But –'

Henry put his hands on his hips.

'All right, Father. "Hapū" it is.'

'Now I've lost my place,' said Henry, scanning the page. 'Ah, yes "... anxious to protect their just rights and property".' He leaned back. '"Their just rights" – how will we translate that?'

'Does he mean the rights of the chiefs?'

'I presume he does.'

'The word for chief being "rangatira" ... could we say "rangatiratanga"?'

'I suppose we could, although to me it means chiefly greatness or chieftainship. We will put that down for now and come back to it later.'

'We need Uncle William's dictionary.'

Henry turned and looked at his son. 'We do indeed. But for one thing, Uncle William has not yet completed his dictionary, and for another, he is many miles away. We will just have to manage on our own. Now, for "protect" I think we can use the word "tohu" here, since it means to preserve –'

'So here we could say "tohungia"? And for property we would say "wenua" – lands?'

'I think so – yes, that would do very well.'

Edward was already looking at the next line. 'I say, Father, it all runs on – there are no commas or full stops. That makes it very hard to follow.'

'I know, Son, but it's a legal document and that's what they do. Now let's write down what we have so far.'

After an hour they had a rough translation of the prologue.

Marianne brought them tea. 'How are you getting on?'

Edward groaned. 'It's hard work, Mother.'

'We have a few sticking points. As I've explained to Edward, for some words there are no precise Māori translations – sovereignty, for example. Edward has come up with "rangatiratanga" for the just rights of the chiefs and tribes and we will probably keep to that.'

'But surely "rangatiratanga" only refers to the chiefs,' said Marianne. 'It wouldn't apply to the common people, would it?'

'You're right, that is a problem. But then we come to "the recognition of Her Majesty's sovereign authority over the whole or any part of these islands", which we also have to find a way of saying. As I've explained to Edward we should avoid the expressions for which there's no appropriate word in Māori, but in this case we can hardly miss out such an important phrase.'

'So what will you say?'

'I think for sovereignty here we could use kawanatanga.'

'Governorship?'

Henry nodded. 'We use that in the Bible to talk about the role of Pontius Pilate with regard to the people of Israel, so it's already a word that's familiar to Māori people. Also, since Captain Hobson is applying for the authority to be a lieutenant-governor, I think that's appropriate.'

Marianne came over to him and laid her hand on his shoulder. 'I fear you've been given an impossible task.'

Henry smiled up at her and covered her hand with his. 'But we're equal to it, because our dear Lord has sent his Holy Spirit to be on our side.'

Now they came to the Articles. The first, which they headed up 'Ko te tuatahi', dealt with the relationship between the chiefs and the queen.

Again they were faced with the problem of what exactly the chiefs were ceding: 'all the rights and powers of Sovereignty which the said Confederation or Individual Chiefs respectively exercise or possess'.

'Surely that's their rangatiratanga,' said Edward.

'But what chief would give up his chiefly greatness? It's impossible and they would never sign.'

'But if that's what Captain Hobson wants . . .'

'He will not get it. And if he does not gain full control over the country he cannot maintain order and, worse, he cannot regulate land sales and prevent the land sharks divvying up the country. And then –' he threw his pen on the table, took off his glasses, rubbed them with a handkerchief and replaced them before turning to his son '– we have a disaster.'

There was silence.

'What say I ride over to Waitangi – we still have a few hours of daylight left – and ask Mr Busby for his opinion?'

'That's very kind of you to offer, Son; and tomorrow morning, when I take the document over, I'll show it to Busby to check he is happy with our translation. But for now I think we can manage on our own.'

'So what do we do?'

'I suggest we use "kawanatanga" again, which is a word the people know and will accept. The thing is, Edward, by and large I think this treaty will do the job: according to Article Two their lands, forests and fisheries are safeguarded and they don't have to sell unless they wish, and then only to the Crown, which will stop the land sharks. They have an official relationship with the Queen of England herself, as set out in this article, and in the third, as you will see, they have all the rights and privileges of British subjects. They may not realise the advantage of that now, but I'm sure it will be of great benefit in terms of obtaining justice when there are problems with the new settlers – as no doubt there will be.'

'But Father, if you're saying the queen, or rather Captain Hobson, is the governor and has all the sovereignty, but the chiefs still have their rangatiratanga, which sort of means sovereignty – isn't that contradictory? Creating problems for everyone?'

Again Henry sighed. 'Maybe it is. However, I think the main thing is to get across the spirit and tenor of the treaty, rather than tie ourselves down to specific abstractions, which in any case is impossible because the words in Māori simply do not exist. And, remember, we have requested the assistance of our heavenly Father, by whom we are guided and who is watching over this sacred work.'

The next morning, Wednesday 5 February, Henry set off on foot for Waitangi. Past the houses at Paihia he went – first the large stone house with dormer windows William had built with his own hands and that was now occupied by William Colenso and his printing press, then the chapel; after that Charles Baker's property. William Fairburn's house was no longer there, for he and his family had left six years ago to help set up a mission at Te Pūriri on the Firth of Thames.

Henry breasted the low rise that separated Taiputaputa from Horotutu Beach and reached the Waitangi River: then over the humpback bridge that had been built very enterprisingly – for it was probably the first bridge to be built in New Zealand – by the missionaries George Clarke, James Hamlin and Richard Davis to link with the rock and pebble-strewn shore on the other side. Then he took the track that led up to the back of Busby's house.

He went through the gate, along past the wings that Busby had now added to the two-roomed house that had originally constituted the Residency, and followed the path through gaily planted flower gardens, round to the front. Then, for a minute, he stopped.

James Busby certainly knew what he was doing when he chose this site. The house faced east over a large, flat, almost semi-circular area, encircled by an expanse of sky-blue sea studded with verdant islands – the Bay of Islands at its very best. Today – and it must be said the air seemed particularly sharp and clear, as if the very land knew that something momentous was about to happen – Hobson's man-o'-war dominated the harbour, its masts fluttering strings of brightly coloured flags. It was surrounded by waka scudding about; these stroked by teams of chanting warriors, their kaituki standing up in the middle of the canoe or with their legs straddling the thwarts, directing the rhythm of the paddlers. Smaller British craft, too, were on the move. Everyone was converging on Waitangi.

The middle of the lawn was dominated by a large tent made of sails and adorned with flags and over the top of which fluttered the red, white and blue of the Union Jack.

Around the tent strolled parties of Europeans, the women dressed in their best outfits for the occasion – full skirts swinging from tiny waists and bonnets curving over their faces.

All was cheerfulness and activity. Even the cicadas, those noisy little insects, kept up a particularly loud chatter.

Māori squatted in groups according to which tribe they belonged. Judging from their intense expressions and flourishing of arms there were some lively debates going on. What would their reaction be to this treaty? It could go either way; but Henry knew whatever happened it was going to be a demanding day.

He clutched a little more tightly the flimsy pieces of paper he held in his hand. He walked past a group of police in uniform who were standing guard on the verandah, and entered the Residency.

Hobson and Busby were in the drawing room, engaged in conversation.

'Ah, Mr Williams!' said Hobson, coming forward to shake his hand.

'So glad to see you, and perfectly on time!'

'I wasn't nine years in the Navy for nothing.'

'Quite! Now, I see you have the vital document.'

Henry laid the treaty on the table in the centre of the room. 'Before we go any further I would be grateful if Mr Busby could cast his eye over my work.'

Hobson turned to Busby. 'Would that be possible, sir? Bearing in mind that time is of the essence.'

Immediately Busby sat at the table and began his perusal.

Hobson drew Henry aside. 'Now, Mr Williams, it was very good of you to undertake this work of translation at such short notice.'

'I was delighted to be of assistance.'

'Since you have been so closely involved in producing this document, would you be prepared to see it through?'

'In terms of . . . ?'

'I mean in presenting the treaty to the Māori people – reading it to them and explaining matters where necessary?'

Henry hesitated. 'I wasn't expecting to take quite such an active role in the proceedings.'

'But in this case, when I am unable to speak to them in their language . . .'

Henry groaned inwardly. 'Very well, sir. I will do my best.'

Busby looked up. 'This translation seems perfectly in order. I have just one change to suggest, or rather the same word which is repeated. You have used "huihuinga" when speaking of the Confederation of Chiefs, which means to congregate or meet, whereas I would suggest "whakaminenga" as being a more formal assembly.' He signalled to a servant to bring a parchment over.

Henry seated himself, once more to write out the treaty.

While he was doing so there was a commotion at the door. Someone had pushed past the policemen and entered the room.

In strode the Catholic bishop, his hand outstretched to Hobson. He was followed by one of his priests.

Hobson greeted him warmly.

Henry shot a questioning glance at Busby. Instructions had been for no one else to enter.

Busby shrugged and shook his head.

Then Hobson invited all who were waiting outside and had not yet met him to be introduced. Amidst the hubbub Henry motioned to Busby: 'The Jack is still flying. Should it not be lowered before we begin proceedings?'

Busby nodded and spoke to Nias, who was standing by. The captain of the man-o'-war disappeared.

When he returned Hobson called for silence.

'Come, gentlemen,' he said. 'It is time to begin.'

21

Hobson, accompanied by Nias on one side and Busby on the other, led the way. In their high two-cornered hats and uniforms of navy blue jackets with gold epaulettes and a double row of gold buttons down their chests, Hobson and Nias were impressive in appearance and appeared to be united. There was no sign of the disagreements and tantrums that people said were simmering between the two.

Behind the dignitaries, there was jostling. The Catholic bishop and his priest so quickly followed on the heels of Hobson, Busby and Nias that the CMS missionaries – Colenso, King, Taylor, Clarke, Baker and Kemp – who had been waiting outside the Residency were shut out. They fell back with Henry.

Before them was the tent, now filled with people. In the middle was a narrow, raised wooden platform to which the procession was directed. Hobson sat in the centre of the dais and Henry was seated on his right, with the CMS missionaries finding space to stand behind him. On Hobson's left was James Busby, next to him Pompallier and next to him were the Wesleyan missionaries. On a table was draped the Union Jack and around this and the dais stood officers from the man-o'-war and the members of Hobson's retinue.

Meanwhile, the people who had been milling about on the lawn were filing in. Amongst the Europeans Henry spied Marianne, Edward and other members of the family ranging themselves around the outside of the tent. Behind them were the vividly coloured flags of different nations that had been affixed to the sides, and which were illuminated by rays of sunshine beaming through apertures in the roof, adding even more drama to the scene.

In front, on the ground, were the chiefs and their followers. What a picture they made! Some wore capes made of longitudinal stripes of black and white dog hair; others were draped in obviously brand-new blankets in an array of colours – crimson, blue, brown and patterned – that Henry had never before seen. Others wore plain cloaks of flax or European clothes. The black, luxuriant hair of the people was decorated with the contrasting white of feathers from seabirds and some of the chiefs hoisted spears embellished with white dogs' tails, bright red pieces of cloth and red feathers.

Considering that many of them had been engaged until quite recently in battles to the death with each other, it was amazing to see them sitting together on the grass.

The tent was full of the sound of chatter: in English, Māori – and French. Henry looked along the row to where the bishop was sitting. The word was he'd been distributing new blankets to the chiefs at Kororāreka and telling them not to sign the treaty. Today Pompallier was wearing his official dress: a long, dark-purple robe on which reposed a gleaming gold chain and crucifix, in contrast to the sober black suits of himself and the other missionaries. He thought the latter more appropriately attired.

Why did he feel such antipathy towards someone who was a man of God like himself? For a start, he and the other missionaries were annoyed the Roman Catholics had moved into an area where they'd already been working for many years and where they were beginning to make progress; the Catholics could have gone anywhere else in the country where there was so much need. And then, there was no disguising it: they were competitors.

But enough of that; he must concentrate. He looked down at the chiefs before him, their expressive faces etched with the moko that proclaimed their daring and ferocity. These were the people he had come to serve and, after many years of living and teaching amongst them, they trusted him. But now he'd been asked to do a task – translating on the spot – that he knew was going to be challenging.

He took two deep breaths and prayed: 'Oh God, in my hour of need, do not forsake me. I beg thee to guide my brain and my tongue as I carry out my duty.'

Hobson stood up and there was a lull in the chatter. First he addressed himself to the Europeans.

'This meeting has been convened in order to inform the native chiefs of New Zealand of Her Majesty's intentions towards them, and of gaining their public consent to a treaty which I will now propose. Mr Williams here –' he gestured to Henry '– will act as my interpreter.'

He then turned to the chiefs. 'Her Majesty Victoria, Queen of Great Britain and Ireland, wishing to do good to the chiefs and people of New Zealand, and for the welfare of her subjects living among you, has sent me to this place as Governor.'

He waited while Henry repeated his words in Māori. That was not too difficult since Hobson had used the same words as in the prologue to the treaty.

'But,' he continued, 'as the law of England gives no civil powers to Her Majesty out of her dominions, her efforts to do you good will be futile unless you consent.'

This was more demanding: 'civil powers?' . . .' dominions?' . . . 'futile?' Now he was struggling. But he kept his composure and out of the depths of his limited knowledge came words he hoped made sense to his listeners.

Hobson continued: 'Her Majesty has commanded me to explain these matters to you, that you may understand them. The people of Great Britain are, thank God! free; and so long as they do not transgress the laws they can go where they please, and their Sovereign does not have the power to restrain them. You have sold them lands and encouraged them to come here. Her Majesty, always ready to protect her subjects, is also always ready to restrain them.'

Hobson stopped and waited while Henry slowly and carefully translated his words, knowing full well that some of his European listeners would be aware of the gaps in his interpretation.

'Her Majesty the Queen asks you to sign this treaty, and so give her that power which will enable her to restrain them. I ask you for this publicly – I do not go from one chief to another. I will give you time to consider the proposal I shall now offer you. What I wish you to do is expressly for your own good, as you will soon see by the treaty.

'You yourselves have often asked the King of England to extend his protection to you. Her Majesty now offers you that protection in this treaty.'

Henry translated, then looked at Hobson, who nodded to indicate he had finished his introduction.

While Hobson was rearranging his sheaf of papers, again Henry gazed down at the people before him. Some had turned to their neighbours and were obviously discussing the message he had translated for them; others were staring straight ahead. Had they understood? It occurred to him that the chiefs would have been better prepared to deal with the arrival of the Europeans if they'd learnt their language. But the missionaries had not come to teach them English: they wanted to speak to them in Māori in order to impart the good news of the Gospel.

'I will now read the Treaty of Waitangi,' Hobson announced. He cleared his throat: 'Her Majesty Queen Victoria, Queen of the United Kingdom of Great Britain and Ireland . . .'

Henry stood beside Hobson as he read in English. Then it was his turn. His hands shaking slightly, he held the paper on which was written the version that he and Edward had worked on the night before.

As he spoke to the Māori people there descended upon the tent a profound and attentive silence.

'I want you to listen very carefully,' he said, 'to what I am now going to read. Do not be in a hurry to sign this treaty: but I want to tell you that we, the missionaries, fully approve of it; that it is an act of love towards you on the part of Queen Victoria, who wants to secure to you your property, rights and privileges. I also believe it will be a fortress for you against any foreign power that might want to take possession of your country.'

Then he held up the paper and proclaimed: 'Ko Wikitoria, te Kuini o Ingarani, i tana mahara atawai ki ngā Rangatira me ngā Hapū o Nū Tīrani, i tana hiahia hoki kia tohungia ki a rātou o rātou rangatiratanga, me to rātou wenua, ā kia mau tonu hoki te Rongo ki a rātou me te Ātanoho kua wakaaro ia he mea tika kia tukua mai tētahi Rangatira hei kai wakarite ki ngā tāngata Māori o Nū Tīrani . . .'

After the prologue he went on to read out Articles One, Two and Three, after each explaining the meaning in his own words.

When he had finished Hobson asked him to tell the chiefs he would like to hear from anyone who wished to speak on the subject, or who had any questions.

But instead of speaking the chiefs rose to their feet and came forward to shake hands with Hobson. They were aware, if no one else was, that before any further proceedings began it was important to make contact with the man who had come to address them.

While the chiefs were greeting Hobson Busby got up from his seat and stepped forward, addressing them in Māori: 'I wish to make it clear to you,' he said, 'that the governor has not come to take away your land, but to secure your ownership of that which you have not sold. As I've often told you, any land not bought from you in the right manner will be returned to you who own it. The governor will do this.'

Henry was somewhat surprised by the ex-resident giving them an assurance he could not enforce. He was also struck by the fact that Busby referred to Hobson as governor when in fact he did not yet officially hold that position.

The chiefs returned to their positions and there was a moment of silence. Then Te Kēmara stood up, no doubt chosen as the first to speak since he was the most senior chief of Waitangi, having owned land at Te Tī, on the mouth of the Waitangi River. He was also a tohunga.

Te Kēmara strode up and down the space left by the chiefs for this purpose in front of the dais. He might have been elderly but he spoke with enormous energy and passion, his eyes rolling and his whole body gesturing.

'Health to you, O Governor!' he cried.

Hobson turned to Henry.

He began to interpret – fortunately it was easier to translate from Māori into English. But then Te Kēmara spoke more and more quickly, his passion rendering his pronunciation difficult to follow, and repeating himself several times. Henry decided to wait until he'd finished.

'This is my message to you, oh Governor! I am not pleased with you. I do not want you here – no, no, no. I will never say Yes to your staying in this country. If we were all to be equal, then perhaps I would say Yes; but for the Governor to be up and Te Kēmara down – Governor high up, up, up, and Te Kēmara down low, small, a worm, a crawler – No, no, no! Oh Governor! My land is gone, gone, all gone. The inheritances of my ancestors, fathers, relations, all gone, stolen, gone with the missionaries. Yes, they have it all, all, all!'

There was a shockwave within the tent. The Europeans began to murmur to each other.

But Te Kēmara wasn't finished yet. He pointed at Busby, then at Henry. 'That man there, Busby, and that man there, Williams, they have my land. The land on which we are now standing this day is mine. This land, even this under my feet,' he said, stamping on the ground '– return it to me.'

He ran up to Henry and pointed at him. 'You – you bald-headed man – you have my land!'

Henry felt his heart pound and the blood run to his face. Te Kēmara and several other chiefs had sold land at Waitangi to him for the mission, and also the land called Te Tī; last year Henry had gifted this latter back to him and his hapū as a reserve for tribal purposes.

Now he kept his features expressionless and stared back at Te Kēmara. Then he translated his words into English. The chattering from the Europeans became even louder.

The chief turned his attention to Hobson. 'You English are not kind to us like other foreigners. You do not give us good things. And I say to you, Go away and leave it to Busby and Williams to settle matters for us Māori as they have up to now.'

Then Rewa, one of the most important chiefs in the Bay, stood and spoke. 'How d'ye do, Mr Governor?'

At this burst of English, so unexpected, the atmosphere was lightened and everyone burst into laughter.

But Rewa, too, had a serious message. He shouted: 'This is my word to you, oh Governor. Let my lands be returned to me that have been taken by the missionaries – by Davis and Clarke and by others besides. This country is ours, but the land is gone: I have only a name – only a name! Nevertheless we ourselves are the governors – we, the chiefs of this our fathers' land. Do we want this land to become like Sydney and all other lands taken by the English? No, no! I, Rewa, say to you, oh Governor – go away!'

Henry turned and raised his eyebrows at the missionaries standing behind him. They grimaced back.

Rewa now lived at Kororāreka, not far from Pompallier's house.

Then it was the turn of Moka, also from Kororāreka and the younger brother of Rewa. He too told Hobson to go away and asked for his lands, sold to Charles Baker, to be returned to him: he also asserted that the trader James Clendon and Gilbert Mair had even now gone to buy land in spite of Hobson's proclamation.

Henry interpreted while a hubbub grew among the chiefs.

Hobson intervened. 'Please tell the chiefs,' he told Henry, 'that all lands unjustly held will be returned, and that all claims to lands purchased after the date of the proclamation would not be considered lawful.'

Then one of the Europeans came forward. He said that Henry was not interpreting all that was being said by the chiefs with respect to the missionaries and land, and that Johnny Johnston would be better as a translator. Johnston was the owner of the Duke of Marlborough, a grog shop at Kororāreka.

Johnston declined, but said Henry should translate more loudly so everyone at the back of the tent could hear.

'Captain Hobson,' said Henry, 'may I speak on my own behalf?'

Hobson assented.

He turned and faced the European settlers.

'A great deal has been said about the missionaries holding land, but the commissioners who are about to sit will examine the lands held by us, and our titles to these lands, as strictly as they will any others. In fact, I have already requested that ours should be the first to be examined.'

He cleared his throat. 'You people from Britain should recollect that were it not for the missionaries you would not be here today, nor be in possession of a foot of land in New Zealand. If any one person has a prior claim to land in this country, that person must be the missionary, who has laboured for so many years in this land when others were afraid to show their noses!'

At this a roar arose from the settlers.

He began to shout. 'I have a large family – eleven children – more, probably, than anyone present, and what are they to do when I am taken from them if they are not to have some land?'

Ignoring the hullaballoo, he continued: 'All I shall say at present is, I hope that those who hold lands obtained from the Māori people will be able to show as good and as honest titles as the missionaries can for theirs!'

Busby followed him. He said he'd only bought land that the Māori pressed him to buy, and he always paid them liberally; he did not make any extensive purchases until he was out of office and discovered that even after he had served the British Government for fifteen years it had not made any provision for himself and his family.

Amidst the din, making his way through the ranks of chiefs was Tāmati Pukututu, a chief from Kawakawa who supported the missionaries. Now he reached the space in front of the dais and acknowledged Hobson.

'I say, Stay, oh Governor!'

The noise quietened down and Henry felt a sigh of relief escape him.

'These chiefs tell you to go away because they have sold all their possessions and have no more to sell. But I say, Remain! – you and Busby, and also the missionaries.'

He was backed up by Matiu, but Kawiti, chief of the Ngāti Hine tribe, told Hobson to go away. 'We Māori people do not want to be tied up and trodden down. We are free. Let the missionaries remain, but as for you – return to your own country.'

Another, Wai, also told the governor to go. 'Will you remedy the selling, the exchanging, the cheating, the lying, the stealing of the white men? If they listened to you and obeyed – ah, yes, that would be good! But have they ever listened to Busby?' he said, pointing to the ex-resident, 'and will they listen to you, a stranger, a man of yesterday?'

After translating this Henry glanced sideways and saw that Hobson was looking uneasy.

Then three white men began calling out from different parts of the tent, saying they could not hear and asking again for Johnston to translate.

Hobson invited him to do so and Johnston gave a rendition of the speech by Wai, the last speaker. But at the end he said, 'It's all lies.'

Hobson asked Henry to continue translating.

The tide seemed to turn. Pūmuka told Hobson he wanted him to remain as a foster-father to him. 'I wish to have two fathers,' he said '– you and Busby, and the missionaries.'

In spite of being the brother of Moka and Rewa, Te Wharerahi supported Pūmuka.' Is it not good to be in peace? We will have this man as our governor. What! Turn him away? No, no!'

But then Hākiro from Kororāreka challenged Hobson. 'Why are you sitting here? We are not your people – we are free. We will not have a governor. The missionaries and Busby are our fathers – we do not want you!'

Now it was the turn of Tāreha, again from Kororāreka and the father of Hākiro. Even among Māori he was an unusually tall and robust man, dressed in an old piece of floor matting and carrying in his hand a bunch of dried fern root. 'We will not be ruled over,' he declaimed in a deep, resounding voice. He held up high the fern roots: 'See, this is my food, the food of my ancestors, the food of the Māori people. But you try to tempt us with baits of clothing and of food.' He raised a canoe paddle. 'If all were to be alike, all equal in rank with you . . . but you, the governor up high' – and here he held up the paddle – 'and I down, under, beneath! No, no, no! So I say, Go back, return, go quickly!'

Judging from the expressions on the faces of the chiefs, Tāreha made a strong impression. But then came Rawiri, who began in English: 'Good morning, Mr Governor. Very good you!' Then in Māori: 'Our governor, our father! Stay here, that we may be in peace.'

This was echoed by Hōne Heke, who was married to Hariata Rongo, the daughter of Hongi Hika. Heke had been a bright, although somewhat mischievous, pupil at the Kerikeri mission school. He then lived at Paihia, where he often turned to Henry for advice, which he continued to do even after he'd moved to Kaikohe.

Now his face was solemn and he spoke with great emphasis, accompanying his words with measured gestures. 'You to go away, Governor – no, no, no! For then the French people or the rum-sellers will have us. We Māori are as children. It is not for us, but for you, our fathers – you missionaries – it is for you to decide what will happen. I say, Stay, Governor, and be a father for us.'

Hakitara spoke next, saying a few words to the effect he was in favour of the governor remaining. But his soft voice was drowned out by the discussions among both Europeans and Māori that had arisen after the speech of Hōne Heke.

However, when Tāmati Wākā Nene stood the noise died down. He was a high-ranking chief from Hokianga, as well as being connected to many other major chiefs in the north. Although very much involved in the campaigns waged against southern tribes, he was a kind person who had protected the Wesleyan missionaries and was also a friend to those of the CMS, especially Henry. He had taken his baptismal name of Tāmati Wāka, suggested by Henry, after a patron of the CMS, Thomas Walker.

Now he gazed down at the Māori people crowded round him and Henry was struck by the chief's dignity and commanding appearance.

Nene began: 'What do you say – the governor to return? Tell me, oh chiefs, how are we to act? Is not the land already gone? Is it not covered, all covered, with men, with strangers, foreigners – even as the grass and plants – over whom we have no power? We, the chiefs and people of this land, are down low; they are up high, exalted. You say the governor should go back? Had you spoken thus in days gone by, when the traders and grog-sellers came – had you turned them away, then you could well say to the governor, Go back! and it would have been tika – right – and I would also have said it with you. But now, as things are, I say No, no, no!'

He turned to Hobson. 'I, Tāmati Wāka Nene, say to you, Stay. Remain for us a father, a judge, a peacemaker. Dwell in our midst. Do not listen to what the chiefs of Ngā Puhi say. Stay here – our friend, our father, our governor.'

Henry finished translating his words for Hobson, who smiled and nodded at the chief.

Then it was the turn of Eruera Maihi Patuone, he whom Henry had baptised the previous month. He was the elder brother of Tāmati Wāka Nene and, like his brother, he was a good-natured man who, although now elderly, had the same impressive demeanour.

'What shall I say on this important occasion?' he began, 'before all these great chiefs of both countries?' He faced Hobson. 'Here, then, this is my word to you, O Governor! Stay! – you and the missionaries and the Word of God. Remain here with us, to be a father for us, that the French have us not. Remain, our Governor. Stay, our friend!'

At this there was a commotion and Te Kēmara, the first chief who had spoken, leapt to his feet. 'No, no! Who says, Stay! I say, Go away, return to your own land. I want my lands returned to me. It would be good if you could say my lands should be returned to me; let us all be alike in power – then, oh Governor, remain. But the Governor up, Te Kēmara down low – no!'

He ran up to the front and confronted Hobson. 'Besides, where are you going to live? There is no place left for you.'

At this Busby intervened. He said in Māori, 'The governor can occupy my house.'

At this Te Kēmara hesitated for an instant: the thought of having the governor at Waitangi under his patronage was obviously compelling.

But then his expression changed and again he faced Hobson. With fiery, flashing eyes he eyeballed him and crossed his hands, imitating a man in handcuffs. He shouted, 'Shall I be thus? Thus! Say to me, Governor, speak!'

Hobson stared back, nonplussed.

Te Kēmara held his crossed hands up to his face. 'Like this, eh? Like this? Come, come, speak, Governor. Like this, eh?'

Henry was doing his best to interpret for Hobson, who by now was looking distinctly alarmed. He saw that the police had stiffened to attention and were ready to intervene.

But then Te Kēmara seized Hobson's hand with both of his and began to shake it with great vigour, grimacing as he did so.

'How d'ye do, eh, Governor? How d'ye do, eh, Mister Governor?' he said in English.

He did this over and over again.

Hobson sat there with an uncertain smile, allowing his hand to be pumped up and down while those around him were laughing. He turned to Henry with a questioning look.

'Just keep calm, sir,' Henry murmured.

Finally, when Hobson was able to free his hand from that of Te Kēmara, he announced that this seemed to be a good point at which to end the meeting.

More laughter.

'I now give public notice,' he said, 'that at ten o'clock on Friday the seventh of February, that is, in two days' time, this meeting will reconvene.'

Someone called out, 'Three cheers for the governor!' and from everyone – white and brown – there was hearty applause.

22

On the evening of 5 February the chiefs, who were camping at Te Tī, the flat land on the south side of the Waitangi River, gathered to discuss the kaupapa: would they or would they not sign the white man's treaty?

Along with some of the other missionaries Henry was invited by the people to attend.

They were not in a good mood. The food that had been provided – flour, sugar, pigs and potatoes – although it seemed a vast quantity to English eyes, was not enough to feed them. They had not brought their own supplies and the nearest places to obtain these were several miles away; or else they would have to go to Kororāreka, where they would come under the influence of people who were opposed to the treaty. All they were given was tobacco, and that had been so ineptly distributed that some gained more than their fair share, some too little and others none at all.

The chief Kawiti, one of those who missed out, was particularly annoyed and decided to leave.

So, too, did those involved in the dispute over Whananaki. Henry was well aware of the situation. Four years before, the Ngā Puhi chief Waikato – he who had accompanied Hongi Hika to England – who had never lived in this place on the coast south of the Bay of Islands, but who had a tenuous connection through a distant ancestor, had decided to make a sale there: a European trader wanted to buy land on which grew a kauri forest. The people of Whananaki did not want to sell and appealed to Henry, who told them to ask James Busby to mediate. Both parties met at Waitangi outside Busby's house, but an argument broke out when the ancestry of Waikato was questioned. This chief and his followers brought out their guns and fired on the Whananaki men, women and children, who were unarmed. Two people were killed and others were wounded. There was nothing the powerless Busby could do to punish Waikato: he wrote to the Governor of New South Wales asking for a militia to come over, but this was refused. Instead Waikato made the sale and the local people lost their land.

Now, brought together for the reading of the treaty, the groups involved began to argue again, and eventually Waikato and his whānau departed.

Whananaki was, thought Henry, the kind of situation he hoped signing the treaty would help to resolve. Once the country was subject to the rule of law, speculators could be controlled and any wrongs committed would be punished.

Now some of the Europeans, fearing they would lose their properties, arrived at Te Tī to stir up the chiefs. They told them that under British rule they would lose their country and be made taurekareka – slaves.

The people asked Henry for his opinion.

Again he and the other missionaries went through the treaty, explaining it clause by clause and assuring the chiefs that under the care of the British Government they would become one people with the British. Wars and illegal acts would be prevented and they would all be under one sovereign, Queen Victoria, and one law, both human and divine.

'In my opinion,' he told them, 'you should sign this treaty. It will be of benefit to you and will preserve you as a people.'

After further discussion among the chiefs, during which several said they would be 'dead from hunger' if they waited any longer, it was decided they would sign the treaty the next day so they could return home.

The missionaries deliberated. With the lack of food to feed the people and the fact that they were beginning to drift away, it did indeed appear a good idea to hold the next meeting the following day, instead of on Friday.

On Thursday 6 February, at nine thirty, Henry and the other missionaries again set off for Waitangi.

About five hundred chiefs and their tribes and hapū in their respective groups were present, scattered about the lawn in front of the Residency; in spite of the debates and decision of the night before they were still in lively discussion, it appeared, about the pros and cons of accepting the treaty.

By eleven o'clock there was still no indication from the man-o'-war that Hobson was on his way. The chiefs were becoming irritated.

At midday a boat from the man-o'-war landed on shore. When Henry informed the occupants everyone was waiting for Hobson, they said no one on board knew anything about a meeting. Busby despatched a boat to the ship and finally Hobson appeared.

Henry and Busby watched as his boat arrived at the little bay below the Waitangi peninsula. The governor-general-to-be was slightly dishevelled and in civilian clothes, although he wore his bicorn hat. None of the officers from the ship was with him.

'Good day to you, gentlemen,' he said, adjusting his hat. 'I must say I was not expecting a meeting today.'

'There has clearly been a misunderstanding,' said Busby.

'However,' said Hobson, 'as it now appears there is to be a gathering,

I will take the signatures of the chiefs who are here and who wish to sign. But we must also have a public meeting tomorrow, because I gave notice of this at the end of yesterday's proceedings.'

They walked up the sloping path from the beach to the flat area outside Busby's house. Hobson headed straight for the tent and ensconced himself at the table on the dais; Henry sat beside him, and also Busby. Apart from themselves, several missionaries and about twelve settlers, there were no other Europeans present.

By now the people were angry at being made to wait for so long and it took a while to persuade them to assemble and re-enter the tent.

Finally they were settled.

At this point Hobson stood up and said, 'I can only accept signatures today. I cannot allow any discussion, because this is not a regular public meeting.'

Someone plucked at his arm. 'I have a message from His Most Reverend Excellency, that he and his priest are waiting at Mr Busby's house and desire to be present.'

'Oh! Very well.'

The two Catholic clerics arrived and sat, as on the previous day, on Hobson's left.

Hobson turned to Henry. 'I believe the treaty has now been copied out on parchment by the Reverend Taylor. As it has been rewritten, may I request that you read it once more.'

Again Henry read the treaty in Māori.

When he had finished Pompallier began conversing in a low voice with Hobson. The latter turned to Henry. 'The bishop wishes it to be publicly stated to the natives that his religion will not be interfered with, and that free toleration will be allowed in matters of faith. Could you therefore say that the bishop will be protected and supported in his religion — that I shall protect all creeds alike?'

Henry was silent for a moment. Then he began, 'Nā, e mea ana te

Kawana . . .' meaning 'Now, the Governor says . . .'

Then he hesitated. He turned to George Clarke, but Clarke seemed not to understand.

Colenso, who was on Clarke's other side, intervened. 'Why don't you write it down first, as it's important.'

Henry found a piece of paper and wrote: 'E mea ana te Kawana, ko ngā whakapono katoa, o Ingarani, o ngā Weteriana, o Roma, e tiakina ngātahitia e ia.' Translated into English, it meant 'The Governor says the several beliefs of England, of the Wesleyans, of Rome, shall be protected by him.'

Again Colenso interrupted. 'I suggest you insert "me te ritenga Māori hoki".'

Henry stared at him. '"And Māori customs also"?'

Colenso gave him a look. 'To balance out "the beliefs of Rome".'

'Ah!' Henry added the words and gave the slip of paper to Hobson, who passed it on to Pompallier.

The bishop read it and nodded. 'This will do very well,' he said.

Then he and his accompanying priest bowed to Hobson and departed.

Now Hobson called for all the chiefs who wished to come forward and sign the treaty.

No one moved.

Hobson looked from Henry to Busby and then at the chiefs squatting on the ground, staring back at him.

The silence was becoming embarrassing.

Busby showed Hobson a piece of paper. 'I have here a list of names of the chiefs who are present. Shall I read them out?'

'Please do', said Hobson.

Busby began. 'Hōne Heke!'

This was a stroke of brilliance, because of all the chiefs present, he was probably the most favourable towards the treaty.

Hōne Heke rose to his feet and began advancing towards the table.

But as he did so, Colenso, who had been writing steadily throughout the proceedings – presumably making a record of what was said, although no one had been formally requested to do so – threw down his pen and leaned across to Hobson.

In an urgent tone he said: 'Will Your Excellency allow me to speak to you before that chief signs the treaty?'

'Certainly,' replied Hobson.

'May I ask Your Excellency if it is your opinion that these natives understand the articles of the treaty they are now being called upon to sign?'

'If the native chiefs do not know the contents of this treaty it is no fault of mine. I have done all that I can do to make them understand it, and I really don't know how I can get them to do so.'

'It is no easy matter, I well know, to get them to fully comprehend a document of this kind; still, I think they ought to know something of it to constitute its legality. I have spoken to some chiefs who have no idea whatever about what is intended, and there are others who have only just arrived.'

Busby put in: 'The best answer to that would be found yesterday in the speech by Hōne Heke here. He said the native mind could not comprehend these things and must trust to the advice of their missionaries.'

'That is the very matter I am raising,' said Colenso. 'The missionaries should explain the matter in all its bearings to the natives, so that it is their own act and deed. Then, in case of a reaction taking place, the natives could not turn on us missionaries and say, "You advised me to sign that paper, but never told me what the contents were."'

'I very much hope,' said Hobson, 'that such a reaction will not occur. I think the people under your care will be peaceable enough, and I'm sure you will endeavour to make them so. And as for those who are not – we must do the best we can with them.'

Colenso was silent for a minute, then nodded. 'Thank you for the patient hearing you have given me. What I had to say arose from a conscientious feeling on the subject, and I now consider I have discharged my duty.'

Hōne Heke was still standing, waiting to sign.

Hobson turned to Henry. 'What shall I say to them?'

'Now?'

'When they sign.'

Henry thought quickly. What about the words he'd addressed to the chiefs the night before, telling them they would become one people with the English?

'I suggest: "He iwi tahi tātou."'

'Which means?'

'We are now one people.'

He wrote it on a piece of paper. He said it again and Hobson repeated it.

Busby pushed the parchment towards Heke, who signed the treaty.

Hobson stood and shook hands with the chief. 'He iwi tātou tahi!' he said triumphantly.

'He iwi tahi tātou,' corrected Henry.

'Koia anō!' replied Heke, smiling.

He returned to where he was sitting, but several others also came forward to sign their names, or make their marks, and to each Hobson repeated his newfound phrase.

While this was happening, two other chiefs, Marupō and Ruhe, came out to the space in front of the dais and spoke for a long time. They were against signing. They strode up and down, stamping their feet, making gestures with their arms and hands, and declaiming in the best Māori oratorical style. Marupō was stripped down to his loincloth and continued to speak until he was exhausted. Then, to Henry's surprise, he approached the dais and made his mark on the parchment. Ruhe did the same.

There was a pause. Finally Te Kēmara approached the dais. 'I would like to say,' he announced, glaring around him, 'that Pīkopo' – meaning the Catholic bishop – 'warned me not to write on the paper. For if I do, he said, I will be made a slave.'

But in spite of that, Te Kēmara signed the treaty.

That left Rewa, who said he would not sign. But the other chiefs remonstrated with him, as did some of the Church of England missionaries.

Slowly he approached the dais.

'Mr Governor,' he said, 'I shall now make my mark. But I would like to tell you that Pīkopo told me not to – in fact, he tried very hard to persuade me not to agree to your treaty.'

In the meantime other chiefs came forward who had only just appeared – their invitations arrived late and they had to walk a long way in order to get there. In spite of not having been present the day before to participate in the discussions, they too signed the document.

By the end of the day forty five chiefs had signed, most of them from the Bay of Islands or nearby. The only ones who had come from any distance were Tāmati Wākā Nene and his brother Eruera Maihi Patuone, from the Hokianga; and Te Kauwhata, Wharau and Te Ngere from Whangaruru. Furthermore, not many of those who signed were chiefs of the highest rank.

Notwithstanding, the people gave three hearty cheers for the 'Kawana'. For now, indeed, he was truly the Lieutenant-Governor of New Zealand – or, at least of part of it.

Patuone made a public presentation to Hobson of a mere, to be sent to Queen Victoria, and then the governor departed with the chief, whom he had invited to dine with him on board the man-o'-war. Colenso was left to distribute gifts, which this time he organised in an orderly fashion – a small quantity of tobacco and two blankets for each chief – muttering to Henry in his usual wry manner, 'Sic transit Gloria Nova Zelanda!'

The next day, Friday, it poured with rain.

Henry reflected that because of the weather they could not have held the meeting as Hobson proposed; and the chiefs would not have been able to wait until Saturday and would have returned to their villages.

Only narrowly had the Treaty of Waitangi gained acceptance.

On Saturday morning the man-o'-war hoisted a profusion of flags in the British colours and fired a royal salute of twenty one guns, the boom echoing round the Bay of Islands.

And thus was born the new British Colony of New Zealand.

23

Marianne walked back to Paihia with him.

'How very embarrassing,' she said.

'I thought it went quite well, all things considered.'

'But when they challenged you.'

'Over the land? Oh! Yes . . .'

During the 1830s the tribes were still battling each other, armed with the weapons sold to them by white men eager to take their land. Until they ceased putting all their energies into war they would never be able to progress into becoming people who followed Christ and realised their true potential. Therefore, whenever he heard of a feud breaking out in the North Island Henry immediately journeyed there, to try to steer those involved into the ways of peace.

At the end of 1831, Ngā Puhi were on the warpath. The year before the daughters of Hongi Hika and Rewa of Kerikeri had quarrelled with the daughter of Kiwikiwi on the beach at Kororāreka, over the affections of a whaling captain. Because any individual of a tribe must always be avenged, right or wrong, the argument escalated into fighting, with battle lines being drawn between the northern and southern hapū of Ngā Puhi.

The northern subtribe, under Hōne Heke, Ururoa and Tītore, attacked the southern people, led by Kiwikiwi, Te Morenga and Pōmare II. During the fighting, known to Māori as the 'Battle of Kororāreka' and to the whites as 'the Girls' War', a northern Ngā Puhi chief Hengi was shot, unarmed.

Henry had walked into the middle of the fight to try to stop it, shouting as loudly as he could, but the din from the gunshots was so colossal no one heard. He then went to fetch Tohitapu, but that chief was not prepared to put his body in the way of the bullets. Henry returned with a young chief: the firing ceased, and Rewa waved to both parties to stop fighting. The warriors surrounded him and gave him their full attention. They agreed he was right and they had been urged on by Satan.

One of the northern Ngā Puhi chiefs, holding a small stick in his hand, made a long chant, at the end of which he broke the stick and threw it down at the feet of the opposing fighters. One of their chiefs then did the same, thus signalling the end of the battle.

The dead and wounded numbered about one hundred. To Henry's dismay he found that people in the same families had been fighting each other.

The next day, a Sunday, all the houses along the beach at Kororāreka were set on fire. After this many waka full of men, women and children, including Tohitapu and Rewa, departed, heading for Paihia. The service in the chapel was delayed because treatment needed to be given to the wounded.

Northern Ngā Puhi, who had won the battle, proposed that the Kororāreka block should be given to them as reparation for the death of Hengi. This was agreed to and peace was established – although fighting was to break out later on between Tītore and Pōmare over the boundary line.

However, the two sons of Hengi, who had not been at the battle, still wanted blood payment. Goaded by the ancient law of utu and, in Henry's opinion the Evil One, they sailed south and descended on groups of Ngāi Te Rangi at Mayor Island and Motītī: there they killed the men and kept the women and children as slaves. While they were feasting on the bodies Ngāi Te Rangi warriors from Tauranga attacked the two sons and their party and, in turn, ate them.

Ever since then the Ngā Puhi people in the Bay of Islands had been agitating for revenge for the deaths of these two young men, even though their tribe were the original aggressors. They were now preparing to sail south to attack Ngāi Te Rangi, who were not nearly as experienced in gun warfare – and this time they intended to annihilate them.

Henry, horrified, did his best to talk them out of the expedition. He was unsuccessful, but to his relief they agreed to being accompanied by the missionaries, who offered to act as mediators.

Henry no longer had the *Herald*, which after serving him well for two years was wrecked four years ago on the bar of the Hokianga Harbour. It had been replaced with a schooner, the *Active*, and now, in January 1832 James Kemp used this to carry supplies. The missionaries also had the cutter *Karere* – which on the open sea rode the water like a duck, but with its shallow draught it could enter creeks and it would be used as a messenger between the boats and the people at home. In an open boat rowed by their crew, Henry and William Fairburn set off before dawn in the midst of a fleet of forty or fifty waka taua, each with their full complement of warriors.

Progress was slow as the men were particularly careful when on a war expedition not to enrage the gods. If they shipped even a little water they made for the shore, fearing that Tangaroa, the god of the sea, was angry; the same thing happened when a gale blew, for it meant that Tāwhirimatea, the god of the wind, was upset. They dared not have any cooked food on board, they could not eat while sailing, nor could they smoke their pipes.

Sometimes they stopped to visit tribes on shore, and there they were joined by the chiefs Tītore and Rewa. Around Mangawhai the warriors pointed out many places where there had been settlements but now the people were no more: they had all been decimated by war.

At one place they went on shore to burn the remains of old sheds they had spotted, as well as some sticks and flax, all of which were tapu or sacred because of the deaths that had occurred there. That night one of their chiefs had a dream in which Tāwhirimatea appeared and scolded him, saying he had stirred up the winds and if they continued to sail the god would tip over their waka and the sea would be rough for a long time. They decided to wait until the sea was calm.

By now there were about four hundred warriors, with another four hundred ahead of them. As preparation for the battle ahead, they set up a haka.

Each of the parties waited in different spots along the beach: then one party moved slowly, holding their muskets erect, towards a designated place. They were joined by another group, and another, until all except one were standing together. These last people rushed furiously at the main party – body against body – then turned and formed one group.

Now it was time for the haka itself.

The men began to emit fearful screams and yells. They threw their bodies into fantastical attitudes, distorting their faces and turning their tongues nearly to the back of their heads, all the while rolling their eyes inside out. Each one jumped as high as he possibly could, at the same time tossing up the stock of his musket so as to display the brass he had polished to perfection.

They did this two or three times, to shouts of exultation from admiring onlookers. Then they sat on the ground, leaving a space in the centre so they could be addressed by the chiefs, or anyone else who wished.

However, there was still talk of waiting many more days until the sea was perfectly smooth. Henry lost patience with this and, as the wind was south-southwest, which would blow him north, he decided to take the *Karere* back to Paihia.

There he was delayed by contrary winds, but eventually he set off again. At Tairua he finally found the flotilla coming out of the harbour, his boat and crew among them.

They pulled in to Whangamatā, which seemed a very pleasant place with lots of forests and streams and a good anchoring spot for small vessels – but without any inhabitants. In former days there were many, he was told, but they had all died. His companions showed him the sites of recent battles.

Poor creatures! he thought. The land must be polluted with blood and every man's hand is against his brother. Only the Lord himself could release them from their cruel bondage and make them willing to turn to him.

The next day was Sunday. Henry was woken before dawn by the warriors talking excitedly. He enquired about breakfast and was told nothing could be cooked because both fire and water were now tapu: the tohunga or priest was about to consult the oracle and was preparing for the ceremony.

He went searching and found eight chiefs gathered in a glade in the bush, all naked. At first they told him to go away, but relented when he persuaded them he was a white person and therefore not involved in the outcome.

The chiefs stuck sticks, each about a foot long, in the ground to correspond with the number of canoes. Then they set up more sticks to represent the number of waka belonging to their opponents. Each stick was tied to two others, and if it fell it was a sign of bad news.

Everyone was told to withdraw, except the tohunga, an old and very thin man.

The chiefs obviously regarded the ceremony with great seriousness – they put as much faith in it as, say, the direction of the wind.

Finally the tohunga reappeared. When the chiefs went to see the results they were inconclusive, with about a third of the sticks lying on the ground.

Seeing it was Sunday, and now that things had quietened down, the missionaries rang a bell to indicate a church service would be held. About a hundred people attended and afterwards some told Henry they were fed up with the expedition.

By the following Saturday they were within two miles of Otūmoetai, the pā of Ngāi Te Rangi. At midnight the order was given to attack and the fleet proceeded up the harbour, the noise they made negating any advantage they might have had by moving in darkness.

The whole surface of the waterway was covered by waka taua. Behind them the countryside had been set on fire, the blaze lighting up the sky and reflecting in the water. Truly it seemed they were issuing from hell.

In the morning, naked again, the Ngā Puhi warriors advanced. Firing broke out from them and was returned by Ngāi Te Rangi. The battle lasted for three hours.

Finally Ngā Puhi returned, having expended their ammunition, and bringing one slain warrior. Several of the chiefs sat down by their waka and seemed dejected: during the voyage down many had assured Henry they'd had enough of fighting and would be glad to see a party of European soldiers come among them to preserve peace throughout the land.

Henry tried to talk them into making peace now, but this was rejected. So when daylight dawned he decided to leave the warriors to it and return to the *Active*. From there he watched as Ngā Puhi pushed close up to the pā, about two hundred yards away from the palisades. The firing continued for more than two hours.

He feared for Ngāi Te Rangi. Dear Lord, he prayed, I beg you to spare this people.

He and William Fairburn watched as the battle raged. About fifty Ngā Puhi were in a strong position, hiding amongst bushes and long grass, but Ngāi Te Rangi warriors managed to dislodge them. Meanwhile, children in the pā were running round picking up the shot as it fell.

The next day he and Fairburn went up to the pā and checked the fortifications, which they noted were well constructed. Back in the boat they saw close struggles on the beach.

At night there was a dramatic scene as from the pā came bitter cries and lamentations, and the occasional firing of guns. Ngāi Te Rangi were mourning their dead.

Next morning the missionaries went back up to the pā and found the defenders in better spirits than they expected.

They then returned to Ngā Puhi, to try to ascertain their intentions. They listened as the chiefs made their speeches: everyone was for war and every kind of evil feeling was expressed. Tohitapu was as bad as anyone. However, when one chief accused the missionaries of passing information to Ngāi Te Rangi, he was shouted down.

Fearing Ngāi Te Rangi had no chance and not wanting to witness the horrors that accompanied victory in war, Henry and Fairburn decided to depart.

Back in Paihia, when they brought the bad tidings everyone at the settlement was cast down: all seemed dark and dreary and without hope. One battle would only lead to another and war spread across the country like wildfire.

But Henry could not rest. Something told him he must keep trying.

William Fairburn offered to come with him and together they boarded the *Active* and for the third time Henry sailed for Tauranga to see if there was any hope of turning the people's hearts from war.

They reached Tauranga in the evening and anchored to the leeward of the great mountain Mauao. When the sun rose more than a dozen waka, crowded with Ngā Puhi, came alongside them, apparently in attack mode.

The *Active* hoisted a white flag and when the warriors realised who it was they set up a haka and invited the missionaries to meet them on shore. Tītore came on board and when the tide turned guided them up the harbour to the camp.

There they met the principal Ngā Puhi chiefs, Tohitapu among them: this last was still bragging about his deeds in battle and exaggerating enemy losses. However, the rest of them were in much less of a warlike state, many sitting shaking their heads, saying they were tired; others were hungry. Their enemy had put up more of a fight than they expected and the big guns they'd brought were ineffective in storming the pā.

Henry went from the camp to the pā and back again, although without effecting a peaceful end to the battle. Ngā Puhi held a discussion, with some wanting to abandon the operation while others were all for continuing. It appeared the latter were winning the day, so Henry and Fairburn, aware they were needed back home, decided to return to Paihia.

The wind being in their favour, they made for Great Barrier Island, in the outer reaches of the Hauraki Gulf, as there were two good anchorages there. However, as they drew close to the land a raging storm blew up. The gusts were so strong they feared they would lose the masts, so reluctantly they brought down the sails and let the *Active* drift, which she did at great speed.

Darkness set in and Henry was full of apprehension. Shipwreck seemed a likely possibility. There were no Christian Māori in this part of the country, so even if they were able to struggle to land, they would be in danger. He thought of the family at home, who might never learn their fate.

Oh my God, he prayed, you have been my refuge in distress, my help in time of need. It is only you whom winds and seas obey.

During the night the wind moved to the north. With the dawn they saw high land looming above them and, thinking they were near Cape Colville, made towards it, only to discover it was the north head of Port Charles where there was no shelter.

A heavy sea was running through the channel and they decided to put up their sails and try to get around the head.

There was a moment in which the sea became calm. 'Ready about!' called the captain. He put the helm down – 'Lee O!' – and round she came.

Eventually they made the Mercury Islands. Though they were close to a sheltered bay, they were unable to enter. They dropped anchor and spent a long night with the ship tossing violently, knowing they were very exposed and in extreme danger.

Finally the day dawned but fog had descended and there was no visibility. The sound of waves breaking on land came from nearby and they knew they had to act. Then for a minute there was a break in the fog. They saw they were close – far too close – to an 'iron-bound', i.e. rock-strewn, coast towards which the raging wind was pushing them ever closer. The square-rigged ship, top-heavy with a mass of sails, was leaning and the flapping of the canvas was like gunshots.

The captain, struggling with the wheel, shouted, 'Wear to!'

With his experience in sailing Henry knew there was no room for this manoeuvre when land was so near. 'Wearing to' meant allowing the stern of the ship to turn so the wind came from behind. In this situation they would lose control and be driven straight onto the rocks. The vessel would be smashed to pieces and they would certainly be killed.

'No!' he shouted. He grabbed the wheel from the captain. 'Put her into stays!' he bellowed.

There was pandemonium as the crew rushed to obey.

Henry stood on the slippery deck, his sturdy legs wide apart for balance, and turned the wheel so that instead of the back of the ship, the bow or front was headed into the wind. He gave the order to tack: there was a heart-wrenching moment as they waited for the foresail to fill with wind and the ship came round. Then, just in time, he steered them away from the rocks.

He had not even had time to pray.

As they sailed away he was suddenly aware his heart was pounding and his whole body was shaking. Even in the turmoil there was one thought that dominated his mind: if he perished here, what would happen to his family?

He had, in fact, been aware of the problem for some time, as had Marianne, but he'd been so preoccupied with establishing the mission he'd not had the opportunity to consider the matter further. His children were still young and dependent and while he was there he could support them all. But once he was gone, there were few avenues open to them. They could become missionaries, but they needed to show aptitude for this work and in any case there were limited opportunities. He did not want them to become traders because many in the Bay of Islands had a reputation for being unscrupulous; nor did he want them in the Royal Navy or the Army. He also did not want them thrown on the mercy of the CMS: even though there were good-hearted people who would do their best to support them, in the end when they grew up his sons needed to be able to fend for themselves. And as for his daughters – if they did not find a capable husband life would be very difficult indeed.

He had brought these people into the world and now it was his duty, as far as he was able, to ensure their future.

Eventually Ngā Puhi returned from their expedition to the south. There had been neither victory nor defeat, but they were weary and dispirited. The God of the missionaries, they said, had been too strong for them. Instead of swelling with bravery, their hearts had turned round, jumped up and sunk down with fear.

The missionaries were delighted. Throughout the Paihia mission everyone gave thanks that their efforts had borne fruit: the hearts of the people had broken free and the Evil One had been routed.

But now that he'd come face to face with the possibility of his sudden death, Henry set himself the goal to provide for his children when he was gone.

In New South Wales the CMS there had given a free grant of 2560 acres for each son of a missionary, and 1280 acres for the daughters. The Paihia people had requested a grant of two hundred acres for each of their children, and the CMS in London agreed, but put so many conditions on these grants they were unworkable. Instead they gave fifty pounds each as an 'apprentice fee', but this was clearly not enough for the children to live on for the rest of their lives.

In the year following his expedition south, with the knowledge and, it appeared, approval of the CMS, with his own money Henry bought land at Pakaraka from Te Morenga, who built him a house made of raupō and fenced in some paddocks. The chief and his people declared themselves very pleased to have 'Karu-whā' among them; in time Henry intended to set up a school there and even begin the foundations for a town. As well as providing a home for his children, it would, he hoped, for those living nearby be a light in the wilderness.

Gradually he bought more land until he felt there was enough to support his family, while leaving enough for the Māori people. Although he was told the land was bad he persisted in working on the property, ploughing and sowing seed, and was delighted to find the resulting crop was much better than expected. He bought sheep and cattle, and to the raupō house and barn already there added a blacksmith's forge, a cowshed, a shed for the sheep and stockyards. He knew he should not be paying so much attention to these developments, rather than concentrating on the public work of the mission; but in order to do this he needed firstly to be free of anxiety about his children's future.

They were nearly home from their walk: Henry turned to Marianne and put an arm around her shoulders.

'Don't worry about the accusations, my dear,' he said. 'We have nothing to fear. I acquired the land at Pakaraka fairly and paid, as you know, a good price. And I'm sure that when the government inquires into my purchases and sees I have an honest title, and that the land is to be shared out among our children, no one will say I have been over the mark.'

24

The governor was ill.

Soon after the signing of the treaty Hobson insisted on riding over to the Hokianga Harbour, on the west coast. He wanted more signatures — obviously aware that the few he had garnered so far were not a mandate for declaring sovereignty over the North Island.

Henry wasn't asked to accompany the party. But he heard that the nine-mile ride had been extremely arduous. They'd fought through impenetrable forests and jumped their horses over fallen trees. When on their return journey they reached Waimate, Nias took to his bed with influenza; Hobson appeared to have survived but complained of having spent the whole time wet through.

Notwithstanding, their journey had been worth the effort, with about two thousand Māori people and British settlers at Hokianga to greet them and an additional seventy chiefs' signatures added to the treaty.

Because it was already settled, Hobson and his retinue installed themselves in Paihia. However, the governor was keen to establish a permanent capital and seat of government for his newly formed colony. He asked Henry for his opinion.

'I know there is talk of keeping it here, in the Bay of Islands', he said, 'but I don't recommend this course.'

'May I know why?'

'For one thing, Your Excellency, it is at the extreme end of the island and therefore distant from the rest of the country. For another, there are too many people here already, with their interests and land speculations well established. You're better to go somewhere with a clean slate.'

'I believe you've travelled extensively throughout the North Island. Is there any place you could recommend as suitable?'

'Five years ago I explored the Waitematā, which is a harbour about a hundred nautical miles south from here. It has an open stretch of water surrounded by a vast extent of fine country, gentle and undulating. In fact, because of its attractiveness it is known to the Māori as Tāmaki-makau-rau.'

'Meaning?'

'Tāmaki loved by many.'

'In that case I presume it is already well settled.'

'When I visited there were no inhabitants, neither European nor Māori.'

'How could that be?'

'The Europeans have not yet discovered it — although no doubt they will, very shortly. And the local Māori people have been decimated by the raids of Hongi Hika, the remaining few dispersed; although I believe recently they have begun to return.'

'I see!'

'Furthermore, it seems to me the site has peculiar advantages, in that it's blessed by good access to the rest of the island. From the Firth of

Thames you can reach the Hauraki Plain, while to travel to the north you can go via the Kaipara Harbour, where there are extensive kauri forests —'

'Ideal for masts and spars,' put in Hobson.

'An excellent building material in all respects. And then,' Henry continued, 'via the Manukau Harbour and the Waikato River, which rises in Lake Taupō, it is possible to voyage by boat to the very centre of the island.'

'I much like the sound of the place you describe,' declared Hobson, 'especially after my experience in the last few days, beating through jungle!' He thought for a minute. 'It would be advantageous to see this harbour as soon as possible. Shortly I intend to travel south in order to collect more signatures to the treaty, leaving on the twenty first of February. I wonder if you would care to accompany me?'

On board ship was Hobson's official party. This consisted of his secretary James Freeman, the treasurer George Cooper and the surveyor Felton Mathew, all officials from Sydney provided by Gipps and whose main interest as far as Henry could see was in land speculation. Then there was Nias, once described by the *Sydney Gazette*, not known for mincing its words, as 'a mean-souled abortion of humanity'.

Now, once more thrown together within the confines of a ship, the two captains resumed their quarrelling. Hobson was furious that Nias would not give him the respect he thought he was due, particularly now he was Governor-General of New Zealand. Nias refused to acknowledge Hobson as his superior while he was captain of the ship on which they were travelling.

They sailed down the east coast of the North Island, stopping now and then to go ashore to show the treaty to any chiefs they found and ask for their signatures. Of these they gained a considerable number.

Finally they reached the Hauraki Gulf. Puffed along by a northeasterly breeze, the ship glided past the shores of a large island the name of which, Henry told them, was Waiheke. He pointed out the bays with white-sand beaches that lined its forested shores and where vessels would find good anchorage. Then they entered a channel between the islands of Motuihe on their port side and Motutapu on the starboard.

The sea lapped around them, rippling from the ship's bow as she cut through its clear, blue-green depths.

Henry went to stand beside Nias as he turned the wheel from one side to the other, guiding the ship. 'Today it is calm,' he told the captain, 'but when the tide turns and you're heading into a southwesterly, you have a tough job on your hands.'

Nias gave a dismissive sniff. Evidently he didn't need advice from anyone, not even in unknown waters.

Hobson came to join them.

He put a hand on Henry's shoulder. 'I must say it is looking very promising, just as you said.'

They rounded a point and there it was, spread out before them. To starboard was the low, sloping, triangular island of Rangitoto that Henry explained was created by lava flowing out of the volcano when it erupted. To port was another small island with a high peak, probably another old volcano. And before them to the west lay a great, wide harbour basking under a bright blue sky, where cotton-wool clouds floated above the sprawling land on the horizon.

'What did you say was the name of this harbour?'

'Waitematā,' said Henry. 'I believe it's after a tiny island that you will perceive as you go further upstream, wai meaning water and Te Matā —'

'As for the city that I shall found here,' said Hobson dreamily, 'I think I will bestow upon it the name of Auckland.'

Nias gave a disapproving grunt.

'Any particular reason, Your Excellency?' asked Henry.

'Auckland – Lord Auckland – was the name of the great lord to whom I owe the honour of my present eminent position.'

Now Nias was really snorting.

It was at this point that Henry was asked to take the ship's boat and travel over to an area called Maraetai, on the mainland south of Waiheke Island, where was living a tribe from whom it was hoped he could collect signatures.

Four days later, his mission having been accomplished, he returned to the ship.

As his boat drew near he noticed there seemed to be an unusual amount of toing and froing on the decks. He clambered up the rope ladder and as soon as he set foot on the deck he was greeted by Nias.

There was a peculiar expression on the face of the captain – a mixture of shiftiness and triumph.

'He's going!' he said.

'What! Who?'

'Hobson!'

Henry stared blankly.

'Had some kind of seizure this morning – lost the use of his speech and completely paralysed all down his right side. Clearly unfit to do his duty.'

'But he seemed perfectly all right – however, it does sound like a stroke.' Henry looked sharply at Nias. 'Did you have another row?'

'You can't blame me, if that's what you mean. The fellow's always been as weak as a sickly hen. Anyway, he himself says he'll have to resign and I'll not stop him.'

The ship's doctor, Alexander Lane, arrived and Nias disappeared.

Lane looked after the captain and shook his head. 'Paralysis hemiplegia,' he said, 'brought on by undue excitement. The two of them have been at each other's throats since they came on board and this morning was too much for His Excellency.'

'They had another argument?'

'More like a violent quarrel.'

At this point they were joined by Mathew. 'The two of them are both obstinate, wrong-headed fellows,' he said, 'neither one fit for the office they hold.'

'So what happens now?' asked Henry.

'We'll take him back to the Bay of Islands,' said Mathew, 'where his friend Willoughby Shortland can decide what's to be done with him. But it's the end of the road for our great governor-general.'

'And your opinion, Doctor?'

Lane heaved a regretful sigh. 'I think he ought to return to Sydney, where he can receive proper treatment.'

Henry looked from one to another. Nias, Mathew, even Hobson's own doctor, were totally uninterested in supporting the governor. For their own reasons they'd already decided he was too sick to govern and wanted him gone.

But how ill was he? Certainly there'd been the episode when he first arrived and announced he was indisposed and unable to draw up the treaty.

And then there'd been that strange incident in the afternoon after the signing on the sixth of February.

William Colenso had related to Henry how after the signing of the treaty he walked with Hobson down the path to the sandy beach below, where the governor's boat was waiting. Suddenly there appeared an elderly chief who'd only just arrived: he grabbed the gunwale to prevent the boat being dragged further down the beach and turned to gaze into Hobson's face. 'Auē!' he exclaimed. 'He koroheke! E kore e roa kua mate!'

Colenso said that, being one of the few people present who

understood Māori, he was asked to interpret.

He tried to brush it aside, but the governor persisted: 'Pray do tell me the exact meaning of the words. I much wish to know.'

So Colenso duly translated: 'The chief says — "Alas, he is an old man and will soon be dead."'

Henry was well aware of the belief that the old tohunga had the gift of seeing into the future. But he refused to be swayed by any prophesy. 'I would like to see the governor,' he told the officials.

In the dark cabin Hobson's deep-set eyes and finely arched eyebrows gleamed from a pale face as he reclined on his bed.

Henry gazed down at him. 'I hear you've had a stroke, Your Excellency.'

'It is most unfortunate,' whispered Hobson, 'but I fear I am in no condition to carry on.'

'As governor-general?'

Hobson nodded weakly. 'I need to go back to Sydney. My wife and children . . .'

'It's a good sign that you are now able to speak, Your Excellency. Do you think you can sit up?'

Hobson slowly raised himself so he was leaning on his elbow.

'I strongly feel it would be most unfortunate, Your Excellency, if you were unavailable now, at this crucial time. With the treaty you have laid the groundwork and begun a process that will see British Government established in New Zealand. And, most importantly, you have won the trust of the Māori people. If you were to depart so suddenly, they would lose faith in you and in the ability of the British to govern.'

Hobson looked alarmed. 'But —'

'I'm aware you have had a stroke, and quite a major one at that. But you are young in years and I'm sure that with a few days of rest and treatment you will soon recover. I suggest you return now to the Bay where our surgeon will take care of you and you'll be back on your feet in no time.'

There was a tear in Hobson's eye. 'Eliza...'

Of course, he needed his family: Henry could relate to that. 'I think the best solution would be for your wife and children to travel from Sydney to the Bay and meet you there. Surely that would be possible?'

At this Hobson seemed to brighten.

Henry turned to go.

'Mr Williams! The signatures... to the treaty. What will happen now?'

Henry considered. 'We must continue the work. That is imperative.'

'My major concern... It is urgent –'

'Yes?'

'Port Nicholson – the New Zealand Company...'

Henry nodded reluctantly, knowing what was coming.

Hobson struggled to a sitting position. 'The only person able without my presence to face up to that Company and gather signatures –' Hobson paused for breath – 'from the local chiefs is yourself. I beg you, sir, to carry out this mission on my behalf.'

25

Henry knew very well that at Port Nicholson neither he nor the treaty would be welcome.

There the New Zealand Company had set up a 'Colonial Council' that made its own laws and claimed its power came from the authority transferred to them by the local Māori chiefs. In a way it was laughable, the stuff of comic opera. It was an illegal republic, and it sprang from the aspirations of two shady men.

Edward Gibbon Wakefield conceived the idea of 'systematic immigration' while in Newgate Prison. Henry had heard the story of why he'd been jailed for abduction – he kidnapped a fifteen-year-old heiress, luring her away from school by concocting a letter from her mother saying she was gravely ill. Then he told the girl her father was in serious financial difficulty and the only way to solve this was by marriage to himself. The pair eloped to Gretna Green, where they were married, although the marriage was later annulled.

It seemed a far-fetched tale, but apparently Wakefield had extraordinary powers of persuasion and could even hypnotise people. He was aided in this venture by his brother William, and the two of them were arrested and imprisoned for three years.

Undaunted by the damage to his reputation – and perhaps to redeem himself in the eyes of the world – once he was out of prison Wakefield continued with his scheme and convinced a group of businessmen, politicians and aristocrats to set up the New Zealand Association, later called the New Zealand Company. Its tenets were that emigration should not be piecemeal, but carefully controlled; and the land would be bought cheaply by the Company from Māori and on-sold to settlers for a much higher price, the profits being used to publicise and develop the settlements.

In charge of the settlement at Port Nicholson was William Wakefield. This latter had now attained the rank of colonel, gained from his years as a mercenary soldier fighting in Brazil for the King of Portugal, and then for Queen Isabella of Spain in the Carlist wars. But by all accounts he showed no ability as a leader.

Word was that the settlement so far had been a disaster: immigrants had been lured to New Zealand with grandiose and sometimes fraudulent advertising, and thousands of lots were sold before anyone left England. When they arrived the settlers found the land they had bought in advance at Petone was a swamp. Some of the lots could not be accessed or were surmounted by Māori pā. And then the river, which had been renamed Hutt after the chairman of the New Zealand Company, when there was heavy rain rose up and flooded out the area. To Henry's mind the whole set-up was as big a fraud as the South Sea Bubble.

Also, he'd discovered the manner in which the purchases had been purchased from local Māori was severely lacking. No one in the New Zealand Company knew anything of the language: the deeds of purchase were written in English and apparently it was left to Dicky Barrett, the owner of a local hotel who knew a few words of pidgin Māori, to translate. Neither party understood the other and the chiefs were unaware they were signing away the land on which they lived.

In England the CMS vigorously lobbied against the proposals

for settlement by the New Zealand Company, regarding its leaders as entirely unsuitable and fearing they would exterminate the Māori population.

In New Zealand Henry had assisted in blocking their purchases. He warned the tribes in Whanganui, Taranaki and Port Nicholson not to sell land to the Company; and in order to prevent it getting into their clutches had arranged for trusts of Māori lands to be administered by the CMS for the benefit of the people.

Now he chartered a small schooner and sailed down to Cook Strait, bearing a copy of the treaty.

Port Nicholson was a large and beautiful harbour enclosed by high hills on which flourished trees and ferns right down to the water's edge. There was only a little flat land, on the northern side, at Petone, where the New Zealand Company had set up its headquarters. When his vessel anchored in the harbour Henry spotted the settlers' huts and their belongings – casks, chests, even pianos – scattered along the foreshore.

Above the settlement fluttered a flag with a red St George's cross on a white background, the first quarter with a red cross on a blue background pierced with four white stars – the flag of the United Tribes of New Zealand.

Whatever was intended by this flag, it certainly didn't mean the settlers accepted the treaty.

When he landed at Petone and searched out the local chiefs no one would sign, saying they'd been warned not to by William Wakefield.

It was obvious the situation required a careful strategy. Rather than approach Wakefield directly, Henry decided first to do some reconnaissance. Dr George Evans, who was not a medical man but had a doctorate in law, was apparently the person to see. Evans rejoiced in the title of Lord Chancellor and was second in command to Wakefield.

However, he was not living at Petone but had already moved to the southwest of the harbour, the place to which the New Zealand Company had recently decided to relocate its whole settlement.

Henry commandeered a boat and rowed himself round to Thorndon, as the spot was now called. He found the lord chancellor in residence in a Māori whare.

When he introduced himself Evans did not rise from the desk where he was sitting, but greeted him with a stony glare.

Henry adopted a conciliatory tone: 'Word has it, Dr Evans, that your company is making great progress.'

Evans' jowly chin lifted higher and he continued to stare at Henry without speaking.

'However, one does hear conflicting reports . . . I would be very interested to receive an account from your point of view.'

Evans gave a sudden thump on the table and stood up, his hands on his hips. 'We know why you're here, Mr Williams – you've come to cause trouble!'

'Not at all. I would simply like to –'

Evans began to pace around the room, his hands behind his back. 'The fact of the matter,' he declaimed, 'is that we have nearly a thousand colonists here and our settlement is well advanced. We intend to provide each settler with one town acre and one hundred acres in the country, with which they are very satisfied.'

Satisfied? It wasn't at all what Henry had heard. But he said in mild tones: 'And you feel you have sufficient land with which to supply them?'

'As to that!'

Evans grabbed a scroll that had been standing in one corner. He spread it out on the desk: it was a map of New Zealand, and on it was marked a large area covering both sides of Cook Strait.

'Ours, Mr Williams!' Evans gave a sweep with his arm: 'From thirty eight degrees to forty two degrees parallels of latitude – twenty million acres! I might say that our directors at Home are very much delighted with our purchases.'

No doubt they were. Henry stood there, noncommittal, perusing the map. He pointed. 'I see this area – which would appear to cover a good third of the whole country – includes Whanganui, Kawhia, Rotorua and Tūranga.' He turned to Evans. 'Have you, I wonder, actually had any communication with those to whom these lands belong?'

'Not as yet. But that will be arranged.'

'And the tribal lands belonging to the people in the Port Nicholson area, where they still live? I believe there has been a problem.'

At this Evans stopped pacing and swung round. His jowly face had turned beetroot-red. '"Problem!" What are you talking about, Mr Williams?'

Henry continued to look him in the eye. There was a minute's silence, then Evans collected himself. 'There is no problem at all, Mr Williams,' he said smoothly. 'In fact, we share your concern for our native people. You are apparently unaware that in the township we intend to set aside one hundred and ten acres expressly reserved for the natives, as well as an equal number of country sections.'

Now it was Henry's turn to be taken aback. 'The people will live with you, within the settlement?'

'That is the plan, Mr Williams. And in doing so we expect they will learn to act in a civilised manner.'

Henry was not so convinced of this. But the information did put an entirely new complexion on the situation.

Once again, it appeared, the Lord had come to his aid. Now he saw a way through.

He took a breath.

'As you may already know, I am the owner of sixty acres in this area.'

'We are very cognisant of that! With the land you claim as yours being situated right in the middle of our proposed township, particularly now that the area of Petone has proved to be, shall we say, not as satisfactory as we hoped – you are causing us enormous inconvenience.'

'I purchased it from the chief Reihana, who asked me to buy it and hold it in trust for him.'

'That's your story, Mr Williams.'

'I wanted to make sure the local people still had a tūrangawaewae – a place to stand – in their own land. But now that you have reassured me with respect to their situation, I think, Dr Evans, we might have a solution.'

Evans stared at him sideways, his eyes narrowed. 'A solution? With regard to . . .?'

'With regard to the land that I own here. We may be able to come to an arrangement.'

At this Evans appeared nonplussed and Henry decided to leave the conversation there. As he left the whare, the lord chancellor following behind, the fluttering flag caught his eye.

'By the way, the flag you have flying – of the United Tribes.'

'Well, then?'

'I wonder why it is flown here, of all places.'

'Why ever should it not, Mr Williams! It is a symbol of independence, and when the tribes sold their land they passed to us that independence – hence the flag.'

Now it was time to tackle William Wakefield.

Back at Petone, Henry was shown into a house where several men were seated. He carried with him his copy of the treaty.

The men stood up and one came towards him, stopping without shaking hands. Colonel Wakefield had a large nose and a small, pursed mouth and he gazed at Henry with cold, watchful eyes. He indicated the rolled-up paper in Henry's hand. 'And what have we here?'

Henry held it out. 'It is the Treaty of Waitangi, sir. Would you care to read it?'

'How dare you bring that rubbish into my house!' Wakefield theatrically backed away as if the paper were doused in poison.

'It is an official document drawn up by the government to establish a legal British presence in New Zealand.'

'Pah! A device to amuse savages!' Wakefield turned towards the other men, who guffawed dutifully.

'I think, sir, you should take this treaty seriously. Your land purchases —'

'Our purchases were made before Hobson set foot in New Zealand.'

'Did you not know that Governor Hobson has made a proclamation?'

'I care nothing for his proclamation!'

'That all claims to title are invalid unless confirmed by the Crown.'

'I tell you, Mr Williams, we are not bound by any "proclamation" that Hobson may make, nor by any pantomime he might indulge in with the natives in some far-distant spot in the country. At Port Nicholson we have established our own government.'

High treason, Hobson would call it, thought Henry. However, he wasn't about to pick a fight over that particular hot potato. Instead he stood there steadily, not allowing Wakefield to dominate him.

'Be that as it may,' he said, 'my instructions are to take the treaty to the chiefs of this area, and to seek to obtain their signatures.'

'You will be waiting a long time, as I have forbidden them to sign.'

'Very well, if that is your wish. However, I have a proposal to make.'

'A proposal!' Once again Wakefield turned to the men for more laughs. Then he turned back to Henry.

'We know you missionaries! You don't want anyone else to have land because you're desperate to keep it for yourselves. You're nothing but a pack of grasping hypocrites!' He crossed his arms and eyeballed

Henry. 'Well then, Mr Holier-than-thou, *Reverend* –' he dwelt on this last word with emphasis – 'Williams, what wonderful proposition do you have to offer?'

'I would thank you, Colonel Wakefield, to speak to me in a civil manner.'

Wakefield sneered at him. 'I speak to all as they deserve.'

At this Henry headed for the door. 'I shall not address you further on the matter while you indulge in such language. I have already spoken to Dr Evans and told him I may be able to meet the wishes of the Company. I am seeing that gentleman again in a few days and I will wait to hear what he has to say.'

Dr Evans expelled a regretful sigh. 'I have been requested by the Company to explain that we do not agree Reihana has any claim to the land in question.'

'No claim! That is ridiculous.'

'He is only a slave and has no right to it.'

Once more he was facing a battle. Really, dealing with these 'gentlemen' of the Company was much like standing up to Tohitapu, except that feisty warrior was far less devious.

'I am well acquainted with the customs of New Zealand,' he said. 'And I maintain the right of Reihana to the land, which was his long before Colonel Wakefield arrived in this country.'

Evans harrumphed derisively.

Time to depart. However, he would still have the last word: 'I did hope, Dr Evans, we could have arranged this matter quietly. However, if you think otherwise we can only conclude that I have shown my willingness to enter into an accommodation, whereas you have declined my offer. Therefore you, and the other gentlemen of the New Zealand Company, must take the consequences.'

26

After five days not one chief had signed the treaty and Henry saw no point in remaining in Port Nicholson. Apart from which, perhaps it was time for a little brinkmanship.

He ordered a boat to take him back to the ship and began to put his belongings together.

The ploy worked.

Wakefield appeared at his cabin door. He removed his hat and entered.

'I hear you are about to depart, Mr Williams, and I have come to make an apology.'

Henry waited without speaking for him to continue.

'I regret that I should have given way to my hasty feelings this last Saturday. And I would not want you to leave the port with an unfavourable impression. In fact, I am ready, if you wish, to make a public apology.'

Aha! The fox had walked into the trap. Henry knew Wakefield badly wanted the land at Thorndon, which was necessary for the new township to be a success, and he would make any sacrifice – at least, as long as it was confined to words.

'Yes, Colonel, I do very much regret that you allowed yourself to be carried away by your feelings. However, your apology is sufficient and I desire no more. Now – I would like to discuss the sixty acres I own in Port Nicholson; I bought the land to protect the interests of Reihana, but I realise it is a most important and valuable area without which your town would suffer. Is that not correct?'

Wakefield grunted assent.

'In my previous conversation with Dr Evans I learned that you have made arrangements for reserves to be set aside for the Māori people here?'

'That is correct, Mr Williams. These reserves amount to one tenth of the land we propose for development.'

'In that case I see no further reason for me to hold on to the land. As a result of these reserves being made I could present my property, free of charge, to the Company.'

The sour look on Wakefield's face began to dissipate.

'Free of charge?'

Henry nodded.

'That is very generous of you, Mr Williams!'

'But in order to show that the land is mine by right of purchase I would reserve one acre for myself and one for Reihana.'

Henry signed the Deed of Gift, which delineated the tract of land in question as being 'in the place now commonly called Thorndon, extending from the beach to the mountain called Tinakore, and bounded on the south side by the brook called Pipitea, and on the north side by the brook called Raurimu'.

After the signing the gentlemen of the New Zealand Company were clearly elated, shaking hands with Henry and with each other. Even Wakefield's face bore a thin smile.

'We cannot allow this act of magnanimity to pass unnoticed,' one of them said to Henry. 'Surely you would like country sections to be attached to these two acres?'

'Not at all. I am quite happy for things as they stand. However, you might, if you thought proper, make some acknowledgement of the transaction.'

'No problem, no problem at all!' they chorused.

'And, of course, I would be obliged if you could encourage the chiefs of Port Nicholson to sign the treaty.'

Henry turned to go, but just as he reached the door, Wakefield called him back.

He saw that the colonel's mouth had returned to a cold, hard line: the colonel realised he'd been outsmarted.

'By the way, Mr Williams, I should inform you that the name for our new town has been decided upon. It is to be called Wellington, after the great duke.'

'The hero of Waterloo – that seems appropriate.'

'It is not so much for his bravery in war that we have chosen to honour him. It is because of his enthusiastic and ongoing support for the New Zealand Company. Anyone who supports this project is our friend – but I warn you, Mr Williams, as far as my brother and I are concerned, anyone who is against us is our enemy.'

After gaining the signatures of thirty two chiefs at Port Nicholson, plus many more in Queen Charlotte Sound, Waikanae and Kapiti, including that of the great chief Te Rauparaha, finally Henry was back in the Bay.

He and Marianne stood there, a man and a woman with their arms around each other, in their house by the sea. He could feel her body trembling and when he loosened his embrace to look better at her he saw the tears in her beautiful blue eyes.

'It has been too long,' he said.

'Every time you leave I think I will never see you again. And –'

'Yes?'

'Problems always seem so much greater when you've not here to help solve them.'

'What sort of problems?'

'Oh, nothing really. It's just those officials of the governor's – always parading around and causing a lot of noise and bother. They've taken over the space where the people used to gather when they wanted to talk to us. And now they've cut down the trees.'

'What trees?'

'The pohutukawa trees at the end of the bay where the rocks are – you might have noticed when you came into shore.'

'I was looking out for you. Why did they cut them?'

'The policemen said they needed better visibility so they could protect the governor.'

Henry sighed with annoyance. He was heartily fed up with the officials causing trouble with their petty decisions, forever asking for help and intruding on his and the family's space. In March they'd even left the government's treasury chest in his care and it was still in the house – no doubt an extra worry for Marianne in his absence.

He held his wife away from him and looked at her closely. Her skin was still flawless, but there were dark lines under her eyes and a few more strands of grey had appeared in her hair.

Again he hugged her to him. 'I think it's time we left them to sort things out for themselves.'

'No more politics?'

'Absolutely none! This is the last time I go on errands for Hobson, or anyone else, for that matter. From now on I'll stay right by your side – if that's all right with you, Mrs Williams.'

Marianne dropped him a mock curtsy. 'Delighted I'm sure, Mr Williams!'

At least the governor appeared to have recovered; in fact, when he arrived at Paihia and found his wife waiting for him on the beach, he reportedly fair leapt into her arms.

But Hobson was still not in a fit state to take complete control and behind his back the surveyor-general, Felton Mathew, and the colonial secretary, Willoughby Shortland, who had now taken up the position of acting governor, were claiming he was too mentally deranged to discharge his duties. Henry had also heard there was a plot afoot on another matter – to make Okiato Point, near Kororāreka, the capital of New Zealand and to get Hobson to pay an inflated price for the land.

Having already advised the governor against the Bay of Islands as a site for the centre of government, Henry was surprised at the choice of Okiato. However, it belonged to James Clendon, a British merchant and shipowner who seemed to be closely involved with Mathew and Shortland. For his three hundred acres Clendon was asking twenty three thousand pounds.

Mathew wrote a report dismissing Busby's suggestion of Waitangi – too exposed, and ships could only land safely when it was calm; while Kororāreka was too shallow. He did not mention Auckland, which Henry thought had already been decided upon.

Then it was announced a shipload of immigrants was due to arrive. They would need somewhere to build houses and settle. Hobson was anxious and could not make up his mind. Felton Mathew helped matters along by making an offer for the land at Okiato without the governor's knowledge, and after recommending the purchase kindly drafted an agreement for him to sign.

Maybe Governor Gipps in Sydney smelt a rat and vetoed the purchase. On the other hand it may have simply been a matter of Gipps resenting Mathew going over his head to the colonial secretary in London to ask for permission.

In spite of Gipps' objection the sale eventually went through, although the payment was not on the scale originally hoped for. Clendon received two thousand, two hundred and fifty pounds, plus ten thousand acres at Papakura, south of the Waitematā Harbour: Mathew said the American consul, a post Clendon also held, had been 'scandalously used by the government'.

The governor no longer seemed to be interested in gaining more signatures for the treaty: perhaps he found it all too difficult – or was he in a state of panic? He was exceedingly perturbed about the antics of the New Zealand Company, and eventually in May, on the basis of signatures already gathered, Henry heard that British sovereignty had been declared over the whole of the North Island.

Then Hobson was warned by Gipps about two individuals in Sydney – a lawyer, William Charles Wentworth, and a merchant by the name of Johnny Jones – who claimed to have bought almost the whole of the South Island from the local chiefs.

Finally came word the French were heading for a place named Akaroa on Banks Peninsula in order to claim New Zealand for themselves.

Suddenly everyone wanted the land.

Hastily, after sending a ship down to collect signatures from only three places – Ōnuku in Akaroa, Ōtākou on Otago Harbour, and the island of Ruapuke near Stewart Island – Hobson declared sovereignty over the South Island, saying he based this on its discovery by Captain James Cook.

Hobson made these proclamations even before Henry had returned from gathering signatures for the treaty. Had he wasted his time voyaging round the North Island, plus visiting the tribes in Queen Charlotte Sound, and facing up to Wakefield and his cronies – only for Hobson to take the bull by the horns and make an overall announcement?

The best thing to come out of all this, as far as Henry was concerned, was that the officials were definitely to move from Paihia to Okiato Point, which would become the first capital of New Zealand. Hobson had decreed, no doubt to curry favour with the powers-that-be in London, that in honour of the Colonial Secretary, Lord John Russell, Okiato would henceforward be known as Russell.

Whatever they called it Henry was delighted to see them go. Now Paihia could return to its habitual quiet and peace.

And he could get on with his work for the mission.

But in September he learned that Colonel Wakefield was not yet finished with him. The former wrote a letter to *The Times* of London in which he accused Henry of obtaining the sixty acres at Port Nicholson in an underhand and fraudulent manner, and of demanding a slice of land for himself before he would come to an agreement. 'I cannot express to you,' said Wakefield, 'the feelings of repugnance entertained by the respectable colonists who came in contact with Mr Williams, on account of his selfish views, his hypocrisy, and unblushing rapaciousness.'

So that was the 'acknowledgement' the Company had promised him!

And the next year, William Colenso wrote to the Church Missionary Society, obliquely complaining about Henry's purchase of land at Pakaraka and the amount of time he spent there: Henry saw the letter because it had been agreed that all correspondence with the CMS would be made public.

Colenso said to the CMS: 'It is almost a matter of impossibility for a man to be a missionary among the heathen and a possessor of lands and cattle, etc, etc, the same having to be looked after or attended to by himself.'

27

Bay of Islands, 1844

Disaster.

Hōne Wiremu Heke Pōkai, the first person to sign the Treaty of Waitangi, had lost faith in that treaty. At Kororāreka he cut down the flagstaff bearing the British flag and the treaty was, he said, 'all soap – very smooth and oily, but treachery is hidden underneath'.

Henry could understand. Heke was a high-ranking chief who insisted on maintaining his authority. Not only had he been annoyed by government customs charges being put on shipping, which meant he could no longer levy his own dues; he was also upset that Hobson had now moved the capital from Okiato to Auckland, with the loss of mana it entailed. But, probably the most infuriating of all, he and the other chiefs were being treated by the local Europeans with disrespect.

Then there was a group of Americans who resented the British taking control so they took to stirring up trouble with chiefs like Heke. They told him the flagstaff was a sign the Queen had taken over New Zealand and the Māori people were now slaves.

Probably they also told him how they'd got rid of the British from their country and recommended the Māori people do the same. Whatever the case, Heke had taken to flying the American flag on his waka.

Henry had a good relationship with Heke, who he knew still regarded him and his brother with great affection. Before the first cutting down of the flagpole William, who'd come up from the East Coast, managed to persuade him not to act, and Heke kept to his promise – in a manner of speaking: Te Haratua, his right-hand man, chopped it down instead.

When Henry arrived back from the East Coast, where he'd exchanged stations with his brother, he found an atmosphere seething with discontent.

Because of the volatile situation the police magistrate for the Bay of Islands asked him to go to Opua to meet the chief Kawiti, who had arrived with his war party from Waiomio and was intent on causing trouble. As a pretext, he was demanding utu for an incident that had occurred at Kororāreka and following that had stolen eight horses.

At Opua Henry faced up to Kawiti and his taua. He stayed there for four days insisting they give back the horses and finally they agreed.

The flagstaff had been resurrected, but on 9 January Heke came to Paihia complaining about the government, and the next day went to Kororāreka and cut it down again.

The police magistrate asked Henry to intervene and he went to the camp of Heke to remonstrate and came away reassured.

Back in September 1842 William Hobson, first Governor of New Zealand, had died of a heart attack. He was replaced by Robert FitzRoy, who arrived a year later.

Alarmed at the situation that was now developing in the Bay of Islands, FitzRoy ordered more troops from Sydney and in the meantime sent a detachment to the Bay of Islands to demonstrate British military power.

Henry knew that such a display of force would only exacerbate matters. Two government officials came to him to discuss re-erecting the flagstaff and he told them not to as it would only be removed.

But it was rebuilt and on 19 January, again Heke cut down the flagstaff.

At Kororāreka Henry met the chiefs Tāmati Wāka Nene and Rewa. They were not disposed to discuss the situation but invited him to attend an assembly of chiefs where Ururoa from Whangaroa would be present.

There Henry moved among them, speaking to each chief in turn, trying to persuade them not to join Heke. They listened to him courteously but they were angry.

That night all the chiefs present criticised the government, with even Tāmati Wāka Nene and Rewa complaining that the cause of their troubles was the treaty.

Henry then stood up to speak. He went through all the clauses of the treaty, explaining them one by one and asking the chiefs to find one instance of where they had been deprived of their rights or where their interests had been betrayed by the government.

Eventually they accepted his arguments and Ururoa assured him he would not go with Heke.

Henry informed the police magistrate of the outcome of his attempts at reconciliation, and of his success in gaining the allegiance of Wāka Nene, Rewa and Ururoa. Governor FitzRoy sent him a letter saying, 'I consider that this country and Great Britain owe you deep gratitude for your untiring efforts to put mistaken people onto the right track.'

However, Kawiti and his followers were still active.

Henry went to see the chief, but it was clear Kawiti was planning a major confrontation with the government.

On 4 March Hōne Heke appeared back in the Bay and set up camp near Kororāreka, joining forces with Kawiti. Four days later Henry and the police magistrate went to their camp in a last-ditch effort to prevent an attack.

By now the eighteen-gun HMS *Hazard* from the Royal Navy had arrived. A message was sent to Lieutenant Philpotts, commander of the ship, informing him an attack on Kororāreka was imminent, but Philpotts treated the warning with contempt.

At dawn on 11 March about six hundred warriors armed with muskets, double-barrelled guns and mere stormed the British soldiers guarding the flagstaff on Maiki Hill. Caught by surprise, the defenders were all killed and for the fourth time the flagstaff was chopped down.

Simultaneously, Kawiti and his followers attacked Kororāreka.

Fierce battles were fought between soldiers and warriors, and women and children were evacuated. When both Māori and Europeans began to loot the abandoned buildings Philpotts gave the order to bombard the town. Then the taua began to burn every house in the northern part: Heke had given instructions that the southern part, including the Anglican Christ Church and the Roman Catholic Mission, were to be spared.

From Paihia Henry heard the sound of cannons. He and two others immediately left for Kororāreka, where they found the place strewn with the bodies of the dead and wounded.

The *Hazard* was still protecting the women and children as they escaped, and under cover of this fire Henry made his way up Maiki Hill, where he found the bodies of the soldiers defending the flagstaff, and also that of a child, half Māori, half European.

Hōne Heke appeared. With a sideways jerk of his head he indicated the bodies, then he took one by the feet. Henry took the head and together in silence the two men carried each one down the hill and deposited them in boats for conveyance to the British ship.

It was quite probable that Heke himself had violently extinguished the life of these people not long before. Henry supposed it was because he'd seen his friend struggling to deal with the bodies that he'd come to help.

With Māori sympathetic to the government with him in his boat, Henry tied up by the *Hazard* and while he was waiting alongside the crew on board began shouting insults.

Henry was worried they would start firing at the friendly Māori. He caught sight of Lieutenant Philpotts and called to him to stop his men.

But Philpotts looked down at him and shouted, 'Traitor!'

The next day Henry went with two of his sons, Thomas and John, to help those who had escaped Kororāreka retrieve what belongings they could. While they were there the *Hazard* began firing into the town, and in response the Māori attackers set fire to the rest of the houses.

To the booming of guns from the ship, stumbling through smoke and burning ash, his nostrils stinging with acrid fumes, Henry continued helping the settlers.

He passed the Anglican church and saw that although it was still standing its wooden walls were splattered with bullet holes.

Ha! In the light of the flames that were engulfing the township appeared a man with a tattooed face, flourishing a mere. The naked warrior bent his face to Henry's and there was a strong smell of rum on his breath.

The Māori had found the alcohol stores. Once they were intoxicated they would be completely out of control and extremely dangerous.

He ran to fetch his sons and the settlers: 'Go! You must get out immediately!'

Henry was the last European to leave the ravaged town: and that night at Paihia he offered shelter to about fifty refugees.

Later he wrote to Edward Marsh, describing the events he had witnessed and of which he despaired: 'How many are ruined by this fatal stroke! I am sorry, sorry, sorry, and well nigh overdone.'

And how the charge of 'traitor' hurt. He supposed it was because of his friendship with Hōne Heke.

The charge was echoed in an Auckland newspaper, where he was abused as an 'Arch Traitor, False Prophet and Reverend Impostor'.

The battle of Kororāreka was only the beginning.

A small military force arrived, sent by FitzRoy to attack Kawiti in his stronghold at Waiomio. Henry was invited to the council of war and managed to persuade the British not to attempt such a foolhardy expedition across several rivers. He told them, 'You may get to Waiomio, but you will never return.'

Then they decided on an attack against the pā of Puketutu, which Hōne Heke had now built near Lake Omāpere. Again Henry, knowing how rough was the terrain, warned them it would be impossible to accomplish without great loss of life. He tried to negotiate with Heke, but the chief would not accept the terms offered by the British.

The attack on Puketutu failed, with twenty eight Māori and thirteen British killed.

Then Ngā Puhi hapū of the Bay of Islands and those of the Hokianga, long-standing rivals, turned on each other.

Tāmati Wākā Nene of Hokianga had given an assurance to the British that Kororāreka would not be attacked and the chief felt that in doing so Hōne Heke had betrayed his trust. He saw also that, with Kororāreka gone Heke had ruined their chances of making any economic gain.

For his part Hōne Heke taunted Wākā Nene that in supporting the

British he was 'fighting for blankets'. This was an insult to the mana of the powerful chief and had to be avenged.

Hōne Heke had built a pā at Te Ahuahu and while he and his men were away replenishing their supplies Wākā Nene seized the pā.

On 12 June 1845 Hōne Heke tried to retake Te Ahuahu and this battle resulted in the loss of many lives.

During the battle Heke was seriously wounded – shot through the thigh – and was taken to the healing spring at Ngāwhā to recuperate.

Henry walked up north to see him. When he arrived he found Heke lying on his side, obviously in great pain. His attendants were occupied in removing the pus that flowed from the wound and burying it in the ground: with a chief of such great mana any bodily fluids needed to be carefully treated because they were highly tapu.

He knelt down. As he did so he was aware of the incongruous sight he made: a middle-aged, bespectacled Englishman speaking in Māori to a renowned warrior, trying to persuade him to stop fighting. But he had known Heke since he was a boy and there had always been a bond between them.

Now Heke slowly raised himself on his elbow and looked Henry in the eye. 'E tino mōhio ana koe, Karu-whā,' he said, 'he toa tū taua ahau – kore rawa e mutu taku whawhai.'

He was a fighting man, and would continue to be so.

Meanwhile, when the British heard that Heke had been incapacitated they decided to strike as soon as possible. This time it was on yet another pā built by Heke – Ōhaeawai.

But by now the Māori fighters had learnt to build their fortifications in a manner that could withstand the bombardment: on the top of a hill they sheltered in pits and tunnels sunk under the ground and the palisades surrounding the pā were covered in flax leaves, which slowed down the speed of the musket balls. Behind the outer palisades and in front of the inner ones were trenches where the warriors could shelter from fire, reload their weapons and continue their defence.

Designed by Kawiti, the whole pā was extraordinarily well defended and Henry wasn't surprised when the British assault on Ōhaeawai failed. To underline the victory the defenders emerged from the pā and performed a triumphant haka.

When he arrived at the battlefield many wounded soldiers were being carried into the camp. He helped attend to them, bandaging their wounds and trying to ease the pain of men in agony.

When evening fell he was asked to go to the pā to bring back the bodies of those who had been killed, but Kawiti shouted at him to go back.

The next day he tried again, with the same response.

But on the third day the defenders of the pā raised a flag of truce and Henry and another went. Forty one bodies, ripped to pieces by bullets, lay scattered among the bushes. Their bright red uniforms, designed to disguise any blood-letting, had made them sitting targets for the men firing from the pā.

Henry went to retrieve one crumpled body in the uniform of a naval officer, lying face down on the ground. He turned him over and there, his face white in death and eyes bulging with shock and pain, was Philpotts.

He stood there for a few minutes. Then he murmured, 'Father, forgive him, for he knew not what he did.'

He knelt down and closed the staring eyes. Then he took a knife out of his back pocket and gently cut off a lock of Philpott's hair, and also picked up his eyeglass, which had fallen on the ground. He gave the items to the man accompanying him and asked him to see to it that the items were sent to Philpott's family.

Death was hideous. War was insane. When would men see sense?

FitzRoy was to be recalled.

This was a blow to the missionaries, for the governor had always supported and trusted them, and tried to base his policies on their advice.

It was rumoured that the reason for his recall was the machinations of the New Zealand Company in England and the vociferous complaints by its settlers in Wellington. They hated the way FitzRoy 'pandered' to the missionaries, particularly to Henry, and they wanted someone to take a strong stand against the Māori 'rebels'.

Henry had lost a major supporter. After the abuse from Philpotts and the slander in the Auckland newspapers he had written to FitzRoy, who replied, 'To say that Henry Williams – the tried, the proved, the loyal, the indefatigable – of being a "traitor", of having acted "traitorously" seemed to me so utterly absurd, to say the very least, that such an idea could not be entertained by me for one moment.'

Captain George Grey landed in Auckland to take up the position of governor on 14 October 1845 and within a few days of his arrival appeared in the Bay.

Henry met him and when he looked into his eyes, he knew. In Governor Grey he had an enemy.

28

Auckland, December 1845

George Grey seated himself at his escritoire in Government House. He had many matters requiring attention, but for a minute he tapped the end of his quill against his teeth and stared out the window.

It was raining. Rain! It never stopped here. Eliza said living in Auckland was like being stuck in a shower bath. He'd tried to explain to his wife that the place was on an isthmus, with the Pacific Ocean on one side and the Tasman Sea on the other, and when the clouds from either sea struck the land they emptied their contents right here.

Of course she wasn't interested. She was a beautiful woman and her attention began and ended with herself. She was also young, with twenty two years to his thirty three: he hoped that one day she would grow into the role of gracious wife of the governor.

On the other hand you could say he himself fulfilled the role perfectly. It was his destiny to be a leader of men – in fact, a hero – and at present it was his task to shape this farthest outpost of the British Empire.

He reached across to the front of his writing desk and gently fingered the medal for gallantry that reposed in its specially made box. It had been sent to his mother by the Duke of Wellington after his father's death. Colonel Grey was engaged in a battle against the French in Spain and died leading the bayonet charge over the ramparts of the citadel of Badajoz. It was a victory, but there was an extremely heavy loss of life. When his eight-months-pregnant wife heard the news she was so shocked she went into labour a few days later and young George was born on 14 April 1812.

And then there was the gold snuff box placed next to the medal: this had been presented to his mother's father by his fellow officers to commemorate his daring exploit in rowing through the Spanish fleet during a siege of Gibraltar.

Two precious items — both signifying the courageous past of his ancient and aristocratic family, and the enormous expectations they now held of their golden boy.

And so far he had certainly not disappointed. He enrolled at Sandhurst, where they were very impressed with him and from which he graduated with a special mention of his 'superior merits and talents'. He served the army in Ireland, but after seeing firsthand the misery of the Irish peasants under British rule, he decided the best solution for them was to emigrate to a place where they could make a new life for themselves.

Then he'd been bitten by the bug: Australia! — its fascinating wildlife and stone-age people. He'd managed to persuade the powers-that-be to allow him to take an exploring party there and search for an inland waterway that was rumoured to exist in the northwest of the country. Then he led another expedition to Shark Bay. Neither venture was successful as there proved to be no great river flowing across northwestern Australia; and although he claimed there was a large and fertile plain inland from Shark Bay, no one at the time believed him.

He and his men had endured extraordinary hardship, struggling over arid terrain in searing heat and violent rainstorms. One man died and

Grey only survived the second expedition because he was rescued by a group of Aborigines. By the time he arrived in Perth he had almost lost his good looks and was unrecognisable. But he was also mentally hardened, because he had discovered along the way that the men with whom he had suffered such privations blamed him for their plight and disliked him.

However, he had successfully played the role of Great White Explorer, and he was content with that. Also, he'd become famous because he'd written a very entertaining book about his 'adventures' in Western Australia.

He'd also had the opportunity to come into contact with the Aborigine people, who survived in these harsh conditions and who were able to follow him and his party without them being aware of their presence.

Come into contact! He'd certainly done that. He put his hand down to his left hip, where the sharp ache had still not gone away, and felt the indentation – a hole the size of a child's hand – that had been made by a spear. The Aborigines were clearly not happy at these strangers invading their territory and, their faces painted menacingly, they threatened them with their spears. George had responded by firing a shot over their heads and at first that had the desired effect.

But then the Aborigines began attacking and one of their spears had pierced his body. Enraged, George covered his hip so they would not know he'd been wounded, grabbed his revolver and fired. One of the men fell and his fellow warriors ran to lift him, ever so gently, and carry him away.

That night he heard the men shouting and the women wailing and as well as the physical pain of his own wound, he too felt their pain. He had never before killed a person and it was a shock to his whole being.

He began to take an active interest in the culture of the Aboriginal people and compiled a vocabulary of their languages. He also wrote a paper outlining his theories on how the Australian Aborigines could be civilised and how the two races – British and Aboriginal – might be combined.

Then he was offered a post as resident magistrate at Albany, two hundred and fifty miles south of Perth. He accepted the position because it would give him a chance to demonstrate his ability to govern.

While in Albany he met and married the sixteen-year-old daughter of the previous magistrate. The striking-looking Eliza Lucy Spencer, with her large dark eyes and jet-black hair would, he expected, be a useful helpmeet and adjunct to his career.

Finally, thanks to his connections back home, at the age of twenty eight he was appointed governor of the colony of South Australia.

There, of course, he had excelled. The colony was in a bankrupt state and George, with the confidence of youth, quickly decided the way to deal with the finances was to cut expenditure to the bone. The settlers were not happy with his actions, but he blamed all problems on the previous governor and dealt with settler grievances by downplaying their petitions to the British Government, and on the other hand misrepresenting the intentions of the Colonial Office towards them.

After five years he'd vastly improved the financial situation of the colony and the white people of South Australia loved him – well, most of them – and they were heartbroken when it was announced he was leaving. Unfortunately the race relations side of things had not gone according to plan, because the Aborigines had continued to attack the overlanders – the drovers bringing sheep from New South Wales – and the settlers counterattacked.

Then he was offered a new post in a bankrupt colony where relations between Europeans and the natives had reached a critical point. But, as the local newspaper had remarked on the occasion of his departure, 'We are sure that you will succeed even in such a blighted and wretched place as New Zealand.'

George was entirely confident he would succeed: bringing order out of chaos was his forte. And then, with the outstanding governance of both the colonies of South Australia and New Zealand under his belt, he would have the pick of any post in the whole of the British Empire.

And now here he was. 'Blighted and wretched' was not a bad description of his new home. Auckland, for a start, where wind and rain followed in quick succession, or concurrently, had a very small population and labour was in short supply. Food had to be imported and there was no adjacent forest to provide timber for building, and no river bringing fresh water.

Well, that had been Hobson's decision: Te Kawau, the chief of the tribe of Ngāti Whātua, went up to the Bay of Islands to ask the governor to move to Tāmaki – he wanted protection from Ngā Puhi, who in spite of the death of Hongi Hika still struck fear into people's hearts. After vacillating about whether or not to remain at Okiato, Hobson finally decided Auckland was the place. He brought his officials down, negotiated the purchase of three thousand acres from Ngāti Whātua and in March 1841 pronounced it the capital of New Zealand.

That, of course, annoyed the settlers in Wellington, who thought the government should be in the centre of the country, in other words, where they were. They were already up in arms after Hobson sent Willoughby Shortland to tear down the flag of the Independent Tribes and tell the people they must withdraw from their illegal association and submit to representatives of the Crown. The New Zealand Company crowd were a continual source of problems: they hadn't kept to their promise of providing one tenth of their land as a reserve for the natives, and in fact from the way they behaved you'd think the local Māori were just nuisance interlopers who had no claim over the land at all.

George was all for ordinary people prepared to work hard and make the best of themselves, but he had no time for speculators.

But back to Hobson. In George's opinion the first Governor of New Zealand was a disaster, although he had managed to cobble the Treaty of Waitangi together, and he was quite right to declare sovereignty over the whole country – the South Island on the basis of discovery by Captain Cook.

He'd also acted decisively with the French attempt at colonisation, sending a warship to Akaroa to raise the Union Jack and establish British authority – just in time. Captain Charles François Lavaud arrived five days later.

And in Sydney Gipps had dealt severely with Wentworth and Jones, the pair who claimed to have bought the South Island. Gipps announced that 'purported sales of land from savages' would be declared null and void; and when he was challenged by Wentworth he told him he would never get 'one acre, one foot, one shilling' for the land and he was not yet safe from a prosecution for conspiracy – all of which solved the problem for Hobson.

But then in 1842 the governor had died of a stroke.

Next they brought in FitzRoy. At least he was an aristocrat, but in his own way he was equally hopeless. The Wairau Affray had occurred under his watch, when two years ago the New Zealand Company tried to take over the Wairau Valley in Marlborough for settlement and the tribe of Ngāti Toa, who claimed the area, had objected. Arthur Wakefield, another brother of Edward Gibbon, went there with a party of about sixty men. They were met by the feared chief Te Rauparaha, renowned for his ability as a war leader and possessor of a large cache of muskets, and his nephew Te Rangihaeata, and there was a stand-off between the two parties.

FitzRoy did nothing to sort out the matter and the whole affair ended in bloodshed. Twenty two British men were shot by Māori, including Arthur; and in the eyes of the settlers this shooting of men who had already surrendered was a heinous crime. However, there'd been no attempt at retribution, FitzRoy declaring the settlers had provoked the fighting. Te Rangihaeata had killed the prisoners to avenge the death of his wife, shot during the affray.

Well! George would make sure that Te Rauparaha was dealt with very firmly. He would find some pretext to have the chief kidnapped and imprisoned, without charge if necessary, until his mana had been diminished and he was no longer a threat. Also, it was important to show the Māori race who was in charge of the country, now that FitzRoy had been replaced by himself.

On the other hand, just as he had with the Aborigines, he made a special effort to learn about Māori culture. To this end he invited the lively and good-looking Wiremu Maihi Te Rangikāheke to bring his wife and family to live at Government House and share his vast knowledge of tribal history and myths, songs and proverbs. George later published these but did not acknowledge their source. Under the guidance of Te Rangikāheke he also learnt the Māori language.

Because of this he was able to establish a rapport with many other chiefs. He reassured them as to his intentions with regard to the Treaty of Waitangi and was held in high esteem by Māori all around the country. He told them they had nothing to fear, for he was a man who always kept his word: and they believed him. They did not know he had the facility of being able to empathise swiftly and deeply with those who addressed him, but would just as quickly forget them and their needs as soon as they were gone. He was focused solely on taming this wild and mysterious land and he would sweep all else aside in order to achieve his aim.

Now to the main problem facing him at present – the Flagstaff War. There'd been several skirmishes so far, the first at Kororāreka, when the town was sacked and looted by both Māori and British, with the settlers having to be evacuated. At Puketutu the British had besieged the new pā of Heke and then retreated; and finally at a place called Ōhaeawai, a six hundred-strong force of soldiers, seamen and militia attacked Kawiti in his pā. Even so the British were outsmarted and suffered a humiliating defeat.

Altogether not a satisfactory look for the government! So George had voyaged up to the Bay of Islands to assess the situation for himself. He met the northern chiefs and praised Wākā Nene and Patuone, who had fought on the side of the British. He also offered peace proposals, originally drawn up by FitzRoy, to Kawiti and Heke. Kawiti said the problem was caused by Wākā Nene clinging to past problems among Ngā Puhi; and Heke wrote that God had made New Zealand for the Māori and England for the English, and enclosed a war song. Neither accepted the proposals.

At the Bay he'd also met the Reverend Henry Williams. In George's opinion the fellow was a missionary of the worst kind: he himself was a good Church of England man, of course, but he did not allow his faith to dictate all his actions and he certainly didn't seek to impose it on anyone else. But those of the evangelical variety were extremists, frowning on everything from crosses to candles to stained-glass windows and they looked down on anyone who did not share their views.

The hoary older missionary – he would have been in his early fifties and apparently a veteran of the Napoleonic Wars – was definitely of this ilk. And the way he dared to look at George! He stared him right in the eye – it was as if he divined the arrogant and ruthless creature that lurked behind the apparently amiable exterior.

In return, George disliked this man immediately. He much preferred the new Anglican bishop of the Church of New Zealand, George Augustus Selwyn, who was of a similar age to himself and had a far more reasonable attitude.

At this point a beam of light fell across his desk. The rain had gone, for now anyway, and from his window he looked down over lush, green slopes to the Waitematā Harbour, sparkling in the morning sun. In truth, on a good day Auckland and its harbour were second to none.

But back to Henry Williams. The fact was although George was on good terms with the Māori chiefs he did not have their total trust and respect. That mantle rested on Williams, who had lived in their country for the last twenty-odd years and through his work among their people was admired the length and breadth of the country. If George Grey was to be the absolute head of the country, looked up to and obeyed by both European and Māori, the power of his rival had to be broken.

He dipped his quill in the inkwell and the pen began to scratch out its message across the page.

By whatever means it took, he would destroy this man.

29

The Old Serpent was rearing up and baring his fangs.

Grey managed to gain the allegiance of most of the northern chiefs, but Kawiti and Heke, the latter now recovered from his hip wound, refused to accept his terms for peace. Instead, they and their taua moved to the hill of Ruapekapeka – 'the bat's nest' – and built a pā in an impregnable position high on a hill and nowhere near any settlements. They constructed a treble blockade and underground shelters to withstand enemy fire. Then they waited for the British troops to come.

Come they did, with Grey at their head, although it took them two weeks to sail up the Kawakawa River, haul their massive cannons over rough, bush-entangled territory and clamber up the hill. Finally they and their artillery were in place. They opened fire at the end of December 1845 and the siege lasted for two weeks. Then, when the British finally stormed the pā – on a Sunday, much to Henry's disgust when he heard – they found the warriors had gone.

But when the British reconnoitred they found Kawiti and his followers at the back of the pā. Maybe they'd returned to worship because it was a Sunday and did not expect to be attacked. Or maybe it was a ruse to take the troops by surprise.

The defenders hid in the forest and began firing at the British troops. There was a bout of heavy fighting. Then, again, the warriors disappeared.

The British lost twelve men with twenty nine wounded, but claimed victory. The Māori lost at least twelve men but claimed victory too, and Kawiti and Heke were hailed by their people as heroes.

This time Henry did not attempt to intervene – what was the use? Even though Grey hadn't fought a campaign before he had supreme confidence in his abilities as leader. He would never accept advice, and certainly not from Henry.

And so Henry had written to Kawiti, trying to persuade him not to join in battle with the British.

During the fight at Ruapekapeka, someone must have picked up his letters to Kawiti and passed them to Grey.

The governor used them to make his first assault. He made it known that letters, written by Henry, had been brought to him and that they were 'of a treasonable nature'.

Some of the Europeans rejoiced that 'the old traitor had been caught at last'.

Henry fought back. The letters were written, he said, at the request of FitzRoy, who was still in the country, and he had kept copies so it was quite plain his letters were not treasonable. In order to clear his name he asked the CMS to hold an inquiry into the matter. He also wrote a pamphlet, 'Plain facts relative to the Late War,' in which he denied Grey's claims.

He requested an interview with Grey so he could refute the accusations in person, but this was refused.

Instead, Grey counterattacked by saying the Christian Māori belonging to the CMS had been the ones fighting the government troops.

Henry sent him a list of the chiefs who had fought against the British, almost all of whom were non-Christian or Catholics. Grey then accused him of attacking the Roman Catholic Mission.

In the 1840s the New Zealand Company was extremely influential in Britain, where sixteen of its directors and shareholders were in the House of Commons and the Whigs, who supported the CMS, had lost power to the Tory Party. The CMS was reluctant to upset the Company because it knew the latter would campaign actively against anyone who opposed them.

In New Zealand Grey made use of the Company's antagonism towards Henry. This organisation had not ceased to attack him since his confrontation with Wakefield. They accused him of taking land illegally from the Māori people in Whanganui, and of claiming sixty acres in Wellington to which 'he had not a shadow of right'. Henry refuted both claims, pointing out that Wakefield would not have allowed him to keep an acre of this land if their claim were true.

The settlers in Wellington were especially angry because their land claims were being investigated and their attempts to obtain legal titles were stymied. George Clarke, as Protector of the Aborigines, tried to ensure the rights of Māori were upheld: the settlers blamed him, the two previous governors and the missionaries in general, in particular Henry as their head, for every problem and failure they encountered.

When FitzRoy was recalled and George Clarke was dismissed by Grey, an effigy of each man was publicly burned.

George Grey played on this antagonism.

Without any evidence at all, he began to announce that the main reason Heke and Kawiti had mounted their rebellion was because of the 'large pretended purchases of some of the missionaries'. He elaborated on this with a series of official reports, which culminated in a 'confidential' despatch to William Gladstone, at the time the secretary of Colonial Affairs.

Grey sent Gladstone a list of twenty four grants that exceeded the permitted 2560 acres per person. He said that eight of these grants related to the claims of CMS missionaries: 'I feel myself satisfied that these claims are not based upon substantial justice to the natives, nor to the large majority of British settlers in this country. Her Majesty's Government may also rest satisfied that these individuals cannot be put in possession of these tracts of land without a large expenditure of British blood and money.'

The despatch was received by the new secretary of Colonial Affairs, who passed it to the chairman of the CMS in England. The committee was horrified and sent a letter to the missionaries in New Zealand, demanding an explanation.

And somehow the supposedly confidential despatch also found its way to an Auckland newspaper, which printed it. That led to an outpouring of hatred and vituperation against the missionaries.

As head of the mission, Henry wrote a letter to the governor challenging his accusations: 'Considering that His Excellency's despatch conveys a charge of a very grave and serious nature against the missionaries in the north, of having been accessory to the shedding of human blood for the possession of land claimed by them and their children . . . I am authorised to say that the missionaries shrink with horror from such a charge, and are prepared to relinquish their claim altogether upon its being shown that their claim would render the possibility of such an awful circumstance as the shedding of one drop of human blood.'

He put seven questions to the governor, asking him to prove his allegations.

Grey did not reply. Instead he continued to attack, twisting the truth with slander after slander, lie upon lie.

Henry was blamed for the publication of Grey's 'Blood and Treasure' despatch. In spite of him having nothing to do with this, he was rebuked by the CMS.

Grey tried to stir up the Māori people in the north, telling them the missionaries had stolen their land. Not one of the chiefs responded by criticising Henry or complaining about the land he'd bought from them. When Grey's officials tried to find evidence of Māori objections to Henry's purchase, there was none.

However, the stationing of British troops at the mission station of Te Waimate had caused resentment and suspicion among the chiefs, and some of them turned on Henry, accusing him of having misled them with his explanations of what signing the treaty would mean.

Because of the fighting, the work of the missionaries had dwindled before their eyes. The soldiers and the Māori warriors plundered the food supplies, so those producing them gave up. This led to starvation and disease and many of the people died: in some cases half of each settlement disappeared. The churches and schools the missionaries had laboured so hard to set up, and which had flourished for so long, were now almost empty.

Then Grey co-opted Bishop Selwyn. George Augustus Selwyn had arrived in the Bay in June 1842. At first Henry had been impressed by this first bishop of the Anglican church in New Zealand – he was a pleasant-mannered, charming man, although of somewhat severe countenance, but full of energy and apparently very supportive of the work of the mission.

But gradually Henry realised that unlike the CMS missionaries the bishop was not at all of the evangelical persuasion, which valued simplicity and a low-key form of worship. In fact, as someone remarked, he was there to create a hierarchy, not a church.

Henry found, too, that Selwyn expected the Anglican missionaries to include Europeans in their ministry, but they refused, saying they'd come to New Zealand for the sake of the Māori people.

And then, after Grey had written to Selwyn requesting his support against the missionaries who had acquired land, Selwyn turned against them and, as their head, Henry.

There was no need for further acquisition of land to support their children, the bishop said, and also the grant by the CMS of fifty pounds to each son and forty pounds to each daughter when they turned fifteen was the equal of two hundred acres for each son and one hundred and fifty acres for each daughter, and that should be enough for them to live on. Apart from that, he said, echoing Grey's accusations, land purchases by missionaries had 'in some cases alienated the affections of the natives from their missionary' and had 'subjected us all to the most injurious suspicion'. In other words, they were the cause of the Flagstaff War.

Henry challenged Selwyn to prove his allegations, but the bishop said he 'reserved the right to offer proof at a time of his own choosing'.

Blows were being rained down on his head from all directions. And then came the final bombshell.

30

Henry was rounding the tip of the peninsula, travelling to Paroa Bay by boat when he spotted his children's ship, named *The Children*, appearing through the heads on its return from Auckland.

He told his crew to ship oars and wait until they came alongside. John called out they had something for him and he stood in the boat as his son clambered down the rope ladder and handed him a letter.

It was from the CMS. He sat down and read it. Then he put the letter in his pocket and commanded the crew to go about.

As they crossed the sea back to Paihia Henry's heart was pounding and his hands were shaking. Over and over in his head ran the contents of the letter he had just read – and if he had to admit, there were tears in his eyes. Was it really true: could the CMS really have done this to him?

The houses on the shore were drawing closer and he gave himself a shake. For Marianne, for the sake of the family, he must be brave.

Once on land he stood for a moment, surveying the settlement he had founded: the row of houses along the foreshore with their neat gardens and cultivations, and the flag flying on the hill behind.

He opened the gate to the home that had been built and rebuilt with so much effort and walked up the winding path past the flower beds he'd planted. He'd managed to keep the dark red Sweet Williams going and they greeted him cheerily, unknowing.

Marianne opened the door and came rushing down the path. 'What's happened? Have you forgotten something?'

Silently he shook his head and after hugging her tightly he took her hand and led her into the house.

They sat in his study and he could see anxiety already clouding her beloved face.

He took out the letter and handed it to her.

'Terrible news,' he said.

'What?'

'The CMS have expelled us.'

'No!'

She bent her head and began to read. Then she laid the letter in her lap and stared at him, her face full of horror.

'It is cruel and unjust. How could they?'

How could they indeed. He thought back to the hardships he and Marianne had endured – leaving their home and loved ones knowing they would probably never see them again, setting up here at Paihia, raising children in the midst of ever-present danger: then there were the regular reports he had assiduously written and sent to the people in London, often in the midst of a crisis.

He let out a deep sigh. 'I suppose those who are in the CMS now are not the ones who sent us out: I believe Josiah Pratt died six years ago. The present staff are unaware of the dangers that we faced at the beginning on their behalf, and of the work we have done since.'

'Even so . . .'

'And they have been pressured.'

'By the governor?'

'By Grey, and the New Zealand Company, and Selwyn.'
'Do you think he's won?'
'Grey?'
She stared at him with intensity.
'I meant – Satan.'

Henry gazed out the window, seeing but not seeing the impervious sea. Certainly things had been piling up against him. His land purchases, for example: Governor FitzRoy had granted him nine thousand acres, which he'd handed over to his children, but in buying that land he'd given ammunition to the New Zealand Company and George Grey. Had he been manipulated by the Devil, who'd put forward a compelling reason, like the welfare of his family, to tempt him into this situation?

And then, the Treaty of Waitangi. Again, in espousing this he'd acted out of a sense of duty, believing that as a British person he should support the British Government. With regard to the Māori people he hoped this treaty would be a sort of Magna Carta, setting out their individual rights in a formal document. From now on they would all have equal rights, both chief and slave, and he'd expected that the British Government would honour the promises it contained.

But the floods of settlers entering the country had come with the intent of bettering themselves. Their main interest was in acquiring land, to which the treaty was merely an obstacle. Furthermore, they regarded the original inhabitants as inferior to themselves.

He may have helped tame one howling wilderness, but now another wilderness had been created.

The settlers hated him for championing the cause of the Māori; who in turn blamed him for encouraging them to sign the treaty and thus lose control over their own country.

Everyone, it seemed, was against him.

He'd always steered by his own compass, always been so sure he was on the right track. Maybe he was wrong and should have been more humble.

However, with regard to the land purchases he could at least be sure, as far as possible, that his children would not be wanting in the future — and if his reputation suffered, so be it.

And with regard to the treaty . . . Its hasty drawing-up was so haphazard, with the eventual signing seeming like a miracle, that he believed the process must have been guided from above. Therefore he was sure the Lord would see that this treaty endured and eventually fulfilled its purpose.

So no, he was not about to give way now to the Vile Fiend.

He turned back to Marianne. 'Remember the story in the Bible about how the disciples were out at sea when a storm blew up. They turned to Jesus, who was on board, and cried out to him, and he calmed the wind and waves and rebuked them for not having faith. We must remember that no matter how bad things may seem, he is always with us.'

She looked at him and he saw there were tears running down her cheeks, but she managed a weak smile and a nod.

He took her hand and stroked it. 'I know this is hard, but we have to accept it — we must leave Paihia.'

She gave a little cry. 'Leave! Why?'

'The house and the land it is on belong to the CMS. We cannot stay here.'

She swallowed. 'How soon, do you think?'

'Now.'

It was Saturday. They decided not to disturb Sunday's worship by announcing their departure and went about their normal duties, even though inside their hearts were breaking.

Every now and then Henry glanced at his wife and saw her glistening eyes and trembling hands.

He was not much better. At their last church service, as he gave his final sermon Henry looked along the rows of familiar faces. In spite of the disruption caused by the Flagstaff War he'd managed to keep the Māori congregation together and today they were there in good numbers. The Europeans too were well represented. How would Marianne manage without the friends she'd made and the families in whose lives she had become so involved?

On Sunday afternoon he went out the back, to his garden. It was the end of autumn, so the vegetables were spent: the stalks of the runner beans clung to their poles with dry brown fingers and the flowering plants had faded. But he was aware, too, as always, of a stillness in this place, a feeling of deep contentment and peace.

But from Monday onwards all was chaos. The work of packing up was continually interrupted. Many Māori chiefs arrived – among them Pene Taui, who at the battle of Ōhaeawai along with Kawiti had got the better of the British troops, came from inland and Pukututu came from Kawakawa with his whole tribe. The nephews of Kawiti and Taiwhanga, and Te Haratua, the close ally of Hōne Heke, also came. All wanted to express their outrage and grief that 'Karu-whā' should have been treated so harshly and was departing.

Then there were the Europeans. James Busby brought a testimonial, signed by members of the parish, attesting to their appreciation of Henry and Marianne's work and expressing their deep regret at the dismissal.

On their last day they invited several Māori friends to breakfast with them and later Europeans from Christ Church at Kororāreka, where Henry had been taking services, came from across the Bay to make their farewells.

The horses arrived. They would convey them to Pakaraka, where it had been decided they would now make their home with their son Henry and his wife Jane.

When they swung themselves up into the saddles there were cries of lamentation and the people from Kororāreka crowded round. As they rode along the road they had to stop several times to lean down and shake the hands of their Māori neighbours. At various places along the way groups had gathered, waving and crying.

Edward rode by the side of Marianne, John with Henry and Thomas with their daughter Kate. They were accompanied by Pene Taui's men on horseback, with the chief himself following behind. Running alongside were about fifteen children from the school Kate had been taking.

All went with them as far as the Tī. There came three loud cheers from the crew of *The Children*, which was moored on the Waitangi River.

Then they turned inland: less than a week after receiving the CMS letter, on 31 May 1850 the Williams family departed from the Bay of Islands.

31

They arrived before nightfall. Everyone was smiling and waving a welcome, and as soon as they dismounted they were surrounded by their grandchildren.

With many excited giggles the children led them into the house built by Henry and Jane. They crowded into the sitting room. 'Look!' shouted one of the children.

'I can't believe it!' cried Marianne. She put her hands over her eyes, then looked again.

A fire was roaring in the hearth and on either side of it were placed their familiar armchairs. On the mantelpiece reposed their own ornaments and on the walls, as they looked around, hung the very same pictures, all brought from Paihia.

The children took them each by the hand and guided them to their chairs. Jane brought them tea, and then Kate and Lydia seated themselves at the piano and together played a duet.

Henry leant his elbow on his chair, his chin resting on his thumb, and watched his two daughters playing as one, their full skirts spread out over the piano stool, their graceful hands moving across the keys. Now and again they turned to smile at their parents.

As the cheerful notes danced through the room he looked across at Marianne. Again her eyes were full of tears, but this time they sprang from joy.

'Oh, my darling!' she said, beaming at him. 'One would think we'd been picked up, transported through the air and set down in our old place. It's like magic!'

It was amazing how Marianne could rally in the midst of a crisis and find the best of things.

But she was right. It was magic – wrought by the love of their family; and amongst their own the warmth and reassurance they received was exactly what they needed.

But where to from here? He would have to wait and see what the Lord wished for him.

He did not have to wait long.

Tamati Pukututu and the people from his pā at Kawakawa built a road to Pakaraka; Te Haratua, whose pā at Pakaraka had been destroyed by the British troops and who had escaped to Mangakahia, returned. From all around Northland the Māori people flocked to be near 'Karu-whā', or, as they called him now to show more respect, 'Te Wiremu'.

When he'd bought the land there, as well as providing an income for his children Henry had envisaged that a settlement at Pakaraka would be a 'light in the wilderness', and so it had proved to be.

However, he was not content to remain in one place, but also went to Kawakawa and Kororāreka, baptising and celebrating Communion. After twelve months he'd baptised one hundred and sixty three people.

At first at Pakaraka he took services in the barn, but then Edward and Henry set to work to build a little church. The money for the materials came from the sale of his acre in Wellington, and from the family selling a tenth of their land.

And residing within the church was Henry's beloved organ, sent to him by Edward Marsh's father, and which had been brought from Paihia.

Then, one day when Henry was taking a service at Kawakawa, who should arrive from Waiomio but Kawiti. The fierce old chief strode up to the front of the congregation and to Henry's astonishment made a long and impressive speech, announcing he was about to enter the church. He would also, he said, travel to Whangaruru, Ngunguru, Whangārei and Mangakahia, and visit the subtribe of Urikapana, to tell them all to join him.

In February 1853, at Pakaraka, Kawiti arrived to be baptised. With his silver hair he looked very handsome, dressed for the first time, as far as Henry knew, in a black suit and frock coat. The tiny church was crammed to bursting with people from all around, come to witness this great event – even the non-Christian tribes who lived in the vicinity of Pakaraka were there.

Kawiti took as his baptismal name Te Ruki – the Duke, after one of the ship captains.

Pōmare – he who had battled with Tītore over Kororāreka and who had always opposed the introduction of Christianity – had become a Christian a year before he died and encouraged his people to observe Sunday as a holy day. After his death his brother brought his family to worship and they built a house and chapel for Henry.

When Hōne Heke died of tuberculosis, he was brought to lie in state in the little church at Pakaraka, and was buried in a cave nearby.

Henry wrote to the bishop to tell him the good news about Kawiti and Pōmare. His relationship with Selwyn had improved – in fact, the latter had never admitted there was a problem between them and had asked him to be archdeacon of Waimate.

However, the CMS was still obstinate. Henry's brother William travelled to London to present his case, supported by Edward Marsh, and he returned with the news that although the committee accepted the missionaries had not precipitated the Flagstaff War by buying land, they still held to their dismissal of Henry. However, when William informed them his brother had no means of financial support after passing on the land he had bought for his children, they offered to make him a yearly allowance of one hundred and fifty pounds.

On Henry's behalf, William refused. 'It is not a matter of salary, but of character,' he told them.

But later in 1853 Henry received another letter from the CMS: 'Adverting to the confidence which this Committee have ever felt and expressed in Archdeacon Henry Williams as a Christian missionary, and their regret at his disconnection with the Society upon a question which they understand may now be regarded as having passed away; rejoice to believe that every obstacle is providentially removed against the return of Archdeacon Henry Williams into full connection with the Society.'

It was not much of an apology, but it sufficed. 'I must regret,' he wrote back to them, 'that the committee allowed themselves to be carried away by vain speeches and unsound statements: these having "passed away", I have no desire to recall them.'

Eventually he discovered the reason for the turnaround. It appeared that in 1853, when George Grey departed from New Zealand, he travelled in the same ship as George Augustus Selwyn. During the months-long voyage the two eminent men must have had plenty of time to discuss a variety of topics, including, presumably, his own situation.

Wryly he imagined Selwyn wheedling out of Grey the admission that his statements about Henry were untrue. Then it must have been a matter of the two of them, once they had arrived in London, going to the office of the CMS where Grey informed the committee that his claims against the missionary had been 'not quite correct' and requesting that Henry be reinstated.

However it had been managed he was relieved it was all over. He had to admit that sometimes he found himself still ruminating over the dismissal, for the whole affair had been devastating, not just for himself but for Marianne, and indeed the whole family. But now he must put it behind him: after all, was he not in the business of forgiveness?

They were well settled now, at Pakaraka. Their sons had built for them a house that was christened The Retreat – not meaning a defeat in the military sense, but a quiet place where one took stock of one's life and then, once refreshed, continued.

Certainly, in his life right now all seemed to be going smoothly. Edward and Henry were making a success of farming the land, producing enough to support themselves and their families, just as he hoped. They had integrated well with the local Māori people, who accepted them as part of their whānau.

Edward had married Jane, the daughter of missionary Richard Davis, while Henry married his cousin Jane Williams. Marianne had married the missionary Christopher Davies. Samuel, who studied theology at St John's College in Auckland, was now ordained as a minister and living in Hawke's Bay, where he set up a school for Māori boys at Te Aute. He also married his cousin, Mary Williams. Thomas was courting Annie Beetham, and John had just married the daughter of James Busby. The others – Sarah, Kate, Caroline and Lydia – were so far unmarried. The youngest of them all, Joseph, was still in his teens.

Edward took many of the church services at Te Waimate, while his brother Henry continued with the services at Paihia. The church there, not being constructed of lasting materials, needed replacing and the two young men rebuilt it.

Their beloved house at Paihia, the property of the CMS, was also beginning to disintegrate, but it was felt it was not worth reinstating.

Meanwhile, Henry continued to take services at Pakaraka, Kororāreka, Te Karetu, Wakare and Kawakawa. He also journeyed occasionally to Whangaroa, Kaitaia and Whangārei, going everywhere, as was his wont, on foot.

However, eventually this became too arduous for him and he bought a small vessel with which to visit the coastal settlements of Whananake, Tutukaka and Whangaruru; later Mangonui, Kaitaia and Whangaroa. At this last place, to his joy he baptised the chief Ururoa. Everywhere he went he received a hearty welcome, and even those he had thought hardened in sin showed an interest in his teachings.

But in the rest of the country all was not well. The main problem, in Henry's opinion, was the purchase of land by government agents. The Māori people resented the way the Crown paid them very little and then on-sold their land for a great deal more. Many disputes arose and in some cases, battles between tribes, bringing confusion and evil throughout the country.

In Taranaki, in 1860, one chief quarrelled with his head chief and, as a way of getting his own back, offered to sell to the government land that did not belong to him. In spite of the protests of the head chief, the governor of the time, Sir Thomas Gore Browne, went ahead with the sale and when there was opposition, sent troops onto the disputed land to take possession. Fighting between the races, Māori and European, ensued.

Alarmed at the situation, the British Government moved Gore Browne on to Tasmania. In his place they brought back George Grey – now Sir George, for he had been knighted – and of whom, in spite of their past history, Henry had high hopes that he could bring the two races together.

But Grey was no more successful than Gore Browne at keeping the situation under control. Fearing the fighting would spread to Auckland, he brought in thousands of British troops and built the Great South Road as far as the Waikato River. Then he sent in the soldiers to quell the Tainui tribe, hoping to move from there into the King Country, the centre of the Māori King movement.

The fighting escalated, with fierce battles at Rangiriri, Waiarai, Rangiaowhia, Hairini and Ōrākau. There were also battles, equally fierce, in Tauranga and on the east and west coasts of the North Island.

Henry heard of these developments with despair. 'When will it all end?' he said to Marianne. 'Will there ever be peace in this country?'

She shook her head. 'I do not know, my dearest, I do not know. At least in Northland –'

'There is no fighting here at present, but the people are unsettled.'

The two of them were together in their sitting room at The Retreat. He looked across at his wife. Her face still had that cheerful and somewhat impish expression, but her hair was now iron-grey and the lines of age and, he had to admit, hardship, were beginning to appear. They were both old now. How would she manage when he was gone?

At least at Pakaraka she was in the best place. The children would continue to manage the farm and support her, and she would always be surrounded by the love and respect of her children and grandchildren – maybe great-grandchildren, one day.

Marianne was dozing now.

Henry took up his pen, preparing to write to Edward Marsh. 'I feel our work is drawing to a close,' he wrote.

Then he stopped, gazing into the distance. What a wise and faithful friend – brother, in fact – Edward had been to him over all these years, keeping up their correspondence, encouraging, advising, supporting.

He remembered how Edward had warned him when they were embarking for New Zealand: 'Even those who ought to co-operate with you may often disappoint you . . .'

How prescient Edward had been. The CMS, Sir George Grey, George Selwyn – all had let him down. He shivered: it had been cruel, so cruel.

And now he was tired. It was time to lay down his pen – lay down everything – and go to be with his Saviour.

And then one day Marianne would join him and the two of them would be together, in heaven.

32

Trouble had broken out near Pakaraka. Of three Ngā Puhi subtribes, two were led by Te Haratua, the former right-hand man of Hōne Heke. The other hapū was Te Uri Taniwha and they were arguing over the possession of Te Ahuahu, the pā where Tāmati Wākā Nene and Hōne Heke had previously clashed.

Henry was exhausted and failing fast. In spite of this, anxious at the news of the outbreak, he sent Edward, who was now resident magistrate of the district, to stop the fighting.

Over several days Edward went back and forth, trying to dissuade the hapū from attacking each other. Finally they agreed to arbitration and he went off to settle a matter in another part of the district.

But the warriors were fired up now and during the night one of the hapū came back to attack the other.

As soon as he heard, Edward returned. But when the opposing parties saw him approaching on his horse, determined not to be foiled this time one of the chiefs fired and killed a man on the other side.

That was all that was needed. A fight broke out leaving several dead and many wounded and Edward himself only just escaped being shot at before his attacker realised who he was.

Their blood was up now and the only thing for it was an all-out battle. They fixed the day – 17 July 1867.

Because of the laws of utu, this battle would have major repercussions and lead to war throughout the North.

On the day the hapū assembled.

Te Haratua and his men leapt forward to perform the haka. Stripped for battle, higher and higher they sprang, beating their breasts, rending the air with piercing cries, grimacing and protruding their tongues to strike fear into their enemies.

Te Uri Taniwha replied, their haka just as terrifying, their intent as deadly. Bodies would be left strewn around the battlefield, blood and bone and hair intermingled and the finest young men in the prime of their lives would be lost to their tribes.

A horse appeared, its hoofs flying, the face of its rider twisted with emotion and urgency.

He rode between the opposing men and they paused.

'E ngā iwi!' he shouted. 'Ka mate a Te Wiremu!'

Te Wiremu is dead?

The men put down their weapons and stood completely still.

Te Haratua stepped forward, tears pouring down his cheeks. 'Nāku i mate ai a Te Wiremu!' he cried. He turned to both sides, his arms outstretched. He believed it was his fault that Henry had died, because of his anguish at the fighting.

Immediately Te Haratua ordered four chiefs to go to Pakaraka to represent his hapū as mourners. Te Uri Taniwha also left for the funeral, and the fighting ended.

In August a peace ceremony was held. From their pā came forth the hapū of Te Haratua, headed by Abraham Taonui bearing a white flag. They walked to the place where the battle had taken place, and once at the battlefield Taonui took out his Bible and read some passages. He ended with the words, 'Blessed are the peacemakers, for they shall be called the children of God.'

He commanded the people to kneel down while he prayed to God to bless them on the undertaking before them. Then they marched up to the pā of Te Uri Taniwha, where warriors from both sides met: together they numbered about six hundred, the largest gathering of fighting men seen since the Flagstaff War.

First a mighty haka was staged. Then Taonui stepped forward and again read from his Bible. He ordered men on both sides to kneel down together while he prayed for the Lord to bless them.

After this they sat on the ground and for several hours listened to the speeches as chiefs first from one side and then the other gave their finest whaikōrero. Gifts were exchanged as a peace offering.

Next Te Uri Taniwha danced the hari to signify that peace had been accepted. In this dance their movements were not ferocious, but gentle and graceful, and at the end the harmony of their voices died softly away.

Then the main chief of Te Uri Taniwha, Wi Katene, approached Te Haratua, and after a few words with him performed the hongi — nose to nose, breath to breath. He dropped his maro, or loincloth, to acknowledge the people that had been slain. Then Tāne, on the side of Te Haratua, approached to salute Te Uri Taniwha and also dropped his maro.

Finally the women appeared, bearing the kai for a feast. Following this everyone mourned the death of those who had been slain, in the great ritual of the tangi.

Thus was concluded the peacemaking, and the end of fighting in the Far North of Aotearoa New Zealand.

>Nō reira, Henry and Marianne – Haere, haere, haere.
>Farewell, farewell, farewell.

ACKNOWLEDGEMENTS

This novel owes much to the letters and journals of Marianne and Henry Williams as contained in *Letters from the Bay of Islands: the story of Marianne Williams* by Caroline Fitzgerald; *Te Wiremu – Henry Williams: early years in the north* by Caroline Fitzgerald; *Te Wiremu: A Biography of Henry Williams* by Lawrence Rogers; and *The Life of Henry Williams* by Hugh Carleton: also to *Hongi Hika* by Dorothy Urlich Cloher.

I am grateful to the Auckland Institute and Museum for awarding me a grant to write this book, and for allowing me access to their archives.

My heartfelt thanks to my husband Patrick for his encouragement, help and support over the nine years it took me to research and write this book.

Ngā mihi nui ki a koutou katoa.

BIBLIOGRAPHY

Unpublished
Williams Papers, Auckland War Memorial Museum Library

Internet
The Williams Museum website: https//www.williamsmuseum.org

Publications
Bagnall, A.G. and Petersen, G. G., *Colenso*, Reed, Wellington, 1948
Bawden, Patricia, *The Years Before Waitangi*, self-published, 1987
Bentley, Trevor, *Cannibal Jack*, Penguin Books, Auckland, 2010
Bohan, Edmund, *To Be A Hero: A biography of Sir George Grey*, Harper Collins, Auckland, 1998
Burgess, Linda, *Historic Houses*, Random House, Auckland, 2007
Butler, John, *Earliest New Zealand: the journals and correspondence of the Rev. John Butler*, compiled by R.J. Barton, 1927
Carleton, Hugh, *The Life of Henry Williams*, A.H. & A.W. Reed, Wellington, 1948
Chapman, Anne, *Missionaries, Wives & Roses*, Steele Roberts, Wellington, 2012

Cloher, Dorothy Urlich, *Hongi Hika*, Viking (Penguin Books), Auckland, 2003

Colenso, William, *The Authentic and Genuine History of the Treaty of Waitangi*, 1890

Doutré, Martin, *The Littlewood Treaty: the true English text of the Treaty of Waitangi*, Dé Danann Publishers, 2005

Evison, Harry, *Te Wai Pounamu*, Aoraki Press, 1993

Fitzgerald, Caroline, *Letters from the Bay of Islands: the story of Marianne Williams*, Penguin Books, 2010

Fitzgerald, Caroline, *Te Wiremu – Henry Williams: early years in the north*, Huia Publishers, 2011

Hall, T.D.H., *Captain Joseph Nias and the Treaty of Waitangi: a vindication*, self-published, Wellington, 1938

Jones, Alison and Jenkins, Kuni, *He Kōrero: Words Between Us*, Huia Publishers, Wellington, 2011

Lambourn, Alan, *The Treatymakers of New Zealand*, Book Guild, Sussex, England, 1988

Locke, Elsie and Paul, Janet, *Mrs Hobson's Album*, Auckland University Press in association with the Alexander Turnbull Library, Auckland, 1989 (originally 1840)

Māori Biographies, *The People of Many Peaks*, Bridget Williams Books, Wellington, 1990

Marsden, Rev J.B., *Life and Work of Samuel Marsden*, Whitcombe & Tombs, 1913

Middleton, Angela, *Kerikeri Mission and Kororipo Pā*, Otago University Press, 2013

Middleton, Angela, *Pēwhairangi: Bay of Islands missions and Māori 1814 to 1845*, Otago University Press, 2014

Moon, Paul, *Hobson: Governor of New Zealand 1840–1842*, David Ling, Auckland, 1998

Moon, Paul, *Te ara ki Te Tīriti – the path to the Treaty of Waitangi*, David Ling, Auckland, 2002

Nicholas, John Liddiard, *Narrative of a voyage to New Zealand, performed in the years 1814 and 1815*, James Black and Son, 1817

O'Malley, Vincent, *The New Zealand Wars: Ngā Pakanga o Aotearoa*, Bridget Williams Books, Wellington, 2019

Orange, Claudia, *The Treaty of Waitangi*, Bridget Williams Books, 2011

Quinn, Richard, *Samuel Marsden, Altar Ego*, Dunmore Publishing, 2008

Ramsden, Eric, *Busby of Waitangi: H.M.'s Resident at New Zealand, 1833-40*, A.H. and A.W. Reed, Wellington, 1942

Riddiford, Helen, *A blighted fame: George S. Evans 1802-1868, a life*, Victoria University Press, 2014

Rogers, Lawrence M., *Te Wiremu: A Biography of Henry Williams*, Shoal Bay Press, Christchurch, 1973

Trubohovich, Ronald V., *Governor William Hobson: his health problems and final illness*, Auckland Medical Society, 2015

Williams, Henry, *The Early Journals of Henry Williams*, edited by Rogers, Lawrence M., 1961

Williams, William, *The Turanga Journals 1840-1850*, edited by Frances Porter, 1974

Williams, William, *Christianity Among the New Zealanders*, 1867

Woods, Sybil, *Marianne Williams: A Study of Life in the Bay of Islands New Zealand 1823-1879*, self-published, Christchurch, 1977